THE INNER CIRCLE

THE INNER CIRCLE

MAN OF WAX TRILOGY, BOOK 2

ROBERT SWARTWOOD

RMS PRESS

For John Cashman—
Thanks for always being in my inner circle

"It is this, it is this—" "We have had that before!"
The Bellman indignantly said.
And the Baker replied "Let me say it once more.
It is this, it is this that I dread!

"I engage with the Snark—every night after
        dark—
In a dreamy delirious fight:
I serve it with greens in those shadowy scenes,
And I use it for striking a light:

"But if ever I meet with a Boojum, that day,
In a moment (of this am I sure),
I shall softly and suddenly vanish away—
And the notion I cannot endure!"

—Lewis Carroll,
The Hunting of the Snark

The nightmare has changed.

Now I stand frozen in room 7 of the Paradise Motel. In front of me lay two wooden caskets. Written on one of the caskets is **WIFE OF WAX**. *Written on the other,* **DAUGHTER OF WAX**.

They are in there, Jen and Casey. I can hear them calling my name. I can hear them screaming for help. I can hear them saying please please please *don't let us die.*

I want to save them, but I cannot move. It's not like before, where I want to move but my body will not let me. I have the power to take a step forward, I have the power to save them, but I do not.

Because Caesar is in the room with me. He stands between the two caskets, faceless but watching me with a smile. He is carrying out what Simon has started. Making sure I go through with the game. That I make my choice.

Save one, kill the other.

Kill one, save the other.

My wife and daughter continue calling my name, screaming for help.

Pick one, Caesar says. Pick one to live, pick one to die.

But I cannot pick one. I can only stand there, frozen, listening to my wife and daughter screaming and pleading and begging me to save them.

I stand there until I finally wake up and feel—if not for an instant—the slightest bit of relief at the knowledge that my wife and daughter are dead, and that I will never have to make that choice, that I will never have to play Simon's game again.

PART I

SMASH AND GRAB

ONE

We were headed south on I-95, about forty miles outside Miami, when the Kid called.

It was Saturday night, just past eleven o'clock. A heavy rain was coming down, the dark clouds occasionally illuminated by a scattered flicker of lightning.

Carver reached into his pocket, pulled out his phone, put it on speaker.

"What's up?"

The Kid said, "We got a problem."

I was driving the Corolla we'd picked up the day before in Atlanta. It was a small four-cylinder thing that still reeked of cigarettes and coffee from its previous owner. I'd paid one thousand dollars for it, cash, and now here we were, Carver in the passenger seat, the radio off, neither of us saying a word.

A quarter mile ahead of us was Ronny and Ian in the SUV. A quarter mile ahead of them was the target. The target was driving a black Crown Victoria, a camera set up in the foot well of the passenger seat so those who wanted to could see what the man looked like behind the wheel of the car, instead of getting the view of the highway from the mini-camera in his glasses. The target was listed simply as the Racist. He was a large bald man with a thick goatee and tattoos of swastikas and racial slurs all over his body. He'd only been in the game for less than forty-eight hours and had already killed someone.

"What's the problem?" Carver asked.

"Another link appeared five minutes ago. I started saving it right away, and … ah, well, you just gotta see it. I'm emailing it to you now."

Then the Kid was gone.

I said, "Should we call Ronny?"

"Not yet."

Carver had already replaced the phone in his pocket, was now reaching in the backseat for his bag. He pulled the MacBook from the bag, along with the wireless card. Then he had the computer on his lap, opened the lid, pressed the power button. Seconds later the Apple logo appeared and the main screen came up and then Carver was working quickly, opening the web browser, opening his email account, then opening the email the Kid had just sent.

There was a minute or two of silence as Carver downloaded the file. When the download was complete, Carver played the video. At once the atmosphere in the car changed. Carver's body visibly stiffened.

"How bad is it?"

"Bad enough," he said, and tilted the laptop so I could see.

Most of the screen was black except for the usual box in the middle. In that box now was a small room. The camera was positioned in one of the ceiling corners, staring down at a bed. It was the only piece of furniture in the room, besides a single lamp standing in the corner.

And on the bed lay a small dark-skinned girl, who couldn't have been any older than ten. She was completely naked, her arms and legs stretched toward the ends of the bed, straps tying

her wrists and ankles. How long she'd been there was impossible to say, but it was clear whatever fight had been in her was
long gone. She just lay there, her body jerking every couple of
seconds, sobbing the sob of a child who has cried so much she
has no more tears left to shed.

TWO

Despite the heavy rain, it was business as usual at the Fort Lauderdale International Airport.

At least that's what it looked like as Ronny and Ian sped down 95, a quarter mile ahead of Carver and Ben, a quarter mile behind the target. They passed the airport just as a massive commercial jet began to make its descent and Ian, slouched in the passenger seat staring out the window, said, "You ever see *The Twilight Zone* movie?"

Ronny glanced briefly at the landing plane before focusing his attention back on the highway. "What about it?"

"That story at the end, the segment with John Lithgow."

" 'Nightmare at 20,000 Feet.' "

"Right. Well, I first saw it when I was, like, ten years old, and it forever scarred me. I mean, I always hated flying after that."

Ronny said nothing, keeping his eyes on the highway. Miami was only a half hour away, and if they were going to do the Smash and Grab—which was the plan—it would be soon.

"I mean, okay," Ian said, "I've only flown once in my life, right after high school, but it was pretty nerve-wracking. It also didn't help that they put me near the wing, and the entire time I'm sitting there and telling myself there's nothing out there, no monster or whatever. I even pulled the shade so I couldn't see anything, which sort of sucked, because we were flying over the Grand Canyon and that would have been pretty cool to see."

Ronny still said nothing.

"Sorry," Ian said. "I'm doing it again, aren't I?"

"It's okay."

"I don't mean to ramble. I just, you know, I get nervous."

"Don't worry about it."

It wasn't that Ronny meant to be cold to Ian, but he needed to stay focused. He too was always nervous before they did a Smash and Grab. It was how they usually intercepted players. A long stretch of highway was always best. Drive up and tap them on the rear, speed around them, swing back into their lane, and slam on your brakes. Nine times out of ten, the players slammed on their brakes too. And then the clock started ticking, doors flinging open as they hurried out and grabbed the player before the player's escorts arrived. That was how they had rescued a handful of players—including Ben— and how they had rescued Ian Prescott less than a year ago.

The kid was only twenty-two. He had been a Theater Arts major at a college in Indiana. His game had been listed simply as the Actor. The last thing he remembered was going to sleep in his single-bedroom apartment just off campus. Next he'd woken up in his old house, in his bedroom, three states away. A bloody butcher knife lay next to him, along with a cell phone. The phone rang the moment he sat up, and he'd answered it, sleepily, uncertain what was going on. The voice on the other end identified itself as Simon. Simon told Ian to put on the glasses that were sitting on his desk. Then Simon said to pick up the bloody butcher knife. Or else, Simon said, Ian's fiancée was going to die. So he picked up the knife. Listened as Simon said Ian's fingerprints were now on the knife—the same knife that had been used to kill his parents. Moments later Ian was downstairs in the living room, staring wide-eyed and open-mouthed at the dead and massacred bodies of his mother and father.

The whole thing had messed Ian up, which was to be expected. Simon's game always messed up the players. It demoralized them. Broke their spirits. And, if they managed to escape, it forever scarred their souls.

Ronny's phone, placed by the gearshift, vibrated.

"Who is it?" Ian asked.

Ronny gave him an annoyed look, once again wishing he had more patience. It wasn't that he didn't like Ian, but the kid could sometimes be jumpy, especially in situations like these. Carver thought Ian was finally ready after the months of training and one previous outing, but Ronny still wasn't so sure.

He grabbed the phone, saw the display, said, "It's Carver," and put the phone on speaker. "Yeah?"

"We're holding off."

Ronny's fingers tightened around the steering wheel. "His escorts?"

"We haven't seen them yet. But the Kid just sent a file. Apparently a new link opened up and ..."

"What is it?"

"Looks like the next part of the game involves a child."

"Jesus Christ."

"Exactly. So we're going to hold off until we establish a location."

Ronny nodded to himself. "Got it."

Carver asked, "How's Ian doing?"

"I'm okay," Ian said. "Just, you know, nervous."

"Don't worry about it. We're all nervous. I'll call you guys back if anything changes. For now, just stay on the target."

"Got it."

Ronny disconnected and set the phone back by the gearshift. Beside him, Ian was slouched in his seat again, staring back out the window. Ronny glanced at him and thought about how the kid's life had changed forever a year ago. He thought about how he himself, almost five years ago, had woken up in that shed just a few miles from the Mexican border. How his wife and two children had been taken and held captive by Simon. How he had thought just like Ian had thought—how all the players no doubt thought, even the Racist a quarter mile ahead of them—that this was just another segment in *The Twilight Zone* and the monster was outside right now, waiting to get his attention, waiting to show him that it wasn't safe no matter how much he tried telling himself otherwise.

THREE

Actually, inside the Crown Vic that moment, the Racist wasn't worried about monsters waiting outside. At that moment, he was worried about the monster on the other end of the cell phone. The monster whose voice he'd first heard less than two days ago, telling him that his wife and son had been taken captive and that the only way to get them back was to be a good boy and do everything Simon said or else they died.

And Simon, at that very moment, was doing everything he could to set the Racist off.

"Come on, Mason," he was saying, because the Racist's name was Mason Coulter, an ex-con who'd been working as a mechanic for the past five years. "You can admit it to me. I won't tell anyone."

Mason's entire body was shaking. Not so much out of fear or concern but rather anger. An inexorable rage coursed through his blood. This fuck face and whoever else took his family were going to pay. Of this, Mason was certain. How and when, well, that was something to worry about later. Right now, though, if he wanted to keep his family alive, he had to do everything Simon said, which included putting up with the asshole's grating voice.

"No," Mason murmured.

"Yes," Simon said. "Tell me how much you liked the feel of that man's mouth around your cock. I mean, you did come, didn't you? You must have liked it. You must have *loved* it."

"Shut up!" Mason shouted, the sudden outburst surprising even him.

Simon chuckled. "What's wrong, Mason? Do you want to cry? Cry like a little fucking girl?" He paused. "What about fucking a little girl? Would that make you feel better? Would that make you feel more like a man? Because if it came down to it and you were given the choice, which would you do?"

"What?" Mason said. The rain was falling harder and harder, the windshield wipers working full force. "What are you talking about?"

"Well," Simon said matter-of-factly, "between fucking a little girl and killing her, which would you prefer?"

Mason's mouth opened but then slowly closed.

"Just think about that, Mason. Think about which would be easier for you. Or is this maybe a race issue? Like, would it be easier to kill a black girl or would it be easier to fuck a white girl? Or vice versa?" Another pause. "Are you there, Mason? I can see you, but I don't hear you."

Mason swallowed, his massive Adam's apple bobbing up and down. His throat was dry. He wanted water, soda, beer, *something*, but he had nothing to drink. He had nothing at all except the money in the wallet that had been given to him very early in the game. That and the cell phone now seemingly glued to his ear.

"Yes," he finally managed. "I'm here."

"Good," Simon said. "It's very good that you're still with me. Because the longer you're with me, the longer Gloria and

Anthony stay alive. Say, you want them to stay alive, don't you?"

"Yes," Mason breathed. His body still shook. "God, yes I do."

"That's great, Mason. That's fantastic. So just do yourself a favor and play the game and maybe both your wife and son will make it out of this in one piece. Got it?"

FOUR

Eventually the Racist turned off 95 onto the Julia Tuttle Causeway, taking him over Biscayne Bay and into Miami Beach.

Now that our target had gone deeper into the city, we had closed the gap. Ronny and Ian stayed only six car lengths behind, while Carver and I stayed five car lengths behind them. Traffic was everywhere, making it impossible for the Racist to know we were following him. Besides, it wasn't him we were worried so much about but rather his escorts, who we usually spotted by now.

Despite the heavy rain, people were still out and about, hurrying from one restaurant or bar or club to the next. Palm trees danced to the music of the rain and wind. Lightning continued to streak the sky like a strobe.

The Crown Vic slowed in front of a place called The Spur. Then it sped up again, drove for another two blocks, and pulled into a parking lot.

Carver checked his gun as he called Ronny.

"Head down another couple of blocks and park where you can. We'll keep an eye on him."

The SUV continued down the street, lost with the constant

rush of traffic. I slowed as we neared the parking lot. The sodium-arc lamps illuminating the lot were dim, but they were just strong enough to see the Racist's massive bulk as he climbed out of the car.

We passed the lot and came to a red light.

Carver put in his earpiece and said, "Go around the block, find a place to park," and then he was outside, slamming the door behind him.

Finding a place to park in Miami Beach on a Saturday night, even if it is past midnight and raining like hell, is not an easy task. Eventually I did find a space, but it was four blocks away from the spot I'd dropped off Carver, even further from the spot where Carver had trailed the Racist. That place the target had slowed down in front of, The Spur, was where Carver had tracked him, which was seven blocks away.

Before getting out of the car, I put in my earpiece. Then I checked my gun, a Sig Sauer SP2022. I shoved it in the back waistband of my jeans, placed a baseball cap on my head, locked the car and hurried back down the street. I was completely drenched by the time I made it to the main strip.

In my ear, Carver asked where I was.

"I'm almost there," I said, my hands in my pockets, my head tilted down but still aware of every person I passed.

I spotted The Spur forty seconds later. There was a small line outside. They were illuminated by a yellow and red neon sign of a cowboy boot hanging above their heads, its spur flashing blue.

Carver and Ronny were waiting on the opposite side of the street, half a block down. Carver had his cell phone to his ear.

I nodded at Ronny, asked, "Where's Ian?"

"Keeping an eye on the back," he said. Then, his face all at once somber, "This is messed up."

I nodded, thinking he meant the little girl strapped to the bed.

Then Carver finished his call and said, "Ben, give Ronny your piece."

"What?"

"Lose the gun."

It's important to note that in the past two years I'd never once questioned Carver. In many ways, he saved my life, and I owed him a great deal. So when he gave me an order I never faltered or asked why. But now, with the rain coming down hard, with lightning streaking the sky, with us so close to our latest target, I couldn't help myself.

"Why?"

He had turned to say something to Ronny but now paused, looked back at me, and said, his voice hard, "They'll wand us at the door."

I understood then why Ronny had said this was messed up. Not the little girl strapped to the bed—which was indeed messed up, just on an entirely different level—but the fact that Carver and I were apparently going inside The Spur, just the two of us, without any weapons.

The first rule about trailing a target—the most important rule Carver always stressed—was never get yourself trapped. That's why we most often did the Smash and Grab. Because then we were out in the open, with limitless exits. But inside a store, inside a house, inside a club, the exits become limited. It gets to the point that if there was a trap and Caesar's men surrounded us, it would be a hell of a time trying to get out alive. And now, going inside The Spur, where they were bound to wave a metal detecting wand over us, which meant of course we couldn't take our guns, I realized just how messed up—how *fucked* up—this had become.

"Why can't we just wait for him to come out?"

"The girl might be in there."

"She's not."

"She might be," Carver said. "We can't take that chance. We need eyes on the inside, and we need them now."

Carver stared at me hard and I knew there was no point trying to argue. I reached behind my back, withdrew the Sig, handed it to Ronny. He made it disappear into his rain parka.

"Who was on the phone?" I asked Carver.

"The Kid. I had him look up what he could about The Spur."

"And?"

"There's going to be trouble inside."

"How can you be so sure?"

"Because The Spur," Carver said, "is a gay bar."

FIVE

Mason Coulter had the words DEATH TO FAGS tattooed across his chest. Below this, on the left side of his stomach, was a swastika. Beside the swastika, on the right side of his stomach, were two crossed hammers.

These tattoos had not been on his skin three days ago. Before then he had only had two, both prison ink. One was his son's name, the other a crossed out AB. The AB stood for the Aryan Brotherhood, which he had briefly been a member of when he was inside. But he had had no choice in the matter, not if he wanted to survive, and so he had become a skinhead for his wife's and son's sake—at least that was what he told himself at the time—but after he had gotten out one of the first things he had done was had it crossed out. The thought had occurred to him to try to get rid of it completely, but he wanted it there as a reminder, a constant accusatory memento of the life he had once led and the life he had almost once lost.

But now there were others.

On his chest.

On his arms.

On his back and on his legs.

His entire body was *covered* in these tattoos that had appeared on his swollen and raw skin when he woke up two days ago in Alma, Georgia.

He had been in a bathtub, completely naked. A cell phone was on the bathtub's rim. It rang the moment Mason sat up. And who had been on the other end? A voice calling itself Simon. Simon saying good morning, Mason, how are you doing? Simon then asking what Mason thought about his new ink. Simon telling Mason that if he ever wanted to see his wife and son again, he would do exactly what Simon said.

Mason had lurched out of the tub, knowing at once that this wasn't his bathroom. He opened the door and stepped into a bedroom that wasn't his either.

On the bed lay two naked black men. They were both dead, their throats slit. One even had his eyes open, staring up at the ceiling.

"My, my, my," Simon said softly in Mason's ear. "Would you look at that? Two deceased homosexual African Americans." A chuckle. "That's quite a mouthful. Though I guess you'd call them dead queer niggers, wouldn't you, Mason? I mean, that is what a racist would say, isn't it?"

Mason was a tall man, standing six-five, weighing close to three hundred fifty pounds. He had a lazy face, somewhat resembling a bloodhound, but he was the type of man who demanded respect wherever he went, taking no shit from anyone. But now here, standing completely naked in this strange place, talking to this strange man, something broke inside him. An internal dam that he had been building most of his life broke and, though he did not cry, tears welled up in his eyes.

In his ear, Simon said, "Oh no, Mason, don't do that. At least not yet. Right now ... well, compared to what's in store for you, this is nothing to cry about. Now, see those glasses on the nightstand? Put them on."

"But I"—he swallowed—"I don't wear glasses."

"Mason, Mason, Mason," the voice said tiredly. "Do you *want* your family to die?"

"No."

"Then when Simon says do something, you better fucking do it and don't ask questions."

Later that night, after making him snatch a pack of gum from a local convenience store, Simon had Mason drive to a nearby apartment. In that apartment was a male prostitute. The prostitute introduced himself as Izzy. He was a deeply tanned man, maybe twenty-five years old, who had bleached blond hair with black roots. Izzy had welcomed Mason, stroking his arm as he led Mason deeper into his apartment, the place decked out in some retro seventies motif, and it took everything Mason had at that moment not to punch Izzy's lights out. But Simon had said that Mason needed to go through with this, that if he ever wanted to see his wife and son alive again, he would follow through and not back out.

And the first thing Simon wanted Mason to do?

Let Izzy suck his cock.

Which he had no choice but to go through with. Sitting there on a velvet couch, his pants and boxers down around his ankles, Izzy on his knees before him while a fucking lava lamp stood in the corner. Mason's entire body was shaking and he wanted to push this man away, he wanted to at least look away, but he couldn't. Simon said he had to watch, that he *needed* to watch, or else one of Gloria's body parts would be shipped to him.

And so he watched.

He sat there and he watched the young man's head bob up and down, his lips around the shaft of his penis. At one point Izzy even looked up at him, and there was a smile in his eyes, a pleasure that nearly drove Mason insane. And right as he came he couldn't take it anymore—he reached forward and grabbed the prostitute's head, twisted it back and forth, again and again, until he'd severed the spinal column and left Izzy on the ground, paralyzed.

Thirty seconds later the cell phone rang.

"Wow," Simon said. "That's all I can say, Mason. Just … wow."

Now here he was, in a gay club called The Spur. Dance music pounding from speakers all over the place. Neon flashing lights everywhere. Mostly men in tight shirts and jeans moving around the club, talking, flirting, buying each other drinks, but it looked like there were a handful of transvestites too.

He walked up to the bar and ordered a beer.

"Honey," the bartender said, a tall skinny man with a red mohawk, "I never saw you around here before. You new?"

With much effort, Mason nodded.

"Well," the bartender said, smiling at Mason as he pulled a beer up from under the bar and set it on top, "the first one's always on me."

And so Mason stood there and waited. Thinking about what Simon had said to him. How he was to come to this place, The Spur. How he was supposed to order a beer and then just stand around, wait for someone to come up and ask him to dance. And when that happened, when someone came up and tapped him on the shoulder, he was supposed to dance.

"Or else your wife's heart?" Simon had said. "I'll send it to you in a box."

SIX

We spotted the Racist almost immediately. He wasn't that hard to find. There were a lot of big men flitting between the bar and dance floor and lounge, but the Racist was recognizable by just how uncomfortable he appeared. Plus, he wore the telltale pair of glasses that didn't seem to go right with his face.

Some things never changed. I remembered the first time I put on a similar pair of glasses in a motel room in northern California. They'd been on the bathroom sink, and when I'd put them on they were heavy and thick and pinched my nose. But the lenses had been my prescription, and when I turned around I found the message that had been painted on the back of the bathroom door in blood.

For the Racist, the game had been going on now for two days. I knew pretty much everything that had happened to him so far. The waking up in a strange place. The special surprise that helped grab the new player's attention. This was all followed by the first part of the game, something simple, like stealing a candy bar or a pack of gum, or going to a diner, eating a meal, and then walking out without paying the check. Something that wasn't difficult at all when it came right down to it. Something that helped prepare the player for the later parts of the game. Start small, work your way up.

The Racist's game had started at least two hours before the Kid called us. We'd been at the farmhouse, our own special base, just hanging out, more or less waiting for the Kid to call. And then when he did he forwarded an email with everything he had downloaded so far.

The camera positioned in the ceiling corner of the bathroom, staring down at the latest player lying naked in the tub. Another camera positioned in the bedroom just outside of the bathroom, where two men lay dead on a king size bed. Even from the distance of the ceiling to the bed the bloody slits on their necks had been evident.

It wasn't my turn to go this time, it was Jesse's, but Jesse had gone with Maya into town for groceries, and when a game started like this, there was no time to waste. So Carver came to me, told me to come along, and we headed to the airport, where Fred was waiting to fly us to Atlanta. From there I'd managed to secure the Corolla, no questions asked, and then Carver and I were headed south, because all the Kid knew at that point was that the Racist was somewhere in southern Georgia. Meanwhile, Ronny and Ian had gotten into the SUV and started south too, planning to meet up with us whenever they got the chance. Driving nonstop, switching off when the other one got tired. It was the way our missions always went, one team heading out first to see what they could, then a second team—the pick up team—coming in behind for backup.

We'd almost had a chance to catch the Racist in Jacksonville this afternoon, but it just didn't work out. So we'd followed him down 95, just as it was starting to rain, hoping for a simple Smash and Grab to end this once and for all. But that didn't happen. Instead the Kid had called, telling us about the girl strapped to the bed, and now here we were, surrounded by pumping music and flashing lights.

Carver went to the bar. He came back with two beers and handed me one. I sipped it just for show, keeping my focus on the Racist as he moved awkwardly on the dance floor, directly beneath a disco ball. He had a beer in hand and looked like he was being tortured, his face flushed and his jaw clenched, as a transvestite in a yellow and pink polka dotted dress grinded up against his crotch.

Our earpieces were useless with the loud pumping music, so we took them out and placed them in our pockets. Carver and I split up and drifted around the club, keeping an eye on the Racist while also keeping an eye out for his escorts.

After about ten minutes, Simon called.

At least we had to assume it was Simon calling, because the Racist pulled the standard black cell phone from his pocket, looked at the screen, then quickly turned away from the transvestite and strode off the dance floor. He ended up in the lounge, surrounded by fake cacti, a finger to his ear while he strained to listen to the phone. He stood that way for several minutes, occasionally nodding, occasionally shaking his head. Finally he took the phone away from his ear, stared down at the screen, then jabbed a button with his thumb. Stuffed it back into his pocket, glanced once more at the people around him, and started moving.

By this point Carver and I had reconvened on the other side of the club.

I leaned into Carver, shouted into his ear, "What do you think?"

Carver, keeping his focus on the Racist, shook his head.

The Racist had returned to the bar. In seconds a red mohawked bartender was pouring the Racist a shot of Jameson, reminding me of being in the Sundown Saloon back in Reno, ordering two shots of Southern Comfort before Simon made me do something I didn't want to do.

Both of us whiskey drinkers, apparently. As if that bonded us somehow.

"This is it," I shouted.

Carver nodded. He shouted back, "Get the car. I'll call you when I'm headed out. Let Ronny and Ian know what's up."

I headed for the exit. As I stepped outside, passing a bouncer decked in a cowboy hat and chaps, I took the earpiece out of my pocket and replaced it in my ear.

"You guys there?"

Ronny said, "Where have you been?"

Ian said, "Yeah, man, we were getting worried."

"Sorry," I said. "The Village People were having a reunion inside."

"Seriously?" Ian asked.

"Look, the target's on his way out. Ian, get the SUV."

"I don't have the keys."

Ronny said, "I'm headed there now."

"Then meet up with him, Ian. We're going to have a very small window to maintain visual."

I was headed away from the club. The rain had slowed to a drizzle. Traffic was still heavy, tires hissing on the pavement. And above this constant noise came the sudden high-pitched whine of a motorcycle as it approached from down the street. The light at the intersection was turning yellow, then red, and the motorcycle stopped more or less directly in front of me. It was a Ducati sport bike. For some reason my eyes focused on the rider, completely dressed in black, wearing a full helmet. The helmet was also black—everything about the bike and rider was black—and when the dark faceplate tilted in my direction, I had the distinct impression the rider was staring at me.

I just stood there on the sidewalk, staring back at the rider, at once wishing I hadn't given Ronny my gun.

The red light turned green, the glow reflected off the black faceplate.

Traffic started moving forward.

The high-pitched whine cried out again as the rider gunned the Ducati and then was gone.

All at once, shouting came from inside The Spur. The walkie-talkie clipped to the bouncer's belt screeched with static, and an urgent voice said: "Micah, we need you in here now."

The bouncer was already moving, turning away from his post and dashing inside. I found myself starting forward too. Reaching for my gun, but of course I didn't have my gun. I didn't have anything.

I stepped back inside, my eyes darting everywhere, expecting the worst. What I wasn't expecting to find was the Racist charging toward the exit. The bouncer tried stepping in his way, placing a hand on the Racist's massive chest. But the Racist grabbed the bouncer's arm and twisted it behind the man's back, shoved him face first into the wall, and continued on.

Coming right at me.

Behind him, back near the bar, the transvestite in the yellow and pink polka dotted dress was being helped up by two helpful patrons. The transvestite was holding her—his?—jaw, shoulders hitching, trying to fight back tears. It was quite clear what had happened, or at least somewhat clear, but I had no time to speculate, because at that moment the Racist was walking right past me, close enough for me to reach out and touch.

And what, I'd later wonder to myself, if I had? What if I'd stepped in front of him like the bouncer had done and told him I knew exactly what was happening. That I too had once been trapped in Simon's game, thinking there was still a chance to save my family. But that instead I quickly learned there was no outlet, absolutely nothing that could be done to save my family or myself other than walking away.

But I didn't do that.

I just stood there, watching him walk past me, hearing him mumbling under his breath. In the next moment he was gone, stepping out into the drizzle, and it took me a couple seconds before I realized I should be out there too, that I should already have returned to the Corolla to bring it around.

Carver appeared in the space the Racist had occupied only seconds before, pulling his own earpiece out of his pocket.

"What happened?" I asked, but Carver just shook his head and hurried past me out into the street.

SEVEN

After leaving The Spur, the Racist went straight for where he had parked the Crown Victoria.

Ian watched him the entire time, while Ronny fetched the SUV. Ian stood on the other side of the street, a half block down, his hands in his jacket pockets, his head covered with a Red Sox cap, and watched as the Racist started the car, backed out of its space, and left the lot. Seconds later Ronny pulled up in the SUV, Ian jumped in, and then they were off, maintaining a five-car-length buffer.

By that point Carver and I had returned to the Corolla. Ronny kept us in the loop the entire time, informing us that currently the target was headed north on Collins Avenue. Carver pulled up a map of our current location on his phone and directed me on a shortcut to catch up with them.

"We don't have our guns," I said.

Carver stared down at his phone. "We'll be fine."

There was a silence.

I asked, "Just what the fuck happened in there anyhow?"

Carver didn't look like he was going to answer at first. He just sat there, staring at his phone. Something was different about his face, about his entire body language. I'd been working with Carver for two years now and we had been paired up many times tracking a new target. I'd begun to get a good sense of Carver's moods, and his different kinds of silences. But this was a new silence.

"Well?" I prompted.

He blinked and looked out his window and took a deep breath. "The guy just … flipped out. He's a loose cannon. That transvestite went up to him, barely said a word, and he just hit her. Smacked her right in the face, then kneed her in the groin. I know it's hard to believe, but I think Simon's already broken this one. I think"—he swallowed—"I think we might have another Christian Kane on our hands."

There was another silence.

Then, in our earpieces, Ronny muttered, "Jesus Christ."

Carver, nodding slowly, staring back down at the map on his phone, said, "Exactly."

Five minutes later, the rain still drizzling, Ronny said, "He just pulled into a hotel parking lot."

"What hotel?" Carver asked.

"The Beachside. We're going up to the second entrance to park."

Carver closed the map on his phone and called the Kid, putting him again on speakerphone. He said, "Find out everything you can about the Beachside Hotel. That looks to be our target's next location."

"You think the girl's in there?"

"Possibly. Has the page changed?"

"Nope. I keep checking it every thirty seconds but it's still the same. Wish I didn't have to, though. I feel like a fucking perv with this thing on my screen."

"You've seen worse."

"Don't remind me."

"Listen," Carver said, "find out everything you can about the place and get back to me. But do it fast."

He clicked off just as we passed the hotel's first entrance, the same one the Racist had used.

Compared to the rest of the hotels along Collins Avenue, the Beachside wasn't overly impressive. The building was mostly white stucco, no more than twenty stories high. The parking lot was moderately full.

"Ronny," I said, "we're pulling into the second entrance now."

Ronny said, "Take the first left and come the whole way back."

I parked the Corolla two spaces away from the SUV. Carver and I got out and hurried over and climbed into the SUV's backseat.

Ronny had our guns and handed them back to us. "What's the plan?"

"The plan," Carver said, hefting his Glock 30, "is we take him as soon as possible. But first he has to get his room number. Once he has that, we're set."

"And, um—" Ronny paused, clearly not sure how to continue. He sat there in the driver's seat, a large man with a full beard who had once been a trucker hauling food orders for restaurants across the country. His St. Christopher's medallion hung limp from the rearview mirror. "And what about the girl?"

"At this moment," Carver said, making sure to look at each of us in the eye, "the girl is the main objective."

We were silent, waiting for him to say more.

He didn't. Instead he pulled out his phone and dialed the Kid, put him on speakerphone.

"Any info on this place yet?"

"It's been like twenty seconds."

"Any info?"

"No."

"Then forget it. We're headed in now." He disconnected and shoved the phone in his pocket. He checked the Glock's magazine, reinserted it, racked the slide, reached for the door handle. Looked back at us and said, "Let's do this."

EIGHT

Yes, it was true—he had lost his cool. Mason would be the first to admit it. That fucking *thing* had come up to him in the bar, placed a hand on his arm, and started talking to him, asking what he was doing later, if maybe Mason would like to come back to its place. So what was Mason supposed to do, standing there with a he/she/it touching his arm? Probably not clock it in the face and then knee it in the crotch—where it used to have a dick, or maybe still did—but that's what happened.

That was something Mason, at that moment, needed to have happen.

What he didn't need was Simon calling him once he'd left the bar, once he'd gotten in the car and started it up. He didn't need Simon's fucking voice berating him for acting like an asshole in public.

"I mean, goddamn it, Mason, do you want your family to suffer?" Simon had never sounded this worked up, this agitated. "Do you want me to go to Gloria and little Anthony and tear their fingernails off? Do you want me to break their fingers, their hands, and just work my way up their arms? Is that what you want?"

Mason hadn't responded as he sat there in the car, listening to the rain, to his own thoughts.

Simon sighed. "Okay, I get it, Mason. You're tough. Nobody messes with you. But that's the thing I don't think you quite understand yet. Nobody messing with you? That's the way it *used* to be. Now you have no choice. Got it? Unless you really do want your wife and son to die. Is that what you want, Mason? Say it is and I'll make sure it happens right now. I'll even let you listen."

Mason closed his eyes. "No."

"What was that? I'm sorry, Mason, I don't think I heard you."

"*No*," Mason repeated, this time with more emphasis.

"Now that's more like it," Simon said. "So have you decided about that ... *other* thing we discussed?"

Mason said, "What other thing?" Knowing very well what Simon meant.

But of course Simon didn't answer him. He just gave Mason directions, to a hotel farther up Miami Beach. He told him go inside and introduce himself as William Simmons. He told him to accept the key given to him and go up to his room, and that once he got there ... well, now that was going to be the interesting part, wasn't it?

So that Friday evening, about a quarter past two in the morning, Mason Coulter entered the Beachside Hotel. He stepped out from under the light rain to find a marble-tiled lobby with potted plants everywhere. A restaurant called The Cove sat to his right. It was closed, completely dark. A gift shop called The Sand Castle sat to his left. It too was closed, also completely dark.

A man stood behind the check-in counter. He was the only person in the lobby. He was about Mason's age, roughly forty, and wore horn-rimmed glasses. For some reason the glasses didn't look right on him, this pale man with a mop of brown hair staring down at a computer screen. The incongruousness of the glasses reminded Mason of his own glasses, the ones he'd been told to wear. He had never worn glasses a day in his life, and the feel of them on his nose and around his ears was very uncomfortable.

Mason walked up to the counter, taking his time as he went. He remembered what Simon had told him, about the choice he would have to make, and he figured the longer he took to check in, the more of a reprieve he had.

The man looked up at him, smiled a fake smile. His nametag said KEVIN.

"Welcome to the Beachside Hotel, sir," the clerk said, his voice almost as fake as his smile. "How can I help you?"

"I have a room reserved for me."

"Of course, sir," Kevin said, typing something onto a keyboard. "What's the name?"

"William Simmons," Mason said, and at once, like a slap, he realized the importance of that name, why Simon had used it among a million others.

The former preacher William Simmons. Colonel William Simmons. The man who, in 1915, helped organize the new society of the original Klan.

Simon's little inside joke.

"Thank you, sir," Kevin said, his focus on the computer screen, typing again. It was the only noise, that incessant clicking of the keys.

Something didn't feel right.

Of course, many things didn't feel right to Mason, not in the past forty-eight hours, but at that moment, standing in the lobby of the Beachside Hotel, with just him and Kevin, something felt wrong.

He looked to his right, at the glass doors he had just used to enter and the side parking lot beyond. Then to his left, at an identical pair of glass doors leading to the parking lot on the other side of the building. Nothing moved in either direction.

"Busy night?"

"Yes," Kevin said, nodding as he typed, "it's been very busy indeed."

But the thing was, the hotel didn't feel like it had been very busy. There were cars in the parking lot, sure, a lot of cars, but that sense of other people being in one closely confined space at the same time was missing.

Or at least Mason just couldn't feel it.

Kevin held up a black plastic keycard, still flashing that fake smile. "You'll be in room three-thirty-nine. It's on the third floor."

Mason took the key without a word. He saw, just as he took the proffered card, that his hand was trembling. His stomach was churning too, like he had eaten something his stomach disagreed with, but the truth was he hadn't eaten anything in the last twelve hours.

"Have a great stay, sir," Kevin said.

Mason turned away, his stomach still doing somersaults. His gaze swept the empty lobby—the potted plants, the couches and chairs, the overlarge fake sand castle in the corner —before stopping on the one pair of glass entrance doors. There were people out there, the first signs of life in this place besides Kevin and himself.

The glass doors slid apart. Three men walked in.

"Um, Mason?" Kevin said behind him.

Mason instantly froze. He slowly started to turn back to the check-in counter—thinking, *How does he know my name?*— when the submachine gun in the clerk's hands stopped him.

Kevin said, "You might want to duck."

And then started shooting.

NINE

The first thing we saw when we entered the lobby was the Racist. He was just standing there, a plastic keycard in his hand, watching as the glass doors parted in front of us. Then the clerk behind the counter said something, and the Racist glanced back.

Just as the man brought up an Heckler & Koch MP5.

Carver said, "Shit," and immediately grabbed for his gun. Ian and I grabbed our guns too, and then we were diving for cover right as the clerk opened fire—Carver toward the right, me and Ian toward the left. I fell to the floor behind a couch. I waited a moment, flat on the ground, before jumping back up.

The things I noticed in the half second before I started shooting: the Racist on the floor, his hands covering his head; the clerk gritting his teeth as the MP5 in his hands kicked with each shot.

Then that half-second was over and I opened fire. I was aiming for the clerk, right at his head. Three shots later he went down.

"Carver!" I could almost see him on the peripheral, a dark shape wedged in behind a small jungle of potted plants.

"I'm okay," he said. The fake leaves rustled and he emerged, his gun in his hands, slowly approaching the desk.

Without even knowing it, I was moving too, keeping the Sig aimed right at the spot where the clerk had been standing. Ian got up from where he had taken cover and followed.

On the floor the Racist slowly moved. He raised his head, squinting up at us.

Carver approached him. He reached down and tore the glasses off the Racist's face, snapped them in two.

"Hey," the Racist said in a strangled voice.

"What room is she in?"

"Huh?"

Before Carver could repeat his question, the doors to the restaurant burst open and two men appeared. They too had MP5s and immediately started firing.

Carver sprinted toward the check-in counter and dove over it just as a spray of bullets tore up the tiled floor in his wake.

Ian and I dove back toward the closest pillars to take cover.

The two men split up as they fired, one heading my direction, the other heading toward the counter. Both managed to shield themselves with the pillars near the restaurant as Ian and I both stepped back out and returned fire.

Out on the floor, the Racist once more lay flat with his hands over his head.

At once Carver appeared behind the counter, the submachine gun in hand. He opened up, his finger on the trigger, the gun spitting out nonstop rounds, taking off chips of the marble pillars the men were hiding behind.

Both Ian and I saw this as an opportunity.

We started firing too, stepping around our pillars, moving closer.

The men didn't know which way to fire.

They panicked.

As if on cue they started backpedaling toward the restaurant, their only form of retreat. They moved back-to-back and continued firing, but it did them no good.

Our bullets took them down almost at once.

Again, silence.

Carver vaulted over the counter. He nodded at me and Ian and the three of us made a quick circuit of the lobby, checking the restaurant and gift shop and anywhere else someone might be hiding with a semi-automatic weapon. Once we established the place was clear—at least for the time being—Carver approached the Racist, who once again had his head raised, looking around to make sure all was safe.

"Where is she?" Carver repeated.

"Please," the Racist said. "I don't know what's happening. I just—"

"What room did Simon tell you to go to?"

And like that, a kind of understanding filled the Racist's face. He was in the process of standing up, getting first to his knees, then placing one foot on the ground. This was where he stopped, looking like a man about to propose to the love of his life.

"What … what did you say?"

Carver leveled the barrel of his gun right at the man's face. "What room?"

For the longest moment the Racist didn't say anything. Then, his voice trembling, "Room three-thirty-nine. Third floor." His gaze skipped around at our faces. "Who *are* you people?"

TEN

After a sudden volley of gunfire in the lobby of a hotel in Miami Beach, you'd expect there to be some people around. Employees, guests, a random vagrant—anyone to poke their heads out from doors, to maybe scream out loud at the insanity of it all. But there were no doors opening partway to reveal frightened faces. No screams or even murmurs floating down the hallway. Nothing.

The Racist climbed to his feet. Both Ian and I kept our guns on him. The man stood there, clearly confused.

"What the fuck is going on here?"

"We're here to help you," Carver said. "Now go with them. They're going to take you to safety."

"But what about Gloria and Anthony? What's gonna happen to them? What about—"

"They're already dead. I'm sorry to be the one to tell you that, but this is how Simon works. You never even had a chance to save them in the first place."

Ian and I maintained close proximity to the Racist. He didn't look at us. Instead he glared back at Carver, anger and fury in his eyes.

A soft noise suddenly filled the silence. A noise that was almost impossible to hear over the ringing in my ears. But it was a noise I recognized, a noise I understood, and I wasn't surprised at all when the Racist glanced down at the right front pocket of his jeans, at the bulge of a cell phone there.

"Give me that," Carver said. He held out his hand. Kept it there, his palm up, until the Racist slowly pulled the black phone from his pocket and placed it in Carver's hand. Carver answered, "Go ahead, Simon." A pause, then a small grin. Carver said, "Yeah, fuck you too," and dropped the phone to the floor where he stomped on it once, twice, three times.

Maybe a minute had passed since the initial shootout. The astringent odor of burnt cordite was still thick in the air. The ringing in my ears had begun to fade. And still no one had entered the lobby.

"Now," Carver said to the Racist, "go with them."

"But—" the Racist started to say, then glanced at Ian and me, saw the guns in our hands.

"Let's go," I said.

For some reason I expected more protest from this man. I expected some real trouble, especially after what had happened earlier at The Spur. A loose cannon, Carver had said about our latest target, how we might have another Christian Kane on our hands, and he was right. So right now, I figured this man was at the end of his rope and was apt to do anything unreasonable.

But he glanced once again around the lobby, at the plaster and the bits of foam from the couches and chairs. At the two dead bodies lying near the restaurant.

And without a word he started walking.

Heading right toward the lobby exit.

Ian pulled out a plastic zip tie. "Do us a favor and let us put these on you."

The Racist stopped walking, stared directly down at the black plastic binding. "For what?"

I said, "For our safety."

The man shook his head. "No. No fucking way I'm letting you touch me with that fucking stuff."

Carver was behind the Racist an instant later. Kicking the back of his knees, forcing him to the floor. Carver grabbed the man's arm, yanked it behind his back, then did the same to his other arm.

The whole process took less than five seconds.

The Racist fought this, of course, kicking and rocking his body, trying to get Carver off of him. But at the moment Carver had the advantage, his knee right in the small of the Racist's back, grasping both of the Racist's wrists together so Ian could bend down and wrap the plastic zip ties around them, squeeze them tight.

Once it was done, Carver stood up. He yanked the Racist back to his feet. It was surprising to watch, because the Racist was at least one hundred and fifty pounds heavier than Carver.

"We don't have time to deal with this bullshit," Carver said to the Racist, who wasn't even looking at Carver, was instead facing the glass doors. Carver pushed him forward. The man stumbled a little. Ian and I immediately came up behind him, taking one elbow each and leading him across the marble tiles toward the exit.

The electric eye sensed us and the doors slid apart. The SUV was parked at the end of the walkway, Ronny having been in radio communication the entire time, knowing we were headed out with the target. He stood beside the opened side door, a gun held at his side.

"You guys all right?"

"So far," I said.

We were less than ten yards away from the SUV when Ian let go of the Racist. I watched it happen from the corner of my eye. It took only a second, Ian releasing his grip on the target's elbow so he could switch hands. But it was all the Racist needed. He was in motion at once. His arms were behind his back, sure, but that didn't stop him as he swung around, trying to get at us. His teeth bared, his face flushed, he growled as he kicked out first at me, then at Ian.

Ronny didn't hesitate. He rushed forward, withdrawing an EpiPen from his pocket. Instead of containing epinephrine, this pen was filled with a special form of methohexital—a barbiturate—we had cooked up for situations such as these. In one smooth motion, Ronny stabbed the Racist in the side of the neck.

The effect wasn't instantaneous. It would take nearly a minute to knock the Racist out. But it slowed him, and gave us the extra time to hurry him over to the SUV and shove him inside.

Then Ronny turned to me and said, "Go."

Carver was waiting for me in the lobby, his gun in hand. In his other hand was the black plastic keycard.

"Nothing yet?" I asked.

He shook his head.

We started toward the stairs. Both with our guns out, neither saying a word. Now that the ringing had completely left my ears, the silence surrounding us was just too palpable.

Through the fire door then and up the stairs.

First one flight, the second flight, the third.

Carver and I paused in front of the fire door, our guns at the ready. I placed my hand on the knob. Carver nodded once. I pulled the door open, just a little, giving Carver enough space to aim his weapon.

Keeping his gun aimed and his focus through the space looking onto the third floor, he nodded again.

I pulled the door open further, enough so Carver could slip through. I followed. Here there were four elevators, a potted plant in the corner, a polished oak table standing against the wall with a lamp and telephone on top. The carpet silenced our footsteps as we approached a T-intersection of the hallway. There were signs on the wall, pointing which rooms were to the left, which were to the right. The ice machine directly across from us hummed quietly, working its hardest to produce its required one-ice-cube-per-hour quota.

The direction we wanted to go—where room 339 was located—was to the left.

The silence seemed even more oppressive up here. In our ears we could hear Ronny and Ian situating the Racist in the SUV. The noise was low but still too much of a distraction that we took out our earpieces and slipped them into our pockets.

Carver placed his back against the wall, peeked around the corner. He raised a fist—clear.

We started down the hall, Carver covering the front while I covered the back. The hallway was carpeted in a design of seashells. Doors lined both sides.

Besides the humming ice machine, the silence thickened.

We were only five rooms away from room 339 when a door suddenly opened. A man stepped out. He had a rifle in his hands, aimed directly at Carver.

ELEVEN

It was as if time had slowed. The man fired only twice and I watched each bullet as it tore loose from the rifle's barrel and tore into Carver's chest. I watched Carver's body jerk. I watched his shoulders hitch. I watched as he fell to his knees. Then time sped up once again and I stepped forward, raising my gun, and fired.

The shooter disappeared back into the room. My bullets tore chunks from the wall, from the door.

Carver was at my feet. He had fallen onto his side. Groaning. Gurgling. The front of his jacket had been ripped up. He'd been hit right in the chest. Blood was everywhere.

The shooter appeared again, his rifle aimed at me.

I fired at him, taking out more chunks of the wall and door, causing him to disappear back inside.

I grabbed the back of Carver's jacket and backpedaled down the hallway. Pulling Carver with my left hand, keeping aim at the door with my right. Farther and farther back, until the shooter appeared again.

I squeezed the trigger—one, two, three, four shots until there was nothing else.

"Shit," I said, because my magazine was empty, because I knew I didn't have time to reload.

But the shooter must not have realized this. He must have assumed I was taking my time again, waiting for him to reappear.

On the floor Carver was still groaning, gurgling, choking on his blood. I glanced down and saw he still had hold of his Glock.

I risked a quick glance over my shoulder. We only had another ten, fifteen yards before we reached the bank of elevators. Not too far, sure, but distance and time are both relative while you're dragging a dying man and you're out of bullets and the man who's trying to kill you is just biding his time.

I dropped the Sig and went to grab Carver's Glock.

He wouldn't let go.

"Carver, come on!"

But he was oblivious. Still groaning, still gurgling. And staring down at his face, I became aware he was also trying to speak.

"Ba—ba," he was saying, his dark face becoming somehow pale, and at that moment I sensed movement further up the hall. I knew the shooter was going to make another appearance, so I did the only thing I could think to do—I stomped on Carver's hand, the one holding his gun. He let go. I grabbed it and immediately started firing.

This time the shooter didn't have a room to disappear into. He had already begun to advance and had to push himself up against the doorframe of the next room, as if this was somehow going to save him. By that time I had reached the elevator bank.

Somehow I'd made it, dragging Carver the entire way. I yanked on the back of Carver's jacket some more, pulling him back completely, then went to the corner of the hallway, peeked around.

The shooter was peeking from the doorframe too, his rifle aimed toward me.

I reached around the wall, started firing, just as he started firing.

A moment later I was back on the floor with Carver, feeling for a pulse, staring down at his paling face as he continued to try to speak.

"Ba—boo," he was whispering, gurgling, groaning.

"Shh," I told him, glancing at the four elevators, at the fire door, at the ceiling.

I heard heavy footsteps coming my way.

I glanced down at Carver's face. His dark eyes stared up at me, or past me, it was impossible to tell.

His mouth moved, trying to form words, and he attempted again, saying, "Boo—boo—*boojum*."

I stared down at him another moment, a moment that seemed to last a very long time. I realized the footsteps were getting even closer, that they were right around the corner, and before I realized it I'd stood up, Carver's gun in my hands, and started firing again. Walking closer and closer to the corner, taking out even bigger chunks of the wall.

Wherever the shooter was behind the corner, he wasn't going to come out in the next couple of seconds. He was waiting for something, though whatever that something was I had no clue.

I backed up then, right next to Carver, who was still on the floor, blood all over his chest and soaking the intricate design of the seashell carpet.

"Boo—*boojum*," he said again, more emphasis this time, and I glanced down at his face, saw his eyes staring back at me, relating something I never thought I'd see there, something I didn't want to believe was true.

Carver nodded at me, just slightly, and without a word or any further hesitation I started running.

Right as I made it to the fire door I sensed the shooter behind me. I turned back. Watched the shooter step around the corner and stride purposefully toward Carver. The rifle no longer in his hands, instead a silver handgun.

He aimed the handgun right at Carver.

Shot him once in the face.

"No!" I shouted, my back against the fire door, completely paralyzed in that moment.

I meant to bring up the Glock, to run back and shoot the fucker in the head.

But the man was faster.

He had his gun up even before I could, and then he was firing, the shots somehow deafening but somehow wide too, because miraculously I wasn't hit as I sprinted down the steps toward what I hoped was safety.

TWELVE

Ronny heard the entire thing. His attention had mainly been focused on securing the Racist and checking to make sure he didn't have any tracking devices on him, but the transmitter in his ear kept him in constant radio communication with Carver and Ben. So he, just like Ian, heard the shooting. He heard the shouting. He heard Carver dying.

Ian looked up at Ronny, his eyes wide. "Holy shit."

Ronny checked the backseat where the Racist was completely passed out. Then he reached under his seat for his spare piece—a Ruger SR9c—and opened his door.

Ian asked, "Where are you going?"

Ronny was already stepping out, the Ruger in one hand, reaching for the piece he had holstered with his other hand. He looked hard at Ian and saw the fear in his eyes and knew the young man was worthless—more than worthless—but didn't have time to berate him right now.

"Giving them backup," he said. "Stay here and keep an eye out."

"For what?"

"Anything."

He used his elbow to slam the door shut and then hurried toward the entrance, a gun in each hand. He didn't care who might see him. Carver was dying, and Ben very well may be too. Ronny wasn't going to just stand by and let it happen.

The glass doors slid open and he strode purposely through the clutter-strewn lobby—thinking, *Where is everyone?*—when a door burst open.

I slammed through the fire door at top speed, running as fast as I could, and at first I thought the man aiming at me was another one of Simon's. Then, an instant later, I recognized Ronny and ran straight toward him. I saw he had two guns. I threw mine aside and shouted, "Gun!" Ronny tossed me one of his pieces. I caught it in the air and spun around and lowered myself onto one knee, keeping the gun aimed right at the fire door.

Ronny stood only a few feet away, keeping his piece aimed at the door too.

Nothing happened. Besides the blood pounding in my ears, the lobby was silent.

Ronny whispered, "How many?"

"Only one. He came out of nowhere."

"Do you think there's more?"

"I wouldn't doubt it."

"We should go."

"No."

"Yes," Ronny said, stepping forward and grabbing my shoulder, "we should go now. Carver would want it that way."

I didn't move. I kept my aim on the fire door, knowing that at any second the shooter would reveal himself.

Ronny's hand stayed on my shoulder. "Ben, come on."

I counted in my head—one, two, three, four, five—and

then took a breath, murmured, "Fuck," and stood up and ran toward the glass entrance doors, Ronny close behind me.

The first thing Ian said was, "What happened?"

Neither of us answered. I slid into the backseat next to the Racist. Ronny threw the SUV in drive and stomped on the gas. He took a hard right out of the parking lot back onto Collins Avenue and floored it.

"What *happened?*" Ian said again.

Ronny shot him an annoyed look. "Call the Kid."

"What?"

"Call and let him know what happened."

Ian still looked lost. "But I still don't know what happened."

"Don't worry about it," I said, pulling the vibrating iPhone from my pocket. "He's calling me now." I placed it on speaker. "Carver's dead."

"*Fuck.*" Then the Kid was quiet for a moment before saying, "I thought he might be. The page just disappeared."

"What page?"

"Of the girl. It's gone."

We were at least three blocks away from the hotel now, weaving in and out of traffic.

The Kid said, "It was a setup."

"What do you mean?"

"They knew you were coming. They expected you."

"How do you know?"

"The fucking Beachside, dude. Even though you guys were going in, I looked into the place."

"So?"

"It was bought a month ago. All the management, employees, everyone was given a pink slip. They were also given a thousand dollar severance pay. Even the fucking busboys.

Seems the new owners wanted to have everyone going away happy, no hard feelings."

"And?"

"Just last week the new owners—who so far are anonymous, no matter where I've looked—they sold the property to somebody. I forget who, but they got top dollar. So get this. The Beachside? It's scheduled for demolition in three days."

"Son of a bitch."

"Exactly. It was a fucking setup. It's a surprise the rest of you made it out alive."

There was a beat of silence.

I said, "Kid, we'll call you right back," and disconnected the call. Then I said to Ronny, "Pull over."

He eyed me in the rearview mirror. "Are you crazy?"

I leaned forward and jabbed the barrel of the Ruger against the back of his head.

"I'm not going to tell you again."

Ian, sitting turned in the passenger seat, said, "Jesus Christ!"

"Are you going to shoot me, Ben?"

"Just pull over."

"No."

I racked the slide. "Don't test me. I'm in no mood to be fucked with."

As it turned out, Ronny didn't have much of a choice. We had been fortunate so far making it through all the green and yellow lights, but now there was a red with several cars in front of us.

"Don't do this," Ronny said.

I pulled the Ruger away, turned in my seat, started grabbing the spare weapons and ammunition from the back.

"Don't do this," Ronny said again. "I know what happened to Carver sucks, but there's no changing that. He's gone."

I pulled two guns from the back and a few spare magazines. "He wouldn't leave us back there."

"He's *dead*, Ben. It's that simple. He's dead."

"The girl isn't."

Ronny shook his head. "You can't be serious."

"The mission was to save the girl. I intend to finish the mission. Now, do a U-turn and take us back."

"No. It's suicide."

I looked at Ian. "You coming?"

Ian said nothing.

I stared at him hard for a moment, then glanced at Ronny in the rearview mirror. Up ahead, the light changed from red to green. Traffic began to move again.

"I'm not taking you back," Ronny said. "I do that I might as well kill you myself."

"Carver would want it this way."

"No, he wouldn't."

I kept my gaze level with his in the rearview mirror. I reached for the door handle.

"Damn it, Ben, you go and you're dead."

I hesitated. Then I opened the door, saying, "All of us are already dead, Ronny." I stepped out into the drizzle and leaned back in. "We just don't know it yet."

I slammed the door shut.

THIRTEEN

The Kid called almost immediately. Even though I was hurrying back up Collins Avenue, I felt the iPhone vibrating against my leg. Both guns were concealed, as were the magazines. I had my head tilted down just a bit, the drizzle soaking my baseball cap.

When I answered, the Kid said, "Are you fucking insane?"

"Did anyone ever tell you how pleasant you are on the phone?"

"You are out of your fucking mind."

"I'm surprised we haven't started a swear jar for you by now."

"Ben, I know you're pissed at what happened to Carver—shit, I am too—but this isn't the way to make things right."

"Save it. I already heard Ronny's speech."

"Good. Now you can listen to mine."

The Beachside Hotel was about another five blocks away. It was a stationary object in the distance, growing more and more with each step. It wasn't a monolith like many of the other buildings along Collins Avenue, but still it called to me just the same.

"Before you begin your monologue," I said, "has there been any activity about the hotel over the air?"

The Kid was quiet for a moment. "Not yet. I've been keeping an ear on the Miami-Dade County radio since you guys arrived and there hasn't been one call. Either nobody's called—which is unlikely—or Simon's redirecting the calls."

"You have my location?"

Another pause as the Kid checked one of his many computers. The iPhones we carried were untraceable like disposables—no specific network carrier—but were still connected to the Internet. The Kid had a program running on each of our phones that could track our locations. It was so precise he could narrow down where we were in any given place to about a few feet.

"Yes," the Kid said. "Why?"

"Because if you don't want me ditching my phone right now, I'd hold off on the speeches for the time being."

"I just … I think this is a bad idea."

"Do you have Carver's location?"

"It's gone."

"What do you mean?"

"They probably destroyed his phone by now. Either that or turned it off."

The Beachside was now less than four blocks away. Traffic continued past me on the street, their tires hissing on the pavement. The rain continued its light drizzle.

I paused at the corner, glanced back over my shoulder, then crossed the street to the next block. I said, "I'll have to call you back."

"Why?"

"Don't call me back. If you do, I won't answer."

"Goddamn it, Ben, what's going on?"

"I'm being followed."

I'm a completely different man than I was two years ago. Two years ago I was just a house painter that barely pulled in thirty thousand dollars a year. I had a wife and daughter. I had survived only two semesters of college before dropping out. My life was simple but fulfilling, and that's all that really mattered to me.

Then, suddenly, that simple but fulfilling life was stolen. My wife and daughter were taken away. I was thrust into a hell nobody should ever be forced to experience, and many times I was only a few seconds or a few feet from death.

But then Carver Ellison entered my life. Carver and his men saved me and helped me understand that there was no way to win Simon's game. That, despite Simon's promise, my family was already dead.

Two years ago my life changed forever. It was no longer simple, no longer fulfilling. Before, my only purpose was to love and support my wife and daughter. Then, when they were taken away, when I knew they were dead, I realized I had nothing else to live for. Nothing else except to avenge them. I no longer cared about dying, because already most of my soul was dead.

Carver trained me well. I was a good student. I studied and trained and did everything I needed to do to become a great soldier. Most importantly, my senses became heightened. When I walked into a room, I immediately assessed the people in there, the number of exits, the different weapons. And I knew when someone was watching or following me.

That was how I knew right then, as I disconnected from the Kid and slipped the phone back into my pocket, that I was being followed.

I continued down the block, my pace steady, reaching back for the gun strapped in the waistband of my jeans. I kept the gun concealed in my jacket and continued walking, passing the few people still out and about in the drizzle, the Beachside now almost two blocks away. There was a parking lot coming up. I increased my pace and then turned left, pushed myself up flat against the wall, waiting, listening to the night sounds—the traffic, the rain, the wind—and started counting.

Nine seconds later—what I had roughly estimated, the person behind me hurrying at a distance of about fifty yards—a figure appeared around the corner, coming fast, and I grabbed the figure by the throat and threw him against the wall and had the barrel of my gun in his face almost instantaneously.

Then I paused, my shoulders dropping, and said, "Ian, what the fuck?"

Ian looked like he was about to piss his pants. His eyes were real big and he was breathing heavy and it didn't occur to me until a few seconds passed that I should loosen my grip around his neck. When I stepped back and put my gun away, Ian rubbed his throat like I had completely crushed it.

"Well?" I said.

"I had Ronny drop me off."

"Ronny wouldn't drop you off."

He ducked his head and nodded. "At the next red light I told him to keep going and hopped out. I ran the whole way back to catch up with you."

"I know. You weren't very inconspicuous about. So why are you here?"

"What?"

"You heard me."

He looked down at his feet, shrugged. "I'm not … the strongest person in the world. I know that. I know I'm not very brave either. But this … I want to help."

"The girl might not even be there."

"I know."

"Ronny's right—this whole thing could get us killed."

"I *know*. But I just … I have to do this."

"Why?"

"Because I don't"—he swallowed, shook his head—"I don't want to remember this night and know I was a coward."

"You have a piece?"

His face reddened. "I forgot it."

I gave him one of the guns and a spare magazine. Then, frowning at him, I asked, "Didn't Ronny try to stop you?"

"He did. But I told him we would be okay. I promised we'd see him back at the house later."

I glanced back at the Beachside Hotel only two blocks away, then nodded at Ian. "All right," I said. "Then let's keep that promise."

FOURTEEN

The truth was I had no plan. As I'd been nearing the Beachside, no coherent thoughts had been going through my mind. I'd just been seeing snapshots of different parts of my life—Jen and Casey at our home in Lanton, Carver and Maya and everyone else, then just Carver's face as he choked on his blood—and I think a part of me knew what I was doing. That this *was* suicide, sprinkled with a touch of valor. That now, without Carver, whatever life I and the rest of us had was over. That so far we'd been living on borrowed time, and it was time to pay up.

But when Ian showed up things changed. Now it wasn't just my life on the line. Now I also had to worry about Ian, which gave me some purpose, some goal to try to attain. We would do this together—we would try to save this girl's life before she was taken to some other place, to some other game—and in doing so we would keep each other accountable. We would keep each other alive.

So this is what we did the morning Carver died, that Saturday morning around three o'clock, as the drizzle increased to heavier rain and the occasional lightning began streaking the sky nonstop: we split up and hid on separate sides of the Beachside Hotel.

I went for one of the cars near the corner, a Honda Civic. I got on the ground to see if anything was rigged up underneath. Next I glanced inside, looking for an alarm, something that might make noise if opened. There was nothing there, so I tried the door. Unlocked. I opened it and slipped inside, shutting the door so the interior lamp wouldn't be lit more than a few seconds.

I had put my earpiece back in. Ian—presumably in a car or truck of his own on the other side of the hotel—did the same. After about thirty seconds, I heard his voice.

"Ben?"

"Yeah."

"You set up?"

"Yeah."

"You in a car?"

"Yeah."

"You notice anything strange about it?"

I glanced around again, the light not very good, but I immediately understood what Ian meant. The car was spotless. Not exactly brand new, but it was clear nobody was regularly using this thing. No scattered CD cases on the floor or balled-up fast food bags. No menus or car dealership flyers left under the windshield tossed in the backseat.

"This isn't good," Ian whispered in my ear, and I agreed with him. This wasn't good at all.

I called the Kid.

He said, "You okay?"

"I'm fine. Ian's with me now. We're scoping out the hotel. I think every car in the lot is a decoy."

"Say that again?"

I told him how the Civic was spotless, how Ian's was too.

The Kid said, "Dude, I told you it was a fucking setup."

"Thanks for the reminder. Is there any way to get some eyes inside? Like can you hack into the security system and let me know if there's even anybody inside this thing?"

"If this was a regular functioning hotel, sure I could. But the way this thing's set up, I doubt there is any security going on."

"Can you at least check?"

"Fine. Give me a few minutes."

He clicked off.

I asked, "Anything on your side yet, Ian?"

"Nope."

I nodded, figuring as much. After we had peeled out of the parking lot the first time around, until Ian and I returned, maybe ten minutes had passed. More than enough time for whoever was inside this place to disappear. For all we knew, we were staking out an empty building.

The Kid called back. "*Nada*."

"Figures. Have you talked to Ronny yet?"

"Yeah. He's back on 95, headed north."

"Good. Is he pissed?"

"Let's just say you're not his favorite person right now."

Before I could reply, a delivery truck pulled into the parking lot. Its headlights momentarily splashed the front of the hotel as it pulled into Ian's side of the lot.

In my ear, Ian whispered, "You watching this, Ben?"

I said into the phone, "Kid, I'm going to have to call you back."

"What? What the fuck's happening now?"

"Put a dollar in the swear jar." I disconnected the phone and asked Ian, "What is it doing now?"

"I think … yeah, it's coming toward you."

The delivery truck was indeed looping around the hotel. Its headlights now splashed the tall grass and palm trees out by the beach before shining on this side of the parking lot as it made the turn. Brake lights flared as it came to a stop, more or less in the same place Ronny had parked the SUV not even a half hour ago.

The passenger's side door opened and a man jumped out. He headed toward the back of the truck. He opened the back doors, and four men piled out. They were all wearing black. All five of them headed straight for the entrance.

"What are they doing?" Ian asked.

I didn't answer. I squinted and leaned forward. Tried making out what was happening now in the hotel lobby. It was difficult because I couldn't use the windshield wipers, but I could make out one of them—it looked like the one from the passenger seat—was pointing at different places in the lobby. He pointed at one of the other men and motioned for him to come with him as he walked away.

"Ben?"

"Hold on."

This wasn't exactly what I'd expected. Then again, I hadn't really been expecting anything.

Ian whispered, "What are they doing?"

"I'm not sure yet."

Then, when two of the men brought out one bagged body and placed it in the back of the delivery truck, I understood.

"They're the cleaners," I said.

I started counting the bodies they were bringing out—a second body, then a third. I was counting the other men, too. There were the four from the back of the truck, plus the passenger. The driver stayed behind the wheel, sipping something from a Styrofoam cup.

The five men were heading back to the delivery truck when another pair of headlights splashed the front of the hotel.

"You watching this?" Ian whispered.

Again I didn't answer. I was too busy wondering why they'd stopped with the three bodies. What about Carver?

"Ben, it's coming your way."

The headlights this time belonged to an SUV. Not the same Chevrolet Ronny drove, but a GMC Yukon. It came to a stop right behind the delivery truck. Like before, a man got out of the passenger's side. He wore glasses and a black baseball cap. He walked up to the back of the delivery truck. Talked to a few of the men standing there. One of them lit up a smoke.

They stood like that for about a minute, just talking, when the man who'd come from the Yukon took a step forward to look inside the truck. He nodded and turned back around, shook everyone's hand, clapped them all on the back. The four men piled in the back of the delivery truck again, and the truck's passenger shut the door. He said a few more words to the man who'd come from the SUV, then hurried over to the front of the truck and climbed inside.

As the delivery truck pulled away, the Yukon moved up to take its place. The Yukon's passenger stepped up to the driver's side and spoke briefly to the driver. He stepped back and waited until someone else came out of the back, also wearing black. They appeared to speak briefly before turning and heading into the hotel lobby.

"I'm going in," I said.

"What? What's happening? What's going on over there?"

I watched the Yukon for a few long seconds, then opened the door and quickly stepped out. Crouched down and started forward, weaving through the cars. As I did I took out my gun, jacked a round into the chamber.

"Ben?" Ian said in my ear. "What's *happening*?"

I took my earpiece out, shoved it in my pocket. Kept moving forward, closer to the hotel and the Yukon.

I stopped at the last row, crouched behind a BMW. I peeked around the fender at the Yukon. The driver was definitely the only person inside. He just sat there, leaning back in his seat, smoking a cigarette. His attention appeared to be focused on the glass doors leading into the hotel lobby, which was a good thing, because as I got up from my spot—my phone starting to vibrate in my pocket—I quickly made my way across the small expanse of wet pavement, my gun held down at my side. I went straight for the passenger's side door and put my fingers underneath the handle, prayed to whatever gods there were out there that it wouldn't be locked.

It wasn't.

The driver, a young guy with long sideburns, was in the process of taking a drag of the cigarette when I opened the door. The cherry on the end lit up brightly, reflected off the window, and for an instant the reflection was the only thing I concentrated on. Then he started, dropping the cigarette like it'd burned him, reaching for the gun in his shoulder holster.

He said, "What the—" and I jammed the barrel of my gun into his stomach, pulled the trigger twice. Both times his body jerked, his eyes widened, and it looked like he was going to say something else. But his face quickly paled and he leaned forward a bit. He coughed up blood, his body jerking, going through the motions of shutdown. It took longer than I would have liked, standing there with the door open, keeping the gun aimed at his chest in case he tried something else. Finally two minutes passed and he was dead.

I stared past his body toward the glass doors of the lobby. It still appeared deserted. I leaned back and looked at him for a moment. He was still wearing his seatbelt so his body was sagged forward only partway, like he was a marionette. The cigarette he'd dropped was smoldering on his lap, a gray wisp of smoke doing pirouettes toward the ceiling.

I backed out of the Yukon, quietly shut the door. The sound wasn't loud but still I tensed. After all, I'd just fired two rounds into the man, but it had been straight into his stomach, and I was fairly certain the close proximity muffled the shots. At least neither of the two men came rushing outside, guns blazing, but that didn't mean they weren't inside now, waiting for me to enter.

My cell phone had stopped vibrating somewhere in the process of opening the Yukon's door and shooting the driver and waiting for him to die. I was tempted to take it out, check who had called, the Kid or Ian. But time was passing too quickly. If the girl was in fact inside the hotel—and for some reason I felt that she was, that she was very close—it wouldn't take long for these two men to bring her outside.

I hurried directly up the walkway toward the automatic glass doors. I kept the gun at my side, at a position where I could bring it up in less than a second if need be.

Behind me, footsteps.

I spun, the gun now in both hands, aimed right at the man approaching me. The man with long hair hiding under his blue Red Sox cap.

"Jesus Christ," I said.

"What?" Ian whispered. "You just disappeared. I tried calling you."

I motioned at the Yukon behind him. "I was busy."

He glanced back, saw the body slumped in the seat. "I can see that," he said. "Now, what's the plan?"

I headed toward the glass doors again, Ian now beside me, his gun out.

"There is no plan. But there's two of them. I'm pretty sure they're here to take the girl."

"So we take them out once they hit the lobby?"

"Sounds good to me."

I stepped close enough for the electronic eye to catch me and quietly open the doors. We walked inside. The lobby was completely silent. The only things that filled it were the lost echoes of the gunfire that played out here not even a half hour ago, the still lingering smells of cordite and smoke. And floating somewhere in here, maybe still on the third floor, trying to make its way outside into the drizzle and lightning-dotted night, Carver's last word flitted about like a butterfly minutes out of the cocoon.

FIFTEEN

We waited in the lobby, near the bank of elevators. We took up positions behind the pillars, Ian on one side, me on the other. We didn't wait long before we heard the dinging of an elevator and the whoosh of parting doors. Footsteps on the carpet, a hushed noise, and then they appeared, the two men dressed in black walking on either side of the girl.

One of the men wore glasses and a black baseball cap, the Yukon's passenger. He was on my side and the first one to die. Like the driver, he too attempted to reach for his holstered weapon when he saw me, but he never got the chance.

I stepped around the pillar and leveled the gun right at his head. Fired a round into his face. At that exact moment Ian did the same to the man on the girl's right. First my gunshot, a half-second later Ian's, and then it was silent once again in the lobby.

That was when the little girl started screaming.

Only she wasn't screaming so much as sobbing, those tears that I'd at first thought she had wasted now returning full force. She just stood there, no taller than four feet, her body covered in a long dark coat. There were blue flip-flops on her caramel-colored feet, and her long ragged hair was jet-black.

Ian immediately dropped to his knees in front of her and placed a hand on her shoulder. Telling her that it was all right, that everything was okay, but then she began speaking rapidly in another language—what I realized after a moment was Creole—tears in her wide eyes as she stared down at the two bodies of the men who'd been her captors.

Watching Ian, I felt an ache in my heart, remembering all those nights I'd raced from my bedroom to Casey's, hearing her crying out from a nightmare. Like mother, like daughter, they both suffered from night terrors, from the bogeymen lurking in the shadows of their subconscious. I'd always gone to her and woken her up, held her close and whispered that everything was okay, that nothing could harm her. But in the end I'd been made out to be a liar, because the bogeymen had come for her. They'd come for her and her mother and taken them away, someplace where I could never find them, no matter how hard and how long I searched, before the startling revelation hit me that they were dead.

"No, no, no," Ian said, as soothingly as he could, staring into the girl's dark face, into her pretty eyes. She was pretty in fact, her eyes lightly tinted with green, a girl who might have someday grown up into a full-fledged knockout of a woman. Unfortunately that wasn't going to happen anymore, not to this girl who had already suffered God knows what kind of horrors. No doubt she was already scarred emotionally from everything she'd been forced to do, but that wasn't all. How long had it taken before her spirit broke and she'd accepted the fact she had no more reason to live, that the simple act of breathing had become a way of counting down the minutes until she died?

Watching them, I said, "I'll be right back."

Ian seemed to be making some progress with the girl. In

less than a minute, he'd gotten her to change her screaming and sobbing into a whimper. It would have been best to move her far away from these two bodies, from all the blood and brain tissue and whatever else spotting the walls and carpet, but neither of us was thinking properly at that moment.

Now Ian paused in his attempts to sooth the girl and looked up at me. "You can't leave me with her."

"It'll just be for a minute," I told him, already heading toward the stairs. "I need to see Carver's body."

"But, Ben, what if—"

I hit the fire door and walked straight through, Ian's words lost behind me.

Carver's body was gone. Gun in hand, finger on the trigger, I stood by the bank of elevators and listened to the hum of the ice machine. There was blood on the blue carpet, a dark crimson soaking the seashells.

For some reason I'd expected there to be more blood. I'd expected the carpet to be covered in it.

I moved forward slowly, cautiously, remembering the shooter. How he'd stepped out and shot Carver twice in the chest. I even found myself raising my gun toward the corner of the hallway as I approached, glancing down at the blood-soaked carpet and back up at the corner, ready for anything.

Standing over the spot where Carver had spoken his last word, his face paling as he stared up at me, I noticed the trail of blood. It went around the corner. I'd dragged him all the way here, down the hallway and around the corner, so obviously he'd trailed blood the entire way. But staring at the jagged and thin line of crimson, I realized there were actually two trails.

I went to the other side of the foyer, my back against the wall, inching closer toward the humming ice machine. I kept my gun aimed down the hall. Farther and farther, my eyes flitting on the spots of blood. Then I was at the corner, staring down the hall. No movement. I stepped into the hallway and immediately turned in the opposite direction, the gun raised, ready to fire. Still nothing.

I started down the hallway toward room 339.

A couple rooms before room 339, however, I stopped. It was the room the shooter had stepped out from. The door was partway open. There was no light in the narrow opening.

Raising my gun, I kicked open the door and charged in, flicking on the light switch as I entered. A single lamp lit up the empty room. No bed, no chair, no bedside table. Nothing except the lamp. In the bathroom there was nothing either, not even a shower curtain.

I stepped back out into the hallway.

I continued on toward room 339. That door too was opened just slightly. Darkness peered out from the narrow slit between the door and the frame. Since the girl was downstairs now, I didn't intend for any surprises when I opened the door. I didn't kick it this time, but instead gently pushed it open, reached inside for the light switch. It came on in the corner, right where I'd seen it on Carver's laptop screen. The bed was in the center of the room, the sheets white, pairs of black Velcro straps at the head and foot of the bed.

I glanced up at the corner where I knew the camera had been positioned. It was gone now, but the evidence was still there, the vent where the camera had been hiding behind hanging open. It wasn't quite a normal cleanup job—those in Caesar's army were meticulous through and through—but of course the building was scheduled for demolition in three days, so why bother tidying up?

My cell phone vibrated in my pocket. I knew it was Ian even before I pulled it out and answered it.

"Ben, I'm getting nervous down here."

His voice sounded weird, almost like a frail imitation of his own. Behind it I could hear the girl's soft whimpering.

I stood there for a moment, taking in the room, smelling the sweat and the tears and the acrid odor of urine, presumably when the girl had pissed herself from fear and weariness.

"Yeah," I said. "I'm headed down now."

SIXTEEN

Ian had moved the girl away from the two dead bodies and taken her to one of the couches that hadn't been completely destroyed in the initial shootout. He had gotten her to sit on the couch while he kneeled beside her, still talking to her while she murmured in her native tongue. He heard me approaching and glanced up, questioned me with his eyes whether I'd found anything.

I shook my head but didn't say anything. I was still trying to work it out in my mind. I'd seen the men bring three bodies out of the hotel and load them into the delivery truck. Hadn't I? Was it possible I'd somehow missed a fourth body, that Carver's had gotten lost in the mix?

"Come on," I said. "Let's go."

Ian said something else to the girl, his voice soft, trying his best to smile. He stood up, holding out his hand. The girl hesitantly took it. He led her through the lobby, toward the glass doors that parted for us, then closed behind us, sealing in the dead bodies and everything else that had once been a part of the Beachside Hotel's memory.

We walked into the rain, past the Yukon, listening to the wind and the traffic out on the street.

"Right there," I said, pointing at the Corolla near the end of the parking lot. "You might as well sit with her in the back. You'll have to move Carver's stuff into the front first."

"To be honest," Ian said, "I'd rather drive. I just … I don't think I can handle it."

We were walking side by side, the girl between us. As Ian said this he glanced down at the girl, who had let go of his hand and was now walking with hardly any emotion at all.

"That's fine," I said, pulling the car key from my pocket. I handed it to Ian who then picked up his pace, heading straight for the driver's door. I watched him, this twenty-four-year-old kid who'd modeled his entire acting career after Robert De Niro. There had been nights back at the farmhouse, either while all of us played poker or sat out on the porch underneath a clear sky, where he would do his impersonations. Running lines from *Taxi Driver* or *Raging Bull*, he'd always make us laugh, or at least smile, and sometimes that was all we needed to make it through those dark hours. And now here he was, a man who didn't think he could handle comforting this little girl any longer.

I couldn't blame him.

It's difficult dealing with a child, especially when that child isn't your own, and when you've just killed two men to save this particular child—not to mention losing one of your own in the process—there's a new, stronger sense of responsibility attached. Then again, Ian had never been a father. He had never handled a baby newly born, staring down at the tiny miraculous thing and telling himself he wasn't dreaming. He never had to remind himself this was his baby, his own flesh and blood, and with that knowledge came a great fear. That now he was responsible. That now there was no going back.

That every single thing he did from that moment on was going to affect the future of his child.

It was the same fears I'd had when Casey was born. That suddenly, after all the planning and positive thinking, I was now a father and realized that no matter how hard I tried, I was going to fail. That nothing I could do would ever be good enough. That I would never learn how to change her diapers, or teach her how to read, or rock her to sleep. Even feeding her and burping her was something I'd come to dread, my imagination coming up with several ways to fuck with my head on how I would screw up.

Ian opened the driver's door just as I opened the back door. I leaned in to grab Carver's bag, to move it aside to give the girl space.

And stopped.

"Ian, is the bag up front?"

"What?" He slid into the driver's seat, the key just inches away from the ignition. "No, I don't see it. Why?"

"Don't start the car."

"What?" he asked again, sliding the key into the ignition.

"*Stop!*"

He froze.

"Don't move a muscle."

He didn't. Softly, he asked, "What's wrong?"

"Just don't move."

I reversed out of the backseat, slowly, and then lowered myself to the wet pavement. I used my phone to illuminate the undercarriage. Nothing.

"Ben?" Ian said, his voice more than nervous. "What's wrong?"

"Carver's bag is missing."

"So?"

"Somebody obviously took it."

"And that means what?"

"That means somebody may have left a surprise in its place."

I stood back up and glanced at the hood. I considered having Ian disengage the hood but knew that wasn't Simon's style. A bomb hooked up to the ignition would take too long to set, and besides, it could be easily defused. After all, roughly ten minutes had occurred from the moment Ronny fishtailed out of the parking lot to when Ian and I returned, which meant that they would act fast.

Not even thirty seconds had passed since I told Ian to stop, but it felt like an hour. I stood there, thinking, the girl quiet beside me. I leaned back down in the backseat, all the way down to the floor, and shined my phone's screen under the driver's seat.

"Son of a bitch," I said.

Ian, his voice barely a whisper: "How bad is it?"

"Extremely. Looks like a tilt fuse."

Ian groaned softly but said nothing.

I squinted at the device underneath the seat. It wasn't a completely professional job, but it was designed to do the trick.

Ian said, "Am I … am I going to die?"

"Be quiet."

"Ben."

"No, you're not. Now be quiet."

A tilt fuse usually consists of a small glass tube filled at the bottom with a certain volume of mercury. At the cap end are wired two live electrical contacts linked to a battery and bomb. When the device is properly placed, such as in a car, the idea is when the fuse is tilted or moved, the mercury will slide down the tube and close the electrical circuit wired to the bomb. Once the circuit is closed, the electric current will then be able to bridge the previously open gap and activate the bomb.

That was what we had here. From where I was positioned, I couldn't see the entire tube, but it was clear the mercury hadn't shifted yet. If that were the case, all three of us would be dead. But the bomb had been attached to the seat in a way that it would be impossible to move it without upsetting the mercury, now that it had been activated. Which meant it was impossible to deactivate it.

Somehow Ian hadn't set it off when he sat down on the seat. It was possible there wasn't as much mercury in there as I feared. But once he would start the car and back out of the space, that would give it enough movement to detonate.

"Ben?" Ian's voice trembled on that one simple word.

"Quiet."

"Just … take the girl. Go on without me."

"I said quiet."

"But—"

"Ian," I said. "You're not going to die. I promise you that. Just sit still while I figure this out."

He sat still. I glanced over my shoulder to check on the girl. She still stood there, watching me. I knew the best thing right now was to get the girl as far away from this car as possible. But I worried that if I did that, Ian would freak and inadvertently set off the bomb. Carver had already died tonight; I wasn't going to let Ian die too.

I climbed out of the back and stood up straight. Turned to the little girl and said, "Do you understand English?"

She just stared at me.

"I need you to go back to where we just left. Do you see that white SUV parked over there?"

No reply.

"I need you to go stand beside it. Okay?"

The girl blinked.

I turned back to Ian. He was staring back at me, his face pale. He looked like he was going to speak again but I held a finger to my lips.

"Stay quiet and don't move," I said. "I'll be right back."

I grabbed the girl's shoulder and directed her back toward the Yukon. I expected there to be some resistance, maybe even more whimpering, but she complied without trouble. Once we reached the SUV, I opened the back door and had her climb in and buckled her to the seat. Then I hurried around the front to the driver's side. I unclipped the dead driver and pulled him from the seat. He tilted over and fell to the ground. I grabbed his arms and pulled him a few feet away from the Yukon, then stepped back to the SUV and leaned in.

"Stay here," I told the girl.

She just stared back at me.

I ran back to the Corolla. It didn't look like Ian had taken a single breath the entire time I was gone. Tears stood in his eyes.

"Okay," I said. "Here's what we're going to do. I'm going to stand here next to the car and hold my arm out. You're going to use that as leverage as you slowly—and I mean *slowly*—lift yourself off the seat. Any sudden movement, no matter how slight, will get us both killed. Understood?"

He nodded slowly.

"Good. Now let's do this."

He grasped my arm and lifted his left leg and gently placed it on the ground. Next he slowly moved his right leg over as he turned slightly in the seat. He started to lift himself up as I leaned down and used my hand to press my weight onto the seat. Ian didn't fully realize what I was doing until he had stood up completely out of the car.

"Ben, what are you doing?"

"Go."

"But—"

"Take the girl. Make sure she's safe."

He just stood there, motionless.

"Now, Ian."

He stood there for another second or two before turning and sprinting toward the Yukon. I watched him go. Then I started to release the pressure on the seat—slowly, so very slowly—until my hand came off the seat completely and I stepped back and away from the car.

I closed my eyes for a moment, took a deep breath, surprised I was still alive.

Then I turned and started running toward the Yukon.

I was halfway there when the world exploded.

SEVENTEEN

I heard the blast an instant before I felt it.

Like a giant fist, it sent me flying into the nearest car. I hit its rear window so hard the glass spider-webbed. I lay crumpled on the ground, the majority of my body feeling like it had been shattered. I may have briefly passed out, I don't know. All I know was my ears were ringing and I thought I was dying. The next thing I knew someone was shouting my name and I felt hands on me, trying to turn me over, feeling my chest and my stomach and my ribs, asking if anything hurt, and then I was being pulled to my feet and dragged to the Yukon where Ian managed to get me into the backseat.

The girl was screaming again. She wouldn't stop. Ian climbed in behind the wheel and got us moving almost instantly, fishtailing out of the Beachside's parking lot. I was coherent enough to glance out the window and see the destruction. The cars strewn everywhere, the fires, the crater where the Corolla had stood.

Ian was saying something to me—shouting, really, trying to get my attention.

"What?"

"Are you okay?"

I groaned, shifting in the seat, holding my side. "I've been better."

"How did it happen?"

"Don't know. The tilt fuse shouldn't have gone off."

I reached into my pocket for my phone. I expected it to be a shattered mess, but it still looked usable.

"What are you doing?" Ian asked, eyeing me in the rearview mirror.

"Calling the Kid. What are you doing?"

"Fuck, man, I'm just driving."

He was driving much like Ronny had done earlier tonight, swerving from one lane to the next.

"Mind the speed limit," I said. "We can't afford to get pulled over."

He slowed a bit as the phone connected with the Kid's number.

The Kid answered almost instantly. "Goddamn, it's about fucking time you called."

"We have the girl," I said.

"Yeah? And in the process of saving her, did anything, you know, *explode*?"

The girl had stopped screaming, was doing her whimpering thing now. I glanced at her and said, "I almost did."

"What the fuck happened?"

"What have you heard?"

"Not much so far. The only word right now is there's been an explosion at a hotel in Miami Beach."

"Wonder how Caesar is going to spin that."

"That's the least of your problems," the Kid said. "Are you guys in a GMC Yukon?"

I looked up sharply at Ian. "Why?"

"It was just reported stolen."

I shifted again in my seat, wincing at the pain. "The cops

aren't going to bother with a stolen vehicle right now, not after an explosion like that."

"That depends on how badly Caesar wants you guys."

"Meaning?"

"Meaning someone could always call in an anonymous tip saying the Yukon is suspected in the explosion. Where did you pick it up, anyway?"

"It used to belong to one of Caesar's people."

"Are you out of your fucking mind? The thing's probably LoJacked."

I thought about it for a second. "No, it's not. If it had some kind of tracking device on it, why would they report it stolen?"

"Beats the hell out of me."

"Look," I said, shifting again in the seat, my body flaring with pain, "do you have our location?"

"Of course."

"What's the fastest way to get back to 95?"

I heard quick typing on the Kid's end. He said, "Two blocks up, make a U-turn. Then keep going until the bridge and take it and continue straight. It will put you guys back on the Julia Tuttle Expressway."

I relayed the directions to Ian and then said into the phone, "How's Ronny?"

"He's fine. But you guys ... what's your plan for the girl?"

"Still haven't figured that part out yet."

"Yeah, it seems like you haven't figured out most of your plan so far tonight."

"At least we're still alive."

The Kid was quiet for a moment. "Yeah," he said, his voice somber. "There is that."

Maybe ten minutes later, Ian said, "Should we drop her off there?"

The Mount Sinai Medical Center was coming up fast on our right, the massive complex bright in the dark drizzle.

I looked at the girl beside me. She just sat there quietly, staring out her window. I hesitated, then shook my head.

"Keep going. It's best we get out of Miami Beach as soon as possible."

Ian kept the Yukon on the highway, taking us over the causeway headed into Miami.

Less than thirty seconds passed before my phone vibrated. It was the Kid.

"We've got a problem," he said.

"I really wish you would come up with a better opening line."

"The APB on the Yukon? It was just canceled."

I glanced up and caught Ian eyeing me in the rearview mirror again. Only, I realized a second later, he was looking past my head out the back of the SUV. I turned slightly, my body flaring with pain again, and said, "Fuck."

In my ear, the Kid asked, "What's wrong?"

"I'm going to have to call you back."

"Why?"

"There's a cop directly behind us."

A second later, the police cruiser whooped its siren and turned on its flashing lights.

EIGHTEEN

I shoved the phone into my pocket, found myself reaching for my gun. It was gone, no doubt lost in the explosion.

I asked Ian, "How long has it been behind us?"

"Not long at all. It came up really fast."

It was riding our ass now, less than ten feet away, its roof lights blazing with brightness.

I stared out at the highway in front of us. The causeway was maybe three miles long, give or take, and we'd only gone about a mile already.

"Give it all you've got," I said.

Ian whipped his head back at me. "Are you fucking nuts?"

"Those aren't regular cops."

"How do you know?"

"The APB on the Yukon was just canceled. Now, give it all you've got."

Ian turned back to focus on the road. Both hands on the steering wheel, his shoulders tensed. Besides the few cars on the other side of the causeway, we and the police cruiser were the only cars headed west. He pressed his foot down harder on the gas.

The red and white lights flashing behind us continued going for a couple more seconds, then all at once stopped.

Ian said, "What the hell?"

"Give me your gun."

"Why?"

"Just do it."

Ian reached into his jacket and pulled out his piece just as the cruiser swung over into the left lane and picked up speed. I leaned forward, taking Ian's gun, and saw the speedometer. Ian was already doing about ninety, which meant the cruiser coming up on the left was going at least one hundred.

"Push it," I told him, and turned slightly in the seat, watching the cruiser as its nose came parallel with our rear bumper.

The passenger's side window began to lower.

And out of it, like an insect's antenna, came a double-barreled shotgun.

I said shit, or Ian said shit, or maybe both of us said shit at the same time. I grabbed the little girl's head and pushed it down.

The cruiser sped up even faster and ran completely parallel with us. I could see the two cops in the front, both men, looking at Ian in the driver's seat.

"Hit the brakes," I shouted, and for some reason I expected Ian to ask me why, I expected to have to repeat myself, but he slammed on the brakes at once and the SUV started skidding, fishtailing, just as an explosion burst from the shotgun, spraying the front hood.

The girl immediately started screaming, fighting my hand to raise her head back up. I held her down and double-checked her seatbelt. It was secure, so I unbuckled it and pulled her toward me as I moved into her seat. Ian's gun in my hand, I lowered the window, the rain at once pelting my face and glasses.

"Keep it steady," I called up to Ian, who was now hunched over the wheel, his foot back on the gas.

Up ahead, the cruiser's brake lights flared, slowing down to try to meet us once again as we sped up.

I leaned out the window as far as I could, keeping myself balanced with my left arm against the windowsill, my entire upper body out the window, holding the gun in my right hand.

The cruiser was falling back fast and I didn't hesitate, firing at the rear window and the wheels and the window again.

The cruiser's brake lights flared again, just as the rear window spider-webbed. A moment later it sped up, jerking itself into the center lane.

To compensate, Ian started moving over into the left lane but I shouted, "Stay here! Don't let them get on the girl's side!"

The Yukon wobbled a bit in the lane but then righted itself and we sped on, the police cruiser only yards ahead of us.

"Ram it," I said.

"What?"

"Ram it!" I shouted, and I could feel the Yukon accelerate, lessening the distance between its front and the police car's rear —until, suddenly, the SUV's nose poked the back of the police cruiser. But it didn't do much damage—it just sent the cruiser ahead a few feet, fishtailing too as its driver tried to gain control of the wheel, before falling back. Ian went to ram it again when something exploded inside the cruiser and the rear window shattered.

Ian shouted, "What the fuck?"

The police cruiser's passenger had crawled over the front seat, was now taking the barrel of his shotgun and pushing all the shards of glass out of his way.

"Right lane and brake!" I shouted, dropping the gun and moving over toward the girl, putting my arms around her and pushing her head into my shoulder, just as Ian slammed on the brakes and jerked the wheel to the right.

At that same moment the cop fired, the shotgun spraying the hood and windshield, sending fissures through the glass. For an instant it felt like the Yukon was up on two wheels, and I was sure that we were going to flip, that this was how we were going to die. But then all four tires met the highway once again, skidding over the pavement until we were completely stopped.

The girl was screaming into my shoulder, kicking her feet, and Ian was saying something up front, but my ears were ringing again and pain was streaking through my body and for an instant I had the light-headed sensation that I was about to pass out.

Up ahead, the cruiser's brake lights flared as it made a hard and sudden U-turn.

Ian groaned. "What the hell?"

The police car was maybe one hundred yards away, its headlights glaring back at us. Not moving, not doing anything but just sitting there.

I said, "I think he wants to play chicken."

Ian jerked his head back, his eyes wide. "You're kidding me."

I glanced behind us, could see distant headlights further down the causeway. We had maybe a minute or so before they reached us, and then what was going to happen? More than likely innocent people were going to die, and I wasn't about to put those extra souls on my conscience.

I turned back around. The highway stretched between us and the police cruiser, the rain falling through the heavy glare of our headlights. Not far beyond it, the causeway ended, an off-ramp taking drivers toward some destination on the mainland.

I buckled the girl in tight to the seat, then buckled myself in. I said, "Do it."

Ian just stared at me like I had five heads.

I told him what I wanted him to do, and he stared at me a moment longer, then turned back around in his seat. He took a long deep breath, staring out through the rain and spots where the shotgun had blasted.

"Here goes nothing," he said, and slammed his foot down on the gas.

The Yukon jerked forward, its engine roaring, the needle on the speedometer climbing higher and higher. At the same moment the police cruiser jerked forward, coming right at us. The girl continued screaming into my arm, she kept kicking her legs, but I held her as tightly as I could, watching through the windshield as the headlights got closer.

The distance between us and the cruiser grew smaller and smaller by the second. Ian kept both of his hands on the wheel, his foot on the gas, pushing the SUV for all it was worth. A moment before we reached them he lifted his foot from the gas and started veering off toward the left, then all at once hit the brakes and jerked the wheel to the right, punching the gas. It was tight, but the cruiser took the bait, already moving toward the left, hoping to hit us head on. By then we'd already made the switch and the side of the Yukon scraped against the side of the police cruiser, creating the loudest screech of metal against metal I'd ever heard, and then we were around them, pointed straight for the exit.

"Yee-haw!" Ian shouted, glancing back as we sped down the ramp. I found myself glancing back too, watching as the police cruiser's taillights flared angrily again, its driver attempting another hard and sudden one-eighty. The girl was crying out beside me and I turned back to her, briefly placed an arm around her shoulder, then looked up toward the front of the SUV, realized all at once that we were doing maybe sixty or seventy miles per hour and there wasn't much room left on the ramp and that Ian still had his attention on the cruiser behind us.

"Ian!" I shouted, and he swung back around, but already we'd run our course on the ramp. There was hardly any more room left. Ian slammed on the brakes frantically, desperately, jerking the steering wheel first left and then right, and once again it felt like the Yukon was up on two wheels, just hanging there as if by a thread, before suddenly we were tipping onto our side, metal scraping against pavement.

Then darkness.

NINETEEN

The darkness didn't last long.

I could feel something warm on my face, something wet. I opened my eyes but saw only black.

My first thought was: *I'm blind*, but then realized a second later that it was blood in my eyes.

A groan sounded out somewhere in the black, and I blinked again, and again, and again, until I was able to make out shapes. A moment later the world began to take on substance and I saw the back of one of the seats in front of me, less than ten inches from my face. I blinked again and tried to move, but my entire body roared with pain, every muscle and nerve and joint screaming at me to please stop.

"Ian?"

My voice was a kind of gurgle. There was no answer, so I tried moving again, ignoring the pain, the numbness, the sudden realization that both Ian and the little girl might be dead.

They weren't.

I could see both of them moving, through the thin layer of blood coating my eyes. The girl was squirming in her seat, crying, while Ian was somewhere up front, the shape of his head moving back and forth.

"Ian?" I said again, my hands finding my face, wiping the blood away. I realized my glasses had fallen off, but still I could see better now, and with the seeing a new kind of realization hit me that the SUV was on its side.

This, I understood, was mainly the cause of the new pain and numbness circulating throughout my body. My seatbelt had done its job fairly well, keeping me in place, though it had dug deep into my stomach, kind of suspending me in midair. The same thing must have happened to the girl. Up front, though, it was impossible to tell what was going on with Ian.

"Ian," I said once more, trying to get my voice to rise above the girl's sobs.

A groan answered me, a terrible sounding groan that could have meant so many different things.

I squeezed my eyes shut and tried moving my hands again, only they didn't seem to want to move. I had to work at it for a couple of seconds before first one hand touched the buckle of my seatbelt, followed by the other hand, and they worked at that for a while before I understood there was too much pressure being exerted by my body, that it wasn't going to release until I took a lot of that pressure off.

"Oh fuck," Ian breathed up front, or in the back, or on the side—the way the Yukon was positioned, it had really messed up my sense of direction.

"Ian," I called. "What is it? What's wrong?"

"Fuck, fuck, fuck!"

With each emphasis of the word his head jerked back and forth, the motion so quick and sudden I had the crazy idea it would somehow tear away from his neck.

The girl's sobbing seemed to have died down now, or maybe something had gone wrong with my hearing. I glanced up, saw her more or less tied to the seat, her arms and legs flailing about as she tried to grab onto anything for support.

I took a long, deep breath—a breath that caused a thousand needles to pierce into my chest—and attempted to release the seatbelt once again. This time it worked. The seatbelt unlatched and I fell, my legs and knees striking the side of the SUV, which had now become the floor. Then I was crouching, wiping at my eyes again, at my face. I gently touched my forehead and could feel the tenderness there. I took a step and heard the tinkle of glass shards, figured that during the crash the windshield—not to mention the side windows—had imploded, sending the shards right in my face. All said and done, it could have been a hell of a lot worse.

The driver's side of the SUV was the side now resting on the ground. It made it so we would have to crawl up to the passenger's side to get out. Either that, or kick out whatever shards remained of the windshield and crawl out that way.

The girl was still kicking and flailing her arms. I held out my hands to her.

Shh, I said, or tried to say, placing my hands on her arms, on her shoulders, trying to get her to settle down. Her dark green-tinted eyes stared back at me, helpless.

Ian groaned again in the front, mixing a string of curse words together, but I barely heard him. I kept my attention focused on getting the girl down. She had stopped kicking and flailing, was now just hanging there. I stepped up and tried to grab onto her body, hold her up as I worked with the buckle of the seatbelt. A few seconds later I had it undone and then was carefully pulling her out of it.

"There we go," I said to her, trying to smile, trying to act like everything was fine and dandy.

The girl said something in her native tongue, what sounded like just one word, and though it may have meant a countless number of things—*I'm scared*, *Get the fuck off me*, *I like Kool-*

Aid—I wanted to think that word was *Thank you*. Even then, hearing her say it, the word fighting through the blood pounding in my ears and the pain streaking through my body and Ian's nonstop groaning, that was what I believed she'd said.

"You're welcome," I said, still smiling, still with blood on my face. Then I glanced up.

The window of the door a few feet above my head was closed. Through it was the dark sky, the soft pattering of the drizzle. It's strange, the way nature will continue unabated, no matter what kind of tragedy strikes us here on the earth. Someone will get hit by a car, a plane will crash, fifty people will be killed in a bombing, and the rain will continue falling like nothing has changed, the wind will continue blowing like everything is fine, and the world will keep spinning no matter what.

I set the girl down, so she was standing on the glass shards. There wasn't much room and I was aware that her body was touching mine as she turned around in a circle, trying to figure out where to go next. I noticed my glasses on the ground too, right by her feet. I did my best to bend down, grab them, place them back on my face. Then I turned toward where Ian was still strapped to his seat.

And at once I could see what all the groaning was about— how when the Yukon had finally stopped, the front end had smashed into a tree and crumpled Ian's left leg.

"Shit," Ian was saying, or groaning, or whimpering. He sensed me close by and looked over. I could see the pain and weariness in his pale face. For some reason it reminded me of Carver's face while he lay dying on the blue carpet speckled by the seashells, his chest dark with blood.

"I think it's broken," Ian said, squeezing the words out through clenched teeth.

"You think?"

"I know." He tried moving it, cried out instead.

"Don't move it."

Ian glared back at me. He said, "Fuck you, Ben," spittle flying from his lips, his jaw grinding his teeth together.

"But your leg is—"

"Broken, yeah. So fuck you, and fuck whatever it is you want me to do. It's your fault this happened."

It was clear reasoning with Ian was a lost cause, so I turned to the girl, still moving in a circle, trying to figure a way out. I turned my attention back to the rear driver's side door, which was now acting as the SUV's roof. I stood and placed a foot on the side of the Ian's seat and started to push myself up.

"What are you doing?" Ian asked, his teeth still clenched.

I ignored him and continued to climb. I got my feet planted, then extended my right arm as far up as I could, grabbing the door handle and pulling it. This unlatched the door, sure, but gravity was my enemy now, so much so I had to close my eyes and clench my own teeth as I kept my arm extended, holding the door handle out, keeping the door unlatched, and then all at once pushed it as hard as I could.

The door swung up, enough for some of the drizzle to sneak into the Yukon's cabin, and slammed shut again.

"Ben," Ian said, but I continued to ignore him, planting my feet again, this time extending both arms. Pulling on the door handle, taking a moment to get ready, then all at once pushing with everything I had.

The door swung open, as far as it would go this time. Gravity started to pull it back down, but I immediately grabbed the side of the doorframe and jumped up, using my other hand to stop the door as it attempted to slam shut once again.

Groaning, Ian asked, "You got it?"

"Yeah," I said. "I got it."

It took me another minute or so before I was able to push the door back to the point where it wasn't going to try to slam shut. I started climbing, my hands finding purchase on the cold wet steel. I pushed myself up and leaned to the side, started crawling out that way, only my legs still inside. Turning slightly, I could see where we'd crashed. Down near the end of the ramp, right by a small park. The front of the Yukon had gone right into the side of a palm tree.

Outside now, with the rain damping my hair and glasses and jacket, I was able to smell the oil and gas coming from the SUV's cracked engine.

"God*damn*," said a voice behind me. "Looks like you've got yourself quite a mess here, don't you think?"

I twisted around so quickly I nearly lost my footing. But somehow I managed to stay in place. Somehow I managed to hold myself there and stare down at the two police officers watching me. They were leaning against the battered police cruiser, wearing rain slickers and hats, their arms crossed.

One of them pointed at the Yukon. "You better help your friends in there."

I didn't say anything. I was expecting them to pull their guns, to riddle my body with bullets. But they just continued leaning against their patrol car, watching like an SUV on its side in the rain at three o'clock in the morning was no big thing here in Miami.

The cops had already placed flares up by the entrance of the off-ramp, forcing traffic coming from Miami Beach to find an alternate route. There were a few lights on in the buildings around us, a few silhouettes watching from windows.

"Come on," the same officer said. "We don't got all night."

I glanced down through the opening. The little girl was staring up at me, rapidly blinking her eyes because of the drizzle. Ian was staring up at me too, a frown on his pain-contorted face, clearly unaware of our guests.

I started to slide back down into the Yukon when the other officer said, "Whoa there. Not so fast." He pushed off from the cruiser and slowly made his way forward, motioning at the front of the Yukon. "Why don't you come down here and help them out through the windshield. Nice and easy like." He said this with a big grin, his voice taking on an over-exaggerated southern drawl, like he was a hick sheriff of some swampland town.

He crossed his arms again, that grin never leaving his long face. I stared down at him for another couple of seconds, faintly hearing Ian calling my name, before pushing myself up even farther out of the door. I pulled out first one leg, then the other, swung them over what had once been the SUV's roof, and slid down, landing on my feet.

The cop was less than ten feet away from me, still with his arms crossed, still grinning. He knew there was nothing I could do now, nothing that would save me. Even if I had a weapon and tried grabbing for it, either he or his partner would most likely draw faster and put me down within a second.

The grin fading, the cop shook his head and glanced back at his partner. "Hey, Gary, can you believe this guy actually lives up to his name? He's just standing there like a fucking man of wax." He turned back to me. "Ain't that right, Man of Wax?"

"There are witnesses."

"Come again?"

"People are watching from the buildings. You can't kill us."

"One, what makes you think we give a shit about them? And two, who said anything about killing you?"

I said nothing.

The cop lifted his chin at the Yukon. "So who else you got in there?"

Without any hesitation, I said, "The Man of Honor," using the name Carver had been given when he was unwillingly thrust into Simon's game.

The cop grinned, shaking his head again.

"Uh-uh," he said. "I don't think so, sport. The Man of Honor's ticket has already been punched. Yours will be soon, too. So let's not put off the inevitable, okay?"

The drizzle continued. The noxious odors of gas and oil still hung faint in the air. Lightning flickered off in the clouds.

I slowly turned and headed toward the front of the Yukon. The palm tree we'd hit when we tipped and crashed was broken near the base. Its leaves still swayed in the light wind and rain.

The windshield was even more shattered than before. There were spots where there was no glass at all. I stepped up close to these spots, very aware that both of the cops were watching me, and leaned down to see inside.

Ian's face was still contorted in pain. "What the fuck are you doing?" he breathed.

I wanted to say something to him right then. Somehow warn him about the cops waiting by their car. Maybe give him a sign that told him there might still be a chance, as long as he had some kind of weapon on him … but then I remembered he had already given me his gun and that I had dropped it somewhere in the Yukon when we crashed.

I said, "We're fucked."

He frowned back at me.

"They're here."

Ian sighed. He closed his eyes and shook his head. When he opened his eyes again, I told him to watch it.

"What are you doing?" he asked, but I ignored him and stepped forward, placing the toe of my shoe through the largest hole in the windshield. As gently as I could I began kicking the shards away, the glass tinkling, creating a soft duet with the continuing drizzle.

Ian closed his eyes and hunched up his shoulders, as if expecting one of the glass shards to find his throat and open it up. As I created a bigger space in the windshield, I noticed the bloody marks on Ian's face.

"Hey," the long-faced cop shouted, dropping the over-exaggerated southern drawl. "Like I told you, we don't got all night."

He placed his hands on his hips, like an impatient parent, and I kicked at a few more loose shards around the windshield and then bent down.

Ian stared back at me, his jaw working. The pain was still there in his face, but now it was accompanied by fear.

"Come on," I said softly, holding out my hand.

Ian looked at it for the longest time. Then he squeezed his eyes shut as he moved his leg. Seconds later he was moving out from behind his seat, crawling through the windshield. The light wasn't the greatest, but it was enough to really see what had become of his left leg—his ankle smashed, his pants and sneaker bloody.

The long-faced cop said, "Why, Man of Wax, I think you got yourself confused. That's not the Man of Honor. That's, that's"—he snapped his fingers in rapid succession, thinking—"why, that's the Actor. See, I keep up with this shit."

"Shit is what it is," I said.

The long-faced cop had been turning toward his partner who was approaching. Now he turned back to me, his face suddenly cold and tight. Not too far away, a faint distinct whine rose up in the night.

The cop asked, "What the fuck did you just say?"

"Shit," I said. I'd helped Ian as best I could, and now I held him beside me, keeping him balanced as he placed all his weight on his right foot. "You said you knew your shit, and I said shit is what it is."

"So you're a smart-ass, are you?" He looked at his partner. "Gary, I forget. What do we do with smart-asses?"

Gary smiled. "Smart-asses? I think the question is what *don't* we do with them."

The drizzle seemed to increase again. Another brief and

short flicker of lightning lit up the dark sky.

I said, "What do you guys want?"

That low distant whine grew louder.

"*Want?*" The long-faced cop grinned at his partner. "I don't know, Gary. What is it that we *want?*"

The low whine, louder and louder, had become a somehow familiar high-pitched sound.

Still smiling, Gary said, "We want to get paid, that's what we want. And bringing you in, the infamous Man of Wax? That's going to bring a big payday."

Light splashed us as someone ignored the flares set up by the highway and came down the off-ramp. Both cops cursed, the long-faced one muttering, "What the fuck does this asshole think he's doing?"

A motorcycle sped toward us, now less than one hundred yards away. The closer it got, the louder the whine became.

The long-faced cop turned and started walking toward the approaching motorcycle, already waving it along. But the bike —a Ducati—skidded to a sudden stop, its tires squealing off the wet pavement. The rider brought a silver-plated pistol out from behind its back. There was a long black tube on the barrel, an incongruous silencer that created only a clapping sound when the four rounds were fired.

Two at the long-faced cop, two at Gary.

Each one in the chest, one in the face.

Then both cops dropped to the ground and it was just me and Ian and this rider dressed all in black, the drizzle beading off the obsidian faceplate.

The rider put the gun away, cocked its head. It pointed at Ian, then down at its own leg, before pointing back at Ian again. The pointed finger became an opened hand, the drops of rain beating against the flat palm. The rider held it like that for a moment before flexing the fingers up and down, up and down, beckoning Ian.

"Go with him," I whispered.

I could feel Ian, open-mouthed, staring at me. He breathed, "Fuck you."

The rider motioned for Ian again.

I remembered the rider as the one who had stopped just outside of The Spur. I didn't know why, but for some reason I trusted whoever it was.

I said, "I don't think we have any other option."

"I'm not fucking going anywhere with that guy."

"He just saved us from those two cops."

"So? That doesn't mean shit. He could be working for Caesar too, or someone else."

I glanced down at Ian's smashed leg. Then I looked up into his eyes and said, "Sorry."

"Sorry?" He frowned. "Sorry about what?"

I kicked his left leg, a simple but solid tap. He howled in pain. I grabbed him and tugged him forward, dragging him toward the Ducati and rider much the same way he had dragged me to the Yukon back at the Beachside Hotel. He hopped along on his right foot, trying to fight me, pulling back and cursing, but it did no good.

I took him straight to the bike and told the rider, "Take him."

Ian said, "What the hell? Fuck you, Ben. Fuck you—"

But by then the rider had inched up on its seat, had grabbed Ian and forced him up onto the back of the Ducati. The end result was not ideal, with Ian lying down on his stomach, his arms on the left side of the bike, his legs on the right, but the rider didn't hesitate in gunning the engine and sending that high-pitched whine out into the night. The rear tire spun out before catching and then they were speeding down the street, the soft red taillight becoming fainter and fainter, the whine growing softer and softer, like the buzz of an insect as it gets caught up in the wind and is never heard from again.

TWENTY

Almost immediately sirens rose up in the distance.

I stood in the rain, listening to them. Watching the spot down the street where the motorcycle had turned and vanished, taking Ian and its anonymous rider with it.

I thought: *What the fuck did I just do?*

I quickly turned and hurried back to the Yukon. I went to where I had pulled Ian out from the front and said, "Little girl."

Movement inside, her head peeking up over the seat to peer back at me.

I motioned at her. "Can you crawl out between the seats?"

She just stared back at me with her dark green-tinted eyes, and I was sure that she didn't understand me at all. Then she began to move, first putting one leg through the space, then her body, until she was on the front seat and crawling over the deployed airbag and steering wheel. I realized she was barefoot —her flip-flops somehow lost during the crash—and picked her up and pulled her out and carried her over to a spot in the grass where there shouldn't be any stray shards of glass. I checked her feet. There were a few minor cuts, but nothing too serious.

The sirens in the distance neared. It was possible they were headed someplace else, but I doubted it. Caesar was powerful, but he wasn't that powerful. His people could only redirect so many calls before one of those calls slipped through and reached the proper authorities.

And besides, we had an audience. I looked around the area again, saw a few silhouettes still watching from windows. Any one of them could have called the police. Especially after witnessing what just happened.

The two cops lay dead yards away from the parked cruiser. Right now we needed wheels and it was the closet vehicle. But stealing a cop car isn't always the best choice. Especially when two cops have just been killed. Even if they were bent, the other cops wouldn't know it, and even if they did, they probably wouldn't care. Because when one cops gets killed, it opens a wound in the rest of the cops that won't stop until the person who did the killing is brought to justice. And oftentimes, that justice is done in the street.

I looked at the little girl and considered just leaving her here. When the cops came, they would find her and take care of her. Assuming, of course, they weren't corrupt like Gary and Officer Long-Face. That wasn't a chance I was willing to take, not after already going so far.

I motioned for the girl to stay where she was and hurried over to the cops. I took both of their guns, their spare magazines. I ran back to the girl and swooped her up and sprinted toward the buildings. The sirens were even closer now. I saw the oncoming flashing lights a few blocks up as we turned a corner and then I was running as fast as I could.

The Kid answered after only two rings. "Please give me some good news."

"I have the girl."

"That's not good news, Ben. That's old news. What happened with the cops?"

"They're dead."

"Christ. Now you guys are never going to get out of Miami."

"They weren't good cops. They were in Caesar's pocket."

"Do you think that fucking matters?" I could picture the Kid shaking his head. "Where are you and Ian headed now?"

I'd been walking for about five or ten minutes, down one random street after another. I was still carrying the girl and the further we'd gotten from the crash site, the more the sirens had faded, and the slower my pace had become.

"Actually," I said, "that's the reason I'm calling you."

The Kid groaned. "What the fuck happened now?"

"Can you track Ian's location?"

"You mean he's not with you?"

"Can you track his location?"

"Hold on. I haven't been watching it since I talked to you last." I heard the super-fast typing. "Doesn't he have his phone on him?"

I paused. "Why?"

"His location hasn't moved in the last fifteen minutes."

I closed my eyes, immediately fearing the worst. That the rider had taken Ian away only to kill him elsewhere. That Ian's body now lay in some ditch, just waiting for the crocodiles or alligators or whatever the hell they were in this area to come and feast on his remains.

"What's his location?"

"About two miles away from you, back at the end of the causeway."

I let out a breath. "He must have lost his phone in the crash."

"What crash?"

"It's a long story. Look"—my left arm was getting tired from supporting the girl's weight, so I clamped the phone between my ear and shoulder and moved her over to my right arm—"this person came out of nowhere, saved our asses from the two cops."

"Saved your asses how?"

"Shot them both dead. Then he took Ian."

"What do you mean, 'Then he took Ian'?"

"Ian's ankle was all fucked up after the crash. He could barely walk on it. The cops were coming soon. I made a split-second decision."

"So let me get this straight. You just handed Ian over to this guy like he was a fucking puppy?"

We were out on a main strip now, cars driving up and down, their tiring hissing on the wet pavement. Nobody seemed to find it strange that a white guy was carrying a dark-skinned girl in his arms this late at night.

"What's done is done," I said. "At the time, it made the most sense."

Silence.

"Kid?"

"I don't even know what to fucking say to you right now."

"It was the right decision. Trust me."

"*Trust* you? Okay, well then if you know everything, where the fuck is Ian now?"

I was quiet for a beat. "Safe."

The Kid asked, "Why the fuck did you call me in the first place besides to raise my blood pressure?"

"I'm not sure what to do next."

"Oh, I get it. So *now* you want my opinion on what to do."

"You know what, Kid? Go fuck yourself."

I meant to disconnect the call and slip the phone back into my pocket. Before I got the chance, the Kid said, "All right, all right. We're both upset right now. We just need to take a moment to breathe."

We were both quiet for a moment.

The Kid said, "So now what do you need?"

"Transportation. Money. Something."

"You don't have any cash?"

"About forty bucks."

"That will maybe get you a coffee and scone at Starbucks."

"Luckily I'm not looking for coffee or pastries."

The Kid said, "Ben?"

"What?"

"Right now, if you want even the slightest chance of getting out of this, you need to do one simple thing."

"What's that?"

"Ditch the girl."

TWENTY-ONE

But I couldn't ditch the girl.

The Kid knew it too, but he still said it because yes, it did make the most sense if I wanted a chance to get out of Miami. The Kid told me about what had just come over the county radio, that the cops already had my description. Two years ago in Chicago I had been set up as a cop killer. Now the same thing was happening in Miami.

I headed up another block and hailed a taxi. One stopped almost immediately. I opened the back door and bent my head inside.

The driver said, "Where to?" his voice heavy with a Cuban accent.

"The hospital," I said, sliding across the seat and slamming the door shut. "My little girl, she's sick."

The driver stared at us for a long moment. Then he turned back to the wheel and got us moving forward in no time at all.

I set the girl down on the seat beside me. I was afraid she might start speaking again, and that somehow the driver would know what she was saying and do something rash. It was clear the driver didn't quite buy my story—I'd caught the slight mistrust in his eyes—but I had asked to go to the hospital, and that, at least, was a safe place.

The iPhone vibrated in my pocket. I pulled it out, glancing at the rearview mirror to catch the driver watching me.

"My wife," I told him, then answered the phone, saying, "Yes, honey?"

"The fuck?" the Kid said.

"We're in the taxi now. Headed straight for the hospital."

"Right. So here's the deal. I called in a favor from a guy I know down there, only he's all the way over in Immokalee. It's going to be at least two hours before he gets there, probably more."

"And what should I tell the doctor when he asks about insurance?"

This tripped the Kid up for a second. "You're headed to the hospital now, right?"

"That's right."

"You planning something stupid before you get there?"

"Not in so many words."

"Even if you get her to the hospital—or, hell, the police—it doesn't mean that she'll be safe. Simon can easily get to her."

I thought about it for a beat. "He won't."

"How can you be so sure?"

"She's served her purpose. He's done with her." I noticed the driver eyeing me in the rearview mirror, and brightened my tone. "So what should I tell the doctor about our insurance?"

"I'll try to find you a motel nearby, one that charges by the hour and will take cash."

The phone beeped. I checked the screen, then held it back to my ear and said, "My battery's about to die. If you could text me the information, that would be wonderful."

"I'll see what I can do.

"Sounds good, honey. I love you."

The Kid said, "Yeah, you wish," and was gone.

The little girl sat quietly beside me. A part of me did not want to let her go. A part of me saw a glimmer of my own daughter in her, and that part wanted to hold on to her forever.

I said to the driver, "Make a left up at the next light."

His eyes shifted up to meet mine in the rearview mirror. "Huh?"

"This light coming up. Make a left."

He frowned. "But the hospital—"

"Just turn left. It's a shortcut."

"No," he said, shaking his head, "that no shortcut. The hospital only—"

It was the cold barrel of the gun pressed against the base of his skull that caused him to stop talking. His eyes shot up into the rearview mirror again, now filled with fear.

I said, "Turn left."

Without a word he flicked the turn signal on and made the left.

"Now go straight for another two blocks."

"Please, mister," the driver said, "I don't want to die."

"Keep going straight."

The driver kept the taxi moving, taking us away from the main strip.

"See this big tree coming up on the right? Park underneath it."

"Please … please, I have family."

"Park underneath it."

The taxi slowed and stopped underneath the tree.

"Now turn off the car."

Trembling, the driver cut the engine.

"Give me your wallet."

"Ma-Ma-Money?"

"No," I said. "I don't want your money. I want your wallet."

"But I … don't have wallet."

"Your ID, then."

"But why—"

I pressed the gun even harder against the back of his head. "Tell me this. Do you believe I will kill you if I have to?"

He hesitated a moment, and in that moment I hoped he wasn't thinking about his own life, but about his family. About his wife, his children, whatever other relatives there were—I hoped fate had given me this taxi driver as someone I could trust, or at least depend upon for this particular task. Then, almost immediately, that moment was over and he was nodding his head almost imperceptibly, as if he feared one quick movement would cause me to squeeze the trigger.

"Good," I said. "Now do you believe that I don't *want* to kill you?"

Again, a moment's hesitation, then another almost imperceptible nod.

"Then work with me here. Give me your ID."

Still trembling, he slowly moved his right hand away from the steering wheel and reached into his front pocket. As he did this, I glanced at the clock on the dash. It was almost four o'clock. I tried calculating how many minutes we'd been stopped here, in front of a two-story bungalow with an overlarge palm tree dripping heavy drops of rain on the windshield and hood.

"Here," he said in his shaky voice, now with his driver's license pulled from his pants pocket. He slowly moved it toward the back.

I plucked the license from his trembling grasp. It was issued by the Commonwealth of Florida. It pictured the driver and said his name was Damian Sanchez.

"Okay, Damian, so this is you?"

"Ye-Yes."

"Good. Now, Damian, I don't have time to bullshit you, so I'm not even going to bother trying. I'm going to tell you the truth, and whether you decide to believe it is up to you. But your ID here, I'm going to keep it. Because this girl beside me? As you've already probably figured out, she's not my daughter. What she is though is some kind of sex slave. I can't really get into it, but I managed to help save her, and in the process, a good friend of mine died. There are people out there right now that are trying to kill me, that are trying to get this girl back, and I can't allow that to happen. Are you following me so far, Damian?"

The driver nodded again and uttered a noise that may have been yes.

"Very good. Because this girl, Damian? I'm putting her in your care. And all I ask of you is to take her to the nearest hospital. You can tell them whatever you like, I don't care, just as long as she gets taken care of. Do you understand? She has no family, not as far as I know, but then again I can't understand her. Maybe you can. Now, Damian, repeat the basics of what I just told you."

"To … to take girl to hospital. To … to make sure she is safe."

"That's exactly right. And Damian? I'm keeping your ID as collateral. Because I'm going to check up on what you do here. I'm going to hold you accountable. You can go to the police later—I'm sure you will and to be honest I don't care—but first you must take her to a hospital, to a *good* hospital, and make sure she's taken care of. Do you understand me, Damian? Because if you don't, if you do something to harm this girl or somehow put her life in jeopardy, I will hunt you down. Do you hear that, Damian? I will hunt you down and I will make you pay. Do you believe me?"

"Ye-Ye-Yes," he said, his voice still soft, almost a whimper, and a block behind us a car turned the corner, its headlights splashing us, and I decided it was time to go.

I shoved Damian's ID into my pocket and said, "Now give me your cell phone."

"Wh-What?"

"Your goddamn cell phone, Damian. Let's not play this game again."

He didn't move as slowly this time, almost confident now in the fact that he wasn't going to die. This time he reached across the passenger seat and pulled out his cell phone, handed it back to me.

"I'm sorry, Damian," I said, taking his phone, "but I can't have you calling the cops on me right away. Pull that wire out from your radio too."

"The … wire?"

The iPhone vibrated again, two short bursts. I glanced down at the screen. The Kid had texted me the name and location of a motel.

"Goddamn it, Damian, don't play stupid. The wire—you know which one. Pull it out and give it to me."

He disconnected the wire from the radio to the mike, handed it back to me, his hand still shaking. Another set of headlights splashed us again, this time the car passing us, and I knew I was now beyond pressing my luck.

I took his cell phone and the wire and put them in one of my jacket pockets. I placed a hand on the girl's head. I smiled and thought, *Good luck, kid.*

"Damian," I said, keeping the gun aimed at him as I slid across the seat and grabbed the door handle. "You remember everything I told you, yes?"

"Ye-Yes."

"Good. Now here's the real question. Can I trust you to do this?"

"Yes," he said again, this time with no hesitation, and I

took that as my cue to open the door and jump out. Almost immediately Damian fired up the taxi and squealed away. Wasn't quite the calm and inconspicuous exit I'd wanted him to make, but then again that hadn't been part of my instructions.

I stood there for a long moment, watching the taxi receding, its taillights fading, and then I turned and started walking.

TWENTY-TWO

The motel was a complete piece of shit. But it was cheap and charged by the hour and was only thirteen blocks away from where Damian had dropped me off.

The guy behind the glass barely even looked at me while he took my money and handed me a key. He had a TV on nearby, some sitcom turned up way too loud, and the canned laughter followed me out of the manager's office to the side of the motel where I went directly to my room. It was even filthier than I had anticipated and reeked of cigarette smoke. There was a bed, a chair, a table, and a TV. I took the chair and propped it up against the doorknob. It wasn't much, but if someone wanted to break down the door, it would at least be one more barrier besides the cheap chain lock.

I was exhausted, my entire body tingling with pain. The only thing I wanted to do was sleep, but even the sight of the bed grossed me out. Instead I pushed it all the way to the front of the room and stood it up and laid it against the single window. This way if someone tried shooting in, they would hit the bed first. Again, it wasn't much, but it was all I had.

I lowered myself to the floor, my back against the wall,

both of the dead cops' guns in each hand. The single lamp on the table was off and the darkness enveloped me.

The Kid called, said, "Good news. Word just came across the Miami-Dade County radio about a taxi driver telling the police a white man with glasses pulled a gun on him."

"That's the only description?"

"So far, yeah. But it also said the unidentified man left a child with him, and instructed him to take the child to the nearest hospital, which the driver did. After he made sure she was in proper care, he called the police."

"Well done, Damian."

"What?"

"Never mind. Any word yet on Ian?"

"Not yet."

I was quiet for a moment, thinking about this. Then I said, "I'm in the motel room now, waiting on your guy."

"Good. He should be there in the next hour or two."

"Let's hope not any longer. I only have the room for two hours. And my phone's battery is now down to less than ten percent."

"He'll be there." The Kid paused. "Ben?"

"Yeah."

"Just a heads up."

"About what?"

"This guy I'm sending? He's ... different."

"Different how?"

"You'll see what I mean."

I saw exactly what the Kid meant an hour and forty-seven minutes later.

By then my eyes had adjusted to the dark. I had been sitting in the same spot for nearly an hour, my back against the wall, still clasping a gun in each hand. Sounds came through the thin walls, the heavy grunting and moaning and squealing of sex. I had heard it all too often in my past life, when I used to lock myself away in my den and log onto the Internet, and did my best now to ignore it. I tried to stay awake, to stay focused, but found myself nodding off and then immediately jerking my head up.

Then there came a sudden knocking at the door.

Two light raps, just below the door's centerline. It was an odd place for the knocks to originate. Most times when someone knocks on a door, they do so around shoulder level, their elbow cocked at a ninety-degree angle. Then again, most people knock casually, not even aware of it, waiting on their family or friends.

I waited in the dark, silent. Exactly ten seconds passed before the knocking came again, another two light raps.

I slowly rose to my feet, my back against the wall, my hands tight around the guns' rubber grips. I moved silently through the dark, inching my way past the mattress covering the window. I moved it just enough to peek through the curtain. I couldn't see anybody outside.

The knock came again, only once this time, and a strange voice whispered, "Ben?"

I moved to the door, looked through the peephole.

Nobody was there.

"Ben?" the voice whispered again.

I blinked, looked through the peephole again.

Still nobody.

There was shuffling then, feet against the stone walkway. I stuck one of the guns in the back of my waistband, used my free hand to move the chair from its place against the door-knob. I unlatched the chain and opened the door, the gun at my side, stepping out onto the walkway.

A child was headed away from the room. He stopped when he heard the door open and slowly turned around.

"Ben?"

It wasn't a child, but a dwarf, or little person, or whatever the hell they were supposed to be called nowadays. The small man just stood there in shorts and a T-shirt, staring back at me with glasses. In his right ear was a hearing aid.

The little man stared at me for a moment, then seemed to come to a decision. He smiled and stepped forward.

"I'm Titus," he said, extending his small stubby hand. "The Kid sent me."

TWENTY-THREE

Titus drove an old Volkswagen Beetle. It was orange with scraped and rusting aluminum bumpers and hubcaps, dents and scratches along the sides and roof. There was a thick cushion on the driver's seat so Titus could see over the steering wheel. The brake and gas pedals had been extended so his feet could reach them. Several pine scented Little Trees were threaded around the gearshift. The thing looked like its top speed was maybe fifty miles per hour. Not the most ideal vehicle to try to outrun Caesar's long reach, but at least it was something.

Titus was clearly nervous as he weaved us through the Miami streets toward the interstate, checking his rearview mirror constantly. I wasn't sure what he could see from his low vantage point, but I had to give him credit for trying. Myself, I kept my eye on the side mirror, watching for any trailing vehicles. By the time we had gone all the way up I-75 and then started west through the Everglades, I was confident that we weren't being followed.

Neither of us had talked much since we left the motel. The Beetle had a tape deck and played quietly, pouring the soulful rhythm of Jerry Garcia and the rest of the Grateful Dead from the crappy speakers. The cassette tape played through until the end and then Titus, perfunctorily, ejected it and flipped the tape over and reinserted it into the deck.

It was nearly six-thirty in the morning. I had been up for over twenty-four hours. The rain had stopped but clouds still covered the sky, and random beams of the rising sun sliced through the gray. One of the cops' guns lay in my lap, my hand around the grip, my finger still on the trigger.

Titus cleared this throat. "I'm sorry."

"About what?"

"Carver. It really sucks."

I was staring out the window, watching the passing wetlands, and now shifted in my seat to focus on the little man.

"What the hell do you know about Carver?"

He flinched at the intensity of my voice, like he expected me to hit him.

I closed my eyes, shook my head. "Sorry. I didn't mean to say it like that."

"No, I understand."

"It's just been a long night."

"I understand."

"And I haven't had a chance to thank you yet. I don't know anything about you except your name and"—I looked around the Beetle, noticed several familiar cellophane wrappers scattered around the floor—"that you like cheese slices?"

He grinned. "Kraft American cheese. I'd offer you some but I already ate all I had."

"Thanks anyway. So how do you know the Kid?"

"From online."

"No kidding."

He heard the irritation in my voice and gave me a cautious glance. "The Kid probably wouldn't want me saying."

This perked me up. "Now you definitely need to tell me."

"It's no big thing. We met while playing *World of Warcraft*."
I smiled.

"What?" he asked.

"Nothing. I just never knew the Kid was into that stuff."

"He's an insomniac like me. We met a few years ago when we crossed paths and had a small battle. We shit talked each other the entire time and became friends. Then we started going on quests together."

The smile still hadn't left my face. It was strange to smile, especially after the night I'd just had, but for the two years I'd known the Kid, never once had I an inkling he was into any type of games, let alone multiplayer online role-playing ones.

I asked, "Do you have a cell phone?"

"Of course."

"Can you call the Kid for me? My phone's dead."

"I don't have his number."

"I thought you said you guys were friends."

"We are. Online. That's how we've always contacted each other. Besides, I don't really get a signal when I'm passing through this way."

I was quiet for a moment. "What all has the Kid told you?"

I didn't think there was anything threatening in my voice this time, but Titus still gave me another cautious look before answering.

"He wasn't the one who told me. I figured it out."

"How so?"

"I read your story."

"My story?" I said, but of course I knew what he meant. Two years ago, after my life had been stolen, I had written down the events and had the Kid post it wherever he could online. But Caesar had powerful friends in powerful places and managed to nix it from the major sites pretty quickly. It was still on the Internet, though, circulating about, but nobody really gave it much thought anymore, if they ever did.

Titus nodded. "I mentioned I have insomnia, right? So when I'm not working or playing *World of Warcraft*, I like to fly around the world on Google Earth. It's not like I'm ever going to be able to visit a place like Mongolia or New Zealand or even Greenland, but at least I can get a bird's eye view. And when I'm not doing that, I just search the web for neat and interesting stuff. And one day I stumbled across this file that had been posted, this ... this story about a guy waking up in a motel room and finding these words in blood on the back of the bathroom door. So I started reading. And you know, some of it sounded familiar, like that bombing in Ryder, Illinois. So I did some research and realized that all of it was true. And the first thing I did was send it to the Kid, asked him if he had seen it. He said he hadn't but would check it out. And so a day or two goes by and I'm anxious to hear back from him and still he hadn't read it, so again one night I couldn't sleep and I started messing around on the Internet, trying to find these websites mentioned in the story. I couldn't find them at first, but a few days later I was on a quest with the Kid and I mentioned how I was trying to find these websites and he went quiet and didn't say anything. Then he told me it was best I stay far away from them. Of course, I was like, what are you talking about? And that was when he told me."

"Haven't you always known him as the Kid?"

"No. I may be short, but I'm not stupid. When we quest, he goes by a totally different handle."

"I'm almost afraid to ask, but what is it?"

Titus grinned. "Now he would *definitely* kill me if I told you that."

"So then what happened?"

"Well, I didn't believe him at first. I thought he was bullshitting me. But that was when he sent me some of the videos he'd saved. Like some of your game, and some of Carver's, just to prove it."

I flinched, trying not to think about the day I woke up in the Paradise Motel. Even two years later just the idea of my game made me sick.

"But he wasn't trying to brag about it or anything," Titus said. "He was doing it for my own good. You know, to make sure I didn't try to mess around with Caesar and Simon and get hurt. Basically, the Kid thought I didn't know what I was doing."

"Do you?"

"I'm a hacker, just like him. I know my stuff. And I offered the Kid my help, but he always told me it was best that I stayed out of it. Quite honestly, I haven't heard from him much in the past year. He doesn't enter the game hardly at all anymore."

"We've been pretty busy," I said.

"Are you guys any closer?"

"To what?"

"Finding Caesar."

I stared out my window for a long time. "It doesn't really matter anymore."

"How so?"

"Now that Carver's dead ..." I shook my head. "How much longer do you think it will be?"

"Maybe another hour. But that's just to the airport. I don't know what's supposed to happen then."

"What airport?"

"Immokalee Airport."

"Immokalee is where you live?"

He nodded. "Me and Hercules."

"Who's Hercules?"

"My pet raccoon."

Before I could further investigate, Titus's eyes grew wide and he snapped his fingers.

"Shoot," he said. "I almost forgot."

"What?"

He pointed at the glove compartment. "They're in there."

"What are?"

"Besides constantly surfing the web, I also like to tinker."

"Tinker with what?"

"Just stuff. Like, create gadgets, or improve on gadgets. Go ahead, open it up."

I opened the glove compartment. Inside were cassette tapes, all for the Grateful Dead, as well as the usual glove compartment junk—owner's manual, folding map, flashlight, a sunglasses case.

"What am I looking for?"

"That case right there."

I pulled out the sunglasses case, held it up. "And?"

"Open it up, man."

I opened the case. Inside were not sunglasses, but a pair of thin reading glasses, much like the ones I normally wore.

"Okay," I said slowly, hoping he would get to the point.

"You can't even tell it's there, can you?"

"I can't even tell what's where?"

"The camera."

I squinted down at the glasses, then shook my head. "There's no camera there."

Titus beamed proudly. "The Kid sent me a pair of the glasses the players use. Actually, it was the pair he wore when he pretended to be you at the end of your game. Even though he broke them, he kept them, and when I expressed interest in seeing what they were like, he just sent me his."

"And you managed to turn them into this?"

"No way. Those glasses right there, those took a lot of work and money. I just wanted to see how Caesar's people make their glasses. It's pretty basic, really, with a mini camera inside attached to a mini antenna to send the signal. Plus there's a battery, but it only lasts for a few days. That's because they don't expect the players to last very long."

"Okay," I said again. "But ... why are you showing me these now?"

He shrugged. "I dunno. I thought you might be able to use them sometime. They're yours. Even your prescription. I figured it out based on the lenses from the broken pair the Kid sent."

I folded the glasses and placed them back in the case and snapped it shut. "I appreciate the gesture, but again, now that Carver's dead ..."

"Yeah," Titus said, and his smile faded.

We drove on in silence.

TWENTY-FOUR

About a half hour later, Titus said he should have a strong signal now and pulled out a BlackBerry from his pocket. He checked the screen, confirmed that yes, there were several bars, and handed me the phone.

"Do you know the Kid's number?" he asked.

I did.

The phone rang three times before the Kid answered, uncertainly, "Domino's Pizza, will this be for pickup or delivery?"

"It's me," I said.

He let out a breath. "About fucking time. Did my guy come through?"

"So far so good."

"How far are you from the airport?"

I relayed the question to Titus who told me at least another half hour. When I told the Kid, he said, "Good. They should be there by then."

"Who's coming?"

"Maya's flying down with Fred."

"Any word on Ian?"

"Actually, yes."

I sat up straighter in my seat. "What happened?"

"He's fine."

"How do you know?"

"Two hours ago, Ronny was driving up 95 when out of nowhere this black motorcycle comes zooming up on his left. At first he thought it might be trouble—he said he even reached for his gun—but then he noticed Ian was on the back. Ian motioned for him to pull over. He pulled over, and the motorcycle pulled over, and then Ian got off and the motorcycle sped away."

"That's it?"

"That's it. Weirdest goddamn thing I've ever heard."

"How did the rider know Ronny's location?"

"That's what we're still trying to figure out. It does have us worried. Drew and Jesse are headed now to intercept them. Eventually they're going to ditch the SUV."

"Have you talked with Ian?"

"I haven't, but Ronny said he asked him a few questions, like who the fuck the rider was, but Ian doesn't know. He just said the guy—or girl, I guess we can't rule out that possibility —just kept driving until after a few hours they managed to catch up with Ronny. Like I said, weirdest fucking thing, right?"

I didn't say anything. I was relieved to hear that Ian was safe and unharmed—at least not any worse than he already was —but I still had to kick myself for letting him go in the first place. It may have been a split-second decision, but it was still stupid and reckless and could have gotten Ian killed. Thankfully it hadn't, but that still didn't mean I shouldn't feel disgusted with my actions.

"Ben," the Kid said. "Are you still there?"

"Yeah, I'm here."

"I'm going to be coming out to you guys in another day or two. We have a lot to talk about."

I stared out my window, the sun shining off the swamp water.

"Boojum," I whispered.

"What was that?"

"Boojum. It was the last thing Carver said to me before he died."

"Boojum," the Kid said slowly, as if trying to get a sense of how the word tasted. "Are you sure you heard him right?"

"He said it a couple times. I'm positive."

"Boojum," the Kid said again, still rolling it around on his tongue.

"Any idea what it means?"

"Not at all."

"Look into it, will you?"

"Right. Like I have nothing better to do with my time. I'll see you soon, Ben."

I disconnected the call and handed the phone back to Titus, who was giving me a curious look.

"Boojum?" he asked.

I nodded. "Boojum."

The Immokalee Airport is a public use, publicly owned airport in Collier County. It's the type of airport that mostly caters to single engine airplanes. It doesn't have a control tower and it doesn't have much security. Which was a good thing, because I was currently in possession of two stolen police standard-issue firearms.

We arrived just after seven-thirty. By then the clouds had broken up more, allowing even more sunlight. Titus parked the Beetle by one of the hangers. He turned off the car then dug into his pocket for his BlackBerry and handed it to me without comment.

I dialed the Kid and waited two rings before he answered.

"We're here," I said.

"Good. They'll be there any minute now."

"Have you looked into boojum yet?"

"I've been a little too preoccupied."

"Have you talked to Ronny or Maya or anyone since we last talked?"

"Briefly. Why?"

"Did you mention boojum?"

"No. Again, why?"

"Because I've been thinking. Maybe it really is nothing. Carver ... he was dying, and he was just ... it's probably nothing to get our hopes up about."

"I never thought it would be, but I see what you mean. We'll definitely look into it later, but if you want to keep it quiet for now, I'm totally fine with that. Anything else?"

"No." I paused. "Just ... thanks."

"Anytime. Now let me talk to Titus."

I handed the phone over. Titus listened for a few seconds, nodding, and said, "It was no problem. Like I told you before, I'm happy to give any help I can." Then he clicked off and stared down at the phone and started punching the keys with his thumbs.

I stared out my window at the sky, hoping to see Fred's jet approaching but only spotting scattered clouds and a few distant birds.

"You guys have a pilot?" Titus asked.

"In a way. The guy we use works for a private jet company that usually serves celebrities and the ultra rich. Whenever we need a fast flight, the Kid calls them. The guy we use—Fred— he was there the first time two years back at the end of my game. Ever since then the Kid has requested him."

"He doesn't ever wonder what you guys do?"

"Probably, but he never asks, which is fine with us."

Titus had kept his focus on the BlackBerry this entire time, his thumbs typing, but now looked up.

"I think I found it."

"Found what?"

"The significance of boojum."

"And?"

"Well, it could stand for a number of things—like did you know there was a baseball player back in the twenties and thirties nicknamed Boojum?—but I think what Carver meant—if, you know, he meant anything—had to deal with *The Hunting of the Snark*."

"The what?"

"It's a poem by Lewis Carroll. The reason I think it has significance is what you had written about Carver in your story—how he and his wife were painting his kid's room with characters from Carroll's work."

"Where did you find this?"

"Wikipedia."

"Okay," I said with a sigh. "Then what's boojum have to do with anything?"

"According to this, the boojum is a particular variety of snark, which causes any who meet it to, and I quote, 'softly and suddenly vanish away, and never be met with again.' "

I let that sink in for a moment—a long moment, really, remembering the look on Carver's face when he tried speaking that single word as he died—but before I could say anything else I noticed a dot off in the distance. I sat up straighter in my seat, squinting. I couldn't make out what kind of plane it was, but I knew it was Fred and Maya. It just had to be.

"What is it?"

"Thanks for everything, Titus."

I opened my door, started to get out, but hesitated. I had

the two guns and considered giving Titus one of them; if he knew about Caesar and his people—not to mention he had just helped me escape Miami—it was possible his life could be in danger. But I didn't know if the little man even knew how to fire a gun, let alone handle one, and I didn't have time to give him a crash course. The dot in the sky had already become a splotch which was definitely aimed toward the airport.

"Ben," Titus called before I shut the door.

I lowered my head back into the car.

"Remember, if you guys ever need any help, let me know. It would be an honor."

He looked so lonely there for a second, so lost and pathetic, that I wanted to tell him he could come along with me right now. At least that, I hoped, would cheer him up, especially after everything he had just done for me. But the truth was there would be nothing for him to do. Carver was dead and right now none of us knew what the future held.

"I appreciate it," I said. "And if we ever do need more help, we'll definitely let you know."

He managed a smile. "Thanks."

The splotch in the sky had materialized into a jet, a Gulfstream G100 to be exact, most likely the same one that had flown Carver and me into Atlanta just the other day.

Titus said my name again, and I ducked my head back down and once again thanked him, and then I shut the door and started away from the Beetle, placing both guns in the waistband of my jeans, watching the jet as it made its descending approach, growing larger and larger, its wheels lowering and locking into place, and then it touched down and I realized I was walking even faster, almost running, not caring if it wasn't proper protocol to stay off the runway, wanting to just leave here, to go back home, away from all of this, and then before I realized it I was running as the jet slowed nearly two football fields away and began to turn around, and I could

see Fred in the cockpit along with his copilot and he said something to the copilot who nodded and said something back, and
the jet slowed and stopped and the side door opened and the
ladder began to descend and there was Maya, looking out at
me, and I wiped at my eyes because there were tears in them,
just a few, and Maya hurried down the steps and met me halfway, wrapping her arms around me, telling me it was okay,
while I sniffed back the tears and told her that Carver was
dead, that he was dead, that he was dead.

"I know," she said softly. "I know. It's over now. Everything
is okay."

I wiped at my eyes, took a breath. "I just want to go home."

She nodded and took my hand and pulled me toward
the jet.

I hesitated, suddenly remembering Titus, wanting to wave
my thanks to him one last time. But when I turned, my hand
already halfway up, he and the orange Beetle were gone.

PART II

BOOJUM

TWENTY-FIVE

The Kid arrived that Monday morning, two days after our fateful visit to Miami Beach.

Jesse had gone to the airport to pick him up. He'd asked me if I wanted to come along, but I hadn't answered him, just sat there on the porch steps, smoking a cigarette. It was where I was still sitting three hours later when Jesse returned with the Kid, the Ford pickup truck leaving a small cloud of dust in its wake as it bounced up the rugged drive.

Jesse and the Kid got out of the truck, Jesse in his blue jeans and cowboy shirt, his long sideburns and dusty hat, the Kid wearing his designer khakis and red polo, a little gel in his hair. He had a laptop bag strapped over his shoulder, and as he approached the house he nodded at me.

"Ben," he said, pausing at the foot of the steps. "How's it hanging?"

I just sat there, smoking my cigarette.

He said, "I thought you quit."

I didn't reply.

Jesse had grabbed the Kid's overnight bag, was trailing the

Kid up to the house. Now he started up the stairs past me, just as the door opened.

The Kid smiled. "Why, Maya, aren't you a sight for sore eyes?"

Maya sat down beside me on the steps. "You really need to work on your lines, Kid," she said, smiling back at him.

"Yeah, well," the Kid said, shrugging. Then his smile faded and he tilted his head at me. "I thought he quit."

I was still sitting there smoking, now staring past the Kid at the pickup and the trees beyond, but I could sense Maya looking at me.

"Yeah," she said, "so did I."

"Graham around?"

"I think he's out back. With the bees."

"Right," the Kid said. "The bees."

A silence passed. My cigarette was almost done but I kept at it, not wanting to flick it away until this little greeting session was over.

"Right," the Kid said again. "Well, I'll be up in Carver's room. If I see Ronny on the way, I'll talk to him. Otherwise, can you tell him I need to see him?"

Maya nodded. "Sure."

The Kid stood there for another moment, nodding again, smiling. He stared at me once more, said, "Ben, it's good seeing you," then hurried up the steps past me without waiting for a response.

Maya waited until the door closed before swatting my arm with her hand. "Sometimes you can be so rude."

"Sometimes?" I ground the butt on the porch step, flicked it out into the grass.

With an aggravated sigh, Maya got up and retrieved the butt, came back and held it in front of my face. "How many more of these are out there?"

I said nothing.

Maya's normally small and worn face tightened. Her nose wrinkled, which meant she was ready to throw a fit, and I just sat there, waiting for it, almost begging for it. But then her features softened, and she slowly shook her head, sat down beside me on the porch step, placed her hand on my thigh.

"What did it look like?" she asked.

I reached down for the pack of Marlboros beside me on the step. Maya reached across my lap and grabbed my hand and pulled it back.

"Ben," she said.

I looked at her.

"What did it look like?"

"What did what look like?"

"His last word."

I had told the Kid we should keep Carver's last cryptic two-syllable word a secret, and I had intended to, but then on the flight home I had confessed it to Maya. Why, I still wasn't sure, and now I was beginning to regret it.

"Ben, you're gonna have to talk about it eventually. You can't keep something like that pent up inside you."

Maya still had hold of my hand. I used my other hand to pull her hand off, then grabbed my pack of smokes and stood up. "I'm going for a walk," I said, and started away before Maya could say anything else, heading toward the side of the farmhouse and turning a corner.

The sun was glaring down on the east side of the house, so I walked a little in the shade, lighting myself another cigarette. I put the pack and lighter back in my pocket and then just stood there, smoking, staring down the hill that crested the backyard. My eyes momentarily rested on the five grave markers. The place where we'd buried Bronson Lam two years ago, the place where Carver had buried his own son two years ago, and the place we'd buried David Resh and Vanessa Martin less than a year ago. The fifth marker stood for Larry Vaughn, who had been killed outside my father-in-law's house two years ago and whose body we hadn't been able to bring back to the farmhouse.

My gaze shifted past the grave markers, down the hill, at the apiary. Graham was down there now, moving slowly in his white jumpsuit, his round hat and wire veil covering his head.

I started to head down the hill, coming around the rear corner of the house, stepping out of the cool shadows into the warm sunlight, when I heard the screen door on the back porch open.

For some reason, I expected it to be Ronny, or the Kid, or maybe even Ian, but it was Drew, dressed in jeans and his heavy flannel shirt. He came down the wooden steps, heading directly toward the barn, and didn't stop until he glanced up and happened to notice me. A moment of indecision passed, both of us standing there, waiting for the other one to move, before each of us took a step forward and met halfway.

I took one last drag of the cigarette, dropped it to the ground, smashed the glowing end with the heel of my shoe. I nodded at the barn, where we stored the weapons and ammunition and four-wheelers. "You're going shooting?"

A half smile passed over his scared face. "Nothing gets by you, Ben."

Silence.

Drew said, "I saw the Kid inside."

I nodded.

"I'm surprised you're not in there with him."

"What is that supposed to mean?"

"Nothing," he said, and looked away, unconsciously touched one of the many scars on his face.

They hadn't always been there, those scars. Before, when I'd first met him two years ago, his face had been round and somewhat pudgy, his chin making its slow transformation into a double. Only a year before that things had been normal for him, living with his thirty-seven-year-old girlfriend and their four-year-old son in their small row house in Elmhurst, right by the train tracks and the Long Island Expressway. Life hadn't been great but life hadn't been bad either, and then one morning he woke up to find himself in Kenton, Oklahoma, his girlfriend and son taken away, both of them held hostage so he would do everything Simon said. But ever since Carver had come into his life Drew had changed things, working out, eating right, and the chin that had been very close to a double disappeared. He lifted weights every day, ran with the rest of us every morning, and that round and somewhat pudgy face of his had started to become leaner, tighter, more pronounced. Then the night came when all of that changed, and the blade of a knife sliced his face several times, scaring it permanently. Not that he really cared about his face, mind you, but the fact that the damage had been done here, at this farmhouse, away from the world and Simon and his games, was what hurt most, what had become the deepest cut of all, not just to Drew, but to the rest of us.

"Tell me something," I said.

Drew nodded.

"When it comes down to it, what do you think?"

"It doesn't matter what I think."

"Yes it does."

He shrugged. "I don't know anymore, Ben. A part of me doesn't want to quit, but another part of me agrees with Ronny. That now without Carver, what point is there to continue?"

I stared at him for a very long time. Then I said, "Yeah," nodding slowly. "Okay, thanks."

We left it at that. Drew went his way, I went mine. I started down the hill directly toward Graham while Drew headed toward the barn, where he would unlock the cabinet and take out one of the rifles and a box of ammunition and then ride one of the four-wheelers through the trees on a trail that led to the firing range Carver had set up with Graham five years ago. When I reached the apiary, I heard the four-wheeler's engine as it revved to life, just beyond the constant buzzing of bees.

Graham had noticed me walking toward him earlier, was already finishing up his inspection of one of the honeycombs. Holding it in his gloved hands, bees crawling all over the honeycomb and his white suit, he stared at the honeycomb for a while before slowly reinserting it back into the hive. His wooden cane was leaning against the same hive, and now he grabbed it, started to slowly make his way toward me.

The apiary consisted of about fifty hives. Surrounding those large white boxes were white clovers Graham had planted himself, giving the bees enough opportunity to find a substantial amount of pollen without forcing them to fly too far away.

I stood far enough away from the hives that the bees mostly ignored me, only a few coming up to see who I was and what I wanted, then buzzing away when they realized I wasn't a threat. I waited there until Graham caught up with me, moving slowly not just because of the bees but because of the cancer that had once ravaged his left leg.

When he was ten feet away, he extended his cane to me. I stepped forward, took it from him, then watched as he carefully brushed off the bees that still crawled about his body. Once he'd finished, he extended his hand toward me again, and I gave him back his cane.

"The Kid's here," I said. "He was asking for you."

Graham looked up, and through the wire veil I could see his face. He nodded, and we started up the hill back toward the farmhouse.

As we walked, he said, "So why aren't you with him now?"

"Why does everyone keep asking me that?"

"I don't know," Graham said. "Maybe because you're the only one who doesn't agree with Ronny."

"I'm not the only one who doesn't agree with Ronny."

"No, you're not. But many aren't sure what to think. They're still too shocked by what happened. All of us are shocked, and there's nothing wrong with that. But eventually that shock will wear off. Eventually our time of mourning will come to an end. And then a decision has to be made. What Ronny is thinking is not selfish, believe me. He's talked to me about this already, and it's not something he wants to do but feels there's no choice."

We walked a little more in silence, slowly, Graham having trouble climbing the hill with his cane. Off in the distance came what sounded like thunder. But there were no clouds in the sky, and I knew exactly where that sound was coming from, could picture Drew lying on the ground with his rifle, aiming at the target two hundred yards away.

"I just don't think it's right," I said.

"And neither does Ronny. But when it comes down to it, what choice do any of us have? You say you disagree and that's fine, but what kind of argument have you given? Really, Ben, you have to stop blaming yourself for what happened. It wasn't your fault."

"But I could have—"

"No," Graham said, stopping suddenly and turning toward me. He glanced back down the hill, decided we were far enough that he could lift the wire veil from his face. "Stop it, Ben. You always do this to yourself. Always with the buts, with the what ifs."

I said nothing.

"I'd like to think I knew Carver pretty well," Graham said, turning slightly and beginning to walk back up the hill again, "and I can guarantee he wouldn't blame you. Ronny told me what happened. Ian told me what happened. And from what they both told me, all of it was Carver's decision. None of it was yours. So stop blaming yourself."

"But you weren't there," I said quietly.

"No, I wasn't. You were. And you know something, Ben? I'm glad it was you. Because anyone else wouldn't have been able to do what you did. Not the way you did it. Besides Carver, everyone stayed alive."

"Ian—"

"Is still alive. Yes, his leg is broken, and it probably will never properly heal, but he's still breathing thanks to you."

We passed the five grave markers as more thunder sounded out in the distance.

"Let me tell you a secret, Ben. Well, it's not exactly a secret, but it's something I haven't told anybody. When I was eight years old, I was stung by a bee. It was a small sting, right on the bottom of my foot, but I had to be rushed to the hospital. As it turned out I have a strong allergy to bees. And so I stayed away from them most of my life. When my wife and I had people over during the summer, we always stayed inside for our picnics, never went out because I was afraid of what might happen."

We came to the back porch. Since there was no railing, I stayed a few feet behind Graham in case he lost balance as he climbed the steps. Finally we were at the top, and Graham went straight for the swing. He sat down with a heavy sigh. I sat down next him. He took off his hat, set it aside, took off his gloves and set them aside. He unzipped the top of his jumpsuit and sat back a little on the swing, keeping his cane between his legs, staring down the hill at the endless horizon of trees.

"So forty years passed and I stayed away from them. Then when Lois died and I had nothing else, I came out here to live the rest of my life. And one day I was out mowing the lawn and a bee flew around my head. I nearly pissed my pants. Can you imagine that—a fifty-year-old man nearly pissing his pants? I jumped off the mower and ran inside, actually locked the door. And I just waited in there."

He shook his head, produced a small smile.

"I've been in wars, I've investigated murders, I've stared into the eyes of cold hard killers who no longer had souls, and at fifty years old I realized my biggest fear was bees. And I told myself I could not die before I faced that fear. So do you know what I did?" He raised his hand, pointed a gnarled finger down the hill at the apiary. "I decided to become a beekeeper."

He looked at me, his dark eyes searching my face, this sixty-five-year-old man who lived out in the middle of nowhere. And I watched him, I watched this old man who had outlived his wife, who had never been blessed with children, who all he had now were bees, I watched him as he said:

"As far as I know Carver wasn't afraid of bees. But do you know what his fear was? That something terrible would happen to his wife and son. And then all of a sudden they were taken from him and he had nothing else to fear. He didn't even fear for his own life. But he knew the risks, just as I know the risks. And just as I keep working with my bees, Carver kept trying his best to stop these people—Simon and Caesar and whoever else. He knew that one of these days his luck was going to end. And still he kept doing it. So if it's anybody's fault what happened this past weekend, it isn't yours."

"Beekeepers get stung all the time," I said.

"Some do, certainly, but not all. I haven't yet."

I started to nod, but movement caught my attention, a small yellow and black dot on Graham's arm.

"Graham," I said, my voice suddenly tense, and he looked down at where I was staring, at the bee crawling across his white jumpsuit.

And at that moment Graham did the strangest thing: he slowly raised his hand, palm up, against his arm. Held it there, waiting, until the bee crawled onto it. Then he moved his hand until it was right in front of my face, and I could see the bee there on his palm, its black eyes, its wings, what I took to be its stinger.

Graham said, "What is your biggest fear?"

I swallowed, almost mesmerized by the bee. "That my family is dead."

"And do you believe they are?"

Still watching the bee, waiting for it to sting the hand now holding it, I whispered, "Yes."

Graham moved his hand back to his face. He raised it to his mouth, pursed his lips, and gently blew the bee away. When he looked back at me, his dark eyes had softened, the crease in his brow had disappeared, and he looked just like he had when I arrived yesterday, before he stepped forward to embrace me.

"Then why are you still afraid?"

TWENTY-SIX

Four years ago, when Carver had woken up in a crummy motel room in Maine, the bloated body of a baby in the toilet, the realization hit him hard that the life he'd always known was now gone. Believing that both his wife and son were dead, that it was no use playing Simon's game, Carver had simply walked away.

When he met up with the Kid again, when they tried everything they could to stop Simon and his cohorts, he'd asked the Kid to look up Graham Fredrick, a man he'd known briefly in the army, and a week later Carver had come out here, in the middle of the northern Colorado wilderness, shook Graham's hand and explained the situation. Graham had listened intently, never saying a word, until Carver finished with his story. Then Graham had said, "Feel free to stay as long as you'd like," and since then the farmhouse had become Carver's base of operations.

Graham Fredrick had moved here fifteen years before, after his wife passed away. The property consisted of just over one hundred acres, mostly woods, and it was at least ten miles from the closest town, at least three miles from the nearest residence.

The farmhouse was an old two-story stone-sided colonial, built over a century ago. A barn that had been built maybe fifty years ago was slumped half a football field away, its shingles falling off, its paint peeling.

The outside of the barn was the first thing I'd painted two years ago.

It was clear that Graham didn't care much about the barn, that it was only used to store the lawn mower and supplies for his bees and—after Carver had arrived—extra artillery. The flaking paint didn't bother him in the least—it didn't seem to bother Carver or anyone else either—but it bothered me. As a painter I couldn't bear to see it the way it was, not while I was around, not after it quickly became clear my four days of nonstop writing was not going to somehow make the world a better place.

And so I got the necessary materials and spent the next several days taking off all the old paint, sanding down the wooden boards, then painting it again. Next I did the farmhouse itself, all the interior rooms, the downstairs and the upstairs. Neither Carver nor Graham had asked me to do this, and for all I knew they would have preferred I didn't, but by that point I had just started my training, going down to the shooting range, beginning the early morning runs and then Carver's intermediate instructions of tae kwon do and jujutsu, and still I was scared. I was scared of going back into the game, or at least going back as some walk-on character in someone else's game.

The first person Carver and Ronny and Drew saved two months after me was Maya, then Jesse three months after that, and by then I had finished painting the farmhouse, had finished sanding down the floors, the tables and chairs. I had no more excuses, no more reason to stall the inevitable, and so the next time the Kid called saying he'd come across a game—

ever since our surprise attack on the Paradise Motel there had been fewer games—I volunteered.

The person who'd been thrown into Simon's game then was Vanessa Martin, who in less than a year would be raped and murdered by someone else we had saved from Simon's game.

I don't know why, but as I made my way up the stairs to the second floor, I found myself scrutinizing the paint job I'd done two years earlier, noticing a few wayward brushstrokes near the wainscoting that never should have escaped my attention.

Carver's bedroom was at the end of the hall. Its door was open.

I heard voices from within, murmuring voices that belonged to Ronny and the Kid. I approached that opened door slowly, passing by the other bedrooms where the majority of us slept when we were here, always bunking up with someone else. Then my slow steps had brought me to the end of my journey, and I was standing in the doorway, staring inside.

It was a small room—all of the bedrooms on the second floor of the farmhouse were small—but Carver had kept it neat and clean. The bed in the corner, two bookcases stacked with books, a desk on the other side of the room with his computer on top. Carver was the only one besides Graham who had his own bedroom, who had a computer in his room so that he could work at anytime, unlike the rest of us who were forced to use the computers in the basement when we wanted to visit the Internet.

Right now the Kid sat in front of Carver's computer, typing at the keyboard, Ronny standing behind him and staring over his shoulder, and there was something about the image of the two of them right then that struck me as particular, like something out of a Hopper painting.

"How about that one?" Ronny asked, pointing at something on the screen.

The Kid typed, moved the mouse, typed some more. "Nope."

Ronny sighed and closed his eyes, placed a hand to his face and squeezed the bridge of his nose.

The Kid leaned back in his chair—Carver's chair, a simple metal folding chair—and tilted his neck back and forth, squeezed his hands to crack the knuckles and each finger.

Neither of them had noticed me and for an instant I entertained the possibility of backing out of the room, maybe heading to the bedroom I shared with Drew. I could lie on my bed and stare at the ceiling and try to forget the past several days. I could try to forget the past two years. I could try to forget my entire life, go back to the period where I was just one jittery microscopic sperm among a million vying for the egg and let another sperm win the race, become a completely different person, someone who might have a better chance at life, who wouldn't have the pleasure of meeting a woman named Jennifer Abele and eventually producing a child as wonderful as Casey Anderson, who wouldn't one day wake up to the faint and distant sound of a ringing motel telephone.

I cleared my throat.

First Ronny looked at me, his fingers still to the bridge of his nose, his eyes glassy and his face fatigued.

The Kid tilted his head next, stared at me a moment, and said, "Hey, Ben, what's up?"

I stepped into the room. Noticed Carver's bed, which Beverly had made earlier, two books now spread out on top of the dark blue comforter. Both were collections of Lewis Carroll's work. Each contained *The Hunting of the Snark*.

"You told him?" I asked.

The Kid nodded. "I did."

"I thought we discussed this."

"We did. But I thought it was important to let Ronny know about it now."

I walked over to Carver's bed. I picked up *The Complete Stories and Poems of Lewis Carroll*, began thumbing through the pages.

"So what do you think, Ronny? Is there any significance to this boojum nonsense?"

"You don't have to use that tone."

"What tone?"

"The sarcastic one."

The place where *The Hunting of the Snark* was located in the book was already bookmarked, but I paged through anyway. "I haven't the foggiest idea what you're talking about."

"Look, I know you're not happy with my decision. But that doesn't mean I don't think there could be some importance in Carver's last word."

"So you don't think his utterance was nothing more than dying brain cells burning out, sending some kind of screwy signal from his mind to his mouth?"

Ronny's face reddened. He glared hard at me for a long moment and I returned the stare, just waiting for him to say something. He didn't, though, instead shaking his head and clapping the Kid on the back.

"I think I'm going to take a break," he said.

"Wait," the Kid said. "Don't go."

"I'll see you later at dinner."

He turned and left without looking at me. I should know —I was staring him down the entire time.

Once Ronny had left, the Kid said, "Jesus fucking Christ, Ben, have some fucking manners."

I looked around the room.

"Now what are you doing?"

"Trying to find that swear jar."

"Would you stop being an asshole? I know you're pissed off at Ronny, but the truth is he wants to help."

"He wants to split us up."

The Kid said nothing.

"What, now you agree with him?"

"Does it really matter what I think?"

"Of course it does."

"Really? Because right now I'm starting to think nobody's opinion matters much to you but your own."

I snapped the book shut, tossed it back onto the bed. Stood there silent for a long moment, then said, "Okay."

"Okay what?"

"I was being an asshole. I'm sorry."

"Don't apologize to me, dude."

"I'll talk to Ronny later. What are you doing now, anyway?"

The Kid turned back to the computer. "Carver had asked me to set him up with a special email program, so he could send and receive emails that couldn't be traced."

"When was this?"

"About a year ago. It was that one weekend I came by last year, right after ... you know, all that shit went down."

Yes, all that shit. That shit concerning a man named Christian Kane being put into Simon's game. That shit concerning Carver and the rest of us saving him and bringing him back to the farmhouse, explaining to him what had happened, what all of this meant. And three days later, the rest of us all naïve, believing the only true evil was Simon and Caesar and their people, Christian Kane showed us just how dark the human soul can become.

"So let me guess," I said. "You don't know the password."

"Nope."

"Have you tried boojum?"

"Don't be a dick." The Kid paused, then leaned forward

and quickly tapped the keyboard. He shook his head. "Yep, that wasn't it either."

"How do we even know there's anything important in the program to begin with?"

He gave me a blank look. "Dude, it was Carver."

"I thought he wasn't going to keep secrets from the rest of us anymore."

This made the Kid pause. He nodded, his eyes drifting. "Yeah, me too."

"If you created this thing, why didn't you give yourself a backdoor?"

"I did. But I can't do it from here. I'll have to take the hard drive back home with me."

"Do you think it's worth it?"

"I don't know. Depends what he has in here. Could be nothing. Could be something. But to be honest, I highly doubt he'll have an address or something titled boojum. Carver"—the Kid still staring at the screen, his arms crossed—"he just started getting real paranoid there near the end."

"You mean even more paranoid than you?"

"He didn't want anybody getting into his shit, Ben. Not even those people he really trusted, like you and me. I mean, you know what he started thinking after that whole Gravedigger shit went down. He told me he couldn't be too careful anymore."

The Gravedigger was what Christian Kane's game had been listed as. A thirty-seven-year-old man standing six feet four inches tall, weighing close to two hundred eighty pounds, a good majority of it muscle.

He'd been a maintenance worker at a large city cemetery, in charge of keeping the grass constantly mowed, the bushes trimmed, the tombstones clean and unmarked by graffiti. And he was in charge of digging the graves. So it made sense that when he woke up in Simon's game, he woke up in a closed coffin.

I can't even begin to imagine what that must have felt like, opening your eyes and seeing only darkness, your breath shallow, hardly any room to move your arms and legs.

One of the things listed on his game—a fun fact for its viewers—was that the Gravedigger partook in necrophilia. A bit macabre, sure, and even a bit overdone, but we'd guessed it was most likely an outlandish claim to gain more and more viewers. When we finally tracked down Christian and saved him and brought him back, this little ditty was brought up and he confirmed it was a lie, that he'd never performed in that kind of intercourse. And the kicker was, we'd believed him, all of us, even Carver, trying to find good in all things, believing that there was more white than black in a person's soul.

But then Vanessa was forever gone, Drew's face was forever scarred, and Carver went about creating a safe house. A place to put the new players we saved, a kind of jail where we could keep them for at least a few days, until we got to know them, until we understood just what kind of people they truly were.

"Again," I said to the Kid. "Do you think it's worth it?"

"I told you already. I don't know."

"When are you leaving?"

"I'm not sure. I guess that all depends on what happens during the meeting tonight."

"What do you think the outcome will be?"

"That really isn't the question you should be asking right now."

"What question should I be asking?"

"Simple," the Kid said. "Even if Carver was still alive, what chance do any of us really have at stopping Caesar?"

TWENTY-SEVEN

Even before Jesse Bowman became a part of Simon's game, life had not treated him well.

Born the youngest of five children, his mother already fed up after the second, it didn't help Jesse much that he'd unfairly been given a genetic defect. The harelip itself wasn't really that bad—hardly noticeable unless you were standing right in front of him—but still it caused him to carry a lisp.

Jesse was ugly, too—a small and angular face, buck teeth, wide eyes, round ears. Taken separately they might not mean much, but together they gave the kids in grade school more than enough verbal ammunition to scale a full-out assault.

He was teased relentlessly. First about the lisp, and then, when he stopped talking altogether, the fact that he was just plain ugly.

This was what Jesse had to deal with in the first dozen years or so of his life—the kids constantly picking on him at school, his mom or his siblings hardly paying any attention to him at home. So it almost made sense that when he turned thirteen he'd packed some of his clothes and the little money he had in a plastic grocery store bag, waited until it was the middle of the night, and ran away from home.

And where did he run away to? Not the circus. This was Wyoming, after all, so after a couple days of walking, after begging for food, after sleeping in fields, he crossed paths with a traveling rodeo.

They were on their way from Buffalo to Casper, taking the straight shot down I-25, and it took Jesse a very long time to convince one of the cowhands that his folks were dead, that he was orphaned and had nobody else and please please please would they take him along?

The cowhand must have figured Jesse's story was complete bullshit, but he relented anyway, found him some work, and that was how Jesse got his start with the rodeo, how he worked his way up until he had become a semi-professional bull rider at the age of eighteen. He was pretty good too, could usually stay on for the full eight seconds and sometimes even longer. But the fact that he was ugly, that he had a lisp, kept him from going any further. Bull riding was just like every other sport— no matter how good you might be, you had to have a face that the public could appreciate, trust, come to love. And his just wasn't that face.

So Jesse never did make the pros. He did get married, though, to a woman who didn't seem to mind the fact he was ugly. A woman who had first gotten pregnant and then came to Jesse later, claiming the child was his. Only when the child was born it was quite clear the baby's biological father was a man of African descent. But Jesse didn't mind. Sure, he knew he had been lied to, but he remembered how he'd been brought up, and he wanted something better for this child—for his child.

But it was difficult. Jesse had quit school when he was twelve, and even then he hadn't been doing well. Not that he hadn't wanted to learn, but learning didn't come as easy for him as it did the other kids. And his teachers had done him the disservice of passing him every year, not wanting to deal with him, and he floated by, so that by the time he eventually woke up in Simon's game he was twenty-eight years old and had the reading capacity of a third grader.

He wasn't stupid, though. Far from it. He was actually very intelligent, was a strong worker, and completely honest. He rarely talked because of his lisp, and this was the first thing Simon had used to taunt him with, claiming that if Jesse could recite the alphabet clearly, without lisping once, his wife and mulatto son would be released and Simon would give Jesse one million dollars cash.

Jesse couldn't even get past the letter C.

Can't say I blame him. Not for a man so hapless he had been cursed with a name he couldn't even pronounce without revealing his lisp. Not after waking up naked, tied to a mechanical bull, fresh dung spread out all around him on the mats.

His first thought was like everyone else's: where was he? His second thought: where was his family? And when Simon contacted him, told him about the game and the stakes, it became difficult to think, to breathe, to even move, so attempting to say the alphabet without trouble?

Give me a break.

Anyway, just because Jesse couldn't read very well didn't mean he didn't want to. He tried reading books, even attempted to teach himself over the years, but he was always made fun of, usually by the woman who had conned him into marrying her, the one he would later try to save.

So what became Jesse's main source of entertainment? Comic books. Superman, Batman, X-Men—anything with superheroes. He loved superheroes. His favorite was Spider-Man. Out of all the comics he'd come to own in the past year since being taken out of Simon's game and coming to live here with us, his Spider-Man comics eclipsed them all.

So it was no surprise that when I knocked on his door he

was reclining on his bed, the lamp tilted at an angle behind his head to provide enough light to clearly see each panel of Peter Parker's latest adventure.

When he looked up, he closed the comic book with a finger to save his page. He must have sensed my real purpose for knocking, because he sat up and said, "Hey, Ben. You lookin' for Ian?"

I started to shake my head but then stopped. "Yeah," I said. "You have any idea where he is?"

"I think he'th downthairth. Wathin the new guy."

I thanked him and started to back out of the room.

Jesse said my name.

"Yeah?"

"I wanted to ax you thomethin."

He set the comic book aside, taking his finger from between the glossy pages. This I knew was serious. Jesse never welcomed interruptions when he was in the middle of a new Spider-Man.

I entered the room and sat down on Ian's bed. The cheap twin mattress squeaked beneath me.

I sat there for a moment, looking about the room. This had actually been my room two years ago. Back then we had been able to have our own separate rooms. But once we started pulling more players out of the games, bringing them here, space became an issue. We started bunking up. Started switching rooms. Carver had liked the idea of us trading rooms every couple of months. Getting to know each other. It was his form of musical bedrooms. Not like it was a huge deal anyway, because besides clothes and a few books or DVDs, we didn't really have any possessions we needed to move from one room to the next. Only the girls had always kept their own room, Carver figuring it was best he didn't make the sleeping arrangements completely coed.

Jesse was sitting on the edge of his bed, the comic book

beside him. He was staring down at his dry and calloused hands, massaging the palms, the tips of his fingers.

I waited. Just sat there watching him. When it became apparent he wasn't going to speak, I said, "So what's up?"

He looked at me sharply, as if surprised to find me sitting there. He tried smiling, his buck teeth flashing for a moment, but the smile was forced, awkward, almost pained.

"Tho what ... what do you think ith gonna happen to uth?"

"How so?"

"You know. Now that Carver ... now that he'th gone."

"I don't know. Depends on the vote tonight."

"Right. But what if ... what happenth if the vote ith we thplit?"

"Then we split. Go our own separate ways."

Jesse shook his head. "I don't know where I'd go."

"Me neither."

I forced a smile, then got up and started toward the door.

Jesse said, "I felt ... cold."

I turned back around. "What do you mean?"

"When I heard about what happened to Carver. I felt cold."

"Do you ... feel cold now?"

He shook his head, staring down at his hands.

"It'th like thith, okay? There wath thith old cowhand I uthed to work with. Old man we all called Rex. He was like eighty, eighty-five, thomethin' like that. Anyhow, one night he tharted complainin' about gettin' real cold. He kept thayin' he could feel it comin'. Everybody, we all ignored him, figured he was ramblin'. But every night, without fail, he keepth thayin' he'th cold. Finally I ax him what'th wrong. I'm like fourteen then, okay? Been there only a year. And tho I ax Rex, and you know what he tellth me? He thayth he can feel Death comin'. Like Death with a capital D. He thayth that'th what it feelth like when you 'bout to die. You feel cold. And not like you feel cold in the middle of the night, when your blanket ith thin and you're thiverin'. I mean cold, like in your thoul."

He paused, still staring down at his hands, still massaging his palms, the tips of his fingers.

"There at the end, he even thaid he could thee him comin'. Death, I mean. He thaid he could actually thee him comin' for him. One night, it wath only me around, and I don't know why I thayed, but I did. And Rex ith lying there, thaking, thaying that Death ith right there with uth, about to touch him. And you know what Rex thaid? He thaid the hand of Death wath like ice. And ever thince then, that'th thuck with me. That idea about Death. And … and that'th what I felt when I heard about Carver. I felt cold. Like in my thoul."

He looked up at me, his eyes glassy with tears.

"Like … like Death ith comin' for me next. Like it'th comin' for all of uth."

TWENTY-EIGHT

I headed back downstairs. Turned the corner to find Beverly and Maya in the kitchen, both of them at the sink, Beverly washing the dishes and Maya drying them.

Maya had a plate in one hand, a dishtowel in the other. She forced a smile and said, "Hey."

I nodded at her, forced my own smile.

Beverly had her hands in the warm soapy water, scrubbing a copper pan. She smiled at me too, though her smile wasn't at all forced.

I asked, "Beverly, do you have the Racist's dinner ready yet?"

Even though we knew the man's real name, we always referred to the latest player we saved as their show name, at least until we were certain they were on the level.

Her back to me, rinsing the pot, Beverly said, "It's still in the oven. About another ten minutes before it's done."

"Can you have it ready for me then, please? I'm going to head over there next."

Maya said, "Want me to come along?" There wasn't so much hope in the question as simple curiosity.

I took a moment, as if really considering it, then said, "Thanks, but I already asked Jesse to come along with me."

She nodded once, like it was no big thing. She took the dripping copper pot from Beverly and began wiping it with her towel.

I waited a moment, expecting more questions, and when none came I turned and headed downstairs.

The basement was split up into two sections. On one side there was a matching washer and dryer, a hot water heater, a furnace. On the other side were tables lined up against the wall, four computer monitors spread out on top of them. A few book-shelves, a TV, a radio, even a mini-fridge.

I found Ian slumped in front of one of the tables, his left leg propped up on a chair. He was reading a thick book. He didn't hear me coming down the old and creaking steps because of the earbuds in his ears.

Graham had done the work on the leg, making a splint and then bandaging it. Ian couldn't be taken to the hospital, he couldn't get the proper medical attention he needed, so this was the best that could be done.

I stood there for a long while, staring down at the leg, hoping against hope that it would heal properly.

A part of me didn't want to interrupt him, so I just continued standing there. Moving my focus away from his leg to the computer monitors. Only one of them was turned on, split so it showed four different pictures. All were of the safe house, and the Racist inside.

The big man lay on the cot, staring at the ceiling. He was so still it didn't even look like he was breathing.

Ian finally sensed me. He glanced over, his head bobbing slightly to the beat, started to turn back to his book but instead jumped, did a double take.

"Son of a bitch." He closed the book with a snap, sat up straighter in his chair. He yanked the earbuds from his ears, picked his iPod up from his lap and turned it off. Looked back up at me and said, "What the hell are you trying to do, Ben, scare me to death?"

"No." I shook my head, attempted a small smile. "But I didn't want to interrupt you, either."

Ian sucked in a deep breath. He lifted his Red Sox cap, ran his fingers through his hair.

"What are you reading?"

He glanced down at the book on his lap, held it up so I could see the cover. "Just catching up on some history."

It was one of the fifty or so books Carver had purchased two years ago. Mostly history texts that dealt with the Roman Empire. He'd wanted us to read up on the subject as much as we could, and would even test us every few weeks.

I lifted my chin at the computer monitor. "How's our boy?"

"Our boy isn't doing much of anything. Hell, I don't think he's moved from that cot in the past seven hours."

"Do you know if he's read it yet?" Meaning the thing I'd written two years ago, the story of the Man of Wax.

Ian, staring at the screen, shook his head. "I haven't seen him touch it. Not after you first gave it to him."

I nodded but didn't say anything.

Ian sensed the awkward silence and glanced up.

"So," he said.

"So."

We just stared at each other.

Swallowing, feeling a lump in my throat, I said, "So … I wanted to apologize. You know, about what happened this past weekend."

He waved a dismissive hand. "Don't worry about it."

"You know I can't do that. I gave you up. You were right to be pissed at me."

"My leg had just been broken, Ben. I was in a lot of pain. I was pissed at everything. So yeah, it didn't help when you gave me to that guy, but … well, it worked out."

"It might not have."

"But it did. I'm here. You're here. That little girl was saved. That's all that matters."

Neither of us mentioned Carver. Neither of us mentioned anything more of the mysterious rider who'd come out of nowhere to save us.

I asked, "So what do you think about him?"

Ian took another deep breath. He glanced at the screen. "I'm not sure yet. You?"

"I'm not sure yet either. But the past four times I've been in to talk to him, he hasn't said a word."

Above us there were footsteps, Beverly and Maya moving about the kitchen.

I said, "You know what Carver said about him that night? Right after we'd left the club?"

"What's that?"

"He called the Racist a loose cannon. He said … he said he reminded him of Christian Kane."

Ian bit his lip. He glanced at the screen once more and whispered, "It might not matter after tonight anyway."

"What makes you say that?"

Ian shrugged. "Depending on how we all vote."

"What's your vote?"

Ian just stared back up at me, his expression flat. Confirming what I already guessed.

"Do you think that's the wisest decision?"

"I don't know what to think anymore."

"But what would you do? How would you survive?"

Ian suppressed a laugh. "You make it sound like I would be dropped in the middle of the Sahara without water."

"But at least you're protected here. We're a family."

"We are not a family, Ben. We're just a bunch of people who got fucked over in life. Yeah, okay, so we got a second chance, that's great. Carver gave it to us and I appreciate that. But now? Now we get a third chance. How many people can say that?" Ian shook his head. "Do you want to know what I think? Honestly?"

I waited.

"I think you're scared. Shit, I can't blame you. I'm scared too. My life ... it's over. I can't go back home. I can't endanger the lives of any of my friends, or even distant family members. You got to figure Simon and his crew would find out about that pretty fast. So what am I supposed to do? How am I supposed to live?"

I crossed my arms, didn't say anything.

"So yeah, Ben, I'm scared. I'm scared to death. But who knows, maybe everyone will vote differently. Maybe we'll stay together. If that happens, fine, okay, I don't mind staying."

"That's bull."

Ian nodded. "Of course it's bull. I don't want to stay here if I don't have to. Not now. Not without Carver. I mean, seriously, Ben, you think we can continue doing what we've been doing? Who's going to lead us?" He snorted. "You?"

I said nothing.

Ian dropped his eyes. "Look, I'm sorry. I don't mean to sound like an asshole. It's just this fucking leg won't stop hurting. The painkillers we have here aren't strong enough. You have no idea what I'd do for a Vicodin right now. But anyhow, you have to look at it this way. No matter what you think or how you feel, you have to understand this simple truth: now without Carver, nothing will ever be the same again. Nothing."

"You sound just like the Kid."

"Do I? Well, I guess I'm okay with that. I mean, the Kid is a genius, after all."

There was movement on the computer monitor. The Racist

was sitting up, swinging his feet off the bed. He just sat there for a moment, then looked up directly at the camera. Lifted his right hand and gave us the bird.

"Oh look," Ian said. "I think that's your cue."

TWENTY-NINE

The Racist looked like he was dead.

He must have heard me open the safe house door, walk in and close it. He must have heard my footsteps on the concrete floor, the noise of the bottom gate opening as I slid the new tray of food into his cell, took away the untouched tray from this morning.

But he didn't stir. His slow and shallow breathing didn't change.

"Mason," I said.

He continued lying there supine on the cot.

"I saw your little message earlier. I'm assuming that means you now want to talk."

Still no response.

I went to the desk just outside the bars and set this morning's tray of food on top. It had been pancakes and scrambled eggs and bacon with maple syrup. When I'd slid it into his cell this morning the food had been warm. Now it was cold and hard.

I pulled the chair out from the desk and sat down. Placed

my arm on the desktop and tapped a slow but steady beat with my ring, middle, and index fingers.

The safe house was a small, squat building made completely of cinderblocks. Half of the room was the holding cell, which contained a cot, a toilet and sink—these last two tucked away in the corner and concealed by a plastic blind for privacy from the cameras.

To be honest, calling it a holding cell wasn't fair. It wasn't the type of holding cell you'd find in a local police station. Ours also contained a mini-fridge, stocked full of bottled water and fruit, and a telephone that, when picked up, immediately called the farmhouse.

Mason hadn't touched the phone once. As far as I knew, he hadn't even opened the fridge.

Three of the four cameras were positioned in the ceiling corners of the safe house. Two looking straight down at the middle of the holding cell, at the cot and fridge. The other on the other side, looking down at the metal desk and chair. The fourth was outside, right near the door, facing the trees and trail leading up to the safe house.

Today Beverly had cooked the Racist meatloaf covered in ketchup, mashed potatoes and broccoli. Steam rose from where the meal sat on the floor just within the cell. It was getting cold, and something told me it would go untouched until I brought another meal.

A minute passed in silence.

I watched the Racist, his chest slowly rising and falling. He wore the same clothes as he had the night we picked him up in Miami Beach. I'd brought him fresh underwear and socks, a pair of sweatpants and a sweatshirt, all of which lay folded in the corner of the holding cell, but he hadn't touched those yet.

I continued tapping.

Another minute passed.

More tapping.

Mason Coulter said, "You killed my family."

My hand stopped at once, the ring finger already touching the desktop, the middle and index fingers frozen in midair.

"I could have beaten him. I could have won the game. But you … you people had to come and fuck it all up."

I leaned forward in my seat. "Do you seriously believe you had a chance at winning the game?"

Mason said nothing.

"Nobody wins the game. That's the whole point. Simon and his people push you and push you until you have no more give left and you either kill yourself or they kill you. And your family? They're already dead."

Mason bolted up from the cot. His face was red. The lights above him shined off his bald head.

"You don't know that."

"But I do. I've explained this to you already. I even asked you to read that"—I gestured at the bound manuscript on the floor next to the clothes—"but you haven't. Why? Why are you making this difficult?"

"Go fuck yourself."

"We're trying to help you, Mason."

"Oh yeah? A lot of fuckin' help you're doing me, keepin' me locked in here."

"I explained that to you also. This is only temporary. Your cooperation dictates how long we need to keep you in here."

"Yeah? Well if I were you, I'd keep me in here forever. 'Cause the minute I get outta here, I'm gonna break your fuckin' neck."

Mason glared at me another moment before he lay back down on the cot.

I closed my eyes, took a deep breath.

"Mason," I said.

No answer.

"Mason, what's your definition of evil?"

Still no response.

"I know you hate black people. Are they evil?"

Mason continued lying there, staring at the ceiling.

"How about the Jews? What have they done to you personally? How are they evil?"

I focused my gaze on the plate of meatloaf, which was still steaming.

"I don't know about you, Mason, but I never really thought much about evil. It was just a word to me. The difference between right and wrong, yeah, that's easy. But evil? I didn't know evil until the first time I spoke to Simon. Until I heard his voice and realized what it was he wanted me to do."

I shook my head.

"So I began to believe that Simon was evil. That Caesar was evil. But just them, you know? Not the rest of us. Not everyone else that I considered … normal. But then a year ago, there was this guy we rescued from one of the games. He was a real big guy, just like you. His show had been called The Gravedigger. He acted like he didn't give a fuck either. He acted like he wasn't scared. But he was scared. And so we welcomed him into our little family. We explained to him what was going on. How he'd been used simply as entertainment. How he never had a chance at saving his family. It was hard to accept—it's always hard for a player to accept the truth—but he understood. And you know what he said to us? He said he wanted to help us with our fight."

The meatloaf had stopped steaming completely now.

"There was this girl we'd saved only two months before the Gravedigger. Her name was Vanessa Martin. She was twenty-four years old. Very pretty. She'd been a waitress at a diner in Alabama. She had never done any wrong to anyone a day in her life, and then all of a sudden she had woken up in Simon's game. But she was tough. She wouldn't back down. And not even a week passed since we'd saved the Gravedigger, when we had started to train him. He had seemed normal enough, but one night he managed to get Vanessa alone. I don't know what happened exactly—maybe he tried hitting on her, flirting with her, something like that, though until then he had never expressed any interest in her as far as I know—but he took a knife from the kitchen and managed to get Vanessa alone and he … he raped her. He kept the knife at her throat, telling her he'd kill her if she screamed, and he tore off her clothes, wrestled her to the ground, and raped her."

I stood up and went to the holding cell, wrapped my fingers around the cold bars.

"He raped her, Mason, and then he killed her. But he didn't do it fast. He started slow, cutting her in different places first. She must have cried out, or someone must have realized the two of them were gone and suspected the worst, because right before he was able to drive the blade into her throat, Drew burst in on them. The Gravedigger—remember, a guy about your size—he fought him. He stabbed Drew in the stomach and threw him down on the ground and started cutting him. He cut him all across the face. Would have killed him, too, but then Carver came in. Carver took his gun and placed it right against the Gravedigger's head and pulled the trigger."

I paused. Realized my eyes were closed. That I had been seeing the entire thing happening in my mind.

Opening my eyes, I stared down at Mason.

"The Gravedigger's name was Christian Kane. And to me, he was evil. He was even more evil than Simon. Because Simon, he doesn't pretend to be something he's not. Simon knows what he is. But Christian? He pretended he was normal, just like one of us."

Still staring up at the ceiling, Mason said, "You really think I'm a racist, don't you?"

I said nothing.

He sat up and swung his feet off the bed and glared back at

me. "You don't know a goddamn thing about me. You see these tattoos and just assume that I'm the one that put them there."

"If you didn't, who did?"

"Who do you think? *Simon*, that cocksucker. Yeah, I was in prison, and yeah, I killed a black guy in there. And yeah, I was briefly a member of the Brotherhood when I was in the joint. But I did that because I had no choice. If I didn't join them, I was going to die."

"What are you talking about?"

"See, you think you know everything there is to know about me just based on my appearance. But you don't know shit."

"Is that right? Then what about the male prostitute you killed? What about the transvestite you beat up at The Spur?"

"I have anger issues."

"That's bullshit."

"It's true. All my life I've had a hard time keeping my temper under control. See, you didn't know that, did you? But Simon, he knew it, and that's why he put me in those situations. Be honest with me. If some faggot was sucking your cock, would you be happy about it?"

I said nothing.

"Exactly. So don't judge me when you know nothing about me. You want to talk about evil? You want to be so self-righteous to think you're perfect? You ask me, that's evil right there." He tilted his head, keeping his gaze level with mine. "What do you have to say about that?"

THIRTY

"Boojum," the Kid said simply. He paused a beat, letting the word sink in, and then said it again. "Boojum."

The room was silent.

"Some of you are hearing this for the very first time. If that's the case, I apologize. The truth is, so much has happened in the past couple of days that this word—boojum—has become a ... bane, almost. Ben claims it was Carver's last word—"

"It was," I said.

"Let me finish." The Kid held up a placating hand to me, then once again addressed the entire room. "Ben claims it was Carver's last word and maybe it was. But even so, who's to say it means anything?"

Nobody spoke.

The Kid cleared his throat. "I won't get into the different possible meanings of boojum, but the main meaning comes from Lewis Carroll. And if we all knew Carver like I know we did, we all know Lewis Carroll meant something special to him."

Ian leaned forward in his chair. "So what does it mean?"

"It's a particularly dangerous kind of snark. The most dangerous kind of snark, in fact."

Jesse asked, "What's a th-th-thnark?"

"A fictional animal created by Carroll." The Kid shrugged. "You can read the poem it's from later, but the main reason I'm mentioning it now is because even if Carver did mean to tell us something using that word—like some kind of code—we have no idea what it is."

We were all spread out around the room. Beverly, Maya, Ian, Jesse, and Graham sat at the long oak table, where we'd just been eating a meal less than a half hour ago, the lingering scent of pot roast and mashed potatoes and green beans still in the air. Ronny, Drew, and myself stood leaning against the walls in different parts of the room. We all faced the Kid, who stood at the head of the table, one hand at his side, the other in the pocket of his jeans.

"So yeah," the Kid said, "I just wanted everyone to know that. Not that I really expect it to change your minds, but I figure you're all owed the truth. Again, if you weren't told, the reason it was kept from you is because we were trying to see if it meant anything first. And, again, as far as we can tell, it doesn't. At least not yet."

Ian asked, "What does that mean, 'at least not yet'?"

"Tomorrow I'm taking Carver's hard drive with me back home. There are some files locked in there that I want to try to get into. Maybe the answer to boojum will be in those files. Maybe not. Honestly, I'm not too hopeful."

Again, silence.

Graham cleared his throat. "Let's move on, Kid. Yes?"

The Kid nodded. He looked relieved to be past the first part of tonight's business. He even took his hand out of his pocket, and while the motion was slight, I saw him wipe the palm against the back of his jeans.

"Secondly, there is this business of our mystery rider, the

one who came to Ben's and Ian's rescue. We still have no idea who this person is, or what his connection is to us or to Simon or Caesar or to anything."

"Do we know yet how he managed to track Ronny all the way up the interstate?" Graham asked.

The Kid shook his head. "Once Jesse and Drew met up with Ronny and Ian and the Racist, they ditched the SUV. So if there was a tracking device on it, how it got there and where it was located is still a mystery."

Another moment of silence passed.

"Ben," the Kid said, "what's the news on the Racist?"

I thought about it for a long moment. "I'm not sure yet."

The Kid nodded again, but didn't look ready to say anything else quite yet. It was clear his little speech had worn him out. He wasn't comfortable being around large groups of people, and even though we were all friends—family, even—there had still been a tremble in his voice.

"Kid?"

This was from Beverly Rodriguez. She had her left hand raised in the fashion of a timid sixth grader answering a question she isn't quite sure about but wants to answer anyway.

"Yes, Beverly?"

"I mentioned this to Graham already, but it was only in passing. Tomorrow I would like to have a memorial service for Carver."

"Sure, I don't see why not." The Kid's gaze skipped around the room. "Is everyone okay with that?"

Nobody shouted a nay.

After a long beat, when he was sure there would be no last second interjections, the Kid turned toward Ronny. He opened his mouth, started to speak, when Beverly spoke again.

"Also, I wanted to say one more thing."

She no longer had her hand held timidly in the air. Both her hands were folded on the tabletop, the light hanging from the ceiling catching the faux-crystal vase holding a spray of daises and tulips.

"I'm sure you all already know this," she said, looking around the room at us, "but I wasn't always a religious person. I grew up Catholic, but everyone in my neighborhood grew up Catholic. It didn't mean anything. And it wasn't until my later years, when I turned forty, that I started thinking more and more about God."

Beverly Rodriguez was forty-six years old. She'd been the mother of three, two boys and a girl. Born and raised in a heavily populated Latino section of Harlem, she had never left. She got pregnant when she was fourteen, had a miscarriage, got pregnant again when she was fifteen, had another miscarriage. She got tired of having miscarriages, started practicing safe sex, until she got married at the age of thirty-three to a liquor store owner named Juan Rodriguez.

"And the more and more I started thinking about God," she continued, "the more and more I wondered if He really even cared about me at all. Like, who was I compared to everyone else? To all those doctors and lawyers and stockbrokers out there. To everyone. I wasn't a good person. I'm not a good person."

The most interesting thing about Beverly was that she had not been Simon's original choice to play the game. Her husband had. But when he'd woken up, when he had been told his wife and three *ninos* were gone, Juan Rodriguez crumbled. He barely even lasted two hours. He broke down crying, begging for all this to stop, but Simon calmly explained it wouldn't stop. Not until Juan complied and played the game like a good boy. It was then that Juan took the loaded .38 Special he'd woken up beside, placed the barrel in his mouth, and pulled the trigger.

"So I believed in God, but I didn't believe. Not in my soul. Not where it counts. I didn't believe he was my savior. I didn't really start believing it until—not until they took me and my babies."

So Juan was dead, gone, his game finished. To any of the viewers who had paid thousands and thousands of dollars to watch, it looked like that was it.

But Caesar couldn't allow that to happen. Not to his loyal fans. And in what Carver believed was an unprecedented move, the original player's wife—who had been held captive along with her children—was thrust unwillingly into the game, to start up right where her husband had left off.

By all accounts, it shouldn't have worked. On the outside Beverly Rodriguez was a plump, dark-haired, brown-eyed woman who stayed at home to tend to her trio of children. Doing housework was her game, not anything Simon's twisted mind could come up with.

But she loved her children very much, and a mother's instinct is a very powerful thing. When backed against a corner, a mother will do nearly anything to save her own. Sometimes, she'll toe the line past "nearly" and do whatever it takes.

So Beverly was taken away from her children and put in Simon's game. The rules were explained to her, and she was told that if she did everything accordingly, she would see her family again. And like anyone else too naïve to know better, she believed Simon was telling the truth.

That was until two days later, when Carver and David and I came to the rescue. When we stopped her on the street of East St. Louis, the same .38 Special her husband had used to kill himself nestled securely in the bottom of her purse.

Now, just over a year later, having become a kind of den mother to the rest of us—doing the laundry, the dishes, cooking meals; whatever she could so the rest of us could continue our never-ending fight against Caesar and his many Simons—Beverly Rodriguez wiped away the tears that had begun to form in her eyes.

"And the entire thing," she said, sniffing back her tears, "from the moment they first took me and my children, to the moment that man put me in the game, I prayed to God. I asked him to send an angel to save us. And Carver ... he was that angel. I knew once I laid eyes on him he was a good person. A great person. And when he told me that my children were already dead, I saw the sincerity in his eyes, I could almost feel the desperation in his soul, and I believed him. And that's why I'm here today. I'm here because of Carver. We're all here because of Carver."

When Beverly had first joined us, there had been some excitement. Carver had waited until enough days passed—when Beverly had started to make the adjustment, when her mourning period had ended—to ask his questions. Because if Beverly had been kept someplace with her children, then it was safe to assume she might have been kept at a private location. Maybe one of the bases Simon and his people used. Maybe even *the* base, the place where we could find Caesar.

But Beverly could give us no helpful details. All she knew was that she and her children had been locked in a cold, dark room. It had been bare except for a toilet, some sheets and pillows. Cameras had been in the walls, watching them. Every couple hours, a man or woman—their faces had been blank, emotionless—came in to give them food.

That was it. Even when she was eventually taken out, forced into Simon's game, she hadn't seen what was outside that room. They had given her a sedative, knocked her out, and she hadn't opened her eyes again until Simon called her on a ratty telephone hanging off the wall in an abandoned apartment.

"So what is the one thing I've learned in my life?" Beverly asked us. Her heavy but pleasant voice had become a croak. "I've learned that everything in this world—no matter how evil, how perverse—happens for a reason. What happened to my family, to my husband and children, it was God's will. Was it right? Was it acceptable? I would like to say no, but nobody should ever question God. He acts"—her voice hitched—"he acts in mysterious ways. But all of those ways, they are for a reason."

She wiped at her eyes, sniffed back more tears.

"And Carver's passing," she said, her voice suddenly quiet, "that happened for a reason too. We can't question why it happened. We can only accept it."

A long silence followed this. Beverly had dropped her head, had started sobbing even harder. Maya, sitting beside her, placed a hand on her back.

Nobody else said anything. Nobody else even looked at each other, instead finding different spots around the room on which to focus their attention.

The spot I found myself focusing on was near the ceiling, right above the doorway leading to the kitchen. Two years ago, I'd painted the entire dining room off-white. I'm a good painter, I know what I'm doing, so that evening when I spotted the crack near the ceiling, it caused the fissure that had opened in my soul to grow even larger.

The crack was so slight nobody else probably noticed it. But I did. It reminded me about what my father had once said, about why he painted. It reminded me how even though you can paint something clean, make it look new, the bad stuff, the nasty stuff, will always be there underneath.

Ronny broke the silence. He stepped forward. Nodded at the Kid who stepped aside, went to lean against the doorway into the kitchen.

Ronny said, "I guess it's time to get this over with, huh?"

Everyone stopped staring at different spots of the dining room. Their gazes fell on him.

"Before we start," Ronny said, "I want to just add one thing. I loved Carver very much. He wasn't just a leader to me. He was my friend. He was a friend to us all. Heck, he was a brother to us all. So in voting tonight, it's very important to make clear that we're not voting against Carver or his memory. This is for us. We are what is left."

Ronny glanced down at the table, slowly stroked his heavy beard.

"So let's not fool ourselves any longer. We need to look deep inside our hearts and souls and ask ourselves just what kind of chance we had to begin with. This whole thing with Simon and Caesar—it's way bigger than any of us. Yes, Carver was our leader, and he gave us the strength and will to keep fighting these people. But the Lord's honest truth is they can't be beaten. They're just too strong. So tonight, we're not giving up. We're just … we're accepting the reality of our situation. Even if Carver was still alive, and we continued like we've been doing, what difference would we make? The games will go on. Innocent people will die. But right now, what's more important? So far we've lost five people in the last two years—Larry and Bronson and David and Vanessa and now Carver. Honestly, we've been much more fortunate than we probably should be. We could have lost so much more. I think it's time we stop worrying about other people. I think it's time we start worrying about ourselves."

Still stroking his beard, he looked up at me.

"Ben, do you have anything to say?"

I nodded.

"Would you like to come up here to speak?"

"No," I said. "I can say what I need to say from right here."

Everybody turned to look at me. I stared into each of their faces for a moment before speaking.

"Each and every one of us should be dead right now. The only reason we're not is because of Carver. Carver refused to give up trying to stop these people, and neither should we. If we owe Carver's memory anything, it's to keep fighting."

Everyone stared back at me. Then, as if on cue, they all collectively looked away.

I nodded at Ronny.

He said, "I guess it's time to vote."

Graham raised his hand. "Nothing against you, Ronny, or Ben, or even Carver, but I'm not going to partake in the voting. In reality, this doesn't involve me. Depending on the outcome, I will live with whatever. All of you are welcome to stay here. If you decide to leave, I will understand that too."

The Kid said, "I'm with Graham. This doesn't involve me either. I'm cool with whatever."

"Okay," Ronny said. He picked up the pre-cut pieces of paper and pens and began distributing them around the room. "Then let's vote."

The voting didn't take long. Not even two minutes.

Ronny, Drew, Ian, and Beverly voted to disband. Maya, Jesse, and myself voted to stay together. It was as simple as that.

The scale had been tipped, and there was no going back.

THIRTY-ONE

At some point everyone moved from the dining room into the living room. Graham made a fire. We sat on the couches, on the chairs, on the floor. The grandfather clock in the corner ticked, the wood in the fireplace popped. We were all quiet, digesting our meals, digesting the outcome of the vote. Digesting what this would mean now for our future.

Eventually Ronny broke that silence. He started talking about Carver. About the day Carver had saved him. About how scared Carver had been, how nervous. Nothing like the smooth, cool professional he had become in later years.

Others joined in on the storytelling. Everyone had something to say. Even Graham talked about how when Carver first came to the farmhouse, Carver had been convinced Graham would not believe his story. In fact, Carver had admitted to Graham later that there had been a moment when he almost turned around and headed back to the Kid's, so certain that Graham would turn him away.

This was how the hours passed. Carver's official memorial service would be tomorrow, held outside in the backyard, beside the other graves. Beverly would probably make a cross to put next to the one that stood for Leon Ellison, Carver's son.

I was the only person who didn't contribute. I just listened to everyone else's stories. I watched the flames of the fire as they licked the air and spat sparks.

After some time, there were no more words left to say. We all sat again in silence.

The Kid got up from the chair he'd moved in from the dining room and went to stand in front of the fireplace. He placed his hands in the pockets of his jeans, cleared his throat. And then, in a very soft and slow voice, he began to sing.

"*I'm a lumberjack and I'm okay, I sleep all night and I work all day.*"

The Kid stopped there and waited, his cheeks burning, looking around the room.

We all stared back at him.

He cleared his throat again, started to sing once more, this time with a louder bass.

"*I'm a lumberjack and I'm okay, I sleep all night and I work all day.*"

Then he paused again and waited, but he didn't have to wait long.

It was Ronny who started the chorus, Ronny who, in a distant and low voice, echoed that first line.

"*He's a lumberjack and he's okay, he sleeps all night and he works all day.*"

"There we go," the Kid said, nodding and smiling. "That's more like it."

He continued the song—it was "The Lumberjack Song" from *Monty Python's Flying Circus*—stopping where he was supposed to stop, waiting for Ronny and everyone else to start in with the chorus. And it was pretty much everyone else.

Only I didn't join in, sitting slumped on the couch, my

arm propped up on the end, holding my head as I stared past
the Kid at the dancing flames.

Maya sat beside me, and as she sang she would look at me,
sometimes place a hand on my thigh, give a slight squeeze, as if
to ask if I was okay.

I never acknowledged her. I just listened as everyone else
joined in with the Kid, singing the same song over and over,
watching the flames but also watching the scene of Carver's
death, up there on the third floor of the Beachside Hotel,
pulling him down the hallway toward the elevators while
Carver spat up blood.

At one point—when they had started the song for the third
or fourth time, everyone really into it now, all of them clapping
—I got up and left the living room, walking through the
kitchen and out the back door.

I wasn't angry. Not at the Kid or anybody else. The Kid was
more shook up about this than anyone. His whole singing, his
whole trying to get everyone involved, was to release the
tension. It was to cheer everyone up.

I sat on the swing, the place I'd sat with Graham earlier
today, the place I had sat with Carver many times in the past. I
stared down the hillside, out at the trees, out at the distant
peaks.

The sun had set hours ago, leaving a clear night sky, the
stars shimmering from their places in the void. It made me
think about my daughter, about what I'd said would be the first
thing I'd tell her when I found her again. About coming
outside, staring up at the sky, asking aloud whether the sheep
had eaten the flower or not.

I had stopped doing that over a year ago. Even before
Christian Kane came on the radar. The stars had always been
quiet to me, and I was pretty certain they would forever remain
that way.

Maya came outside a few minutes later. She shut the door quietly behind her. She asked, "Can I sit with you?"

Staring out at the dark horizon, I said, "You know you can."

She sat down beside me, leaving a couple inches between us.

She didn't say anything. I didn't say anything. We just sat there in silence, listening to the noises of the night, to the insects and a lone owl hooting somewhere in the trees. Behind us, inside the house, distant voices continued, still singing along with the Kid.

Eventually Maya spoke.

"You've been distant."

"What do you expect?"

"It hasn't just been recently. It's been the past couple of months."

I said nothing and continued staring out at dark trees, listening to the owl.

Maya placed a hand on my thigh and said, her voice fragile and soft, "I do love you, you know. I love you more than I've ever loved anybody."

Maya Smith was twenty-six, eight years younger than me. She was dark-skinned, had dark eyes, had long jet-black hair. She had been beautiful once, back when life was kinder. Now her face was worn and drawn, her body thin from her disease. Yet despite this, there were times when she smiled that you could see the beauty that once resided in her face—a beauty that continued to reside in her heart and soul.

She was Native American, though she did not know from what tribe her people had originated. She was born on an Indian reservation in Washington State—this she knew for a fact—but she never knew which reservation that had been. Spokane, Colville, Quinault, Umatilla, Yakama, Makah—it could have been any one of them, it could have been none. Her mother never told her, having taken her away right after she was born to live in Seattle. There her mother hooked up with a white man twenty years her senior who promised to provide and take care of Maya and her mother.

That was how Maya spent her childhood, living in a white man's house (a man whose last name was Smith, which she ended up taking as her own), going to a white man's school, learning the white man's ways. Maya knew she was different but she didn't know why, and it didn't help that when she got into middle school the kids started teasing her. More than once she would hear hiya-ya-ya hiya-ya-ya in the hallways, always whispered behind her back, and when she turned around the offending parties would stop, already moving away, like they had never uttered a sound.

When she was sixteen, she had had enough of living in a white man's world. She was Indian by blood and she wanted to find out where she had come from, the culture, the people that she could rightly call her own. So she ran away, never to look back, never to speak to her mother or her white father ever again.

"Ben?" Maya said. "Did you hear me?"

"Yeah. I heard you."

"Well? Don't you love me too?"

Maya didn't get very far. Not for a sixteen-year-old girl without any money, any transportation, any clue of where to go next. So she hitchhiked.

She knew the dangers in this. She even carried a pocketknife, in case any driver ever tried to take advantage of her. For the most part, though, not many people picked her up. The few that did told her she should know better than to hitchhike. It was a tiring experience, and she found herself walking most of the time.

She went from reservation to reservation, asking about her mother, trying to find any kind of family. She barely got any answers, only offers for her to stay with them, to not travel by herself. Maya would have none of it.

Eventually she ran out of what little money she had. She couldn't afford any food. She couldn't afford any shelter. She knew she could return home, but she pushed the idea far from her mind. So she began living on the streets. Begging for and stealing what little she could get. She hooked up with a group of homeless girls her own age. They didn't treat her differently because she was Indian. They treated her as an equal. They even helped her learn how to survive on the streets. How to avoid the police. How to steal worthwhile food and clothing. All of them sold their bodies from time to time. It was just something you did on the street. Maya refused to do this. She knew she was better than that. But after a while the girls started distancing themselves from her. No longer did they treat her as an equal, but as someone who thought she was better than them. This was the very last thing Maya wanted—they were her only friends in the world—so she agreed. The girls took her to their pimp.

He was a forty-year-old black drug dealer. When he met Maya for the first time, he smiled widely—his teeth capped in gold—and said he was going to have fun with her.

He broke her in that night. It was what he did with all the girls, to see just how valuable she was, how much he thought she could charge. She didn't want to, but she cried the entire time. This turned the pimp on even more. When he was done, he asked her what her Indian name was. Maya told him she didn't have one. He said that wouldn't do, she needed an Indian name, and called her Suntaker. Because, he said, her face was so pretty it took away the brightness of the sun. Then he fucked her again.

Now, less than ten years later, a completely different Maya sat on the swing beside me, waiting for my answer.

"Well?" she said again, her voice still soft.

I closed my eyes. Thought briefly of my wife, of my daughter, both whom I knew were long gone, whom I would never see again.

I opened my eyes and tilted my head in her direction. Stared at her worn but beautiful face in the dark.

"Of course I do," I whispered.

She took her hand resting on my thigh, placed it against my stubble-haired cheek. "Then why won't you let me in?"

For close to six years Maya lived her life as a prostitute. When the pimp that broke her in got killed in a drive-by, she ended up with a different pimp, one that didn't treat her much better. This pimp got her hooked on drugs, so much so that she tried every form of narcotic there was.

Out of all the drugs she took, she found acid to be her favorite. One time, after dropping, she had seen all these things floating in the air. Very small things, like bugs, flying about here and there. Some were black, some were gray, but others were a beautiful iridescent. They were close to her and she tried reaching for them but couldn't feel them. She said, "Wow," drawing the single syllable out, and as she spoke what looked like a rainbow-colored butterfly fluttered from her mouth.

It was then that she understood what these flying things were. Not bugs, not butterflies per se—though that was what they looked like, all of them floating about—but words. And not just her words, but everyone's words, everyone in the history of the world.

Every word spoken became a butterfly. The color of those butterflies depended on what kind of words they were. If they were good words—wholesome words, words that expressed love and gratitude—they were rainbow-colored. If they were ugly words—hateful and hurtful words—they were black.

Most words, she found in the few hours during her trip, were gray. Words that were neither good nor bad. But between the two, the good and the bad, she found that there were many more black words. So much so that the rainbow-colored butterflies were so few they almost got sucked up by the rest of the black and gray butterflies.

She never saw those butterflies again. No matter how much acid she took, how many other drugs, she never experienced the same thing.

But it stayed with her. Even when she wasn't tripping, she would sometimes find herself squinting her eyes to try to see the butterflies. Mostly she couldn't, but there were a few times when she claimed that she could. That if you looked closely enough, if you knew what you were looking for, you could see the words of the world, all the different words spoken throughout the history of time, just floating about.

I closed my eyes again. I touched her hand touching my face. Held it there for a moment, then pulled her hand away.

I said, "Do you want to know the truth?"

"Not if it's going to hurt me."

I opened my eyes and stared at her, waiting.

"Of course I want to know the truth, Ben. What is it?"

"I don't know if I'm ready yet."

"Do you ever think you will?"

I looked past her, saw the distant and faded memory of my wife and daughter. "I don't know. I hope so."

Her hand in mine, she squeezed it lightly three times, her silent way of saying I love you.

"Take all the time you need. I'll keep waiting."

Maya was twenty-five when she woke up in Simon's game. Her show had been listed as the Suntaker. It was two months after Maya had learned she was HIV positive.

Simon, of course, had used this to his advantage. He'd used it to taunt Maya. That and the fact she was an Indian but didn't know from what tribe. Simon claimed that he did know. That he had done the research, and he knew which tribe Maya's blood came from. But, Simon said, he would only tell her if she played by the rules and won the game. If she won the game, she would not only learn her true identity, but she would get to keep her life.

It was nothing new for Simon, really. He didn't always follow the same formula. In fact, he tried to mix it up as much as possible. The I'm-holding-your-family-hostage routine could grow tiresome, and Simon knew the audience wanted something new, so he tried to keep it fresh.

Maya was only in the game three days before Carver, Ronny, and David rescued her. Before she was brought back to the farmhouse and explained what was going on. By that time she had been addicted to heroin. She had no track marks on her arms, would instead inject the drug between the toes of her feet.

One of the things Simon had used to keep the Suntaker going was the promise of more and more drugs. But now that she was out of the game, in Carver's care, there were no drugs. After only a day she started going through withdrawal, and somehow, between finishing the painting of the farmhouse and barn, taking care of Maya Smith became my responsibility.

I never once complained about it. My wife and daughter were gone, I felt I had no more purpose, and now, taking care of Maya, I realized I did have a reason to keep going. Maya had become my reason.

So I took care of her. I nursed her back to health. And as the days became weeks, the weeks became months, we started to get to know each other very well. Nothing sexual in nature at all, but we started to connect. She fell in love with me, I fell in love with her, but neither of us went forward with our desires. Maya didn't go forward because of her HIV and fear that she would somehow pass it on to me. I never went forward because I felt by doing so would be a betrayal to Jen and Casey.

But now almost two years had passed. Maya and I had started growing even closer. Oftentimes we would sleep together, but not have sex. Just hold each other until we fell asleep, listening to each other's breathing, feeling each other's heartbeats. Sometimes we kissed.

That was as far as it ever went. I was still holding back, and Maya, sensing this, understood. And recently, I found myself falling more and more in love with her, and as that realization blossomed in my head, I started to become afraid again. I started thinking more and more about my lost family.

Then Carver died, and I became even more scared.

Staring out at the dark horizon, holding Maya's hand, I said, "Back in Miami, when we went into that hotel and they ambushed us? My first thought was you."

Maya didn't say anything.

"You were the thing that made me want to keep going. What made me want to survive. Just seeing your face, thinking of you ... that's what made me want to come back home."

She squeezed my hand again, those three light squeezes.

Maya said, "What did it look like?"

I closed my eyes. Thought about being back in the Beachside Hotel. Watching Carver speak his last word.

"It looked like a butterfly."

"You're just saying that."

"It did."

"What color was it?"

I let go of her hand. Adjusted myself on the swing so I could look at her, so I could see her dark eyes staring back into mine. I opened my mouth, started to speak, but then stopped. I listened to the insects, to the owl, to the voices inside the farmhouse. The Kid had stopped singing, everyone else had stopped, and now they were just talking, probably about Carver again.

Finally I whispered, "It was black."

Maya stared at me another moment, biting her lower lip. She nodded, took a breath, and stared out at the trees.

I leaned back in the swing and stared out at the trees too.

"Maya?"

"Yes?"

"I … I love you."

"I know. I love you too."

We continued sitting there then in silence, just watching the night. I squinted my eyes and imagined that I could see our words out there, rainbow-colored, fluttering about the night, rising up toward the stars that may or may not have been tinkling like bells.

THIRTY-TWO

At eight-thirty the next morning, the Kid had his overnight bag packed, Carver's hard drive stored away in a box, and was ready to go. Jesse was going to drive him out to the airport. I volunteered to come along.

Jesse said, "Then you want me to thay?"

We were standing in the front yard, the three of us, only a couple feet from the pickup.

"No," I said. "You can drive. I just want to tag along."

The Kid had taken a shower, had applied gel to his hair, and he stood there now under the bright morning sun, not a strand of hair out of place. He gave me a strange look but didn't say anything.

We got in the truck, Jesse in the driver's seat, the Kid in the middle, and me on the passenger side.

It took nearly an hour and a half to get to the airport, and none of us spoke the entire way. Jesse played his country music, and while neither the Kid nor I cared for it much, we didn't object.

When we arrived at the airport, the Kid said, "Thanks, guys. I'll give you a call later tonight."

I had gotten out of the truck so he could get out, and I stood there holding the door open.

"I'm going with you."

The Kid said, "No, you're not."

"Yes, I am."

I leaned back into the pickup, told Jesse to head back to the farmhouse without me. He looked dubious but I told him it was okay, I would give him a call later when I boarded my returning flight.

"Tell Drew he's in charge of checking up on the Racist," I said, and shut the door, took a step back and waited for him to pull away.

When he did, I turned back to the Kid.

He said, "Have you lost your fucking mind?"

"I just can't be there right now. Especially when they're having that memorial service."

"But you can't come with me."

"I'm the only one that believes boojum means anything. I want to be there for this."

"It might not be anything."

"But it might."

The Kid sighed, shook his head, stared out at the parking lot.

"Fred's not flying this time," he said. "You can't just hop on board."

"I know that. That's why I went online last night and reserved a ticket."

"Yeah? And with whose money?"

I smiled at him.

"That's right," he said. "Mine."

He started walking away, toward the airport entrance, his overnight bag swinging from the strap off his shoulder, the box containing Carver's hard drive cradled in his arm.

"Kid," I said, and there was defeat in my voice. "Please."

He was only a few feet away when he stopped. "And what are you going to do when you find out it means nothing?"

"It won't."

"But what if it does? You can't keep kidding yourself, Ben. You have to move on."

"Okay." I swallowed. "If that's the case, I'll move on. But until then, I can't."

The Kid mulled this over for a beat. "You already booked the flight, huh?"

I nodded.

"Well, then I guess you spent your Christmas present a couple months early." He nodded toward the entrance for me to come along.

When we went through the sliding glass doors, he paused and looked around the terminal. He unzipped his bag and pulled loose his iPad, hesitated, then handed it to me.

"What do I want with this?"

"I figured you could use some in-flight reading."

I glanced down at the iPad. He reached out and tapped one of the apps and a screen popped up, mostly all text.

"What am I looking at?"

"Do you know anything about Carver's life? About how he spent his childhood?"

"No."

"Exactly. None of us did. So when I found out about what happened, I got curious and I started doing some research. It's one hell of a crazy story, I'll tell you that much. A lot of the information I managed to find was originally sealed and was a major pain in the ass to uncover. I'd meant to talk to Graham about it but chickened out."

I glanced down at the iPad again. A voice came on over the intercom announcing that gate three was now boarding.

"What's so crazy about it?"

"For starters," the Kid said, "Carver's mother was a whore. Literally."

I expected him to smile at this, as he usually did when he made a joke. But he just stared back at me. He didn't even crack a grin.

THIRTY-THREE

Carver's mother was indeed a whore. Her name was unknown, her age undistinguishable, but it's a good guess that she was under the age of twenty. She had worked the streets of New York City, just one hooker among a thousand, and as these things go, she got pregnant.

Before she could have an abortion, though, her pimp found out. She was called to see him. Expectations of a beating, of him remodeling her face, quickly faded from her mind. As it turned out, her pimp, while angry, had other ideas for her. She was told to relax, to take a couple months off, and if she was going to work, to just give head, nothing else.

The pimp saw himself as an entrepreneur. There was always money to be made, no matter the outcome. He knew someone who knew someone who paid a pretty penny for children. Newborns went for an especially high price.

Once Carver was born, he was paid for by a middleman (seven thousand bucks), who drove with at least a half dozen other children—all ranging from newborns to two years old—down I-95 toward Washington, D.C. There the middleman met up with another man to complete the transaction, where he would then receive a couple more thousand dollars on top of what he had originally paid for the children.

Only thing was, the man he was meeting was an undercover federal agent. The operation had been under surveillance for eight months. When the middleman came to D.C. to make the trade, he was busted, his "goods" taken away to a local halfway house. (Truthfully, the government didn't care what happened to the children. Once they were put into a government-funded orphanage, any thought of the children left the agents' heads. Their main goal now was to concentrate on the trafficking that was going on between New York City and D.C.)

Carver's time in the orphanage was not a bad one. The staff took good care of him. One nurse, who had graduated from Tuskegee University, had become quite taken with the baby. A name had to be placed on the birth certificate, so the nurse named him Carver, after George Washington Carver.

He spent his first two years at the halfway house before being put in the care of a young couple living in Maryland.

He only stayed with them for six months. Out of nowhere the man was laid off from his job; his wife slipped getting out of the bathtub and broke the lower section of her spinal cord. As much as they loved Carver, wanted to keep him, they had no choice but to give him back to the orphanage.

Carver spent another three years there. Learning to read, learning to write. One monthly report mentioned how Carver was "very attentive" and "showed great promise."

He was nine when he was put in the care of a family who lived just outside of Lynchburg, Virginia. The man was a music teacher at a local high school. He was slim and handsome with neatly trimmed hair and a thin mustache. His wife was a pediatric nurse at the local hospital, working mostly nights. She was a few years younger than her husband, with soft hands and breath that always smelled of spearmint.

Together the couple had taken twelve children into their care over a fifteen-year stretch. They already had two other boys living with them by the time Carver arrived.

A year later, the family took in two more children, fraternal twins. Their names were Stacey and Kelley. They were twelve years old.

Less than three months passed before the father began molesting them.

This was not something new, however, and it was not something Carver—then ten years old—was aware of right away. At the time he didn't find it strange at all that the father, on the nights the mother was working, visited the girls' bedroom. That he would shut the door and lock it. Once Carver asked Stacey and Kelley what the father did with them, and they both claimed they played board games.

Carver thought nothing more of it.

Then he saw the bruises.

It happened by accident. He walked into the bathroom one day and saw Stacey naked. She was just coming out of the bath, reaching for her towel—and the moment Carver opened the door and saw her she stopped and stayed that way, frozen, the water dripping to the tiled floor.

Carver, ten years old, never seeing a girl naked before, did not notice the fact that this twelve-year-old girl had a vagina. What he noticed was the discolorations on the inside of her thighs.

"What's that?" he asked, meaning the bruises, and when she just continued standing there, not saying anything, he said, "Are you hurt?"

"Leave," she told him. "Get out."

Carver left. He waited until she came out wearing her clothes. He asked her again about the bruises but she shook her head.

"Please," she said. "Just forget it."

She ran away and slammed her bedroom door shut.

Later that night, the mother away at work, the father again went into the girls' bedroom. Carver heard the door open and close from where he lay in his bed. He stared at the ceiling, tried listening for any sound. When he heard none, he threw off his covers and started to get out of bed.

"Don't," one of the boys whispered.

"Why?"

"Bad idea," whispered the other boy.

They both remained in their beds, their covers on top of them, their eyes closed.

Carver left the room. He tiptoed down the hallway. It was an old house and sometimes the floor creaked. It took him much longer to reach the other end of the hall than normal.

He came to the closed bedroom door. He placed his ear close to the door, listened carefully.

From inside came noises. What sounded like crying.

Carver listened for another minute. He didn't know what to think. Finally he returned to his room, climbed back in bed.

"What are they doing in there?" he asked the quiet room, but both boys acted as if they were asleep.

The next day, during recess, Carver approached the girls.

"Why were you crying last night?"

"We weren't," Stacey said. "We were sleeping."

"But he was in your room," Carver said.

Kelley said, "We were sleeping."

"But—"

"Carver," Stacey said, her voice urgent, "we were sleeping."

It was left at that.

For the next several nights, Carver couldn't sleep. He lay in bed, listening to the house settle, until he heard the father open and close the girls' bedroom door. Then he would get out of bed, tiptoe down the hall, and listen to what was happening inside. Along with the crying was a faint grunting noise that didn't make any sense to him.

One of these nights, tiptoeing back to his room, he stepped on a loose board. It creaked. The noise coming from behind the girls' door stopped.

Carver hurried to his room, quietly shut the door. He scrambled into bed just as the girls' bedroom door opened and closed. Heavy footsteps pounded the floor.

The bedroom door opened. The shadow of the father was outlined in the doorway. The father stepped in but didn't say a word.

Carver acted like he was asleep. His eyes were closed, and he opened them just a bit. As his eyes adjusted, he saw that the father was bare-chested, wearing only a pair of pajama bottoms.

The father stood that way for another minute, watching the three boys in their beds, before closing the door.

The next day at recess, when Carver confronted the girls, Stacey said, "Carver, please, just forget it. Nothing happens in there."

"Does he do something to you?"

Kelley said, "He doesn't do anything to us. Please, stop bugging us."

Carver went to one of his stepbrothers next. The oldest stepbrother, thirteen years old, said, "He plays with them in there."

"What do you mean? Like a game?"

"Something like that."

"Why doesn't he play with us?"

"Trust me. You don't want him to play with us."

But Carver remained curious. And it wasn't until three nights later that he waited until he'd heard the girls' bedroom door open and close that he got out of his bed and tiptoed back down the hallway.

The same noises were coming from behind the door. The

crying, the grunting, and even a soft whispering, what sounded like the father.

Carver listened. He just stood there and listened. And then fate played a cruel trick on him.

Carver sneezed.

He never had a chance to make it back to his bed. Before he could even turn away, start to take a step, the noises from behind the door stopped. The door opened. The father stood there naked. He grabbed Carver and pulled him back into the girls' bedroom, slammed the door shut, pushed Carver up against the wall.

The father growled, "What do you think you're doing out there?"

Carver did not answer. He couldn't. Not while the father kept one of his hands around Carver's throat, squeezing tightly.

Something changed in the father's face. He loosened his grip around Carver's throat. He smiled and patted Carver on the shoulder and said, "Sorry about that, sport. Didn't mean to hurt you. You just startled me is all."

Beyond him, on the bed, Stacey and Kelley were naked, holding each other, sobbing quietly.

Carver asked, "What are you doing to them?"

The father's smiled widened. "Nothing at all. We're just playing a game."

"What kind of game?"

"It's a secret game. You know how to keep a secret, don't you?"

Carver nodded.

"Good. Because it's important our secret game stays a secret. We wouldn't want that secret getting out now, would we? If that happened, there would be consequences. You know what a consequence is, don't you?"

The smile had left the father's face. His eyes had become cold.

Carver may have been ten years old, but he understood the implication. He nodded again and murmured, "Yes, sir."

"Good." The father patted Carver on the head. "Now why don't you be a good boy and run back to bed."

Carver left. He returned to the bedroom. After he got back into bed, one of the boys whispered, "Told you so."

The next day was Saturday. It was raining. They were all stuck inside. Because the father had to help out with some school music program, the mother stayed home to watch them. She stayed in the kitchen, making dessert for a party at the hospital.

Carver went into the girls' bedroom. He shut the door. He said, "Why were you naked last night?"

Both girls said nothing.

"Why was *he* naked?"

Stacey started crying. "Didn't you hear him?" she asked. "It's just a game. A *secret* game. We can't tell you about it."

"Does he hurt you?"

The girls had nothing to say to this. Carver left. He went downstairs to the kitchen. The mother was there, making her dessert. He stood there and waited for her to notice him. She didn't. Finally he said her name, and when she turned, he asked his question.

"Why does the father go to the girls' room in the middle of the night?"

The mother was in the middle of icing a cake. At this question, she stopped in the middle of writing out the word *Congratulations*. She had just finished the *a* and all it said was *Congra*.

"What are you talking about?" she said.

Carver told her about the secret game.

The mother's face paled. She went very quiet. Eventually she said, "He does no such thing," and turned away from Carver and continued the rest of the word.

Two nights later, the mother having gone to work, the father didn't go into the girls' room. Instead he came into the boys' room. He stormed in and pulled Carver from bed, dragged him out of the room and down the hall, down the steps, through the living room and kitchen, down into the basement.

"I thought we had an understanding," he said. "I thought you knew how to keep a secret."

Carver said nothing.

The father pointed at a large steamer trunk in the corner. "Open it."

Carver shook his head.

The father smiled, his voice going soft and kind. "Open it, please."

Carver, knowing he shouldn't, went to the steamer trunk and opened the lid. It was empty.

"Now," the father said, "get inside."

Carver shook his head again.

The smile slipped off the father's face. His eyes went cold, just like that night back in the girls' bedroom.

"I told you there would be consequences, didn't I?"

It was the very last thing Carver wanted to do. But he saw the look in the father's eyes and knew he had no choice. He could try to run, but the father would catch him. And if that happened, he knew the punishment would be even worse.

Carver got in the trunk.

"Good boy," the father said. "This is for your own good, you know. You have to be taught a lesson. A secret is a secret, no matter what. Do you understand?"

"Yes, sir."

"Good. Now be quiet, don't make a fuss, and I'll come get you in the morning. And this will be our little secret."

The father closed the lid and locked it, trapping Carver in darkness.

Carver learned something important that night: he was claustrophobic. Within a minute he was kicking the inside of the trunk. Shouting. Pushing up on the lid that wouldn't budge. He did this repeatedly until he tired himself out and fell asleep.

In the morning, the father came to get him before the mother returned home from work.

"Hey, sport," the father said, smiling. "So did we learn our lesson?"

Carver said nothing.

The smile faded. "I *said*, did we learn our lesson?"

"Yes, sir."

The father didn't seem convinced. And the next night he brought Carver back down into the basement.

"I don't think we've quite learned our lesson yet," he said, opening the lid to the steamer trunk. "Why don't you hop in there and think about it overnight."

Carver shook his head adamantly. His entire body had begun to tremble at the idea of spending another night in that complete darkness.

"Oh, sport," the father said. "I don't think you get it yet. In this house, you never say no to me."

Carver turned, meaning to bolt for the stairs. The father grabbed his arm and yanked him back. Carver screamed, "No, no, please, no!" while the father dragged him to the trunk. Carver tried kicking, he tried punching, but none of it seemed to help. So he turned his head and clamped his teeth on the father's hand. The father cried out, letting go, and backhanded Carver to the floor. Carver, dazed, was not strong enough to put up more of a fight as the father picked him up and placed him in the trunk and closed the lid.

All the next week Carver did not go to school. He had a black eye from where the father backhanded him. He was confined to his bed. The official reason was that he was sick with pneumonia. The mother had even gotten a note from one of the doctors at the hospital to give to the school.

The mother came to see Carver the first morning.

"Why are you doing this to yourself?"

Carver, his eye swollen, said nothing.

"Your father is a good man," the mother said. She carried a tissue and dabbed at her eyes. "He's trying to teach you to obey so you can become a good man just like him someday."

Later that afternoon, while the mother went to the grocery store, Carver was left alone. He got out of bed. He walked around the house. He first looked through the kitchen, at all the different knives. He went to check the basement but then thought about the steamer trunk and refused to go downstairs. He went into the father's study, looked through the desk drawers.

He found what he was looking for in a shoebox in the father's bedroom closet.

A gun and a box of ammunition.

It took Carver a while to figure out how to open the cylinder. It took him even longer to figure out how to load the gun properly. Once all six cylinders were full, he closed the gun and took it downstairs.

That night the mother went to work. The father, after midnight, went to visit the girls.

Carver lay in bed, staring at the ceiling, while the two other boys pretended to sleep. After a while, Carver threw off his covers and started to get out of bed.

"What are you doing?" asked one of the boys.

"Yeah," said the other. "Haven't you learned your lesson by now?"

Carver ignored them. He knew they would be no help. He went into the hallway. Instead of going right, toward the girls' bedroom, where the crying and grunting was coming from, he went left. Opened the father's and mother's bedroom door and slipped inside. He went to the nightstand, picked up the telephone, and dialed 911.

When the person on the other end answered, Carver whispered, "I need help."

"What's wrong?"

Carver gave the address. "Please come fast. He's trying to kill me."

Carver hung up.

He went back out into the hallway. Started the long walk toward the girls' bedroom. Came to the door and stood there for a moment, not doing anything.

Then he knocked.

The grunting coming from behind the door stopped. The crying continued. There were heavy footsteps, and then the sound of the door being unlocked.

The door opened to reveal the father standing there, naked again.

He glared down at Carver. "You want to go back in that trunk?"

Carver spat at him. He turned and ran away.

The father gave chase. He chased Carver down the hallway, down the stairs. Into the living room, into the kitchen, into the dining room, back into the living room.

"Come here," the father shouted. Naked, he extended his step and grabbed hold of Carver, threw him to the floor. "You just don't learn, do you?"

Carver scrambled to his feet. He ran straight for the couch. The father's long legs helped him reach Carver almost immediately. He grabbed him again, but this time it wasn't fast enough. By then Carver had reached down between the cushions and grasped the revolver he had hidden there that afternoon and pulled it back out.

"Stop!" Carver shouted, aiming the gun at the father.

The father was less than ten feet away. "Come on, sport, you don't want to do that. Guns are dangerous."

"*You're* dangerous," Carver said.

"Now, now, sport. You don't know what you're talking about."

The father, smiling sweetly, took a step toward Carver.

The gun shook in Carver's hands. He said, "You're a bad man."

The smile faded. The father's eyes went cold. He growled, "And you're a nosy little nigger."

It was the very first time Carver had ever been called that name.

The father took another step toward Carver.

Carver pulled the trigger.

Obviously, Carver had never fired a gun before. While he'd aimed it at the father's chest, nervousness caused his hands to shake and the shot went wide, shattering one of the living room windows.

The father laughed. "And you're stupid, too."

No, he wasn't stupid. If he was stupid, he would have shot the father back upstairs, when the father had opened the bedroom door. But Carver didn't want to take the chance of shooting one of the girls in the process. He wanted to make sure they were safe. He even wanted to make sure his two step-brothers were safe. He wanted to make sure everyone was safe.

So Carver readjusted, aimed again, and fired once more.

The bullet struck the father in the chest.

The father stumbled backward. He tripped over his own feet, went sprawling to the floor.

Carver kept the gun aimed until he knew the father was dead. He watched the blood soak into the carpet. Then he set the gun down on the floor and sat on the couch and waited for the police.

THIRTY-FOUR

Not only did the Kid drive a Dodge Neon, but he lived in a small house located back on a county road a half mile off the main highway. It was a one-story ranch style, a single car garage attached to the side. It was painted blue with red trim along its shutters and window frames. Many of its roof shingles were worn and faded. The front lawn featured a stone birdbath, circled by a miniature white picket fence. The grass looked an inch too long.

As the Kid pulled into the driveway and pressed the button to open the garage door, I said, "Huh."

He stopped the car right in front of the garage, waiting for the slow creak of the door as it lifted. "Go ahead," he said. "Say it."

"What do you mean?"

He gave me a blank look.

"I just"—I glanced at the house, at the lawn, back at the Kid—"I was expecting something different."

"Yeah, Ben," the Kid said. The garage door had lifted the entire way and he drove the Neon forward. "Fuck you too."

When we got out of the car, the garage door already

creaking shut, the Kid made me carry the box that contained Carver's hard drive.

"We're going to head straight down to the basement," he said.

"What, I don't get the bachelor pad tour?"

The Kid ignored me and walked inside. We passed the laundry room, started toward what appeared to be the kitchen, but the Kid stopped and opened a door. Flicked on the light switch just inside and motioned for me to head down.

The steps were carpeted a yellowish-orange. The walls had a fake wood paneling motif. I had been expecting a lot of computers and wasn't disappointed. There were eight of them, all spread out around the carpeted basement.

The Kid went immediately to one of the tables and turned on the monitor. He waved at me to bring over Carver's hard drive.

"Huh," I said again.

The Kid sat down on a large leather office chair and started typing. "What now?"

"Nothing," I said. "It's just … it's not like I'd pictured."

"Yeah? And how did you picture it?"

"I don't know." I pointed at a microwave in the corner. "Is that where you make all of your infamous popcorn?"

"Actually, I've been trying to keep away from popcorn this past year. I only use that to make tea."

"*Tea?*"

"Herbal tea's good for you, in case you weren't aware."

"But … where are all the movie posters? I thought Carver said your basement was covered in Terry Gilliam film posters."

"Yeah," the Kid said. "*Was.*"

He continued typing for another couple of moments. Paused and swiveled around in his chair, grabbed the box from my hands and set it on the ground.

"What are you talking about—*was?*"

The Kid took the hard drive out of the box, set it on the table. He produced some wires out of nowhere and started connecting the hard drive to his computer.

"Like I said, *was*. Thanks to you, I had to move."

"What?"

"Two years ago, after you wrote that thing and I posted it? I realized too late you kind of identified me. Not entirely, but enough that if the wrong people wanted to look in the right places, they could figure it out. It was too late to go in and change the records and still stay where I was, so I changed the records and got the hell out of there."

Another leather office chair, not as large as the one the Kid currently used, was by another table. I pulled it over and sat down.

"What are you saying?"

The Kid was still busy connecting the hard drive and computer. He paused momentarily, glanced at me, shook his head.

"Nothing. But it's just—all of you guys think I'm made of money."

"You're not?"

This time he glared at me. "It's not even worth saying 'fuck you' to you anymore, is it?"

He turned back to the computers, talking as he worked.

"But here's the thing—I make good money doing my white hat stuff. Pull in a nice yearly salary, even though it's spec work. But keeping myself covered, and making sure all of you out there at Graham's stay covered too? That nearly puts me in the red."

"You never mentioned this before."

"And what good would it have done had I said anything? I'm not bitching about it, you know, but it just seems you all take it for granted. Like when we pulled that switch on them two years ago, the jet that flew you and Carver to California?

When all was said and done, that whole operation, just with getting the jet alone to fly where we wanted and in the time frame we needed, that cost about forty grand."

I leaned forward in the chair, tried to make sense of what wires he was putting where.

"Well, you're a hacker," I said. "Why can't you just, I don't know, hack into some company's money and siphon out some funds? You know, like they did in *Office Space*. A hundredth of a penny or something like that."

The Kid shot me another glare. "I'm not a thief, Ben."

"I never said you were."

"I've never stolen anything a day in my life."

"Kid, I was just joking. Don't—"

"All the money I ever had I've earned legitimately. Got it?"

I nodded slowly. "Yeah, Kid. I got it."

The Kid continued glaring at me another moment or so, then got back to work.

"And if I need money real bad, you know who I ask? My boy Titus. I can always trust on him to help me out."

"Speaking of Titus," I said, "how much do you know about him?"

The cables now connected, the Kid turned on Carver's hard drive and waited for it to warm up. "What do you mean?"

"Like do you …"

"Know he's a dwarf?" He tilted his head, cocked an eye at me, before he started typing. "Yeah, I know everything there is to know about him. I'm not stupid, Ben. I might have no friends except for you guys, but I'm not starved for attention. I know where Titus lives—which is not in Immokalee, like he says. I know about his trailer, about his pet raccoon, about how his parents fucked him over when he was a kid. Yeah, Ben, I know all of that. Most importantly, I know he's a good guy. He's got heart. I check into people before I trust them one hundred and ten percent."

"Really," I said. "Does that include all your friends in *World of Warcraft*?"

Besides our voices, the only sound filling the basement was the typing of the keyboard. Now that stopped.

The Kid glanced at me, his mouth slightly opened.

I smiled. "Don't worry. Your secret is safe with me."

"*Any*way," the Kid said, "Titus is really good at what he does. Like, *really* good. He's probably a better hacker than me, to be honest."

"Coming from an egomaniac like you, that's impressive."

"I never wanted to tell him about the games and Simon and all that shit. But he found it first, even brought it to my attention. I tried to play it off like I had no idea what he was talking about, but I got scared for him, you know?"

I nodded. "He told me that."

"Did he tell you about his map?"

"What map?"

The Kid paused, moved and clicked his mouse. A new window filled the screen. It showed the continental United States. Different colored lines crisscrossed the map.

"What are all those?"

"Every game I had saved—and believe me, I have a shitload —I sent to him. For each game he determined the location of where each player wakes up in the country, the route they take, where they eventually end up. He mapped it all out, each and every game."

"How many games?"

"Nearly one hundred. See these dots here and here?" The Kid made circles with the cursor. "The bigger ones are the starting and ending points of each game. The smaller dots are the stops each player makes along the way. You know, the shit Simon makes people do. Here's your route."

He clicked on a line that began near the top of California and traveled halfway down the state, then started west, all the way into Indiana, where I had turned around and headed back to Chicago.

"Obviously your game was one of the anomalies, but it should still give you an idea."

I stared at the map. All the different dots and lines. They nearly covered the entire thing. Some states had more dots and lines than other states. A few states only had lines, no dots.

"The Midwest doesn't seem to be too popular," I said. "Look at Kansas and Missouri. Just a few lines, no dots."

"Shit, dude, is that surprising? There ain't *nothing* to do in Kansas and Missouri." He closed out the window and brought back up the window he was working on. He typed some more, then pushed away from the table, started cracking his knuckles and fingers. "There."

On the screen now was a box with rapidly moving words and numbers. The words and numbers were coming so fast it was impossible to make any sense of them.

"What is it exactly?"

"The key inside Carver's email program."

"How long will it take?"

"Shouldn't be too long. Maybe five minutes, maybe ten."

"And then?"

"And then you're one step closer to getting the fuck out of my house."

I smiled, started to say something else, but a noise upstairs stopped me. It was the noise of a door opening and closing, of footsteps tramping over the floor above our heads.

I looked at the Kid.

The Kid looked at me. His face had paled a little, his eyes had widened.

"Who's this?" I said. "Your girlfriend?"

"No, Ben, don't—" the Kid began, but I was already up and out of my chair, striding across the yellowish-orange carpet to the stairs. Hurrying up the steps, opening the door, then taking a left into the kitchen.

And stopping at once.

There were two people there. A young Hispanic woman and an old white woman. The old woman was being supported by a metal walker and the Hispanic girl who held onto her arm.

The Hispanic woman was startled by my presence. When she first glanced up there was a familiarity in her face, like she knew just who I was, but then when she realized I wasn't who she had expected, that familiarity turned to shock.

"Hi," I said.

At the sound of my voice the old woman looked up. She had a very wrinkled face. Her white puffy hair was thin and balding. She squinted at me with eyes that couldn't quite see me.

She asked in a frail voice, "Have you seen my son?"

Speechless, I took a step back and looked down the basement stairs. The Kid was standing at the bottom. His hands were on his waist, and as he stared back up at me, he released a long and heavy sigh, deflating like a balloon.

THIRTY-FIVE

The Kid's mother sat in a high-backed easy chair in the living room. It was positioned to face out the big picture window overlooking the front yard. Her metal walker was beside the chair. She seemed oblivious to our presence—the Kid's, her personal nurse's, my own—and just continued staring out the window.

I whispered, "What is she looking at?"

The Kid and I were in the kitchen, which wasn't really a separate room so much as an extension of the living room. The Hispanic woman—her name was Carmen—was busy fixing lunch for the Kid's mother.

"Not what or at," the Kid said. "It's who and for."

"Okay. So who is she looking for?"

"My brother."

"I didn't know you had a brother."

"I don't."

Carmen had just finished making a sandwich. She placed it on a plastic plate and took it to the Kid's mother. Even when she walked up the old woman didn't notice. Carmen had to lean down, whisper something into her ear, and wait a few seconds before the words registered. Then the Kid's mother smiled up at her, nodded once, and Carmen placed the plate on her lap. The Kid's mother stared down at it for a moment, touched it briefly, and returned her attention to the picture window.

"Alzheimer's," the Kid said. "She's had it a couple years now. Just recently it's gotten worse. For some reason she thinks it's 1989."

"What happened in 1989?"

"My brother died."

I looked at him, this twenty-six-year-old computer genius who wore expensive jeans, designer shirts, always had gel in his hair. His face had grown more somber in the past couple minutes, his eyes dimmer.

"Are you going to tell me?"

He didn't look like he was going to respond. He just stood there, watching his mother. Finally he took a deep breath and said, "I was six. My brother was nine. Our dad had just returned from one of his business trips, this one from Australia. He brought us a boomerang. You'd think he'd buy us two boomerangs, but he was a cheap bastard and only brought back one."

Carmen had pulled up a wooden rocking chair beside the Kid's mother. She sat there waiting for the Kid's mother to take a bite of her sandwich. When that didn't happen, she took the sandwich and gently lifted it toward the old woman's mouth.

"So of course we both wanted to play with it. There was this field about a mile from our house, out near the woods. We went there to test it out. We didn't really know what to expect. Our dad said something about how it was supposed to come back to us, so that's what we were hoping. But I guess we didn't throw it right or … I don't know. The thing ended up in a tree.

Real high up there. Neither of us was supposed to climb the trees because the branches were too high, but that didn't stop my brother."

The old woman kept her gaze out the picture window as she let Carmen feed her. Taking little bites of the sandwich, she would chew thoughtfully for a long time before swallowing. Carmen would lift the sandwich toward her mouth again and sometimes the Kid's mother would turn her head away like an obstinate child, other times she would open her cracked and gray lips and take another bite.

"So he climbed the tree. He went the whole way up. The boomerang was caught in the branches farthest out. He had to shake this one branch for about five minutes before the thing finally got loose. Then when he started to climb back down, his foot slipped and he just … fell."

There was a pink plastic cup on the floor beside the old woman's chair. It had a lid and a straw. After about two bites of the sandwich, Carmen picked up the cup and offered it to the Kid's mother, placing the straw between her lips.

"The drop, it was only about ten, twelve feet high. Shouldn't have hurt him much at all. But as he started falling he tried to catch himself on one of the other branches. He managed to grab one of them but it threw off his center of gravity. He sort of flipped in the air and instead of landing on his feet or back like he would have, he landed on his head. I was standing right there when it happened. I heard his … I heard his neck snap."

The Kid's mother chewed and sipped silently from her chair. Carmen went about her task without any complaint or show of impatience.

"His eyes were still open and for some reason I thought he was still alive. But he wouldn't answer me when I said his name. So I ran home. I ran straight home and found my dad and told him what happened. My dad took me back out to the field. He found my brother and he just … he started crying. It was the first and last time I ever saw him cry. He picked up my brother and carried him the entire way home. He put my brother in the car and drove away to the hospital. He had never even said a word to my mother. She had been home the entire time, gardening or whatever. And then it was just me there, watching my dad drive away with my brother, and I didn't want to go back inside. I didn't want to tell her what had happened."

The sandwich gone, Carmen offered the pink cup one last time. When the Kid's mother refused it, Carmen took a napkin and wiped the corners of the old woman's mouth.

"Anyway, I knew I couldn't stay outside forever, so I went in. My mom was there, but I didn't tell her anything. I just went to my room and shut the door and cried. And my mom, she knew I was home, that my dad had gone off somewhere, but she didn't know where my brother was. So she sat by the window for him. She just sat there. And even when my dad came home, told her what happened, she refused to believe him. I think … I think that's when the screw in her head really started to come loose."

Carmen gathered the plate and the cup and brought them to the kitchen. She went about cleaning up without a word.

The Kid glanced back at her, then at his mother, and whispered to me, "Sometimes she has good days, sometimes bad. Today's another bad day."

I said nothing.

"Go ahead, Ben. Ask your question."

"What question?"

"You want to ask, why don't I put her in a home?"

Carmen washed her hands at the sink. Dried her hands on a towel and walked back into the living room, sat down beside the old woman.

"It's none of my business."

"First," the Kid whispered, as if he didn't hear me or just didn't care, "because she's my mom. And second ... because of Hickory View."

I thought about that brick building, about the Halloween decorations, the Norman Rockwell calendar and the bowl of Hershey's Kisses. I thought about Phillip Fagerstrom and his dark eyes as he stared back at me, his angel of death.

"You don't really expect the same thing would happen, do you?"

"I'm not talking about the building blowing up. But every time I think about putting her in one of those places, I remember what it looked like. I remember how you wrote about it. And that old man, the one that was just coughing and coughing and nobody did anything about it, nobody came to help? I just ... I couldn't do that to her. It wouldn't be right."

We stood in silence for a couple long seconds. Then the Kid muttered, "Fuck it," and turned away, went and opened one of the cabinets. He brought out a box of Orville Redenbacher. He opened one of the bags, tossed it into the microwave, closed the door, and hit the popcorn button.

As the microwave hummed to life, he said, "Believe it or not, I've been trying to stay away from this shit. I don't have the metabolism for it I once had, and I don't have time to go to the gym."

"Then why are you making it now?"

"I'm fucking nervous."

A minute and a half later, the microwave pinged. He opened the door and carefully brought out the steaming bag. The smell of artificial butter was intoxicating. He dumped the popcorn into a large plastic bowl, held it out to me.

"Want some?"

I shook my head.

"More for me then."

He opened the basement door and disappeared down the

steps. I started to follow but stopped, turned to check on the old woman one last time. Carmen sat beside her, a book now opened in her lap, just reading while the Kid's mother continued staring out the window and waiting for a son who would never return.

THIRTY-SIX

I sat down next to the Kid and said, "So what do we have?"

"Not sure yet."

"What's your first impression?"

"That we may have just opened a big fucking can of worms."

The Kid clicked the mouse, typed some commands, and a window popped up on the screen.

"What are these?" I asked.

"Folders. Eleven of them."

"Anything else?"

"Nope. Just these."

"And?"

"Notice how they're labeled?"

I did. Below each folder was a single word, or hyphened word, all starting with the letter B.

Bellman, Boots, Bonnet-Maker, Barrister, Broker, Billiard-Marker, Banker, Butcher, Baker, Beaver. And, lastly, Boojum.

"Recognize where they come from?"

I nodded. "*The Hunting of the Snark*."

Like the Kid, I had already read over the nonsensical poem

a dozen times. It was about a crew of ten lead by the Bellman, whose map of the ocean was a blank sheet of paper, on their hunting expedition of a snark. All of the labels were the ten members of the crew, except for Boojum.

The Kid was already opening the folders, skimming through the emails. He had started with the first one: Bellman.

"Why not start with Boojum?"

"Because if this is the can of worms I think it is, then knowing who Boojum is is the very last thing I want to do."

I wasn't quite sure what he meant, but it didn't matter anyway. Within minutes he had skimmed through all the emails. Apparently there weren't many.

"Looks like Carver was reaching out," the Kid said, and stuffed a handful of popcorn into his mouth.

"For what?"

"Here's how he started out every email."

The Kid made another circle with the cursor, and I leaned forward and read the simple line:

I'm currently on the hunt for a snark named Caesar.

That was it. Carver didn't even sign his name, though the email came through with the sender simply identified as Man of Honor. And if the intended parties knew anything of Caesar and Simon and the games, it was safe to assume they already knew everything there was to know about Carver Ellison.

"Who are they?"

The Kid kept skimming, opening one folder and then closing another. "People high up in the government. FBI, CIA, NSA, Homeland Security. There's even one from the Secret Service, and another from the Pentagon."

"Were there any replies?"

"A few. Luis Thackray of the CIA—labeled under Boots—responded with a standard spam warning form, detailing what would happen if Carver didn't take him off his list immediately. The same with Demetrius McGowan of the

NSA—labeled under Beaver—though his was a little more crude."

The Kid clicked the mouse and again made circles with the cursor. There was McGowan's message, simple and to the point:

Fuck off, asshole.

"Well that isn't very professional," I said.

"Few in the NSA are."

"None of the others responded?"

The Kid opened another window. "Bernard Jardine of Homeland Security did. He's listed as Barrister."

"What did he say?"

The Kid shoveled another handful of popcorn into his mouth and pointed at the line with the cursor.

Who all is in your hunting party?

"What was Carver's response?"

"There wasn't one. At least not here."

"Do you think he contacted Jardine another way?"

"I have no idea, Ben. I know just as much as you do."

"That's bullshit."

"Excuse me?"

"Why haven't you opened the last folder yet?"

The Kid went quiet, looking away from me. Above us, a soft patter of footsteps sounded, no doubt Carmen heading into the kitchen, maybe to refill that plastic cup the Kid's mother didn't seem very interested in. I wondered just how many hours passed through a day where the Kid hid himself down here while his mother sat in her high-backed easy chair, waiting and watching for a son long dead. Surely Carmen wasn't here day and night. Was there a night nurse, and if there was, did either nurse know what the Kid truly did with his time?

"Kid?"

He sighed. "I have a bad feeling about it."

"Pardon me for saying so, but right now I don't give a shit

about your feelings. Carver obviously wanted us to find this and do something about it, so let's do it."

The Kid's hand hovered over his mouse, motionless. He said, "Aren't you going to talk about it?"

For some reason I thought he meant his mother.

"What do you want me to say?"

The Kid glanced at me from the corner of his eye. "You read it, didn't you? I saw you on the plane. You went through every document and news article. You pieced it together just like I did."

"So?"

"What do you think?"

"I think there's more to the story than you're letting on."

The Kid's hand finally settled on the mouse. He moved the cursor around the screen in a wide circle.

I said, "What aren't you telling me?"

"Nothing."

"Don't make me kick your ass in your own house."

He stopped moving the cursor around, leaned back in his chair. "Did anyone ever tell you you would make the perfect dinner guest?"

"Kid."

He took a deep breath, crossed his arms. "Once Carver graduated high school he went to West Point. After he graduated he went straight into the FBI. Started working in the Crimes Against Children program but was reassigned two years later."

"Why was he reassigned?"

"Carver never told me, but from what I can tell he got too involved in the investigations. Wouldn't let certain cases go. The FBI doesn't like to live in the past, and it certainly doesn't want to waste time on cases they don't think they're going to break. So they move on. Carver wouldn't."

"So they put him on the terrorist stuff."

"No, they put him in cyber investigations. Online scams, child pornography, all that clean and fun stuff. Put him in a room with a computer, got him away from doing what he really cared about. Then they moved him to the terrorist stuff. And after a year or two ... well, he forever became known to the Inner Circle as the Man of Honor."

"That's it?"

"Not completely. You remember Carver talking about his supervisor, the one he thought turned him in to Simon?"

"What about him?"

"Did Carver ever tell you his name?"

"No," I said. "But what—" I stopped, sat up straighter in my seat. "You don't think ..."

"His supervisor's name was Edward Stark. I completely forgot about it until I saw the other people on this list."

"Stark as in snark?"

"Only one way to find out."

The Kid clicked the mouse and the folder labeled Boojum opened. And there, inside the file, were several email correspondences from the Man of Honor to FBI Assistant Director Edward Stark.

"I told you I had a bad feeling about this," the Kid said. "Say hello to our boojum."

THIRTY-SEVEN

According to the time stamp on the first email Carver had sent
—to Dominic Kilford of the FBI, aka Bellman—nearly an
entire year had passed. This was a year after Carver and his
people saved me from my game, when he first became aware
that there was an almighty Caesar pulling strings. We had been
able to learn nothing about this Caesar—we hadn't been able to
learn much at all about anything—so Carver had decided to
make his own furtive inquires. Had he known these people in
his past life? Possibly. But even if he had known them, there
was no guarantee they weren't in Caesar's pocket.

A year ago he contacted Dominic Kilford. When there was
no response, he went to the next person. How many people he
had planned to contact in all was impossible to say, but clearly,
based on the way he had labeled the folders, he had intended
on ten. Then, when those ten fell through, he contacted an
eleventh person, his old supervisor at the FBI. The first form of
contact had been only five months ago, with Carver's opening
salvo:

I'm currently on the hunt for a snark named Caesar.

That had been sent, according to the time stamp, at 10:17

PM. I wondered where I had been at the exact moment Carver typed out those ten words and hit the send button. Certainly I had been at the house, probably downstairs in the living room with Maya and Jesse. Maybe we had been watching a movie to unwind. Carver usually went to bed early and shut his door and didn't reappear until early in the morning. In the back of my mind I had probably wondered what he was up to, but knew that if he wanted any of us to know, he would have said so.

Edward Stark's reply came at 9:48 the next morning:

You aren't the only one. I'm sorry about what happened.

Nearly an entire week passed before there was another email. I could almost picture Carver hesitantly typing the few words, maybe deleting and retyping them several times. After trying ten others, here he finally had a lead. But just how solid was it? As far as Carver knew, the man on the other end of this email had been the one who turned him in to Simon. In the end, Carver asked the most important question as simply as he could:

Who is he?

Later that day, Edward Stark replied:

No clue.

For several weeks, there was no interaction—at least, none that hadn't been deleted. Whether Carver had contacted Stark another way, it was impossible to know, but nearly a month passed before Carver wrote:

How high does this go?

For two days there was no reply. Then:

To the top. We should meet.

Again, several weeks passed without any correspondence. This had been during the spring, and I tried remembering what Carver's mood had been like. In the past year he had become withdrawn, but it had been gradual, so much so that those close to him, who talked to him every day, might not have noticed it. I certainly hadn't.

Carver finally responded:

Who turned me in?

Stark replied only a few hours later:

No clue. We should meet.

It was probably this second suggestion that they should meet which caused there to be another gap in their communication, this time nearly two months. There was a very strong chance that Edward Stark had been in league with Simon and Caesar from the beginning. Carver had probably contacted him on a lark, not expecting anything. Now a shadow of doubt had formed. If Stark was in fact clean, meeting might not be a terrible idea. But if Stark was in fact dirty, then Carver would be walking into a trap.

"He never said anything to you about any of this?" I asked.

The Kid shook his head, staring at the computer screen. "Not one word."

The next email, dated only a month and a half ago, was from Carver:

How do I know I can trust you?

Stark replied the next day:

You don't. But you can.

Four hours later, Carver wrote:

How much do you even know?

The next morning, Stark replied:

More than most people, but not nearly enough.

Four weeks passed. Carver wrote:

I would rather talk first. Where can I reach out?

Two days later, Stark replied with a phone number and said:

It's a burner. Call any time.

The Kid said, "Son of a bitch."

"What?"

"Two weeks ago Carver called me. Said he wanted to fly out here for something."

"He didn't say what?"

"No. But now I think it was to call this guy."

There was one email left, dated just last week. Thursday, Carver wrote:

New game has started. Will call once it's over.

"Fuck," the Kid said.

I shook my head slowly, my eyes fixed on those two sentences. "Why would he let him know that? He fucking led us into a trap."

"Maybe he was testing the guy."

"Yeah? Well it got him killed."

The Kid closed out the folder. He went to reach for more popcorn, hesitated, and then sat back in his chair, crossed his arms. We were silent for a long time. Above us, the sound of a television had come on in the living room, what sounded like *Wheel of Fortune*.

I said, "We need to kill this motherfucker."

"If only it were that simple."

"I would give anything to hear this guy's voice. Just to talk to him for a minute."

The Kid looked at me, a thoughtful expression on his face.

"What?"

He smiled. "I have an idea."

THIRTY-EIGHT

One thing about the Kid, he always had a trick up his sleeve.

This time he had three.

The first was not only did he have a secure phone line, but it was so secure that if anyone tried tracing it, the signal would bounce all over the globe before eventually landing up somewhere in New York City's Penn Station.

The second was a program that could analyze the other speaker's voice. Any traces of uncertainty, doubt, even bullshit, the program would detect immediately and would represent via different colored lines bouncing across the screen. The program was, the Kid admitted, 90% accurate.

"Seriously?"

He shrugged. "Okay, maybe eighty percent."

I just looked at him.

"Fine," he said. "Seventy-five percent."

I kept looking at him.

He sighed. "Okay, maybe sixty percent. Fifty at the very least."

"Why don't we just use a Magic Eight Ball while we're at it?"

"Listen, dude, it works. Granted, it would be best if we could monitor the guy's vitals, too, but this is what we have to work with right now."

"Wonderful. What else do you got?"

The third was the thing that really took the cake. Not that the Kid had recorded every conversation he'd had with Carver and me and everyone else who had been taken from Simon's game, but he'd managed to save enough to download those conversations into a special program on his computer. This program was then able to take the different tones and pitches and inflections of each of our voices so that they could be perfectly copied under someone else's voice.

So in theory, if I wanted to talk to someone—like an assistant director of the FBI, for instance—I could speak as clearly and simply as normal. Only the voice Edward Stark heard wouldn't be mine. It would be Carver's.

"Ready?" the Kid asked. He sat in front of his main computer, headphones hanging around his neck.

I sat beside him, staring at the monitor. Trying to think. Trying to get myself prepped for what I had finally decided was a terrible idea.

I nodded. "Let's do it."

The burner's number from Stark's email was already triggered into the computer. There was no guarantee it would still even be in service, or that if it was, Stark would answer. Still, the Kid placed the headphones over his ears and clicked his mouse. The number connected and began to ring.

It rang four times before a voice answered.

"This is Stark."

For an instant—a split second—I didn't know what to say, or do, or even think. I just sat there frozen. Then I said, "Hey, Ed."

Silence. Then, incredulous, "Carver? Is that you?"

The white lines on the computer screen bounced with the cadence of the man's voice.

"Yeah, it's me. How are you doing?"

"I'm fine. I'm just … surprised to hear from you."

The white bouncing lines turned green, and the Kid nodded. This meant Stark was telling the truth.

Stark asked, "How are you doing?"

"I'm great. I wanted to follow up on our email. Do you have time to talk?"

"Yes."

The lines turned red.

"Are you sure?"

"Of course I'm sure."

The lines stayed red.

"I understand you're hesitant to meet," Stark said. "I would be too after what happened. But I can assure you, I'm on your side."

Still the lines stayed red.

I asked, "Who is Caesar?"

"I told you. I don't know."

Still red.

"How high up does this go?"

"Very high."

The lines turned green.

"Why does it seem like we're talking in circles?"

"What do you mean?"

"I don't have time to waste. Either you give me something substantial or we have nothing to talk about."

"It would be easier to do this in person."

"That's not going to happen."

"I'm trying to be your friend here, Carver."

The lines turned red again.

I said, "Was it your friendship that fucked us over down in Florida?"

Silence.

"Do me a favor, Ed. When you see Caesar next, tell him something for me, will you?"

Still silence.

"Tell him the very last thing he will see before he dies is the barrel of my gun. Can you do that for me, buddy?"

I nodded at the Kid, who clicked off before Edward Stark could say—or not say—anything else.

The Kid took the headphones off his ears, let them hang around his neck. He gave me an exaggerated thumbs-up. "So that went well."

I said nothing. I hadn't realized it, but my entire body had begun to tremble. Had I been trembling during my brief conversation with Stark? Had he heard it in my voice?

"Ben?"

I blinked, looked over at the Kid.

"Now what?"

"Now nothing. We got our confirmation who and what Boojum is. That's that."

The Kid just stared at me.

"What?"

"Nothing," he said. "It's just as long as I've known you, you never struck me as someone who gives up this easily."

"First of all, we can't be one hundred percent certain if all those red lines were actual bullshit."

"But—"

"Besides, what else is there to do? Ronny was right. This whole thing is way too big for us. Even with Carver it was way too big."

"So you're giving up, just like that."

"What do you want me to do?"

The Kid shrugged. "I don't know. We could track Stark down, beat him up. Would that make you feel better?"

I grinned. "Maybe a little."

"So now what?"

"Now I guess I head back."

The Kid said nothing.

"All right." I sighed, clapped my hands together. "So ... if you don't have any other ideas, you mind driving me back to the airport?"

The Kid still said nothing.

"What is it?"

"You asked before, about me holding back about Carver? I was lying to you."

I crossed my arms. "Were you now."

"Ben, where did Carver meet Graham?"

"In the army."

The Kid looked at me blankly.

A flickering light bulb suddenly lit up bright in my head, and I said, "But Carver never went into the army."

The Kid didn't say anything.

"Then how ... how did they meet?"

The corners of the Kid's mouth lifted, creating a somber smile. "Come on, Ben. You mean you haven't figured that out yet?"

THIRTY-NINE

Returning to Colorado wasn't as easy as leaving. The earliest flight I could get was very late in the day, and there was a two-hour layover in Chicago (a city which brought back bad memories), and then because of the weather the flight was delayed another two hours. I spent much of that time in a haze, thinking many different things. I barely slept, even on the plane, dozing off for a few minutes and then jerking awake. By the time my flight arrived, it was nearly six o'clock in the morning. I sent a text to Jesse letting him know I was back. He showed up in the pickup three hours later. For some reason I was expecting—and hoping—Maya to be there too, but it was just Jesse.

The first thing he said to me was, "Ian'th gone."

"What do you mean?"

"He left."

"You mean he left for good?"

Jesse nodded.

"And nobody stopped him?"

"How could we thop him? We voted, remember."

We didn't speak for the rest of the way home. I laid my

head back against the rest and watched the passing scenery. My eyelids were heavy and I kept fighting to keep them from closing.

For some reason the farmhouse looked different than it had yesterday. Nothing external had changed, obviously, but it looked emptier somehow, and Ian's leaving had nothing to do with it.

When Jesse parked and cut the ignition, I said, "How was Carver's service?"

"Good. You thoulda been there."

Outside the pickup, I took a moment to savor the fresh air, the pellucid sky, to listen to the wind stirring through the tops of the trees. Jesse had immediately gone straight toward the house, up the steps and through the front door. I started to take a few steps in that direction but then changed course and headed around the house.

I don't know what was driving me at that moment. Maybe it was everything I'd learned yesterday—which was quite a lot compared to what I had learned in the past two years—or maybe it was my brief conversation with Edward Stark. Maybe it was what else I had learned from the Kid, about Carver and Graham. Maybe I was feeling betrayed, lied to, suckered somehow into believing a false reality.

But there hadn't been any maliciousness to it at all. Nobody had ever actually lied to any of us.

I walked past the house and down the hill toward the apiary. Graham didn't appear to be among them, but that didn't mean he wasn't working around one of the hives.

It was early afternoon. The sky was clear, the sun bright. Yet despite this it seemed the bees had quieted down for the day. All the outside work was done and now they were busy inside their individual hives, going about depositing the nectar into the special cells, doing everything automatically because that was their nature, the only thing they knew how to do.

I waited a minute without any luck.

I turned and headed back up the hill. I kept my focus on the farmhouse, but my gaze shifted to the graves. A new wooden cross had been planted there. I stared at it for only a moment before continuing on.

Inside, Beverly was standing at the stove, stirring something in a large metal pot. Maya was sitting at the kitchen table, her one leg curled up under her. She had an elbow on the table, her one hand cradling her head, her other hand swinging a pencil back and forth between her fingers. Before her lay one of the many Sudoku books she and Beverly and Ronny and Graham played during their free time.

Maya glanced up at me first, stared a moment, returned her attention back to the book opened before her. The silent action took less than two seconds but it caused a sharp ache in my heart.

Beverly, her back to me, said, "Ronny's downstairs."

Ronny wasn't who I was looking for, but I started toward the basement anyway. Went down the creaking stairs to find Ronny and Drew in front of the computers. They had been talking but quickly stopped when they heard me coming.

"Hey, guys," I said.

Neither of them said anything. They just stared back at me. Finally Ronny glanced at Drew, who glanced back at him. Ronny touched his beard, played with it for a moment, then took a deep breath.

"You missed the service."

"Did I?"

Drew said, "Are you here to tell us anything?"

"Such as …"

Both men looked at each other again. Drew sighed and leaned back in his seat, folded his arms over his chest.

Ronny said, "The Kid emailed us already, Ben. He figured

he would save you time when you got back. We already
listened to the conversation between you and the FBI guy."

"Wasn't that thoughtful of him."

Neither man answered.

I said, "Did he also tell you about Graham?"

Both of them looked confused.

"Okay, then. So where is Graham?"

"I think he's out in the barn," Drew said. He leaned
forward in his seat. "But first, Ben, don't you think we should
talk about this?"

"What is there to talk about?"

Ronny dropped his hand away from his beard and cleared
his throat. "Well, you were right for starters. Boojum is real.
And this guy, if Drew and I get this straight, was lying through
his teeth."

I looked at them both for a long moment, not sure what to
say. The monitors behind them were on. I focused on the
monitor that showed the holding cell. Two of the four frames
showed the Racist. Unlike before, where he doing nothing else
but lying on his cot, he was now sitting upright, the stack of
papers that told my story in his hands.

"He's actually reading it?"

Drew nodded. "He called last night. He wants to speak
with you."

"Ben," Ronny said. "Let's not stray from the main problem
here."

"And what main problem is that?"

"Boojum."

I took a few steps forward to get a better view of the
holding cell. The Racist was indeed paging through the
manuscript.

"Ronny, when was the last time you saw God?"

He didn't answer.

"When was the last time you actually heard him speak to you?"

Still no answer.

"But you still believe in him, don't you? You still believe he exists, even though you have no proof. It's been the same for me these past few days. I've never stopped believing in Boojum."

Ronny was watching me, no emotion in his eyes.

"And what can we do about it? Probably nothing. Carver's dead. We already voted to disband. And even if we didn't, like you said, what can we do against Caesar's army?"

Both men shifted their gazes away from me.

"Anyway, right now I'm not worried about that. Right now I want to speak with Graham."

Drew asked, "About what?"

"Come with me to the barn and you'll find out."

We found Graham inside the barn working on the riding lawn mower. He wore dirty chinos and a sweatshirt. He heard us and glanced up, nodded once, went back to work.

"Graham," I said.

"Hey, Ben." Not looking up, still going about his task. "You missed a very nice service yesterday."

"I want to talk to you about something."

"So talk."

"Carver's childhood."

Still not looking up as he went about tightening a nut on the rear tire. "Don't know anything about it."

"Because you met him in the army, right?"

"That's right."

"Only thing is, Graham, Carver was never in the army. He went to West Point, then into the FBI. No army."

At this Graham stopped tightening the nut.

Ronny and Drew—both whom I'd given an abbreviated version of Carver's childhood on the walk here—stood silent behind me.

"Why didn't you ever say anything before, Graham?"

Graham took a deep breath and stood up. His joints popped like faint firecrackers. He grabbed a rag from his back pocket and wiped at his brow, his neck.

"I never saw a reason why I had to. It didn't really make a difference."

"Maybe not to us," I said. "But it definitely did to you. It definitely did to Carver."

"So what do you want to know?"

"The truth."

Graham produced a thin smile and shook his head. "You were never lied to. None of you were."

"Carver may be dead, Graham, but his memory isn't. He never told anybody about his past. I want to know what happened afterward."

"After what?"

"After he killed his foster parent."

Graham looked up, almost startled.

I said, "After you and your wife adopted him."

FORTY

"You know, the more I think about it, I wasn't even supposed to be working that night. It was a Thursday and I didn't normally work Thursdays. The other detective—a man named Saunders—he had come down with a really bad flu. Had he been there instead, things definitely would have been different. Maybe none of us would be here right now."

We were still in the barn, the four of us, Graham sitting on the vinyl-cushioned lawn mower seat, Drew and me sitting on two upside down apple crates, Ronny leaning against the locked door that led into the closet we used to keep all our weapons.

As Graham spoke he stared down at his hands, lightly rubbing his fingers against his thumb.

"The call came in around midnight. Not the original call that Carver had placed to bring the police out to the house. I'm talking about the call the two officers placed to me, saying that there was a murder. I went out there not sure what to expect. I'd lived in that town for a good ten years or so, and I pretty much knew everyone there was. I knew of the man and his wife who had taken in all those children, but I didn't know him well.

"And then I got there and I saw just what kind of mess we were dealing with. You have to understand this town was in the southern part of the country, and while a lot of people didn't come out and voice their opinions on segregation, it was always there right under the surface. And now we had a black boy shooting a white man to death. A man who was a well-respected teacher, for Christ's sake."

Graham rubbed his fingers together a little more. His face looked as if it had aged five years in the space of only minutes.

"I guess that's news to all of you too, isn't it? That I was a detective. You have to understand, Carver and I never made a conscious choice to lie about our pasts. We just … we figured our pasts were in the past, so why even bother bringing them up? And Carver, when he first came and told me about what was going on and then first saved you, Ronny, and then you, Drew, he never didn't tell me I couldn't be open about my past. But I sensed it. Carver … he was a haunted man. He didn't want anybody to know about what he'd been through. He only wanted to worry about the present, about the here and now. And maybe, if he could, worry about how the present would affect the future."

"So what happened?" I asked. "When you first arrived at the house?"

Graham forced a distant smile and dipped his head, stared back down at his hands and started rubbing his fingers against his thumb.

"Believe it or not, it wasn't the first murder I'd investigated. Our town was small but it wasn't that small. We had a couple murders a year. But now we had a child murdering an adult, and again, even though it had nothing to do with the act, race was an issue.

"The two uniforms had already gathered the children

upstairs. They didn't want them coming down and seeing the mess in the living room. And so they started talking to them, asking each of them separately what happened. I was there for some of it. I could see how scared those kids were, not from what happened, but from a previous threat. They may have known the man was dead but for some reason this didn't seem to make them feel any better.

"Eventually I came in and took over. I tried my best with all the kids. Even Carver. Carver was the only one who told us everything. He wasn't afraid. And I'll admit, it was strange watching this ten-year-old boy tell us what had happened in this house. Not the story itself so much as how he told it. He never hesitated, he never seemed to worry that we were against him. He knew what he had done was wrong, but at the same time he knew it was the only way. And because of that, he wasn't scared.

"Hours passed and finally we got everything straightened out. It had been clear from the beginning what had been going on inside that house, but first we needed confirmation. Sure, the idea that all these kids were lying to us crossed our minds. But I just had this feeling, this feeling in my gut, and I knew these kids were telling the truth. Especially Carver.

"The thing was, we still had a murder to deal with. We couldn't just wash our hands of it and forget everything. Something had to be done. And this ... well, this was where I could have lost my job—where the other officers could have lost their jobs, too. You see, in the next town over there had been a series of home invasions. Whoever was doing it would go in, wreck the place, steal some stuff, and leave. A few times the people who lived in those houses were home, and they were badly beaten. One man was even killed. The perps hadn't been caught yet, so right then it made the most sense to blame what happened on them. If and when they were eventually caught— they weren't, surprisingly—we would deal with it then. So I called my supervisor, explained what had happened—the truth, mind you—and then I explained about what I wanted to do, how I wanted to change the story. It took some convincing but he eventually relented, made the disclaimer that if anything were to come back and bite us in the ass, he had never been in the know.

"So here's what we decided, the two uniforms and myself— the burglars broke into the house, not knowing the house was occupied. The man, hearing something downstairs, came down to inspect, and that was how he got shot. And the burglars? They disappeared into the night, took their gun with them, and were never heard from again. Like I said, if and when the perps got themselves caught, we would be in a world of trouble. The emergency call served as the only problem in the plan, but when Carver told us what he had said, how he had claimed he needed help, that 'he' was trying to kill him, it was enough for us."

Graham went silent again, still staring down at his hands, which had gone motionless.

"What about the mother?" I asked.

Graham looked up at me, his face blank, like he had no idea what I was talking about. Then, slowly, he began to smile.

"Again, another thing that could have really messed things up. When we had decided on a story, when we had explained to the children what had 'really' happened, I went to the hospital. I found her and asked if I could speak with her privately. I could tell by her eyes she wasn't an honest woman. That yes, on the outside, she looked honest and wholesome, but on the inside she was rotting. She thought my presence there signified a completely different outcome, and she had good reason to think that."

Graham had taken the woman aside and looked at her evenly and said, "Your husband is dead. He was shot to death earlier this evening by an unknown intruder at your home."

Tears stood in her eyes. Her face began to sink. She started to turn away, but Graham gripped her arm and pulled her back.

"Don't shed tears for him," he whispered coldly. "Your husband was a disturbed son of a bitch that molested the children you and he took in under your care. You can go and try to deny it as much as you want, but we both know the truth. And we both know the world isn't going to miss your husband one iota."

Tears still brimmed her eyes, but her face had begun to take shape again, reddening along the cheeks. He could almost feel the anger radiating off her.

"You realize too that you're an accomplice. That even if you never touched one of those kids, you still allowed your husband to do with them as he pleased. In a way, you're just as bad as him, if not worse."

The woman tried to deny it, said that she and her husband had given the children a home when nobody else would, that they loved them and would never hurt them. But Graham could see the truth in her eyes, the denial she had been feeding herself all these years beginning to regurgitate. Before she had been denying what her husband had been doing all this time, and now it changed, denying the fact that she was just as guilty.

Graham left her there at the hospital. He had already decided she wasn't going to be charged. That in the end it would only cause more trouble. That by charging her it would bring all the children into the picture, cause them even more pain than they had already suffered.

He went back to the station, filled out the proper paperwork, made some calls, got all the children taken away from the house to an orphanage two towns away.

He had no intention of telling his wife what had taken place—it was just too awful—but the next day she sensed something was bothering him and asked what was wrong. He told her, and she listened without comment, and when he finished the story she said, "So that boy has no home?"

Graham shook his head.

"Then we must provide him a home. Graham, we must save him."

It wasn't that easy, though. Adopting was a long and arduous task. But it helped that Graham was a police officer, his wife a librarian. It helped that they had tried for years to conceive but were never able to, had even started going through the channels of adoption. And it helped that every weekend Graham and his wife went to visit Carver at the orphanage, that Graham's wife would bring Carver books to read from the library.

Eventually the paperwork was pushed through, the papers were signed, and Carver became a part of the Fredrick household.

Graham said to us, "You have to understand, neither my wife nor myself were trying to make Carver our son. He was already ten years old by that point, and we weren't that naïve. But he was a good kid. We saw potential in him. And we knew that for his potential to really grow, he had to be in a good, safe environment. I'm not saying the home we provided him was the greatest, but it was good enough. We made sure he was challenged, that he was respected, that he felt loved."

Ronny asked, "What about his last name? How did he come up with Ellison?"

Graham beamed proudly.

"One of the books Carver read in high school was *Invisible Man* by Ralph Ellison. It became one of his favorite books. By that time he had been using Fredrick as his last name. We all understood that it wasn't going to last. That if he wanted to keep it, that was fine, but that if he eventually wanted to change it, that was fine too. The truth was Carver had never really had a true last name. He had never had a proper identity. Just like the narrator of *Invisible Man*. So when Carver graduated high school he had it legally changed. And Fredrick? Well, I don't think anyone ever questioned it, but Fredrick became his middle name. Carver Fredrick Ellison."

A beat of silence passed, and I said, "So that's it, then. That's the whole story."

"That's it, Ben. That's all she wrote. You know the rest. Carver always stayed in touch with us. He even came to my wife's funeral. And when I decided to quit the force and move away, move someplace where I could be alone, he was the only one I told. I never thought I'd see him again, but then years later he showed up and ... well, here we are."

Silence then, and I realized Graham was watching me. I held his stare for several long seconds, then glanced down at my watch.

"I think we're missing lunch," I said.

Nobody moved. Nobody said a word.

Graham kept watching me, his face still blank.

"What?"

"You know that quote Carver was always talking about, the one by Edmund Burke?"

I nodded.

"He didn't learn it in any of his high school classes. It was a quote I had up in my den at home, the words burned into a piece of wood. Carver was eleven the first time he saw it and asked me about it. He asked me, how could he become a good man? And I told him he didn't have to worry, that he already was."

Graham smiled, shook his head slowly.

"That's what always drove him, I think. Seeing that quote when he was eleven. Or maybe it was something that had happened even sooner. Like killing that man. I don't know, but every time I think of that quote now, I image a candle surrounded by darkness. And the darkness, it represents evil, while the candle represents good men doing something. But the thing is, good men can only do so much before they tire out and all their work is wasted."

"What are you saying?" I asked. "That Carver was wasting his time?"

"Not at all. None of you have been wasting your time. But … I think we need to accept the reality of the darkness around us. That's something Carver never could accept. He always thought the candle would still be burning, no matter what happened. That no matter how heavy and thick the darkness grew, there would always be a speck of light left."

Graham looked around at us.

"And while I respect all of you—I know all of you are good men—I'm almost glad the vote went the way it did. Because every day the world is growing darker. And I'm afraid that pretty soon whatever light is left is going to be extinguished, never to be lit again."

FORTY-ONE

For lunch Beverly had made the Racist a massive double cheeseburger, topped with lettuce and tomatoes and onions. Steak fries accompanied the burger, along with a long slice of dill pickle and a small plastic bottle of Heinz ketchup.

He took a large and hearty bite of the burger, chewed awhile, and said, "This is really good. She made it just like I'd asked."

In less than twenty-four hours the man had become a completely different person. So much so that I had trouble still thinking of him as the Racist. Now he had graduated to simply Mason Coulter, forty years old, husband and father from a town in Arizona, just another hapless victim in Simon's game.

He had changed out of his clothes and was now wearing the sweatpants and sweatshirt. He was sitting on his cot, eating the meal Beverly had prepared. Apparently he'd eaten his breakfast too, because the plate I had replaced was wiped clean.

I sat at the desk and watched him, not sure what to say. Drew had already told me about how the man had done a complete one-eighty, but it was hard to believe.

Besides his one compliment to Beverly, Mason didn't talk

for the rest of his meal. He saved the pickle for last, chomping it down in three bites and then licking his lips of the juices, a crooked but healthy smile on his face. Finally he looked at me, held up the plate, and nodded.

"Excellent," he said.

"I'm glad you enjoyed it."

"It was really good."

"So you said."

He gave me a curious stare, then got up from the cot and took his plate to the spot where the other plates had been before. He set the plate down and picked up the stack of papers by the pile of his dirty clothes, came back to the cell bars and held up the stack in front of him.

"Did everything in this really happen to you?"

"Yes."

"That's some fucked up shit."

"I agree."

"And your wife and daughter ... you still haven't found them yet?"

"No."

"Do you think they're still alive?"

I sat up straighter in my chair and took a long, deep breath. "I'd like to think they are."

Mason said nothing for a long moment. "So these people, Simon and Caesar, this whole Inner Circle ... they're a bunch of douche bags, huh?"

I couldn't help but crack a smile. "That's right. A big bunch of douche bags."

"What would you do if you were to confront Caesar? If he were to walk through that door right now."

"I'd kill him."

"You wouldn't hesitate?"

"Not at all."

"But what difference would it make? You know, in the end."

"Maybe none. But it would make me feel a hell of a lot better."

Mason watched me, his head cocked slightly, seeming to measure me. Then his eyes shifted at something past me. "What is that?"

"What is what?"

"*That.*"

He was looking at something over my shoulder. Even though I knew what he meant, I glanced back anyway. There, right beside the door, was a plastic screen with two red buttons underneath.

"Those," I said, "are in case of an emergency."

"What kind of an emergency?"

"A bad one."

He kept the frown on his face for a moment, then nodded and asked, "Do you still dream of Michelle Delaney?"

The question caught me off guard. "What are you up to, Mason?"

"What do you mean?"

"The other day you barely wanted to talk to me. Now you want to be friends. What gives?"

"I'm sick of being trapped in here."

"So you figure if you play nice, we'll let you out."

"I guess. But I know you guys are jumpy after what happened before with that Christopher Kane guy."

"Christian Kane."

"Right. And it's just … yeah, I have anger issues. Like I told you, I've had them all my life. That's no excuse for what I did during my game, but there you have it."

"And?"

He tossed the bound manuscript on the cot and raised his hands up to his sides in surrender. "And what?"

At that moment I wished I had the Kid's nifty gadget with me, the one that could analyze Mason's voice so I could see whether or not he was telling the truth. A part of me knew to be hesitant, but another part felt as if he was being on the level.

I leaned forward in my seat, my elbows on my knees, and interlaced my fingers. "The other day you said I misjudged you."

"You did."

"Then tell me about yourself, Mason. Make me understand."

"You mean like my childhood and shit?"

"Just anything you'd like to share."

He stood silent for a while, just staring back at me. Then he nodded slowly and turned and sat back down on the cot.

"I always knew I was going to be a mechanic, even before I got into high school. My old man had been a mechanic so it just made sense, like it ran in the blood. And it's good, honest work. I was never one to try to rip somebody off. I started dating Gloria in my last year of high school. She had this brother, a guy named Adam. He was in this biker gang. And when I say biker gang, understand that I mean an actual biker gang. These guys were the real deal."

"What was their specialty?"

"Arms, mostly. But they would also transport drugs every now and then. Whatever helped pay the bills."

"Prostitution?"

"Not that I knew of, but then again I knew better than to ask questions."

"You end up in the gang?"

"Nah, Gloria wouldn't let me. I wanted to, you know, but Gloria was really strict about it, and I guess I could see why. Adam, though, he was actually really cool to me. He understood how things were, and he told me once that even if his sister was okay with it, he wouldn't let me join. He knew just how dangerous being in the gang could be, and he didn't want something to happen to me. He knew that if that happened, it would kill Gloria. So I started just working as a mechanic in their shop, doing work on their bikes and shit. All of it was legit. I got a paycheck and everything."

"So how'd you end up in jail?"

"Adam. He was doing a last-minute run one night. The guy he was supposed to go with fell out, got really sick or something. So he asked me to come along. Said it would be real simple, just a drop off and that was it. He just wanted me along for the extra protection. I mean, even if I wasn't in the gang, I still carried a piece on me, so I could give him some backup."

"You expect me to believe he couldn't get anybody else to go with him?"

"Man, at that point I was just happy to tag along. I mean, even though Gloria made me swear to never join the club, that didn't mean I didn't want to be a member. From the outside it looked like a pretty sweet life."

"Dangerous, though."

"Well, yeah. But right then, it was just me and Gloria. Had we had Anthony then, maybe I wouldn't have gone along."

"But you did."

"That's right, I did. I went with Adam to the drop. We didn't even make it the whole way there. On the way, a cop tried to pull us over. We both were carrying meth. We took off, went different directions. The cop ended up following me. Chased me for a couple long miles until I ended up in a dead end."

"Then what happened?"

"They busted me for possession with intent to distribute. As you can imagine, that didn't go down too well. The club had a lawyer and everything, but seeing as I wasn't an actual member, they weren't too quick to use him to help me out. I mean, the cops were sweating me to give them names. They knew I wasn't a member, that I was just related to one. They wanted to break me to get to Adam and the rest of the club."

"But you didn't break."

"No, I didn't. Trust me, the last thing I wanted to do was go to prison, but I wasn't about to rat out my brother-in-law."

"What about your son?"

"He wasn't born yet. Gloria didn't find out she was pregnant until I had already had my sentencing. The way we figured it, our boy had been conceived a night or two before I went on that drop with Adam."

"So what happened inside?"

"There was a rival gang. They knew who I was and what I was in for. They tried to come for me. I managed to fight some of them off, but not all. It happened way too soon once I got inside. The club hadn't been able to get me protection yet."

"And?"

"And the rival gang, they were mostly black. When they came at me, I ended up killing one of them in self-defense. It caught the attention of the AB. They were impressed. I was too scared then to really think straight, so when they approached me, I just went with the flow."

"How long were you inside?"

"Too goddamn long."

"Did you have any other issues?"

"Not while I was still with the Brotherhood."

"And then once you got released?"

"I packed up Gloria and Anthony and got the fuck out of there. We moved three states away. Adam and the club said they were really sorry, that they wanted to make it up to me, and maybe they did, but I wasn't about to trust them anymore. I didn't want them raising my son any more than they already had. So we moved and I tried getting another job as a mechanic, but as you can probably guess it was tough with my record. I did come across one place, but they were associated with the AB. It was the last place I wanted to work, but money was getting tight and I was getting desperate, so I stopped by. They hired me right on the spot. Then five years later ... well, I woke up and my family was gone."

Mason went silent then, his gaze now focused on his hands. Slowly, so very slowly, his eyes shifted up to meet mine. They were completely sincere.

I sat quietly for a moment, thinking. Then I stood up and reached into my pocket and approached the bars.

"A lot of things have changed in the past twenty-four hours," I said, withdrawing the single key from my pocket. "What's going to happen in the next twenty-four hours, I have no idea. But I figure at this point, nobody should be locked up."

I slid the key into the lock but paused, cocked my head at Mason.

"But try to keep your anger under control. Because I am not joking when I say I won't think twice putting two in your head."

Mason nodded solemnly. Then, slowly, a grin spread across his face.

"What's so funny?"

"Nothing. It's just that doesn't sound like the guy I read about in your story."

"Yeah, well, didn't you figure that part out yet? That guy died two years ago."

And I turned the key.

FORTY-TWO

The inscription on my wife's wedding ring read TO JEN, MY OTHER HALF. It referred to a story she had once told me weeks before we got married, a story going back to the beginning of time. A story of love.

It was the same story I found myself thinking about again and again from that day forward, to the day we got married, to the day we had Casey. It was those halcyon days where I truly believed my life was complete, an expensively crafted model with no missing pieces, where everything worked just right. Of course there were times when Jen and I had our disagreements, where Casey misbehaved and had to be scolded. I'm not even going to try to kid myself that none of that ever happened. But even then, on those rare occasions when I became frustrated, angry, perturbed to the point where I'd wonder just what the hell kind of mistake had I made, I would think about Jen's wedding ring, about the inscription, and I would somehow know that everything was all right.

I thought about that every day, from the day my family was taken away from me until now, this very evening, alone in my bedroom. Lying in my bed and staring at the only thing I had that belonged to my wife, which had been shipped to me in a box along with her savagely cut off finger.

I always kept it at the farmhouse. I never took it on missions, for fear that I would lose it. At nights I would place it beneath my pillow, as if my wife's spirit were somehow trapped in that white gold, and that during the night, while I slept, her spirit would meet me in my dreams.

It was nearly ten o'clock. Everyone else was downstairs, watching TV or playing cards. I had wanted to be alone so I just lay there with the lamp on behind my bed, moving the ring between my fingers, holding it at just the right angle so I could make out those five words.

There was a soft knock at the door. Maya stepped inside. Wordlessly she moved to the other bed against the wall and sat down, pulling her feet up onto the bed and hugging her knees.

"Hi," she said.

"Hi," I said.

That was it. Neither of us said anything else. I still had Jen's ring in my hand, unconsciously moving it around with my fingers. When I realized what I was doing, I stopped the motion, made the ring disappear into a fist, and went to place it back underneath my pillow.

"You don't have to do that."

I looked up at her.

"I don't mind, Ben. You know that."

I replaced the ring anyway. Sat back and pulled up my feet, hugged my knees, both of us less than ten feet apart but the distance feeling so much farther.

Maya said, "You ran away yesterday."

My first instinct was to deny this claim, but I nodded instead.

"Do you know why you did it?"

"I wanted to go back with the Kid."

"Please, Ben. You can lie to yourself, but don't lie to me."

The lamp by my head was getting hot. I adjusted it, moving it so the glow illuminated the other side of the room.

Maya said, "I think I know what I want to do. You know, once we all officially disband."

I said nothing and just stared back at her, watched the thin profile of her jaw as she spoke.

"A while back, the Kid offered to help me find my tribe. He said with his skill it shouldn't be too difficult. I told him at the time not to worry about it, but now … now I'm ready. I want to go back to Washington. I want … I want to find my family."

She wiped at her eyes, though I wasn't quite certain there were any tears.

She said, "Do you think …" but then looked away, bit her lower lip.

"Do I think what?"

Refusing to meet my eyes, she slowly shook her head.

I dropped my feet off the bed, leaned forward, started to get up but stayed in place. Jen's ring was always in this bedroom, always when I was here with Maya, either holding her in bed or kissing her, and I had never felt as strong a sense of betrayal as I felt now.

"Maya," I said softly. "Do I think what?"

"Forget it."

"Tell me."

"Please, Ben, just forget I said anything."

"Tell me," I repeated, this time with more force.

She wiped again at her eyes, swallowed hard. "Do you think you … you might, I don't know, want to come with me?"

The question hung heavy in the air. We stared at each other, neither of us wanting to be the first to blink.

I blinked. "Maya, I—"

"Don't."

"But I—"

"Please, Ben. Don't."

She was looking away again, the absent tears now visible on her face, falling down her cheeks, causing her eyes to glimmer in the dimness.

I stood up from the bed. I went and sat down beside her. I tried to hold her but she pulled away, averted her face from mine.

"Maya," I said, and she continued to shake her head, to try to pull away from me.

Suddenly she stood up, started toward the door.

I got up and went after her, grabbed her arm and pulled her back, turned her around so I could see her face.

She was staring down at the floor, still shaking her head.

"Maya, look at me."

Slowly she raised her head, exposing the fresh tears on her face. "Yes?"

"I would love to go with you."

Her face broke again, this time into a smile, and it looked strange there in the dark of the room, her beautiful smile accompanied by the tears lining her face, by what had been only moments ago fear and embarrassment and dejection filling her eyes.

"Yeah?" she said, wiping away the tears.

"Yeah," I said, and took her free hand in mine, gave it three slight squeezes.

We stood there then, watching each other's eyes, neither of us moving, neither of us saying a word, both of us just lost in the moment. And it was a perfect moment, the kind nobody can take away, a kind of comfortable peace where we both knew that, despite everything else, we were going to be okay.

Then the Kid called the next morning, shattering that fragile perfection.

FORTY-THREE

They were waiting for me.

I'd taken Mason to the shooting range to give him some practice with a rifle—why exactly I wasn't sure, as the vote to disband was official, but I needed to do something to keep him occupied for the time being—when Drew called me on the radio and told me to hurry back. So we hurried back, each of us on a four-wheeler, and I left Mason in the barn to put everything away as I hurried inside and down the basement steps to find Ronny and Drew and Jesse and Maya huddled around the main computer.

The webcam was set up and the Kid was on screen.

"Well," he said when I'd joined them, "about fucking time."

Ronny released one of his long and weary sighs. He was the only one sitting down, right in front of the computer.

"Okay, Kid," he said. "Show us what you got."

The Kid looked away at one of his other monitors. There was the sudden sound of his quick typing and then the screen suddenly changed to show the profile of a man.

"He's listed as the Abortionist," the Kid said, and immediately Ronny sighed again, Drew cursed under his breath, Jesse shook his head, and Maya looked at me.

The page was the usual page used in Simon's game. The one that showed a picture of the latest player, that listed his hobbies, his ambitions, what he had once been in life before it was all taken away. No real names, only links to show the family or friends or whoever had been taken.

I asked the Kid, "How long ago did this come up?"

"Less than an hour."

"Do you know the location yet?"

Ronny shifted around in his seat to glare back at me. I ignored him, continued studying the page.

The Abortionist looked to be in his thirties. He had a sharp nose, square-jaw, short reddish hair. His hobbies listed fishing, reading, playing video games with his sons. He was a huge Clint Eastwood fan, especially the early westerns. His occupation was listed as a former doctor who had lost his license in the past couple years but who still occasionally performed abortions for women who could not afford to go to a real clinic.

He was currently playing to save the lives of his wife and two sons.

"Actually, yeah," the Kid said, sounding almost surprised.

I asked him why this surprised him.

"When he left the motel room he woke up in and got in his car and started out, he passed a highway sign almost immediately."

"So where was he?"

"In Las Vegas. That's the New Mexico one, not Nevada. Not that far away from you guys as the crow flies."

Ronny cleared his throat and said, "Unfortunately the crow isn't flying from here anymore."

"I'll do it," I said.

Ronny twisted his neck so quickly in my direction I

wouldn't have been surprised if he'd given himself whiplash. "The heck you will."

Again I ignored him. "Kid, keep an eye on this guy. Also send me as much info as you can."

Even though the monitor still showed the Abortionist's bio page, I could hear the Kid smiling when he said, "You got it."

Ronny said, "You're not doing this, Ben. We voted. We—"

"You voted. You don't have to go."

"It could be a trap."

This gave me pause. My sense of purpose had been waning the past couple of days, my soul drifting on an endless sea of doubt and despair. But this right here—a new player in need of saving—was something I could finally get behind.

"Maybe," I said. "Then again, maybe not."

"He'll have escorts."

"They always have escorts."

"But Carver—"

"Is dead." I held Ronny's stare. "Anybody else in?"

Maya said, without hesitation, "I am."

It took Jesse a couple more seconds before he said, "Me too."

The Abortionist's bio page disappeared and it was the Kid again. "Who's all in?"

I said, "Me, Maya, and Jesse."

The Kid nodded and started typing. "All right. Head out now and—"

"What the hell," Drew said. "I'm in too. That sound good to you, Ben?"

"That sounds great." I looked at Ronny. "So how about you? Last chance."

Ronny, who looked ready to have a conniption, just shook his head.

"Okay then, four it is." The Kid grinned back at us. "Let's fucking do this shit."

FORTY-FOUR

We caught up with the Abortionist less than twenty hours later. By that time it was ten o'clock in the morning. This was in Arizona, speeding down Interstate 10, headed west toward Tucson.

So far the Abortionist had jumped through a number of Simon's standard hoops.

The first was lifting a Milky Way bar at a gas station. Just like it had been for me, like it was for many new players, a way to ease into the game.

The second wasn't so easy.

The Abortionist drove south to Las Cruces, where he was instructed to enter a nondescript brick building on the outskirts of the city. Inside he found a woman strapped to a delivery table, her legs in stirrups. She was pregnant.

Simon told the Abortionist over speakerphone, "You want to see your wife and sons again? You want to see them alive? Then do what you do best, Clark. Give this woman an abortion."

Problem was this woman didn't want an abortion. She was awake for the entire procedure, screaming and crying, pleading with him to leave her and her baby alone. After a while she passed out, though whether from the pain or mere exhaustion it was impossible to say.

The Abortionist—or Clark, as Simon called him—didn't stay around to revive her. He went into the bathroom, fell to his knees, and threw up all over the floor. He lay there sobbing for about five minutes before Simon called to tell him that he had done well, and that if he had any human decency left in his bones, he would put the woman out of her misery before she woke back up.

The Abortionist didn't do this. He left as quickly as possible, speeding to the plush hotel room that awaited him, where he threw up again in the bathroom and cried himself to sleep.

In the morning he was back on the road, heading west into Arizona.

Drew and Jesse were driving lead in the SUV, Maya and myself following about a half mile behind in a Ford Focus. The plan was to do a Smash and Grab but the opportunity hadn't yet presented itself.

The thing you have to understand when catching up to a new player is just how long and aggravating the process becomes. From the Kid's initial call to the actual moment when you get the target within your sights, a lot of chips have to fall just right into place. Because the target is constantly moving, a game piece among thousands, and you have no idea where the next stop will be. So you wait, and you hope, and you just keep driving toward whatever location the Kid directs you.

And here's the real kicker—sometimes the Kid isn't even sure where the target is half the time. He has the tedious and thankless job of sitting in front of his computer monitor and watching every single detail of every single frame. Looking for clues that will help, searching for some sign that will give him a location, and once he has that location he maps it out, triangulates the most probable place, and that is where the target is at that moment in time.

But time is relative.

For one, the game the Kid is watching might not even be a live feed. It might be delayed a day, an hour, even a minute. And while minutes don't seem like much, they can make a huge difference when the target comes to one of those major serpentine highways, the kind that rises and falls, directing its drivers toward different points of the continental United States.

Also—and here's the thing you really have to remember—the Kid is human. He makes mistakes. He has to eat, sleep, shit, which means he doesn't have time to sit in front of the computer monitor every waking minute of the day.

Which means, sometimes, luck becomes a major factor.

Determination is important, too. The constant and steady need to see this through and never give up, no matter what happens.

Because there have been times when we've lost targets. When we've traveled day and night, through towns and cities and states, only to find that the target's game has already come to an end.

But now here we were in Arizona, the sky cloudless and blue, the sun heavy and hot, the Focus's windows down letting in the wind. I had driven for the first leg of the trip; Maya had taken over for the second.

I didn't know about Maya, but I was doing a lot of thinking.

A *lot* of thinking.

Trying to wrap my brain around this whole mess, from what happened in Miami Beach to the here and now. Not even a week had passed but it seemed so much longer, months even, that what we had considered a lengthy abeyance was nothing more than a short break.

First there was Carver's death, his last word boojum.

Boojum then being a word of great mystery, some thinking it complete gibberish, others thinking it some secret key or code.

And it had been a key of sorts, one that led us to an assistant director of the FBI, who claimed he didn't know anything, which, according to the Kid's nifty program, was a lie.

Even so, where did that leave the rest of us? Carver was still dead, we had voted to disband, Ian had taken off, and others were soon to follow.

So what were the four of us doing out here now in the bleak and inhospitable Arizona desert?

I wasn't sure about Maya or Drew or Jesse, but I was thinking about that lone candle in the darkness, the wick becoming shorter and shorter. I was thinking about how the only way for evil to triumph is that good men do nothing, and I wasn't ready for that. Not yet. Not while I still had the power to do something.

Drew called. He said the target was turning off the interstate, heading south.

I started to relay this message to Maya, how we were getting off at the next exit, when I suddenly heard a familiar high-pitched whine.

The radio was off, the only sound that of the wind raging through the opened windows, but the noise was distinct, coming from behind us.

I quickly turned in my seat.

A black sport bike—a Ducati no less—was racing up the left-hand lane.

It was there for only an instant before passing us by, doing at least one hundred, disappearing down the highway and letting the high-pitched whine fade away into nothingness.

FORTY-FIVE

The town was named Hope Springs.

Out in the middle of nowhere, it was the kind of town whose population was less than one thousand. A few cars and pickups traveling along the main strip, but hardly anybody out and about, not in this heat, not when they could find solace from high-powered air conditioners or overworked fans.

Just as we passed a Circle K grocery store, the Kid called.

"He's got a gun."

"What type of gun?"

"Revolver. Looks like a Smith & Wesson."

"You think it's loaded with blanks?"

"How the fuck should I know? But I'll tell you, this doesn't look good. Whatever Simon's been telling this guy, he hasn't been taking it well."

"How so?"

"For starters, the sorry bastard's been crying for the past five minutes straight."

I had called the Kid earlier about the Ducati, told him that while I wasn't one hundred percent certain it was the same one that had saved us in Miami, I was pretty certain. He had said,

Yeah, well, pretty certain won't fucking get you laid at the prom. I was half-tempted to ask him if he had even gone to his prom, but instead told him to keep an eye out for it regardless.

Now I asked him if he'd seen it.

"Nope."

"Are you sure?"

"Yep."

When I'd disconnected with the Kid, I called Drew.

"If he pulls off anywhere, keep driving and circle back around. We'll try to make contact first."

I told him about the Kid's call, how the Abortionist had a gun.

Drew said, "Good luck."

Less than two minutes later, the Abortionist made his turn.

We had just passed through the heart of Hope Springs, and judging by the few weathered and decrepit buildings, not to mention the single traffic light hanging suspended above the intersection, it was a safe bet to say it was an unhealthy heart.

Up ahead, the Abortionist turned into the parking lot of one of the town's two gas stations.

Drew continued forward, didn't even tap his brakes.

The gas station looked reasonably sized. Two islands covered by an overhang to help protect those weary drivers from the harsh desert sun as they pumped overpriced gas. The building itself was white stucco, its entire front mostly glass and plastered with signs announcing sales on soda and ice cream and claiming their cigarettes were priced as low as the state would allow.

Three cars were already parked in front of the building. Another car was at one of the islands, its weary driver not looking so weary, a young woman in a sundress fanning herself with a magazine as she watched the numbers cycling upward and onward.

The Abortionist parked in front of the building. He was

out of his car and walking, his head lowered, when Maya made her turn and parked four spaces away.

He didn't seem to notice us—didn't even seem to hear us— as he neared the two glass doors leading into the store. Presumably he was deep in thought, concentrating on the task at hand, his mind trying to wrap itself around the cactus which had become the next part of Simon's game. He was probably trying to figure out how to go about this and not get pricked, not get hurt, and I can't say I didn't blame him. He didn't look very sure of himself as he walked, his shoulders slouched, but neither would I if I were carrying a small revolver in my right hand.

The Abortionist wasn't even trying to hide it as he opened the door and stepped inside.

"Shit," I said, already flinging off my seatbelt and scrambling to open the door. I withdrew my Sig just as I stepped out of the car, saying to Maya, "Stay here and call Drew. Tell him to get his ass back here pronto."

I slammed the door, hurried up onto the walkway toward the store's entrance.

Tinny music was coming from speakers perched in different spots of the overhang. At the moment Steely Dan was singing about reelin' in the years.

The young woman in the sundress was still by her car, pumping her precious, leaving-a-hole-in-your-wallet fuel, too busy fanning herself to have noticed the gun in the Abortionist's hand.

I couldn't see through the windows, not with all those cardboard signs taped in different spots. All I could see were the racks of snacks, boxes and bags, twelve-packs of soda stacked precariously on top of one another.

A dusty pickup truck pulled into the parking lot, what looked to be a father and son. I wanted to wave them away, tell them to get the hell out of here, when, from inside the store, I heard the first scream.

FORTY-SIX

It wasn't much cooler inside the store.

A half dozen box fans were situated around the place, at the ends of each aisle, picking up the slack of the failing air conditioner. A sign above the counter read *A/C on FRITZ* with a frowny face scribbled in marker below it.

The music playing outside was playing inside too, but most of it was drowned out by those six box fans, all set on high, creating a kind of maelstrom as it used the stale air to crinkle bags of pretzels and potato chips, fan the pages of magazines, send the advertising mobiles hanging from the ceiling off in drunken dances where they never got very far and always ended up in the same place.

Besides myself, there were five other people—a man and a woman, both in their sixties, both Mexican; a guy in his thirties wearing a straw cowboy hat; the counterman, also Mexican; and the Abortionist.

The counterman was behind the counter, his hands held up in front of him. The three others were frozen off to the side, also with their hands raised.

The Abortionist was the only one not partaking in the hand

raising. Instead he had the Smith & Wesson aimed straight at the counterman.

"Come on, please, just give me the money. I don't—I don't wanna hurt anybody. Just please, give me the money and I'll go."

This was what he was saying when I entered the store, when an actual bell dangling above the door with a string tied to it announced my presence with an off-key jangle.

The Abortionist was already in a bad state. Any untrained eye could see that the hand grasping the gun was shaking. Any untrained ear could hear the nervousness and fear in his voice.

He was starting to ask for the money again when he heard the bell jangling and spun around, already starting to say something to whoever else had unfortunately walked in on this early afternoon fracas.

But he didn't say anything. He tried, his mouth moving, but he couldn't seem to form the words.

All he could do was stare back at my Sig aimed straight at his chest.

"Put the gun down, Clark," I said, talking to him but also talking to the thick black glasses on his face, staring at the center where the camera was located and where Simon and Caesar and everyone else in the Inner Circle was watching me right this moment.

He was clearly spooked at hearing his name, but slowly shook his head, the gun grasped in his hand shaking even more.

"I—I—I can't. If I don't do this, they'll kill them. I just—I need the money."

"They're already dead, Clark. I'm sorry to be the one to tell you that, but your wife and sons are already dead."

The Mexican woman began sobbing, whispering a prayer.

Clark shook his head slowly, staring back at me through the

lenses of the glasses, his hand trembling so much now it looked as if the gun had gained one hundred pounds.

"No," he said in a small and soft voice, and dropped his head, his shoulders hitching up, the shaking gun lowering.

"I'm here to help you," I said to him, taking one slow step forward, keeping the Sig aimed right at center mass in case he tried anything stupid, anything rash. In case Simon had already broken him enough that he didn't care who he killed or hurt to get to his family.

I was less than ten feet away, the fans roaring around the store, Steely Dan still pouring from the speakers, when the Abortionist dropped the gun.

His hands went to his face, and he began sobbing, his shoulders hitching even more.

Keeping my own gun aimed, I bent and picked up the Smith & Wesson, placed it in my back pocket.

"Let's go," I said.

He looked up at me, his face red, tears in his eyes. He nodded once and took a step forward.

The Mexican woman was still sobbing, still praying, and the three other men were doing nothing more than curiously watching. They stayed where they were, their hands up, their gazes now on me.

"Sorry for the inconvenience," I said to them.

I took the Abortionist by the arm and led him to the doors. I pushed one open without taking the extra second to look through the glass, and in doing so almost knocked over the man and the boy stepping up onto the sidewalk.

The man said, "Whoa," and caught the boy, an amused expression on his face. The amusement didn't last long. A moment later he saw the gun in my hand and immediately reached for the gun holstered to his belt. Whether he was an off-duty cop or just an average American citizen expressing his second amendment rights, I didn't care to find out.

I shouted, "Don't move!" and aimed the Sig right at his face.

He froze.

"We're leaving now," I said. "We're doing so peacefully. No need to make things worse."

The man said nothing. His other hand gripped the boy and pushed him back behind his body.

"I got him."

This was from Drew, standing outside the SUV now parked beside Maya in the Focus. He had his gun out, the barrel trained on the man.

This wasn't going down nearly as well as I had hoped, but there wasn't any time to worry about it. Right now we had to get out of here as soon as possible before the police showed up. Not even twenty seconds had passed since we stepped outside, but I was sure the counterman—or someone else inside the gas station—had already dialed 911.

"Get in the SUV," I told the Abortionist.

He wiped at his eyes. "Huh?"

"Get in the SUV now."

Before he could take a step in the SUV's direction—Jesse opened the driver's door to get out and help—a thought occurred to me and I reached out and snatched the glasses off his face.

"Hey," he said, startled, trying to grab for them, but I dropped them to the ground and smashed them with the heel of my shoe. He looked up at me, dumbfounded. "Why'd you do that?"

The music from the speakers in the overhang had changed. Steely Dan had faded to be replaced with Buffalo Springfield, telling us that something was happening and whatever it was wasn't exactly clear.

Jesse came up behind the Abortionist. He gently grabbed

his arm and the back of his neck to start leading him to the SUV.

"Let's go," I said again, pointing the way, and that was when I heard the low oncoming rumbling from the street.

Jesse and Drew and Maya heard it too. They all glanced toward the main drag—Jesse pausing as he led the Abortionist toward the SUV—right as a red Corvette convertible came roaring down the main strip.

It happened so suddenly that we forgot all about the man and the boy.

It happened so suddenly it gave the man enough time to grab his gun and pull it from its holster.

"Stop!" he shouted.

I didn't even get a chance to look back at him. I could see him from the corner of my eye—his gun aimed at me—but that was it. My focus was instead on the Corvette as it swerved into the gas station parking lot. On the two men inside, both wearing sunglasses. On the passenger and the Heckler & Koch MP5 in his hands.

The Corvette screeched to a halt, parallel with the gas station, and both men jumped out, the passenger brandishing the MP5, the driver a Glock.

"Fancy meeting you here," the driver said.

From the corner of my eye, I watched the man turn toward the two men from the Corvette. "Stop!" he shouted again.

The passenger said, "Who the fuck are you?"

"Deputy Ray Porter. Now drop your weapons!"

The driver laughed and said to the passenger, "Talk about wrong place, wrong time."

From the corner of my other eye I watched Maya open her door silently, step out, place one foot on the ground.

I said, "Deputy Porter and his son aren't involved here. Let them go."

"That depends," the driver said, "on how big of a hero he thinks he can be."

"Deputy Porter," I said, "for the sake of your son, stand down."

"I said drop your weapons!" the deputy shouted.

Ahead of me, Drew had positioned himself to sight over the SUV's hood. Jesse, still with one hand on the Abortionist's arm, withdrew his gun.

The Corvette's passenger said, "Ben, this cop here is making things difficult."

"What do you want?"

"For you to surrender—for *all* of you to surrender. You do that, you get to see your friend again."

The boy started crying, hiding behind his father.

"For the love of God, Deputy Porter," I said, "don't be stupid. Take your boy inside."

Deputy Porter shouted, "This is your last warning! Drop your weapons now!"

The woman in the sundress, who'd been methodically fanning herself as she pumped gas, stood frozen by her car. Her eyes were wide as she watched the unfolding drama. I wanted to yell at her, tell her to get in her car and just drive away, but before I could the Corvette's driver shook his head.

"Like I said—wrong place, wrong time."

And he tilted his gun and shot Deputy Ray Porter right in the forehead.

His boy screamed. The woman screamed. The Abortionist screamed.

I shouted, "Now!"

Maya opened up first, striking the Corvette's passenger in the chest. His MP5 sprayed the front of the gas station, shattering glass. Drew fired at the driver who had already turned away to take cover behind the Corvette, while Jesse and I hurried the Abortionist toward the SUV.

I created a mantra in my mind, repeating *let's go let's go let's go*, while bullets zinged everywhere, puncturing metal, shattering more glass.

Once I was certain Jesse could handle getting the Abortionist loaded—this was about three seconds since the gunfire had started—I pushed away and raised my gun, aimed at the passenger who was still standing, still spraying the MP5.

I fired, one two three shots, and still the Corvette's passenger was on his feet, his finger stuck against the trigger, spewing bullets everywhere. He went down a second later, taking the MP5 with him.

Jesse and the Abortionist had taken cover behind the SUV, Jesse shielding the man with his body.

I started that way when I realized the gunfire wasn't over. The driver was still alive.

He popped back up behind the car, jumped inside, firing wildly as spun the wheel with one hand and punched the gas.

Maya had moved from her position by the Focus and advanced on the Corvette as it squealed out of the parking lot, Maya shooting first at the driver and then at the back of the car, trying for the wheels if possible, trying for anything.

Moments later the Corvette had made it back on the main strip, nearly colliding with a pickup heading south, the pickup's horn blaring.

Maya turned back, lowered her gun, started toward the SUV.

The Abortionist, sensing the gunfire was over, tried getting back up but Jesse was still shielding him with his body.

"Jesse, we're clear," I said.

Jesse didn't move.

"Jesse?"

Still nothing.

The tinny music had faded away once again, from Buffalo Springfield to The Doors, Jim Morrison going on about breaking through onto the other side. Just behind this the boy was still screaming, as was the woman.

Maya and I hurried forward, but Drew was the closest, only feet away. He leaned down and turned Jesse over.

Jesse's entire front was dark with blood. His eyes were open, blinking slowly. His mouth was open, and he was gurgling blood.

I fell to my knees beside him. I touched his forehead, felt for a pulse.

It was very weak.

"Jesse," I said, and grabbed for his hand, held it tightly.

"B-B-B-Ben," he said and his voice was frail and as thin as a piece of parchment.

"Jesse, it's okay, it's okay," I said, telling him the same words you tell anyone who's been mortally shot, who's very close to knocking on heaven's door.

He continued to blink slowly. His eyes rolled around in his head, left and right, up and down, until they found me.

"I'm … c-c-c-cold," he whispered.

And died.

FORTY-SEVEN

I stood up almost immediately. Stared past the SUV toward the main strip.

"Ben?"

I turned away and started toward the Focus. Paused and turned back. Leaned down and grabbed my gun off the ground and then stood back up.

"Ben, what are you doing?"

A part of me—the sudden numb part—wanted to continue ignoring Maya. Instead I jabbed my finger at Jesse and the Abortionist and said, "Get those two loaded up and get the fuck out of here."

"But what about you?"

"I'll be fine," I said, already heading for the Focus. I climbed inside, tossed my gun and the Abortionist's gun on the passenger seat, fired up the ignition, and then tore out of the parking lot in the same direction the Corvette had been headed less than a minute ago.

There wasn't much traffic on the main street—a few cars and pickup trucks—but still I needed to swerve around them as I pressed the gas pedal to the floor. I knew the Focus couldn't compete with the Corvette, not when it came to horsepower, but at that moment I didn't care. Hope Springs was barely a dot on the map. The only way to enter and exit the town was via the main street, which eventually turned into the highway. From there, it was miles of endless asphalt until the next town loomed on the horizon.

My cell phone vibrated in my pocket. I made no move to answer it. It was either Maya or the Kid, and right now I didn't want to deal with either of them.

Less than a minute later I reached the outskirts of Hope Springs, and the highway opened up. In the distance—maybe a half mile away—was the red Corvette. It was a peculiar choice for Simon's men, almost too conspicuous, but again, it had massive horsepower. My only hope was that during the shootout something vital had been struck. My fingers were crossed for the fuel line.

I pushed my foot down on the gas even more, as if that would make the car go faster. The speedometer was rising—going from ninety to ninety-five, ninety-five to one hundred—but at some point it would reach its breaking point. Still, there was nothing between the Focus and the Corvette but empty highway, and as the seconds ticked by, the distance between us began to shorten.

Until, suddenly, the distance vanished almost at once.

One moment the Corvette was off in the distance ahead of me, barely even a red speck, and then the next moment I was coming up on it way too fast.

It didn't occur to me until a second later that the Corvette had stopped completely. That was when I saw the oil directly behind it on the highway. That was when I saw the driver climbing out of the Corvette and bringing up his gun and aiming it right at my windshield.

I slammed on the brakes just as the driver opened fire. The windshield spider-webbed. I flinched, jerking the wheel. The tires caught in the oil—its fuel line or something had definitely been hit—and then the car started into a spin, its tail end just missing the Corvette. The Focus kept spinning until it slid off the highway completely and then skidded to halt in a cloud of dust.

For an instant, I didn't move. I *couldn't* move. My seatbelt had tightened, making it nearly impossible to breath. The windshield was all fucked up, and the dust was thick outside the windows, so I couldn't see much. Both guns were now on the floor of the passenger side. I went to reach for mine—I wasn't about to trust the Abortionist's Smith & Wesson—but the seatbelt held me in place. I unsnapped the seatbelt, leaned down, grabbed the gun, but didn't sit back up.

I waited.

I counted ten seconds in my head, letting the dust settle, then, still staying low on the seat, bent to open the driver's door. It disengaged, opened just a little bit. I placed my foot against it and count five more seconds before I kicked it open.

The shot was almost instantaneous, shattering the window. There was a pause, then another shot. Another pause followed this and I dove out of the car, head first, rolling and then coming back up, my gun aimed on where those first two shots had originated. I fired twice, then waited as the dust settled.

The driver wasn't there.

Behind me then, the crunch of shoes against dirt, and the driver said, "Don't fucking move."

I stayed still for a second, then jerked back, rolling away, and brought up my gun. It was kicked out of my hand. The driver stepped forward, aiming his gun at my face, but I knocked it away just as he fired it near my ear—*BANG!*—and the slide snapped back, the magazine empty. I grabbed onto his wrist and jerked it down onto my knee, the driver screaming as the bone snapped, and then I rose to my feet and kicked him in the chest, sending him to the ground. By then the dust had thinned enough to see clearly—the Corvette up on the highway, the Focus off to the right, my own gun just feet away—and I started toward the gun.

Behind me, I heard a *snick!* and turned to see the driver back on his feet, a switchblade held at his side with his unbroken hand.

He charged at me.

I squared my feet, waiting, and then twisted away at the last moment, dodging the knife. I kneed him in the stomach, heard him groan, but he was much quicker than I took him for. Despite his injury, he managed to slice my arm and elbow me in the face. I stumbled back, my glasses askew, and he was on me again, throwing me to the ground. I used my arm to keep the knife away from my face, but the driver kept it there, the blade pointed at my eye. I struggled, and he struggled, sweat beading on his brow, breathing heavy, his teeth gritted, the point of the blade lowering closer and closer ...

I jerked my head away, pushed his hand gripping the blade to the left, and snapped my head forward into his nose. He stumbled back, letting go of the knife, and I climbed on top of him, used the heel of my sneaker to grind into his broken wrist.

He screamed.

The gun lay only feet away, the knife even closer. I grabbed the knife, flung it away, then stood and went for the gun just as a familiar whine rose up in the distance.

I glanced up and readjusted my glasses.

The Ducati was headed this way, coming from Hope Springs.

I picked up the gun and turned back to the driver. He was still on the ground, holding his broken wrist. I leaned down and grabbed the front of his shirt and pulled him up and stuck the barrel of the gun in his mouth.

"You fucking killed that boy's father."

Despite the gun in his mouth, the driver looked back at me with amusement.

"And you killed one of my people. A close friend."

The driver began to laugh.

I slid the gun back out of his mouth and knocked it against the side of his head. "What's so fucking funny?"

He spat blood and grinned up at me. "You, Ben. You're a fucking joke."

The distant whining had stopped. For the first time I was aware of it and glanced up and saw the rider straddling the bike on the side of the highway. In his hand was a gun—maybe the same gun that had killed those two bent cops back in Miami Beach.

"What do you want?" I shouted.

The rider made no reply.

"I don't need your help. I'm taking care of the situation."

The rider lifted the gun and fired. The ground only feet away from me spat dirt.

"What the fuck?"

The driver saw my lack of attention as an opportunity. He used his undamaged hand to punch me in the face. I fell back, dropping the gun. He scrambled and picked it up, started to aim it at me.

The rider's second shot didn't spit up more dirt. Instead it struck the driver in the shoulder, sending him reeling to the side.

I sat back up. The driver was feet away, his hand still on the gun. I stood and took the few steps to where he lay and kicked him in the stomach. He let go of the gun, and I picked it up and again aimed it at his face.

A third shot echoed across the desert, and once again the ground near my feet spat dirt.

"*What the fuck is your problem?*"

The rider made no response. Coming down the highway

was an SUV. Not the same SUV Jesse and Drew had driven into Hope Springs, but a Cadillac Escalade. As it approached the rider, it didn't slow but swerved off the highway and bounced over the dirt until it came to a stop right in front of us.

The driver's-side front and rear doors opened and two men stepped out. Both of them were Korean. They barely even acknowledged me as they grabbed the driver and dragged him to the SUV. By then the driver had stopped laughing; a flash of fear entered his eyes. He tried speaking but one of the men punched him in the face and he went silent. They had him loaded in seconds. One of the men ran around the back of the SUV to the other side, and the other one started to slide behind the wheel but paused. He stood still for a moment, then turned his head just slightly.

"I'm sorry about your friend," he said, not looking at me. His English was plain, with a hint of an accent.

Then he climbed into the SUV—I could see a third man in the front passenger seat, staring ahead—and slammed the door shut. The Escalade spun out in the dirt. It sped back onto the highway and continued west, away from Hope Springs. The rider stayed where he was for another few seconds, straddling the Ducati, the gun still in his hand, before he holstered the weapon and revved the engine and tore off after the SUV.

FORTY-EIGHT

It had started raining early that Saturday morning, and had continued into the late afternoon, thick, heavy drops falling from the dark and gray impressionist painting that was the sky.

I was on the back porch of the farmhouse, sitting on the swing, staring out at the trees and distant peaks. The moisture in the air felt good, especially in comparison with the stifling Arizona desert where I'd just been less than twenty-four hours ago, and the fresh smell of wet earth was surprisingly pleasant.

Three o'clock in the afternoon and I'd been sitting out here since noon, since we'd had our small memorial service for Jesse. Standing out by the ever-growing cemetery, rain pattering on the umbrellas, Jesse was lowered into the hole Drew and Mason had dug that morning. Not quite six feet, but it was still deep enough, and with heavy ropes the wooden casket Graham had made yesterday was lowered into the ground.

A pack of Marlboro Reds was beside me on the swing. The pack had been unopened when I first sat down. Now the pack was half empty, placed on top of the crinkled cellophane wrapper so it wouldn't blow away.

I'd finished my last cigarette fifteen minutes ago, decided it was time for another. I was just lighting up when the door opened and Maya stepped out.

She walked to the edge of the porch, right on the threshold between wet and dry. She stood there for a long time, staring out at the trees, cupping her elbows. Eventually she turned and came to the swing and sat down beside me. Without a word she took the cigarette from my mouth, placed it between her lips, took a drag, then stared at the end of the cigarette and the wisp of smoke on the end crawling up toward the ceiling.

Like me and Carver, she had stopped smoking awhile back, but some vices are hard to quit.

She handed the cigarette back to me. I finished it, flicked it out over the porch railing.

We sat in silence for several minutes before I cleared my throat.

"Want to know what I've been thinking about?"

Maya did not answer.

"I've been thinking about my daughter. I was remembering that when she was two she asked me one time why it rained. She was picturing that there was actually water up in the sky, like one giant bathtub, and every once in a while God or whoever else was up there pulled the plug and drained the tub."

Thunder rumbled out in the distance, almost lost behind the constant patter of rain.

"And when she asked me I told her the best I could, trying to remember everything I learned in school, about moisture and heat rising and all that. And she sat there on my lap while it rained outside and listened to me and didn't say a word, even when I was done explaining. And I could see the disappointment in her face, a kind of betrayal, as if she was hoping there was a giant bathtub in the sky, and the whole explanation of why it rained was because God or whoever else just decided to pull the plug."

Another rumble of thunder, this one less distinct, the storm finally starting to head away.

"Casey ... she was a great kid. She always just ... she was always asking questions about why things were the way they were. And it wasn't one of those kid things where they ask just to ask, because it's what's expected of them. She really wanted to know. She wanted to learn. Like why does it get cold in the wintertime and hot during the summer. Why is the sky blue. How does the Internet work. I mean, she asked questions that I'd never asked when I was a kid, just ... you know, content with what was there. I'd never cared why it rained. I just knew that when it rained you closed the windows and tried not to get wet. But that wasn't Casey. Casey ... well, she was just like Jen. Jen liked to question things too. She wanted to know how everything worked, why things happened the way they did."

I fell silent, thinking about that myself, about why things happened the way they did, and applying that to my entire life. Applying that to Carver's life, to Jesse's life, to my wife's and daughter's lives, to the lives belonging to all the innocent people I'd encountered over the past two years, people caught in the crossfire. Asking the unanswerable question *Why do things happen like they do?* and understanding that even if there was an answer it probably wouldn't be good to hear it, that it might make us even more frustrated about being alive.

The back door opened. Ronny stepped out this time. He went to stand in the same spot where Maya had stood earlier, his arms folded, his shoulders back, watching the rain and the tops of the trees swaying in the wind.

Maya looked at me, asked me with her eyes if she should leave. When I nodded and watched her get up, start toward the door, I realized that she hadn't said a word to me the entire time she was out here. She hadn't said one word, yet she'd communicated with me just the same, from the look in her eyes, the posture of her body, the way she clasped her hands in her lap.

Then she had entered the farmhouse and my already withering soul felt a little lighter, less substantial, and I understood I truly did love Maya. That I was in love with her, this woman who somehow carried around a piece of my soul so that every time she was with me I felt more whole, more complete, more like the man I had once been in a previous life, content with the world and the things that happened in it.

I took the pack and lit up another cigarette. I sat there puffing away and waited for Ronny to get to it.

I didn't have to wait long.

"How's the new guy?" he asked. "What's his name ... Clark?"

Wasn't quite what I had been expecting, but oh well.

"So far so good," I said. "He's still freaked out. Especially about what happened back in Arizona. He made me promise I wouldn't bring my gun with me next time I go see him. I never had it with me before, but like I said, he's spooked."

His full name was Clark William Gorman, Jr. He'd given me his social security number, his home address, even the password to his and his wife's joint AOL email account, all of which I'd passed on to the Kid and which he'd looked up confirming it all checked out.

I'd gone to see him before the memorial service, and he had changed into the clothes we'd provided, and when I left him he started to read the story of the Man of Wax.

Unlike Mason, Clark actually needed glasses. He hadn't known his prescription off the top of his head, otherwise we would have tried to have a pair of glasses ready for him when he arrived. Instead we had a number of glasses in a box, enough that after trying on about ten of them Clark found a pair that worked okay and which he was wearing now.

"And what are we going to do about him?" Ronny asked.

"I don't know. What are we going to do about Mason?"

There was no answer to either question and we both knew it. Surprisingly, Mason had adjusted very well, that anger inside him never once showing itself. It had only been two days but he helped out around the farmhouse when needed, doing any type of task like helping Beverly in the kitchen or helping Graham when Graham needed to build the casket for Jesse.

Another silence fell between us. The rain continued to fall from the gray clouds, still thick and heavy. More thunder sounded out in the distance. For some reason I thought about the bees down at the apiary, all of them tucked away in their individual hives.

Eventually I said, "Go ahead, Ronny. Say it."

"Say what?"

I took one last drag of the cigarette, flicked it over the railing. Waited.

Ronny sighed, slowly shook his head. "It's not worth it."

"Say it anyway."

"I won't."

"It's my fault. Go ahead and say it. It'll make you feel better."

"Ben, I'm not going to do that. Your mistakes … it's not my job to keep you accountable. I've learned all about forgiveness through God, and—"

"Don't fucking talk to me about God."

He stared at me, his eyes slightly narrowed, his bearded jaw set.

"God has never done one good thing for me."

The rain was letting up, the tapping on the top of the porch overhang less persistent now.

Ronny said, "I'm sorry you feel that way."

"Yeah, well. What are you really out here for?"

"Beverly and I are leaving."

"When?"

"In a couple days. Maybe a week. We've already discussed it with Graham and the Kid. Both are fine with it."

"Of course they are."

"Why are you so dead set against this? Why can't you accept change?"

"I can accept change. My whole life is one big fucking change."

"I will miss you, Ben. And I will be praying for you."

"Thanks, Ronny. I don't know how my soul has gotten this far without you."

He didn't say anything else. He just sat there beside me for a little while longer before he stood and went back inside, leaving me alone with the rain tapping the overhang and the dwindling pack of cigarettes beside me on the swing.

FORTY-NINE

Clark looked even more dejected when I brought him his dinner.

By that time the rain had stopped, God or whoever else reinserting the plug in the gigantic bathtub in the sky. Still the trees were wet, dripping drops on the holding cell's roof, a soft and arrhythmic beat.

Drew had come with me, nodded hello to Clark, but then after a minute decided the holding cell was a bit too cramped and went to wait outside.

Clark whispered, "What happened to his face?"

He was on the cot, the plate of Salisbury steaks on his lap. He had a knife in his left hand, a fork in his right. The way he was cutting the steaks into small bites, chewing quietly, all that was needed to complete the picture of perfect etiquette was a napkin tucked in the front of his shirt collar.

"That's a story for another time. How are you feeling?"

He took another small bite. Glanced up at me with wariness in his dejected eyes.

"Not well," he said, and placed his knife and fork on the plate. "I'm feeling … sick."

"Your stomach?"

"My stomach, yes, but also my heart. My head. My entire *being*. My whole body feels sick. I read about half of that"—he gestured at the manuscript on the floor—"and I just ... I keep thinking about Susan and Brett and Matthew. About what's happening to them right now. I just—I can't stop thinking it's somehow my fault."

"None of it's your fault. You did the best you could. In the end, you wouldn't have been able to save them."

"But how do you know?"

"I used to be exactly where you were. I used to think there was still a chance, that there was hope. But ... do you know what hope is? Hope is hopeless."

Clark shook his head. Tears brimmed in his eyes. He took off his glasses to wipe at them.

"My wife and sons," he said, looking down at his lap, "they're my life. They're all I know. They can't ... they *can't* be dead."

At moments like these there's nothing for you to say, so I said nothing. I looked away from him. Listened to the irregular beat on the holding cell roof. Listened to the distant, faint sound of thunder.

Clark looked back up at me, wiped at his eyes, his nose. He gestured again at the manuscript. "How long ago did that happen?"

"Two years."

"And ... are you different?"

I nodded.

"How so?"

I thought about it for a moment. "In my old life, the one with my family, I never once thought I would touch a gun, let alone fire one."

"But you did?"

"Yes."

"What else?"

I sat there silent, not wanting to continue. But this man needed to hear the truth. He deserved that much.

"In my old life, I never once thought I'd ever hurt someone, let alone"—I cleared my throat—"kill someone."

His face instantly went white. "You've … killed people?"

"Yes."

"But … why?"

"They were bad people."

"But don't you"—he shrugged, trying to find the words—"don't you feel guilty?"

I took another moment to think about that. "Not really. At first I did. It wasn't something easy to accept. But after a while … I just became numb to it."

He swallowed. "When are you going to let me out of here?"

The drops of rain continuing to tap … tap, tap … tap.

"How long have I even been in here?"

That distant sound of thunder fading away and then growing stronger.

"Ben?" He waved at me through the bars to get my attention. "Hello?"

The leftover drops of rain continuing to fall but the sound of thunder growing stronger and stronger.

Clark stood up from his cot. He walked to the bars of the cell. "Are you okay?"

The growing sound of thunder, and I was thinking about all the times I had been in here, not that many but enough to know that it was always quiet, except when it rained and when it thundered and what I was hearing now was not thunder.

"Ben? What's wrong?"

Carver had specifically built this holding cell in the middle of nowhere. Besides the occasional sound of an airliner jet flying thirty thousand feet up in the air, there almost always silence.

"Hey"—Clark hit the bars with his fists—"Ben, are you okay?"

The drops of leftover rain continuing to fall but the sound of thunder even closer.

Clark said, "Do you know what you look like sitting there?"

I'd been watching Clark from the corner of my eye, watching him get up from the cot and make his way to the bars, watching him strike the bars with his fists to get my attention. But now I turned my head, focused my gaze on his face— his face no longer resembling the man we'd rescued from Hope Springs, Arizona, the man who had been scared out of his mind and worried for the fate of his wife and two sons.

Now his face was accompanied by a slight and subtle sneer. The tears that had been so prevalent in his eyes seconds ago were gone. He took off his glasses and tossed them in the corner. He rubbed the bridge of his nose, rubbed his eyes not of tears but the irritation the prescription had caused his vision.

"You look just like a man of wax." He smiled. "I have to admit, you guys are good. You knocked me out so I wouldn't be a problem when you brought me here. So I wouldn't even know where this place was. And you no doubt scanned me for any tracking devices. That's smart, too. I remember reading about it when your story first appeared online. So you know what we did instead?" He opened his mouth wide and used a finger to tap one of the rear molars. "Had this baby inserted. Was completely dead until I woke up and turned it on. Didn't see that on your cameras, did you?"

The door behind me burst open.

Drew rushed inside and shouted, "We have to get out of here!"

Clark barely even acknowledged the disruption, keeping his gaze level with mine. "After all this time, all the bullshit you put us through, now it's over."

I didn't know when it happened, but I had risen to my feet.

Clark said, "You know the best way to win a game of cat and mouse?"

Outside, the thunder that wasn't thunder was so very close.

"If you're the cat, you become a mouse. Let the other mice lead you back to their den."

Drew stepped up beside me, grabbed my arm. "Ben, let's go."

"I don't know why we didn't try this earlier," Clark said. "This worked perfectly. Remember, Ben, misdirection—the public falls for it every time."

The thunder was so close now it was distinct—not just one helicopter but two.

I nodded at Drew, turned, and started toward the door leading outside.

"You know, Ben," Clark said, "I was the one that took you and your family from your house."

I stopped.

"Your wife was in her underwear. I remember they were these pink silk panties."

The helicopters were directly above us, their rotors thumping the air.

"She was a beautiful woman. One of a kind. Great breasts, too. I'll admit it, I copped a feel. Nice and supple. A lot nicer than your daughter's."

I spun back around and started toward the holding cell.

Drew stepped in front of me. "Just leave it. We have to go now."

"By the way," Clark said, standing with his fingers casually wrapped around the bars, "there's something you don't know about me. I love to torture. I get off on it. In fact, I was the one that cut off your wife's finger. She kept crying the entire time. She kept blaming you, Ben. She kept asking why you weren't coming to save her."

I tried pushing past Drew. Drew kept holding me back.

"I said to her softly, 'Don't worry about it, baby. You're not gonna feel a thing.'"

Drew was stronger and bigger than me. I wasn't going to be able to push past him. I stepped back and said to him, "Give me your gun."

Clark chuckled. "You were being so kind to me, Ben, not bringing your gun when I'd asked you not to. Because guns really scare me, don't you know? They scare me to death."

Drew said, "It's outside on the four-wheeler."

Clark's smile started to fade. "Four-wheeler?"

I said, "You assholes think you're so smart? You're not smart enough."

I nodded again at Drew, and we turned and started toward the door.

"She was a real beauty, that wife of yours," Clark said. "At least she was before I started in with my knife."

Drew hurried through the door to start up the four-wheelers, leaving me alone. I stopped before the door, though, and stood completely still.

"You know exactly what I'm talking about, don't you, Ben? I know you watched it. You watched me stab her here, and stab her here, and stab her here."

Everything in my shaking body wanted me to turn back and storm the holding cell. I had the key. I could open the cell. I could beat Clark to death with my fists.

"Right here, Ben, right here in the throat. That's the best place to stab someone. That way they drown to death in their own blood. That's what really gives me a fucking hard-on. And after your wife, I went and did the same to your little bitch of a daughter." He laughed. "But what am I saying? You watched it all, didn't you? Of course you did. Say, Ben, how many times did you watch me kill your family?"

Beside the door was the plastic screen covering the two red

buttons. I pulled it up and hit the first, nearly smashing it to pieces. But still it did its job, frying the cameras that sent the signal to the farmhouse. Outside, I heard Drew starting the four-wheelers, their engines mostly undercut by the helicopters. Once I hit the second button, we would have sixty seconds.

I turned back around, my hands clenched into fists, my entire body fuming.

"Is your name really Clark?"

He smiled and shrugged. "Why don't you stay and find out?"

"Well, whatever your name is, when you and I meet again? I'm going to fucking kill you."

And I turned, smacked the second button, and sprinted outside.

FIFTY

There were only two helicopters, what looked through the trees to be Black Hawks, and they were doing just what I had suspected—circling around, trying to find a place to land.

Only problem was for them, there weren't any places to land. Not for at least three miles in any direction.

This was, after all, Colorado. Trees covered half the state. After the Christian Kane incident, Carver had become paranoid something like that might happen again. Even worse, Simon might try to send one of his own men into the game. With that fear in mind he had us build this holding cell in the middle of nowhere. A holding cell that had taken months to construct, multiple trips with very little equipment because all that fit through the trees were four-wheelers. Four-wheelers that we used every time we came out here, toward the sound of the generator that provided electricity for whoever was inside.

Because if the mice were smart and brought another mouse back to their den, they wouldn't bring it back to their real den until they were sure—one hundred percent certain—that the mouse was really a mouse and not a cat disguised as a mouse.

But Carver, being ever so paranoid, didn't stop there. He

created a failsafe on the off chance a cat did manage to make it through to the mouse's den. He set up several flash bombs around the holding cell, some very close, others hundreds of yards away. They were triggered to go off sixty seconds after the emergency button inside the holding cell was engaged.

Drew was already on his four-wheeler, gunning the engine. He looked back at me, started to shout something, but then his gaze shifted. He grabbed for his gun, aimed it high, and fired.

I looked up. A rope had appeared through the treetops. A man in black was rappelling down the rope. When Drew's bullet hit him, his body jerked and went still.

I hurried over to the second four-wheeler. On the seat were my radio and gun. I secured the gun in the waistband of my jeans. I grabbed the radio and placed it to my mouth. There was no cell reception this far out, but shortwave radios worked from here to the farmhouse. I keyed the radio and shouted, "*Ronny, Maya, whoever—bring the pickup to mile marker eighty-five. Be there in twenty minutes!*"

Drew fired at another man in black rappelling down another rope. One of the helicopters returned fire.

"*Go!*" I shouted at Drew. I climbed onto the four-wheeler and gunned the engine.

We took off into the trees … just as the sixty seconds elapsed and all around us the flash bombs began to erupt.

If the men in the helicopters had heat sensors—and we had to assume they did, as Caesar's people had all the cool toys—they would be able to track us from the air. With the flash bombs, we might just be lucky enough to escape their cover.

The daylight was fleeting but there was still just enough for us to see. Besides, we knew the trails. Carver had made it a point to create a few that crisscrossed just in case, and he had us ride them enough times that we knew all the turns. One of the flash bombs went off right by the trail. I flinched, thinking the helicopters were bombing us. Then I was past it, followed by Drew, and we rode up and over the hills and fallen tree stumps, branches slapping at our faces.

Several minutes later we stopped and abandoned the four-wheelers. Normally we took them to a completely different location, where we stored them in a hidden shed and then walked a half mile to our vehicle. Now we were never coming back here, and we were not chancing anything.

We hurried through the trees. We could barely hear the helicopters off in the distance. By now the men in the helicopters would have made it through the trees to the ground. They would have made it inside and found Clark—or whatever his real name was—behind the bars. But that would be it.

Drew and I hustled for another ten minutes until we reached the highway. It was mile marker eighty-three—my guesstimation had been close enough. The stretch of road was deserted. I was about to pull out the radio when movement caught my eye. A tractor-trailer appeared around the bend. It was pulling a long bed of logs. The thing was stacked high, the heavy metal prongs on each side of the flatbed keeping them in place.

"Try them again?" Drew asked.

I nodded and put the radio to my mouth. Then I spotted the red pickup trailing the logging truck. Drew and I broke cover and sprinted up the slope.

Seconds later the logging truck roared past us. The red pickup eased to a stop. Ronny was behind the wheel.

"What happened?" he asked.

Drew climbed in first. I slammed the door shut and shouted at Ronny to move it. Ronny punched the gas.

"What *happened?*" he asked again.

"They came for us."

"How?"

"The son of a bitch had a tracking device in his goddamn

molar." I lashed out, slamming my fist against the dash. "Motherfucker!"

We drove for another minute in silence. The road twisted and turned. I didn't know why, but when the dark sedan came speeding around the bend in the oncoming lane, something dropped in the pit of my stomach.

"Fuck," I said.

Ronny glanced at me. "What's wrong?"

The sedan came up fast. For a moment I had the childish thought that if I closed my eyes and didn't look at the sedan, it wouldn't be real. But I kept my eyes open. I looked.

For a split-second as the sedan whipped past us, the two men in the front wearing wraparound sunglasses like the Blues Brothers looked back.

"Hit the gas," I said.

Ronny knew better than to question me. He heard the urgency in my voice. He pressed his foot down even more on the gas pedal, and the pickup accelerated.

I glanced back through the pickup's rear window. The sedan's taillights were already flaring. The car appeared to rock back and forth for a moment, teetering, before the driver executed a hasty one-eighty.

"Here they come," Ronny said, his gaze momentarily on the rearview mirror.

I reached for the glove compartment. Inside were two spare magazines—we always kept extras in our vehicles. I took them both out and handed one to Drew. Then I pressed the button to lower the side window.

"What are you doing?" Ronny asked.

"Heading out to get some fresh air." I glanced at Drew. "Want to come with?"

Drew nodded.

I stuffed the magazine in my pocket, went to grab the caution bar. This part of the highway was not level and straight.

The pavement was still wet and slick. Any false move and I would be toast. I squeezed the caution bar tight, took a deep breath, and pulled myself through the window.

It wasn't as easy as I thought it would be, not with Ronny already driving nearly eighty miles per hour. I almost lost my balance once when I attempted to put my right foot on the window, but then I managed to crawl back into the pickup's bed. I pulled the gun from my pocket, checked the magazine, slapped it back in place.

The sedan was coming right up our ass. The passenger's window lowered, and one of the Blues Brothers leaned out with a gun.

I moved toward the back of the pickup bed on my knees, aimed, and opened fire.

Despite Ronny swerving the pickup around the curves and my heart blasting away in my chest, my aim was steady. The bullets struck the sedan's windshield—each bullet making a sort of splat in the glass—but that was as far as they got. There was no penetration. The driver barely even flinched.

The passenger, who had ducked inside during my volley, leaned back out. He opened fire.

I flattened myself on the pickup's bed. My foot hit something solid. As Ronny began swerving the pickup even more, trying to evade the bullets, I glanced back and saw Drew lying flat too.

"*What happened?*" he shouted.

"*The windshield's bulletproof!*"

Ronny hit a tight curve, tapping the brakes enough to send us rolling across the pickup's bed. There was a lull in the sedan's gunfire. I peeked up and redirected my aim, this time going for the grill.

The burst of bullets was temporarily drowned out by a logging truck roaring past in the opposite direction. This truck had a shorter bed, with even thicker logs stacked in the back.

These were not contained by heavy metal prongs, but by two thick chains.

I checked the highway ahead of us. Another one of these logging trucks was coming our way.

"*Drew!*" I shouted, and lifted my chin at the oncoming truck.

He glanced back, then nodded at me. "*Keep me covered!*"

I turned back to the sedan. The passenger was leaning out the window again. I fired, first at the windshield, then again at the grill, until I ran out of bullets. I let the magazine drop, slapped in the spare, opened fire again.

The space between the sedan and pickup was maybe two hundred feet. It was going to be tight. I glanced back and saw Drew kneeling with his left arm balanced on the side of the bed, waiting for the right moment. I knew if anyone could make this work, it would be him. He was our sharpshooter. This was what he trained for. Even if, when it all came down to it, we were relying on luck.

The logging truck roared past and Drew opened fire. I saw the bullets tearing into the chains and logs. The first chain snapped. The second didn't.

"*Shit!*" he shouted. He looked at me, and his eyes went wide. "*Ben!*"

I hit the bed just as another round of bullets tore into back of the pickup. Ronny started swerving again.

I shouted back at Drew, "*Are you out?*"

He shook his head, pulled the spare magazine from his pocket.

"*We're going to have to take out that windshield! Give it everything we have!*"

The pickup suddenly increased even more in speed. The entire bed vibrated. Ronny, who had been keeping low behind the wheel, slid open the rear window.

"*Here comes another one!*"

I closed my eyes. Not another sedan. We were barely keeping this one away, and we were almost out of bullets.

Ronny shouted, "*Make it count!*"

I looked at Drew. Drew looked at me. Ronny swerved the pickup again, creating another lull in the sedan's gunfire. It gave me enough time to sneak a peek. Nothing was behind the sedan. But ahead of us was another logging truck, coming fast.

Drew saw it too. He was already getting into position.

"*I'll cover you and then go for the rear chain!*"

He nodded.

I aimed again at the sedan's windshield. My finger tightened on the trigger. I fired twice, then turned to my right, settled my arm on the side of the bed, and took aim.

It literally happened in a flash of slow motion. The logging truck passed us. The world exploded into a giant cacophony of gunfire. Bits and chips of wood spat up from the logs. Like before, the first chain snapped. Like before, the second chain didn't.

At least, it didn't at first.

The logging truck roared past just like its predecessor. Unlike its predecessor, it didn't keep going. The driver slammed on the brakes. The rear began to fishtail. The sudden halting jolt was enough to snap the second chain. The logs started rolling off the flatbed.

They rolled right into the highway.

Right into the sedan.

The sedan was already going at least eighty miles per hour. Maybe that was its undoing. The driver never had a chance to stop. Instead he swerved into the oncoming logs. The momentum and velocity was enough to flip the sedan, sending it reeling off the highway into the trees.

Drew and I both watched it happen. It took only a second. Then the road curved and the whole thing was gone from view.

We went to the front of the truck. The rear window was still open. Miraculously it hadn't been hit.

I leaned my head in. "You okay?"

Ronny nodded. "What about you guys?"

"We're fine."

"That was intense."

"Tell me about it." I looked up through the windshield. "Pull off at the next road. We're going to need to ditch this thing."

"And then what, walk ten miles through the woods?"

"That or call Maya to come pick us up. Either way, those guys no doubt called in our location. One of those Black Hawks might be coming along at any moment."

Ronny was silent behind the wheel for a second. "I can't wait to be done with this stuff."

"I know what you mean."

He looked at me. "Do you?"

There was more to the simple question than I cared to admit. I decided to ignore it for now and said, "But before we officially disband, I think we all need to take a trip to Washington, D.C."

"Why?"

"I figure before we all part ways, Carver's memory deserves some payback."

"What are you talking about?"

"Boojum," I said. "The son of a bitch that sold Carver out. I think it's time we finally meet him face to face."

FIFTY-ONE

"This is Stark."

"Hey, Ed."

"Carver?"

"I was thinking about our last conversation."

"Where are you?"

"I'm here."

"Here? Here where?"

"Washington."

"What—what are you doing in Washington?"

"I want to meet."

"You do?"

"Yes. Are you busy?"

"Actually, right now I am, yes."

"I'm at the Holocaust Museum. I want you to meet me outside the main entrance in ten minutes."

"Ten minutes? I can't make that."

"I already called you a taxi. There's one waiting outside your building right now along Pennsylvania Avenue."

"How do you know where I am?"

"Ten minutes, Ed. Don't be late."

"Carver, I can't—"

I clicked off, slipped the iPhone into my pocket. The Kid had rigged the same voice manipulation application onto the phone that was on his computer. Like before, while it was my voice coming out of my mouth, it was Carver's voice going into Edward Stark's ear.

As promised, a taxi was parked in front of the J. Edgar Hoover Building on Pennsylvania Avenue. It had pulled up right when I called Stark. That had been a minute ago. Another minute and it would have to move along. More than a decade had already passed since 9/11, but still people were extra cautious. Especially the FBI.

I stood across the street, on the corner of Pennsylvania Avenue and 10th Street, the Office of the Attorney General behind me. I wore a gray suit, dress shoes, my prescription sunglasses. In my left hand was a briefcase. It was Monday, and in Washington a suit and briefcase won't bring you a second glance. Probably won't even bring you a first glance.

I knew Edward Stark was inside the Hoover Building. I had watched him enter it two hours ago. Now it was nearly ten o'clock in the morning. Everyone was in position. Either he made his appearance or he didn't. If he did, things would progress as planned. If he didn't, we would need to improvise.

Less than a minute after I disconnected my call with him, Edward Stark appeared. He came out of the entrance doors, a tall broad-shouldered man wearing a suit. He paused for a moment, scanning the street. He spotted the maroon taxi. He took a step toward it but stopped. Seemed to think something over, then started walking again toward the taxi.

He didn't get inside it.

Instead he went to the curb directly behind the taxi and raised his hand to the oncoming traffic. Another taxi—this one a blue Town Car—eased to a stop. Stark climbed in the back, and the Town Car merged with traffic.

I touched my earpiece. "We're a go."

Across the street, the maroon taxi pulled away from the curb. Drew was behind the wheel, a driver's cap on his head. He knew I was standing on the corner but kept his focus on the street as he drove past.

I turned and started south down 10th Street.

Based on this morning's traffic—D.C. is flooded with traffic—it was going to take the blue Town Car several minutes to get to where it was going. Stark had no doubt told the driver to go to the Holocaust Museum. And that was where the driver would seem to be taking him.

Except the driver had a detour planned—turning left onto 12th Street, then, waiting for the light, turning left again onto Constitution Avenue. It was in the opposite direction Stark would want to go—the Holocaust Museum was west, while he would be headed east—but there wasn't much he could do about it. Not while the car was in motion. And when it came to the light at the next block, I was already waiting at the curb.

As the blue Town Car slowed and stopped, I stepped toward it, my hand slipping into my pocket. I opened the door and climbed in beside Stark, who, judging by the way he was reaching for his gun, knew he was in trouble.

"Hey there, Eddie," I said, and jabbed the methohexital pen into his neck.

The light changed, and traffic began to move forward.

Ronny, behind the wheel, merged us with it.

FIFTY-TWO

When Edward Stark awoke, he was tied to a metal folding chair, naked except for his boxer shorts.

We had already scanned him for any tracking devices—not just his clothes but every inch of his body in case one had been slipped beneath his skin—and he appeared clean. We also checked and then double-checked his teeth, and besides two capped molars, they were normal.

Besides two cell phones—a BlackBerry and the burner he had been using to communicate with Carver—he had his wallet, his credentials, a tiny tin of Altoids, a dry cleaning receipt, and his gun. The piece was a standard issued Glock 22. It, like everything else, had also been scanned.

Plastic zip ties kept his ankles in place to the chair legs. His wrists were bound behind his back. On his chest, right above his heart, was an inch-wide patch taped to his skin. It, just like a smaller patch taped to his temple, was attached to wires running to a laptop set up directly behind him. Maya sat behind the laptop, monitoring his heart rate and his brainwaves, the program all courtesy of the Kid. Ronny and Drew were outside keeping watch of the perimeter.

I sat on a metal folding chair directly across from Stark. His head was hanging down. When he started to raise it, blinking, I leaned forward.

"Hello, Eddie."

He looked up at me. First there was confusion in his eyes, followed quickly by understanding. His eyes widened slightly. He tried to speak but couldn't. Not with the strip of duct tape over his mouth.

"I don't want to draw this out. The past two weeks haven't been very good to me, as you can imagine. Getting shot at, almost getting killed—these are all things that damages a person's psyche. So why am I here now? To tell you that you win. Well, not *you* so much as Caesar. Whatever the fuck Caesar has planned, we can't stop it. I'll be the first to admit that. All of us—the ones that haven't yet been killed—will soon be going our separate ways. Before we do, though, I wanted to meet you. In many ways, we're all connected to you. I mean, if it wasn't for you fucking Carver over, he never would have started his battle against Simon and Caesar, and he never would have saved us from the games."

Stark stared back at me calmly. Almost too calmly.

"Now, if you think about it, we all probably would have been thrown into the games regardless if anything had ever happened to Carver. But the fact is, we were thrown into the games, and Carver got us out, and our families are all dead, and those of us still alive are still fucking pissed about that."

On the ground beside my chair was a knife. I picked it up.

"Two years ago I never once considered myself a violent man. But … well, things change. I used to think torture was disgusting and vile. That what the government did at Guantanamo was just wrong. But you know, I've started to understand something. There comes a point when you just don't give a fuck anymore. And unfortunately for you, I've long since stopped giving a fuck."

I crouched down in front of Stark. I placed the blade of the knife against his pinkie toe. His foot twitched, but that was the only reaction.

"My wife's finger was sent to me in a box. Did you know that? They even kept her wedding ring on it."

Steel pressed against flesh, but I hesitated. I thought about Jen and I thought about Casey and I thought about just how damaged I had become. It wasn't that I had wanted to become the person I was now, but that I'd had no choice. Mercy was a word with no definition.

I pressed down on the knife. Stark's foot twitched again. His entire body didn't buck in pain as I had imagined it would, not even when the blade severed the toe. The duct tape over his mouth muffled a slight groan. His eyes slid shut. But that was it.

Beneath his chair was a box of gauze. I took some and placed it against the wound and applied pressure.

"I don't know how long we're going to do this," I said, standing back up to look him straight in the eye, "but the last thing I want right now is for you to pass out from the pain. Though, let me guess. Assholes like you don't feel pain. That's why you've hardly even made a sound yet."

Stark just stared back at me. He didn't move or make any noise. Then, softly, he made a sound. Just one syllable.

"What's that?"

He made the sound again.

I glanced past him at Maya. She didn't seem ready to meet my eyes. She'd known what the plan was from the beginning, and she had gone along with it, but she was clearly disturbed by my actions. On some level, so was I. But that didn't stop me from continuing.

I turned back to Stark. "Right now we're in the basement of an abandoned warehouse just outside of D.C. If I take this tape off, you can scream all you want, but nobody will hear you."

He made the sound again, that one simple syllable.

I took a loose corner of the duct tape and peeled it off his mouth. I did it slowly, much slower than was needed, until there was very little tape still sticking to his skin and then I ripped that off.

"Ben," he said. His eyes were glassy. His body trembled slightly. He was in pain but was trying his best not to show it.

"That's my name. What about it?"

"You have the wrong idea."

"Is that right?"

"I'm not who you think I am."

"And who do I think you are?"

"In league with Caesar."

"You're not?"

He shook his head. "God, no."

I glanced past him but Maya was still looking away. Her gaze was on the laptop screen but it was clear she wasn't really watching it.

Without a word I walked past him to the folding table, stepping over the wires. I leaned down close to Maya and whispered in her ear, "Do we have a problem?"

She blinked, sat back, looked up at me with surprise. The reaction was of someone snapping out of a daydream. She stared at me for a long moment. "No," she said, but her voice was so quiet I barely even heard it.

"If you don't think you can continue with this, go outside and relieve Drew. He can take over."

"No"—her voice still soft as she shook her head—"I'm fine."

It was then I first noticed the laptop screen. The graph it showed was the same from the Kid's computer. Even with the lines bouncing with Stark's voice. Before, when I had spoken to him on the phone, the lines had been a combination of greens and red like a Christmas decoration. Now they were all green.

I grabbed the laptop and hurried back to Stark. I pulled my chair closer and set the laptop on the seat and tilted it so only I could see the screen.

"What's your name?"

He stared back at me, confused. His eyes shifted between me and the laptop.

"What's your name?" I repeated.

"Edward Lee Stark."

The lines were green.

"When were you born?"

"August nineteenth, 1954."

The lines stayed green.

"Tell me a lie."

"What?"

"Tell me a lie."

"I don't—" He paused, thinking. "I know who Caesar is."

The lines went red.

"Bullshit," I said.

"I don't know his real name, who he really is. I don't even know what he looks like. I just know he exists. And that those very high up in the Inner Circle call him Augustus."

I watched his eyes, looking for any signs of deceit. I checked the computer screen again. All the lines were green.

"You don't seem surprised to see me."

He shook his head.

"But as far as you knew, you were speaking to Carver. Both today and last week."

"I knew it wasn't Carver both times. In fact, I was hoping it would be you."

The lines were green.

"What do you mean, you were hoping it would be me. I don't even know you."

"No," Stark said, "but I know you."

"How?"

"What you wrote two years ago. About your game."

"You saw that?"

"Yes."

"And just because you read that I'm supposed to, what, believe that you're telling the truth?"

"Ben, I am not the enemy here. I did not fuck Carver over, either."

The lines stayed green.

"You turned him in," I said.

"I didn't. At least, not on purpose. At my position at the time, I had several different bosses above me. I had been told that if anything strange ever came across the Internet, I was to thank whoever found it and say it would be reassigned elsewhere. And I really believed it at the time. Then Carver came and showed me what he did and I told him it would be reassigned and I thought that was it. I sent it up to my bosses. They told me it would be taken care of. Then, later, Carver came back and showed me even more. I began to suspect something was wrong, so I told him I would put him in charge of the investigation. Next thing I knew, I was notified that Carver had been transferred. They didn't say where, but that he was doing important work. I'm not sure I even believed them then, but I knew better than to make waves. I did email Carver the next week, and promptly received a reply saying he was swamped and would get back to me. He never did."

"That wasn't Carver."

Stark shook his head. "No, it wasn't. But at the time I believed it was. Then a couple years passed and I was sent your story."

"Who sent it?" I asked, but immediately I knew. It all made sense now. While the Kid had helped post it wherever he could online, Carver had made it a point to briefly contact his old supervisor. The man who he believed had been responsible for

Carver losing his family. He had sent it as a way of saying, *I know what you did and I will never forget.*

"Carver," Stark said. "At least, I assume it was Carver. It was sent from an anonymous Hotmail account. I replied but there was never any response."

"So when did Carver contact you next?" I knew the answer to this too but wanted to hear it from Edward Stark's own lips.

"Less than a year ago. He emailed me out of the blue. I wasn't even sure it was him at first. I was worried Simon and the rest of them were on to me."

"How so?"

"After I read about your game, I started my own investigation. I knew if your story was true—and I believed it was, having double-checked the stories about the bombing in Ryder, Illinois, and that cop getting shot in Chicago—then this went very high up. I ended up in contact with Francis Houser. Her nickname is Frank. She's a congresswoman for the state of North Carolina."

"What does she have to do with any of this?" It didn't occur to me then that I hadn't been checking the laptop screen. I did now, and saw that all the lines except that one for the forced lie were green.

"She's a member of the Inner Circle."

I wasn't sure what to say to this.

"Don't worry," Stark said, "she's on our side. It was her husband who was a member, and even he hadn't been fully aware of what he was getting into at the time. He's dead now. Died of a heart attack a few years back. She became a member by proxy. She's been helping me try to figure out a way to bring this entire thing down. But it's difficult. This whole thing, it's just way too big."

"You mean in our government?"

"I mean *globally*. There are games all around the world. Some are bigger than others."

"How many members are there in the Inner Circle?"

"The Inner Circle itself isn't very large. There are maybe a thousand members, all said. But those who watch the games? There are *millions*. And more sign up every day."

"I thought the games were top secret."

"They are."

"Then how can they allow so many people to join?"

"Do you still look at pornography?"

"What?"

"Do you?"

"No."

"But when you did, did anyone know?"

"Besides my father-in-law and Simon, no."

"It's the same way here. People know when to keep a secret. They know because their lives depend on it. That's made very clear from the start. If word gets out, whoever leaked it will be killed, as will their family and friends. Some have tried, just to test the system. They're all dead."

"You know what I just realized?" I asked.

"What's that?"

"You haven't once asked for Carver."

"Why would I ask for him? I know he's not with you."

"Exactly."

There was a silence, both of us waiting for the other one to speak.

Stark said, "You don't know, do you."

"About what?"

"Carver."

"Carver is dead."

Stark shook his head. "No, he isn't."

"I was there. I saw him get killed."

"You may have *thought* you saw him get killed, but he wasn't. He was shot, yes, but he's not dead."

My eyes shifted to the laptop screen, at all those green lines, then up to Maya who was staring back at me with alarm.

"What the fuck are you talking about?"

"I'd been hoping you would contact me," Stark said. "I didn't know how to get in contact with you. Not after I found out about it."

"Found out about what?"

"The Coliseum. That's what they're calling it. It will be the first of its kind."

I shook my head as if trying to clear it. "You're not making sense."

"When you had called the first time, I worried they were on to me. I knew it wasn't Carver. I knew about what happened down in Miami Beach. So then I thought it might be you, but I couldn't just come out and say it."

"*Hey*," I shouted. "What are you talking about? What about Carver?"

"He's alive."

I stood in front of Stark, the laptop beside me, but I was no longer in the warehouse basement. Instead I was back in Miami Beach, on the third floor of the Beachside Hotel, having just watched Carver get shot, now trying to pull him back to safety.

"They set the entire thing up to trap him," Stark said. "They didn't want to kill him—at least not yet."

I was dragging Carver over the blue carpet speckled with seashells, keeping my gun aimed, waiting for the shooter as Carver coughed up blood and tried to speak.

"They've been keeping him alive ever since. For the Coliseum. Like I said, it's the first of its kind."

I got Carver around the corner by the elevators, leaving a trail of his blood in our wake, and still he was attempting to produce his one word, still he was coughing up blood.

"The games have been going on for decades. The Inner

Circle has existed for just as long. But never before have they all come together in one place."

After firing down the hall, trying to keep the shooter at a distance, I was back with Carver and staring into his paling face and hearing him speak his last word.

"Whatever Caesar has been working towards, it's almost complete. He plans to present it to the Inner Circle this weekend."

I was listening as Carver repeated his final word, this time saying it louder, and the look in his eyes changed, expressing something that I never thought I would see, something I didn't want to believe was true.

"But before that, Caesar has a surprise for them, though by now everyone knows what it is. They know it's Carver, and they're all excited."

I saw myself leaving him, running toward the fire door, sensing movement behind me and turning back.

"For the past five years Carver has become their ultimate antagonist. They are all rich and powerful people, and he is not, and yet he has managed to hurt them time and again."

I saw myself turning back, watching the shooter as he raised the silver handgun and fired at Carver's face. I heard myself shouting no and wanting to raise my own gun but not having the chance because the shooter was faster. I saw him firing at me, the shots deafening but somehow wide too because I miraculously wasn't hit as I tore through the fire door … the fire door, I now remembered, which hadn't been marked at all when I returned to find Carver's body gone.

"Caesar plans to kill him there, in front of everyone. Don't you get it yet, Ben? Carver's dying will be the official beginning of the end. It will be the grand finale."

PART III

THE COLISEUM

FIFTY-THREE

From the outside, the Fillmore Theater looked just like any other building along West 43rd Street.

It stood right in the middle of the block, four stories high and made completely of granite. Narrow rectangular windows overlooked the street from every floor. Glass double doors made up the main entrance. Off to the left, when facing the building, was the entrance for the underground parking garage.

Nondescript would be the best way to describe the Fillmore. Just one anonymous building among a thousand anonymous buildings huddled around Manhattan. It was the kind of building you might glance at when you passed by, but nothing about it would leave a lasting impression in your mind.

It was just a building—nothing more, nothing less. The only thing special about it was that tonight it was where the highest and most elite members of the Inner Circle would gather, to witness the games played firsthand, to sit before Caesar and all his wisdom and hear what he had to say and then watch with awe as he took Carver Ellison's life.

It was Saturday morning and Ronny and I, like we'd done the past three days, passed the Fillmore on foot. We were on the other side of the street, walking side by side. Neither of us spoke as we continued down the sidewalk, our stride purposeful, Ronny chewing a piece of gum while I smoked a cigarette. Then we came to the corner and waited for the light to change.

"Anything?" Ronny asked.

I took one last drag of my cigarette, dropped it to the dirty sidewalk and ground it out with the heel of my sneaker.

"Nope."

"What about Mason?"

I shook my head.

The light changed and we continued on with the rest of the swarm of people crossing Ninth Avenue.

Ronny had shaved his beard four days ago when we first arrived to the city. He said it was the first time he'd shaved it since he was in high school. Not even on his wedding day had he shaved it, despite his wife's protests. Looking back, he said he should have granted her that simple wish. He said the reason he didn't was the cleft in his chin that he had always been self-conscious about, ever since middle school when the kids would call him Butt Chin. But he had decided he needed a change. He was forty-five years old and he figured he had more important things to worry about. After he'd shaved it, spots of tissue paper dotting his meaty jowls, he'd asked Maya what she thought and she had smiled and said he looked good enough to eat.

Right now Ronny was wearing a Yankees baseball cap low over his face. He had on a light jacket, his hands in the big pockets. In the left pocket was his semi-automatic.

I wasn't wearing a hat. The sky was overcast but still it was bright enough to allow me to wear my prescription sunglasses without looking like a complete jackass. It had allowed me to check out the Fillmore as we'd walked past, searching for any movement from any of the windows, from the main entrance, from even the gaping maw of the parking garage. Nothing. Just like it had been for the past three days. Would have been nice to get a place across the street, an apartment or office where we could set up our surveillance, but this was New York City, and in New York City it practically took a miracle to get a half-decent parking spot.

We crossed Eighth Avenue, heading against the one-way traffic. The city is usually loud, but it grew even louder as we neared Times Square. The constant traffic and the people and the construction that was never on the street you were walking but a block or two away, though if you ever tried searching for that construction you might find yourself walking for an hour with only weariness and impatience to show for it.

And the smell wasn't any better. I'd been in almost every major city across the country, and there was something about New York—particularly Manhattan—where it seemed a thousand different smells had gotten together over time to create a perpetual and ubiquitous stink that refused to leave the sidewalks and streets and alleyways. Even the groups of smokers crowded outside offices and restaurants and bars couldn't seem to fight that ever-growing stench with their own spreading clouds of nicotine-induced smoke.

We came to Seventh Avenue and waited for yet another light. Traffic surged with even more earnest as it headed downtown, mostly swarms of yellow taxis weaving in and out and between other taxis and cars and buses farting exhaust.

I took a moment to light up another cigarette and scanned Times Square. Maya had mentioned just last night how it was like the heart of the city. It kept the city alive, she said, Seventh Avenue and Broadway and the rest of the streets ventricles feeding blood into all of Manhattan, keeping it beating and breathing and alive.

The light changed and we continued forward. Cars honked, people shouted, snatches of music showered us with persistent beats. Actors and actresses and models stared down from their frozen perches around the Square. Advertisements for soda and sitcoms and musicals bombarded consumers from every direction. The Jumbotron currently hawked the trailer for the latest Disney film. It was enough to make you wonder when they were going to require all the cops walking around the Square to wear some kind of patch or other form of advertisement on the back of their uniforms, maybe something promoting Starbucks or McDonald's.

We continued on to Sixth Avenue, then one block south to Bryant Park. We headed around the park to the New York Public Library, where we waited near the steps with practically everyone else in the city whose only job it seems is to hang out on public library steps.

Ronny glanced at his watch. I took one last drag of my smoke and dropped the butt to the ground.

"How long?" Ronny asked.

"Soon."

He nodded, chomping on his gum.

I lit another cigarette and watched the traffic choking the street. After a couple of minutes, I spotted Edward Stark in the flood of people crossing Fifth Avenue. He was dressed down—jeans and a jacket, sunglasses and baseball cap—but what really gave him away was his limp. The limp I had given him earlier this week.

"Here he comes," I said.

Ronny stood up straighter, keeping his hands in the pockets of his jacket, his fingers no doubt wrapped around the semi-automatic.

The thing was, despite all we had learned Monday, and all we had learned the past four days, we still couldn't allow ourselves to trust Edward Stark. He seemed on the level, and he probably was, but after everything we had experienced since entering our own individual games, our trust in the human species had become broken. So while we'd agreed to work with

Stark, so much so that he was helping lead us into enemy territory, we still couldn't bring ourselves to trust him one hundred percent.

Stark nodded to us but didn't say anything as he continued up the block. Ronny and I followed. Our pace was slow, because Stark's pace was slow. Despite everything, I truly felt bad for what I'd done to his toe, and knew there was nothing I could do to show my regret besides having already offered up my apologies.

We came to the end of the block and stood directly behind Stark as everyone waited for the light. Then the lights changed and the flood of people started moving. Stark swerved toward a black limousine idling behind a taxi. He opened the back door and climbed inside.

Ronny and I exchanged a glance.

I motioned at the limo. "After you."

Ronny ducked his head down first to peer inside, then climbed in after Stark. His right hand—the one cradling the semi-automatic—never left his jacket pocket.

I unconsciously noted the Beretta currently resting snug in the waistband of my jeans as I slid in right after him, shutting the door behind me. Then I just sat there beside Ronny, while across from us sat Edward Stark and the woman who was our ticket into tonight's Coliseum.

"Hello, Congresswoman," I said.

FIFTY-FOUR

"Just for the record," Congresswoman Francis "Frank" Houser said as the limo began to slither its way through the city streets, "I think this is a terrible idea."

"What's that?" I withdrew an eyeglass case from my jacket pocket, switched out the sunglasses for my regular glasses. "Carpooling?"

Her gaze on me turned frosty before it was redirected at Stark. "I knew this was a mistake."

"Ben," Stark prompted.

I cleared my throat. "Congresswoman, I appreciate you taking the time to meet with us, even if it is last minute."

"I couldn't get into the city any sooner. Edward explained that to you, didn't he?"

"He did."

"Besides, I'm not even officially here this weekend. As far as my constituency is concerned, I'm visiting a friend and her family at their home in Florida."

"I know." I glanced at the closed partition between us and the driver. "We've been keeping tabs."

She gave me a curious look for the first time, this woman in her late fifties with pale skin and dark short hair. She wore a blue pantsuit and a white blouse. Her wedding and engagement rings still sparkled on her finger despite the fact her husband had died of a heart attack three years earlier. The soft and silky scent of her perfume was a nice alternative to the stale city stink we'd been breathing in outside.

"Can I ask you something, Ben?"

"Absolutely."

"Do you have a death wish?"

I smiled. "Is that all you're worried about?"

"I don't think you understand the great magnitude of this situation."

"Oh, I think I do. So does he"—I tilted my head toward Ronny—"as well as the rest of my team. Keep in mind, we all survived Simon's game."

"Simon's game?" She snorted. "Simon's game is *nothing* compared to this. Tonight every member of the Inner Circle will be present. These are not just wealthy investors bored with their time, either. These are leaders and dignitaries of very well-known countries, including our own. Some of the richest and most powerful people in the world will be there. And they won't be alone. There will be more security tonight than what they normally have at the White House."

"So then why the Fillmore?"

"Excuse me?"

"If all these important members are meeting for the first time in one place, why put them together in a building located in the middle of the Theater District? Why not somewhere more remote?"

"Well, for starters, because they can. That right there should give you a sense of their arrogance. Also, New York is the greatest city in the world. It's the mecca for culture and entertainment. And it doesn't hurt that this week the United

Nations is in session. This is why I stress there will be a massive amount of security."

"Congresswoman," I said, leaning forward in my seat, "are you trying to scare me?"

"No. I'm simply trying to open your eyes to the reality of your situation. What you're planning tonight—it's suicide."

"And what, again, do you think is a terrible idea?"

"*All* of it," she said, exasperated. "Us meeting together like this. The *purpose* for our meeting. Everything."

"You could have said no."

Again her stare on me turned curious. Before this week, I hadn't even been aware of her existence. Since then I'd read countless articles, watched clips of her on political websites, and she came across as one of those Washington, D.C. anomalies: an honest politician.

"You're right"—she nodded thoughtfully—"I could have said no. I probably *should* have said no."

"But you didn't."

"No, I didn't."

"Why not?"

She was quiet for a moment. Her hands were in her lap, her ankles crossed. The posture was one that tried to convey she wasn't a threat. I had seen enough interviews with her where she did the same thing. She sat in a way that made it appear as if she was open to any question, to any line of thinking. She made herself appear almost timid, innocuous, while at the same time she was assessing the situation and trying to determine all the different outcomes.

"As I believe you already know," she said, "the only thing necessary for the triumph of evil is for good men—and, it is my duty to add, women—to do nothing. Does that sound familiar?"

I nodded. "Edmund Burke."

"Actually, it's not. I mean, it's *attributed* to Edmund Burke, yes, but there is no written proof that he is in fact the very first person who said it. Imagine that—your legacy being associated with words you never actually spoke or had written. And really, when it comes right down to it, does it even matter?"

"I think we're getting off track."

"Are we? Because, quite honestly, I think we're right on track. The fact is, it's my duty not only as an elected congresswoman but as a woman—as an American *citizen*—to do whatever it takes to protect this country. So that's why I agreed to meet with you, Ben. I may not like it, I may think this is a terrible idea and that it will get us all killed, but I can't rightly sit back and do nothing. I've already done nothing for long enough. Now, ask your questions."

"Okay," I said. "Who's Caesar?"

"I don't know."

"But you've been in the Inner Circle for years."

"Nearly twenty."

"Nearly *twenty*," I said. "And in all that time, you've never once talked to him."

"Nobody talks to Caesar."

"Then how do you know he even exists?" Before she could respond, I said, "You know what, forget I asked. Let's focus on something else."

"Such as?"

"Your rape and subsequent abortion."

The silence that hung in the limo then was as thick and heavy as the granite that built the Fillmore.

Stark murmured, "Jesus Christ."

How many seconds passed, I wasn't sure, because I kept my full attention on the congresswoman. And she on me.

"Ben," Stark said, shifting in his seat, "what the hell are you doing?"

"Currently having a staring contest with Congresswoman Houser. You want dibs on the winner?"

"He's trying to rile me up," the congresswoman said, not breaking my stare. "He doesn't trust me, just as I'm sure he doesn't trust you, Edward. Isn't that right, Ben?"

"One day I woke up in a motel without my family and learned I couldn't trust anybody."

"What about your friend Carver? Do you trust him?"

"He has his moments."

Silence again ... and then the congresswoman blinked with a sigh.

"Very well," she said. "What do you want me to tell you? It happened in college. I was nineteen. The man who raped me raped several other girls. He didn't use protection, and I became pregnant, and so I had an abortion. The whole traumatic episode was made public years ago when I decided to run for office, which I'm guessing you already know."

It was true—I knew all about it, or at least as much as was documented. She had tried keeping it quiet at first, but when she ran for Congress her opposition dug deep into her past, as the political opposition is wont to do, and unburied the remains of her unborn and unwanted child. To the congresswoman's credit, she didn't back down. In fact, she had used it to strengthen her campaign, running on the issue of a woman's right to choose. The fact she had been raped only led to more public sympathy.

But that wasn't the reason I asked. The reason I asked was I wanted to see her eyes when she spoke. It would help me with my next question.

"How did you become a member of the Inner Circle?"

She smiled. "Finally, after much trotting, we get to the point."

"I try not to disappoint the ladies."

"We could have done this over the phone."

"You're right, we could have," I said, and waited.

She sighed again. "It was my husband who became a

member. He took many trips to Manhattan on business. One of the men he drank with—a close business associate, I guess you could say—eventually keyed him into it."

"Was there an application process?"

She gave me a bored look. "I haven't the slightest idea. But he did keep it a secret from me. At least at first he did. I don't think then he understood exactly what it was he had gotten himself into. In fact, I *know* he didn't understand what he had gotten himself into. The reason I found out about it was because of the money he was donating."

"Donating?"

"Well, that was what he told me, and what he told our accountant so that he could write it off as a tax deduction. Apparently that's what everyone else in the Inner Circle does."

"Did he watch the games?"

"At first, yes. But then he quickly stopped. They disturbed him greatly. My husband was always an easygoing man. I sensed almost immediately a shift in his mood."

"How did you find out about it?"

"He confessed it to me one night. He told me everything. He said at first he was intrigued, because this was a group that wanted to change the world for the better. Everything was falling apart, but they wanted to make things right. So why wouldn't he want to join them? But then … then he was introduced to the games. He didn't think they were real at first, but very soon he realized that wasn't the case. They were very real. And he was scared. Not so much by the games, he told me, but by the people who were in charge of the games. But he knew he couldn't stop being a member. He had heard rumors from his friend that there had been others who had been disturbed and who wanted to leave but who'd had … accidents."

I thought of Claire Abele who'd had one such accident after she had given me her blessing to marry her daughter. I only found out later that it had been her husband who had made sure she died for her sins against him.

"So then what happened?"

"We kept it a secret. We knew by that point there was nothing that could be done. And the Inner Circle … despite the money we gave them, they were generous to us. When I started getting into politics and ran for city council, I received a large anonymous donation. It practically helped cover all my costs. The same thing happened when I ran for Congress. In many ways, the Inner Circle helped put me where I am today."

"Despite the fact they were also killing innocent people."

"What would you have had me do? At that point we were helpless. We merely did what we could to survive. Besides, they never asked anything from us. It wasn't like they were lobbyists."

"That's a nice way to rationalize it."

"I seriously thought I could make a difference. Like many politicians just starting out, I was naïve. I thought, despite everything my husband had gotten into with the Inner Circle, I could make things better for our country. But the truth is, our country is broken."

"What happened to your husband?"

"He had a heart attack."

"I know that. But why?"

"What do you mean, *why*?"

I just stared back at her.

Understanding crossed her face, and she slowly shook her head. "If you're thinking they killed him, they didn't."

"Are you sure?"

"Positive. At least, I'm as positive as I can be. But I did suspect it at first. I was—and am still—very paranoid."

"So how does our FBI friend enter the story?"

"Edward didn't tell you?"

"I was waiting to ask until we were all together."

"I see." She allowed a small smile. "Maybe you are more paranoid than me after all."

I said nothing.

"Well, I never really watched the games, but I would let them play every so often. I knew my continuing participation was required, even though my husband was gone. Because the Inner Circle had already given me so much money for my campaigns, I was notified that I was now a member and expected to make regular donations. As you can imagine, I knew better than to protest."

"I think we're getting off track again."

Her lips tightened, and she sighed. "It was your game."

"My game?"

"Yes. That's what eventually led me to contact Edward."

For the first time since entering the limo I frowned. First at Ronny, then at Stark, then back at the congresswoman. "Would you care to elaborate?"

"As you already know, your game made a lot of waves. Until then, I hadn't been aware of Carver Ellison. Again, I never watched many of the games, and those that I did watch I had on in the background until they were done and I could turn them off. So it ... shocked me at first, to know that there were people like Carver not only aware of the games, but doing what they could to stop them. It made me feel ... almost hopeful for the first time in a long while."

She tilted her head down, smoothed her pants with her hands.

"From everything that happened in that game, I wondered how they were going to be able to keep it all quiet. There wasn't anyone I could tell, or talk to about it, so I had this idea. I created Google Alerts for you, and for Carver, and your game names, and even the name of that retirement home that was bombed. I knew it was a risk, that they monitor everything, but I also knew it was a risk worth taking. Then, weeks later, I received an email that directed me to your story."

It was then, she admitted, she realized she had crossed a line and there was no going back. Creating those Google Alerts had been a risk, yes—a very huge risk, in fact—but even if something had come up, she could have ignored it. But now here was something that threatened to destroy the Inner Circle, and she readily devoured it. She read it through once, twice, three times. Each time she cried. And each time she wondered if there was anything she could do to somehow change things.

"So then what happened?"

"I decided to contact Carver's supervisor at the FBI. Only I didn't know who his supervisor was—you hadn't given a name in your story. But I knew what section he worked in, at least from what you had written, so I began to quietly make inquiries. I claimed I was looking into ways to make sure my constituency would be safe against child pornographers and even online terrorism. I asked around, and was eventually put in contact with Edward. I began to suspect he was indeed Carver's supervisor, but I couldn't quite tell whether or not he had purposefully set Carver up. Then I realized there was no need for subterfuge—I was a member of the Inner Circle, after all. One day while we were alone I simply asked him about Carver."

Here Stark cleared his throat and leaned forward, taking over the story.

"Truthfully, she scared the shit out of me. As I told you, by then I had begun to suspect something had happened to Carver, and here now I became even more paranoid. I denied it at first, because quite honestly, I didn't know much about it. I asked how she even knew about Carver—by that point it seemed nobody even remembered him, even though he had been gone for only a year. The congresswoman looked me straight in the eye and said—" He looked at her. "Do you remember what you said?"

She nodded. "I asked, 'Are you a member of the Inner Circle too?' I knew it was a risk, but I knew that if he *was* a member, everything would be fine. We could, I don't know, laugh about it and be on our way. But if he *wasn't* a member, then that would be okay, too. And I watched his eyes, just like you've been watching my eyes, Ben, to see if he was lying. Tell me, do you believe me so far?"

"I'm not sure yet. I guess that depends."

"Depends on what?"

"Are you going to help us?"

"That's a good question," she said. "I'm still asking myself the same thing."

FIFTY-FIVE

The limo let us out down near the Financial District, a few blocks away from the World Trade Center Memorial. I lit up a smoke almost immediately.

Ronny said, "Maybe you should cut back on the smoking."

"Maybe you should cut back on the gum chewing."

"I'm being serious."

"So am I. That can't be at all good for your jaw." I tilted my head down the street. "Come on."

We started walking down the block. Nearby was a subway station.

"So what do you think?" Ronny asked.

"I'm not sure yet. You?"

"She put on a good face, but she seemed scared."

"That she did."

We came to the Rector Street subway entrance. I pulled out my phone and dialed the Kid's number as I took one last drag of my cigarette.

"We're headed back."

"How long?"

"Probably an hour."

"How did it go?"

"Pretty much as expected."

"Is she going to help?"

"She says she still needs to think about it."

"What the fuck," the Kid said. "She *does* realize the fucking thing is happening tonight, doesn't she?"

"Stark said he'll call later, either way."

"I'm glad we could wait until the very last minute. Bet you wish you'd taken along my program, huh?"

He meant the program used both times we'd spoken to Edward Stark, first over the phone and then face-to-face. The problem was the Kid, despite his assurances to the contrary, could not place the program on one of the iPhones fast enough. Besides, we'd agreed to only use burners while in the city, to ensure nobody could listen in on our calls or somehow manage to track us. Also, I wasn't sure what level of nervousness the congresswoman would have shown when I whipped out my phone and told her to keep talking, that this would alert me every time she lied.

"I'll see you when I see you." I slipped the phone back into my pocket, caught Ronny giving me a look. "What?"

He opened his mouth but hesitated. Shook his head.

"What's wrong?"

"Nothing."

Now it was my turn to give him a look. "Don't you think it's time for a new piece of gum?"

He shook his head, and we started down the steps into the subway station.

We took the N train up to Union Square, transferred to the 4, and rode that up to Lexington Avenue. Then we waited for the N, which took us back downtown, where we ended back at

Times Square. There we waited for the 2, which then took us uptown.

Were we being too overly cautious? Perhaps. But if I'd learned anything in the past two years, being overly cautious was better than being dead. Carver had trained us to keep an eye out for possible tails, but in a city of over eight million people, a dog would have a hard time keeping track of its own tail, let alone someone meaning to track and kill you.

Eventually we came to our stop. We scanned the terminal, made sure we were clear, and headed up to the street.

"Let me guess," Ronny said as we climbed the stairs, "you're going to light up the moment we hit the sidewalk."

My hand was already in my pocket, reaching for my smokes. I glowered at him. "Not anymore I'm not."

He offered me a yellow stick of Juicy Fruit. "How about an alternative?"

"Why, Ronny, I thought you would never ask."

We waited on the sidewalk for another minute, both of us chewing our gum, waiting to see if anyone else might linger. When it was clear we definitely didn't have a tail, I pulled out my phone and dialed the Kid. I told him we would be there in ten, and then I disconnected the call and walked over to the nearest overflowing trashcan and added my gum to the detritus.

I shrugged at Ronny. "That doesn't keep its flavor long at all, does it?"

We started up the block. When we turned at the corner and headed east, I asked, "So what's on your mind?"

"I told you it was nothing."

"No, it's definitely something. What is it?"

"It's just …"

"Yeah?"

"What the congresswoman asked you about—you being suicidal."

"What about it?"

"Are you?"

We came to an intersection and waited for the light. I pulled out a cigarette and took my time lighting it.

Ronny waited.

The light changed and neither of us moved. Those few around us did, heading in different directions. It wasn't that busy where we were, but there were people around, and for some reason I didn't feel like talking.

"Do you remember what you said to me back in Miami?" Ronny asked. "After we thought Carver was dead and left the Beachside?"

I took a long drag, let the smoke drift out through my nose. "Enlighten me."

"You said all of us are already dead. We just don't know it yet."

"Really? That's kind of badass."

"Ben."

"What?"

"You're slipping."

"I know what I'm doing."

"I think you think you know what you're doing, but I'm talking about spiritually."

I rolled my eyes, surveyed the street, started across to the other side.

Ronny kept pace beside me. "This isn't a God or Jesus thing, either. It's just … you know what you're doing—I have no doubt in my mind about that—and I know you have all the right intentions. But I think deep down, you want to die."

I took another long drag of the cigarette and flicked it into the gutter. "Are we done?"

"I know you think you have nothing left to live for, but that's not true. There's never any good reason to want to die, Ben. None. God put us here to live—"

"I thought you said this wasn't a God or Jesus thing."

"Listen to me," he said, grabbing my arm and pulling me to a halt. "I don't want to die. Drew doesn't want to die. The Kid doesn't want to die. *Maya* doesn't want to die. Are you seeing a pattern?"

"Let go of my arm."

He sighed and released his grip. "It's crazy what we're planning to do tonight—everybody thinks so—but we're doing it with a purpose. Our purpose is to save Carver and stop Caesar if possible. We all know the risks. We all know that it's possible some of us may die. But the difference, Ben? None of us *wants* to die."

"They're dead."

"What?"

"Jen and Casey. They're dead."

Judging by his expression this wasn't at all what he had expected to hear. "What are you talking about?"

"I watched them die."

"Ben, you're not making any sense."

"Do you remember a month after my game, after I had written about what happened and the Kid posted it everywhere online?"

"What about it?"

"Right before Maya's game, Carver took me somewhere. Do you remember? We got in the pickup and just drove away for several hours."

Ronny nodded, slowly, waiting for me to continue.

"We met the Kid at a motel over in Denver. It was just him in the room, him and his laptop. He said a message had been posted marked specifically for the Man of Wax. The Kid found it, watched it, and called Carver. They debated for a few days whether to even tell me about it, but then Carver decided it was best."

"Ben"—Ronny shifted uncomfortably on his feet, his arms crossed—"what was it?"

I opened my mouth, started to speak, but then went completely still.

Ronny stared hard at my face. "What's wrong?"

"Grab your gun."

"Why?"

A familiar high-pitched whine was singing out among the chaotic tumult that was New York City.

"We have company," I said, already reaching for my Beretta, and turned toward the street just as the Ducati came screaming our way.

FIFTY-SIX

We were on a side street, only a few vehicles parked along the curb. There was an open spot right beside us and this was where the Ducati came skidding to a halt, its rider once again in black.

At the same moment, tires screeched behind us.

I kept my body squared toward the bike, the Beretta now at my side, and tilted my head just enough to see the Escalade now parked askew at the curb. The driver and passenger doors opened, and two Korean men stepped out.

"Ben?" Ronny said quietly beside me.

Whoever these guys were, I couldn't rightfully call them enemies. Not after my last two encounters with them—the rider in Miami Beach, who had saved me and Ian and the girl from the two bent cops, and then in Hope Springs, Arizona, when the rider and the men in this SUV had taken one of Caesar's men away. We might not necessarily be on the same team, and we certainly weren't friends, but still I had the sense they weren't here to do us any harm.

That isn't to say my grip on the Beretta didn't tighten anyway.

The men kept the Escalade's doors open as they slowly approached. Both kept their hands, empty, at their sides.

"Stop right there," I said.

Both men stopped at once.

I watched them a moment, then glanced back at the rider on the bike wearing the black faceplate helmet. Past the rider, down the street, traffic whipped back and forth. Fortunately for now, the street was deserted of innocent bystanders.

Keeping my body squared toward the Ducati, the gun still at my side, I tilted my head back toward the two men and asked, "What do you want?"

The passenger said, "For you to come with us."

"You're joking."

"We are not."

My focus was now on the passenger. He was the one who had spoken to me back in Arizona, who had said he was sorry about my friend.

I started to ask what it was they wanted when his gaze shifted slightly past me. His eyes narrowed. His face tightened. Then, quite suddenly, he and the driver had guns in their hands.

"Ronny!" I shouted, and we both brought up our guns, aiming them at the passenger and driver.

Only the passenger and driver weren't focused on us. Instead they were focused on the rider.

Maya, it turned out, was standing behind the Ducati, her gun pointed at the rider's head. The rider clearly hadn't heard her or even known she was there until the two men pulled their guns. For a moment nothing happened. Then, at once, the rider jerked back, falling off the bike. The bike thudded hard against the street. The rider popped back up, smacking the gun from Maya's hand. The rider stepped forward but Maya was already moving, sidestepping the rider, spinning and grabbing the rider's jacket and jerking backward as she swept out the rider's feet. The rider hit the pavement hard, and then Maya was on top, keeping a knee pressed against the rider's chest, a hand held against the rider's neck, her other hand reaching for the gun which lay only feet away.

Less than five seconds had passed.

The passenger and driver still had their guns aimed. The passenger's eyes shifted to meet mine. Beside me, Ronny kept his gun trained on the two men. I waited a moment, debating, then cleared my throat.

"Maya, stop."

She paused, her hand only inches from the gun. "Who the fuck are these people, Ben?"

"Good question." I turned to the passenger and driver. "You guys care to explain?"

"We are friends," the passenger said.

"Is that right?"

"I would hope by now you realized we are not a threat to you."

"Says the guy holding a gun."

"You are holding a gun as well."

"Fair enough." I lowered the gun to my side. "You too, Ronny."

"Ben."

"Just do it."

Ronny lowered the gun but didn't put it back in his pocket.

"All right, fellas," I said, "we've met you halfway. Your turn."

The passenger and driver lowered their weapons.

I nodded. "So far so good. Maya?"

She had loosened her hold around the rider's neck, the rider who just lay on the ground, not even struggling. "What?"

"Why don't you stand up for a second?"

She didn't move at first, but then leaned back and rose to

her feet. She stood straddling the rider for an extra second before she stepped away.

"Help him up," I prompted.

"Her," the passenger said.

"What?"

The passenger just nodded toward the rider, who was being helped up by a reluctant Maya.

"Are you okay?" the passenger asked.

The rider tugged the helmet off. I don't know why, but I had been expecting a young Korean man. Instead it was a young Korean woman, her short hair almost as dark as Maya's.

The woman nodded but said nothing.

Up the block, a panel truck turned down the street. We all waited, silent, until it passed. Then I said to the passenger and driver, "So what do you guys want?"

"To talk."

"Then talk."

"Not here. We want you to come with us."

"Sorry, but I have a prior engagement tonight."

"We know. That is why we need to talk to you."

I watched the passenger's face, searching for anything that might give me a good handle on our current situation. Nothing was there, at least nothing I could see, so I took a deep breath, silently counted to five, and asked, "How long will it take?"

"That depends on you."

"I can't be gone too long."

"You will not."

I nodded, still debating, then handed my gun to Ronny and said, "I'll be back."

"Ben"—his voice was a hoarse whisper—"don't do this."

"It'll be okay."

I started toward the Escalade. Maya watched me, a helpless look in her eyes, urging me not to go.

The passenger said, "Please empty your pockets."

"I thought we were friends."

"You and your team are careful. That is why it took us a long time to find you. But we are more careful. Now please, empty your pockets."

I didn't have much in my pockets anyway, just a pack of cigarettes, a lighter, the burner, a MetroCard, my eyeglass case, and a few spare bucks. I handed them all to Ronny.

The passenger opened the back door for me.

I started to get in the Escalade but paused when I saw both Ronny and Maya watching me. Their eyes stressed the fact they both believed this would be the last time they'd ever see me. I hated to admit it, but right then I was beginning to think the same.

FIFTY-SEVEN

Neither the driver nor the passenger introduced themselves. They didn't even speak as the Escalade snaked through the city streets all the way to a park overlooking the Hudson River. There they let me out, and the passenger pointed at a man sitting on a bench.

"You guys have any cigarettes?"

Neither of them spoke.

"How about some gum?"

Still nothing.

"Thanks for the ride," I said, and headed toward the bench.

Surprisingly, the park was mostly deserted. Some children were looked after by a few women—probably nannies—but that was it. I approached the bench slowly, staring first at the back of the man's head, then, as I neared, the side of his face.

Before I could speak, he tilted his head and looked up at me.

"Hello, Ben."

Like the other three, he was Korean. He was much older than the others, maybe in his early-fifties. He wore slacks and nice shoes, a dress shirt and sports coat. A wooden cane rested between his legs.

"Please," he said, inching over to one side of the bench, "have a seat."

I sat down. "You don't happen to have a spare cigarette, do you?"

"I do not smoke."

"I wouldn't ask, but your guys made me leave all my worldly possessions behind."

"I apologize for that. But as I am sure my men told you, we are very careful."

"Of course you are. I don't even know your name."

"My name is Bae. The two men who brought you here are Chin and Seung."

"And the girl?"

This he clearly wasn't expecting. His body tensed slightly, and when he spoke his voice was soft. "She ... her name is Ho Sook."

"She's your daughter, isn't she?"

He hesitated. "How do you know?"

"I used to be a father myself once upon a time."

"Yes. I am truly sorry for your loss. For everything you lost because of your game."

"What do you know about my game?"

"I know from what you wrote in your story."

I stared out over the water at the trees on the New Jersey side of the Hudson. "I think we're getting too far ahead of ourselves."

"Yes, I believe we are."

"Why don't you start from the beginning."

"Very well." Bae shifted on the bench, cleared his throat. "I was a police officer. The city I worked in had major problems with child sex trade. Girls and boys no more than ten years old. I took it on myself to work against this. I wanted to shut it down. I received threats. My family received threats. Child sex trade, you see, is a large commodity. Nobody wanted it to stop. But I would not stop in my work. Then one night my wife was taken. She was taken and beaten and raped. She was left in the middle of the city without her clothes. It was a warning to me. For me to stop. But I could not stop. My wife understood. She knew the work I did was important."

Bae closed his eyes, tilted his face down, rested his chin against his collarbone.

"My wife was beautiful. She gave me two sons. They were four and six. I think … yes, it was because of them I worked so hard. Every time I thought of those children forced to do their work I thought of my own children, and it made me angry. It made my wife angry also and this is why she would not let me stop, even after what happened to her. So I did not stop. And they—"

He opened his eyes, raised his chin.

"They took my children. Both of my boys. They … they sodomized them. They left them just like my wife in the middle of the city. My sons were in the hospital for a month. I wanted to stop then. I wanted to quit work as a police officer completely. But my wife would not let me. She said I had already come this far. She said we had all come this far. I knew she was right, but I would not risk my family's safety. I made plans to have them taken away to a safe location while I continued my work."

He fell silent then, staring out at the water.

"How long before you woke up in the game?" I asked.

He looked at me, his face stone. "The next day."

He had woken up in a small room. A cell phone was ringing beside him. A voice said that Bae's wife and children had been taken hostage and that if Bae ever wanted to see them again he must play a game. Bae, of course, agreed.

The first task of the game was not something simple like

stealing a candy bar or a pack of gum. Told to wear the glasses which had been on the ground when he awoke, Bae was directed to a building. In the basement was a masked man and a boy no older than five. There was a gun in the room, and Bae was told to watch the man sodomize the child and not touch the gun, to not interfere at all. He was to watch the entire time and say nothing, and when it was done to leave and not look back.

"I could not do this. I knew even then my family was forever gone. I was not going to let this man have his way with the child. So I picked up the gun and aimed it at the man and told him to get away. He came at me. I pulled the trigger, but nothing happened. It was empty. That was when the other men came in. They beat me. I tried fighting. They broke this leg"— he lightly touched his right kneecap—"and then left me there. But first the masked man sodomized the boy in front of me. Then he killed him."

The men left Bae alone with the boy's dead body. The cell phone rang again. Bae managed to pull it from his pocket —"My clothes were dirty and soaked with blood"—and listened to the voice tell him that his family was now dead and that soon Bae would be too. The police, the voice said, would be coming for him at any moment.

"They meant to humiliate me, whoever had done this. With my leg broken, I would not be able to go far. I managed to climb to my feet and leave the room and go outside. I went only a block before the first police car arrived. The officers did not see me, but I saw them. They were Chin and Seung."

"Then what happened?"

"I shouted their names. They came to me at once. I quickly explained what had happened, about being kidnapped, about my family being abducted, about the dead boy in the base-ment. Neither of them questioned me. I was their captain for many years. They trusted me deeply. They helped me to their car and drove away before the other officers arrived."

"Did they take you to a hospital?"

Bae shook his head. "I told them it would not be safe. That the men who did this to me were very powerful. I should have known then just what kind of trouble I was putting my own men in. I am responsible for what happened to them."

"Their families were killed too, weren't they?"

"Yes, by 'accident.'" Bae actually made vague quotation marks with his hands. "Chin's family died in an automobile crash. Seung's family died from a gas leak at their home. They happened on the same day. Simple coincidence, no?"

I said nothing.

"But at the moment my men took me away from that awful scene, their families were still alive. That ... that only occurred afterward. After I told them to take me to my daughter."

The children playing not too far away from us ran and hollered and laughed. One of them tripped and fell and started to cry. One of the women—definitely a nanny—finished whatever story she was telling her friend before lithely extracting herself from the bench and hurrying over to the sobbing child.

"Your daughter," I said. "I know she exists, because she saved my life twice already. But didn't you say you only had two children?"

"With my wife, yes. But before we were married I had an affair with a younger woman. I am not proud of what I did. She became pregnant. I could not be associated with her. I told her I would support the child if she remained silent. Nobody knew of our arrangement. Not even my wife."

"Your wife never questioned the missing money?"

Bae smiled again. "I am very careful. I made it so nobody knew about my ... mistake. In my position I could not afford for it to become public. The woman understood. The girl—my daughter—did not care. She never wanted to see me."

"Then how did you two cross paths?"

"One day she was arrested—drugs. Her mother contacted me. I told her there was nothing I could do. She threatened to expose me. I could not let that happen, so I agreed to help. I eventually got Ho Sook released. I told them she was my ... how do you say it in America—a criminal informant. It was the first time we ever saw each other. I immediately recognized her. She had my eyes. She knew who I was, and she did not care."

"Kids," I said. "They always take their parents for granted."

Bae ignored this. "Ho Sook had fallen in with some very bad people. I told her it would be best for her to stay away from these people. She told me to go to hell. I did not see her again, but I kept track of her. I knew the people she associated with—drugs dealers and the sort. So when Chin and Seung wanted to take me to the hospital, I told them to take me to Ho Sook instead."

Chin and Seung took Bae to his daughter. It was in a bad part of town. They were in a police car. As you can imagine, the tension was thick. The gangbangers were about ready to start something with the cops. But Ho Sook intervened. She saw what had happened to her father and came to his side. He explained that he could not go to a hospital. She understood, and took him to one of the doctors that took care of the gang-bangers when they were injured.

"By then it was the next day," Bae said, "and those men who had killed my family went and killed Chin and Seung's families as well."

It was clear to them then that they could never return to their former lives. They could not even call any of their cop friends, for fear that they might be secretly associated with whoever had done this to their families. When Bae was strong enough, he explained everything to Ho Sook and a few of the other gangbangers who refused to leave Ho Sook's side. One of these gangbangers offered up a name. It belonged to a man who specialized in the child sex trade. He was, among other things, a businessman. Chin and Seung paid this man a visit along with two of the gangbangers and brought him back. There they forced the information they needed out of him.

"I am not proud of what we did," Bae said quietly. "But it was something that needed to be done."

I was again staring off at the trees on the New Jersey side of the Hudson. I was thinking about taking the knife and cutting off Edward Stark's toe. I knew all too well about doing things that needed to be done, though that didn't make those things right.

"This man, he told us about the games. He himself was even a viewer. We managed to watch some of the games. Apparently viewers are not supposed to record what happens, but this man did. The man was low level and could not tell us much more than that, but he knew someone higher up. Someone, he said, in the Inner Circle."

They went to this man next. It wasn't as easy as it had been before. This man was much more powerful and well protected. But they managed to abduct him. They forced the information they needed out of this man. They learned more about the games, about the Inner Circle, about Caesar. Then they killed him.

"This was four months ago," Bae said. "The man mentioned something about there being a gathering of the Inner Circle. He didn't know when or where, but that it was going to happen soon. We realized that Caesar operates out of America, so we decided to come here. Ho Sook made the decision to come with us. I believe ... I believe she feels she owes it to me, for once helping her."

"Maybe she did it simply because you're her father."

His smile was thin. "A nice thought, but I do not think so."

"Fine," I said. "But what exactly does all of this have to do with me?"

"We saved your life and the life of your friend in Miami."

"You did, and I appreciate that very much."

"We plan to kill Caesar."

"So do we."

"No, you plan to save your friend. Killing Caesar is secondary."

"Well whichever one comes first we'll do. We're not too picky."

"We watched the games when we came here. That is how we managed to track you in Miami. That is how we obtained one of Caesar's men in Arizona."

"Yeah, I meant to ask you about that. How did your daughter catch up with my guy? He'd already been an hour outside of Miami."

"My other men were following the SUV once it left the Beachside Hotel."

"And Caesar's man from Arizona—you killed him, didn't you?"

"Yes."

"But first you tortured him."

Bae said nothing.

"What all did he give you?"

"That the Coliseum was to be in New York City. At the building called the Fillmore. Tonight."

"That sounds about right."

"How did you learn of this?"

I shook my head. "Sorry, but this isn't my story time. Let's just say I know about it, and I plan to be there tonight."

"We also plan to be there."

"So I've gathered. Where did you get your invitations?"

Bae smiled. "We are, how do you say, crashing the party."

"Then maybe our paths will cross again."

"I am sure they will."

"So can you clue me in again on why I'm sitting here?"

"I felt it would be polite to give you warning. We understand what you plan to do, and I felt it was best to let you know what we plan to do."

"Again, the point?"

"We will hold off killing Caesar as long as we can. So that you can try to save your friend. We know Carver Ellison is a great man. He deserves to live. Or, at the very least, he does not deserve to die in front of those people."

"Speaking of which, it's probably time I got back to my team."

"Of course. Chin and Seung will take you back."

I stood from the bench and started to turn away when Bae said my name.

"One more thing," he said. "Have you heard them yet?"

"Heard what?"

"Those five hundred million bells you wrote about in your story."

"They're from a children's book—a fairy tale. It doesn't mean anything."

"I would not be so sure. What, again, is the purpose of fairy tales? To tell children that monsters not only exist, but they can still be beaten."

I shook my head. "Caesar may be a monster, but this isn't a fairy tale."

"No," Bae said somberly, "unfortunately it is not. This is life, and as most things which happen in life, it makes this a horror story. Let us just hope tonight at least one of us makes it out alive."

FIFTY-EIGHT

Chin and Seung didn't speak at all on the drive back. They let me out a block away from the place they'd picked me up from. As I stepped out, I said, "Thanks, fellas. I'd offer you a tip, but I don't seem to have any cash on me right now."

I started to shut the door when one of them—Seung, I think—spoke.

"Good luck tonight."

I nodded. "You too."

I shut the Escalade's door and started down the block.

Ronny was waiting for me outside on the sidewalk.

"Fancy seeing you here," I said.

He pulled my disposable cell phone from his pocket and tossed it to me. "Stark called while you were gone."

"And?"

"He wouldn't tell me anything. Said he would only talk to you."

"How long ago was this?"

He glanced at his watch. "Twenty-seven minutes."

"Where did you tell him I was?"

"What was I supposed to tell him? I said you were currently indisposed and would call him back."

"You haven't asked yet how my meeting went."

"I'm assuming it went well."

"Meaning?"

"Meaning those guys didn't kill you."

We went inside and started up the stairs. The building had been a shitty warehouse once. Years ago it had been remodeled and was somehow even shittier now. We were currently renting half of the fifth floor. The other half was deserted.

I called Stark and said, "Sorry I missed your call."

"Where have you been?"

"Didn't Ronny tell you? I was indisposed."

"For half an hour?"

"I had a bad bean burrito."

He was silent for a moment, and I thought the connection had dropped out. Then he said, "You weren't very nice to the congresswoman."

"Granted, I wasn't on my best behavior, but on the bright side, I wasn't as rude as I could have been."

"She wasn't quite convinced after our meeting."

I was climbing the stairs, Ronny in front of me. "What are you saying?"

"She wasn't quite convinced, but I did everything I could to convince her. She understands the risks. She knows what might happen to her if this all goes south. But she also knows she just can't sit back and let it happen."

"Again, what are you saying?"

"She's agreed to help." Stark released a heavy breath. "She's scared, Ben. So am I."

"Join the club."

"Where are you now? I'll meet you to discuss the details."

"How about we just discuss them over the phone instead?"

Another pause. "You still don't trust me, do you?"

"What are the details?"

Stark sighed again, and then started to talk.

Ronny had gone ahead of me and was waiting at the top of the landing when I caught up to him, closing the phone.

"We all set?"

I nodded and said, "I have to be downtown by ten." I started toward the door but Ronny stepped in my way. "What?"

"What you were about to tell me before—about Jen and Casey being dead."

"What about it?"

"You need to talk about it."

"I haven't talked about it for two years. I don't have to start now."

I went to step around Ronny but he moved again to block me.

"You do," he said.

"Ronny, don't piss me off."

"Everyone's inside."

I looked at him sharply. "Why?"

"After what happened, we weren't even sure you would be back."

Since we'd come to the city we had kept the team split in case something happened. It wasn't wise to put everyone in the same place at the same time. But now it seemed that was what had happened.

Ronny placed his hand on my shoulder. "You need to let it out, Ben. For your own sake. And if not for your own sake, then at least for Maya's sake. You owe her that much."

I glared back at him, and carefully took his hand off my shoulder. "You know something, Ronny? Sometimes you can be an annoying prick."

He smiled. "If I am, I learned it from watching you.

Just as Ronny said, everyone was inside—the Kid, Drew, Beverly, Maya, and Mason Coulter, who had surprised us all and stepped up in a big way this past week. The man certainly had anger issues, but he was able to control the anger for the most part, and was using it to help us get back at the people that had taken his family away. Now he was dressed like a homeless person, in nothing but rags, filthy and smelling like trash. This was because for the past three nights he had literally been sleeping in a dumpster.

The only person who wasn't present was Graham. As much as he wanted to help, there wasn't really anything for him to do, or anything he could do, not in his condition. It was hard for him to accept, especially as he had helped raise Carver and thought of him as a son, but he acknowledged the reality for what it was and stayed back at the farmhouse.

So it was just the seven of us—six of them and one of me —and when Ronny and I entered, they all turned to look at us.

The Kid said almost immediately, "Did you talk to Stark?"

I nodded. "We're a go."

The tension in the room seemed to momentarily lift. While we had hoped the congresswoman would come through, there had never been any guarantee, and we had already prepared a Plan B.

"So what did those guys want?" the Kid asked.

"To talk to their guy in charge. He's kind of like the Korean Carver."

The Kid raised an eyebrow at this.

"They're going to be there tonight, too. They're aiming to

kill Caesar. They understand our main objective is to get Carver first, so he said they'll try to hold off as long as possible."

"Why don't they just team up with us?"

"I'm not sure. I think they, just like us, have trust issues."

Ronny cleared his throat. "Ben has something he wants to say to everyone."

I shot Ronny a glare but he wasn't having any of it. He just stood there, his arms crossed, waiting.

"Ben?" Beverly said. "What is it?"

I looked at her and started to speak … but then my gaze shifted and my eyes met Maya's.

"Ben?" Beverly said again.

Staring at Maya, I whispered, "My family."

"What about your family?"

I blinked, looked around the room, took a deep breath. "My family … they're dead. Jen and Casey—they're dead."

Beverly shook her head sadly. "But you don't know that for certain. They may still be alive."

"They're not," I said, my voice all at once going cold. "I saw them die. After my game, when I wrote my story and the Kid posted it online, they … they sent out a video. It was encrypted, so only someone like the Kid could find it. Maya wasn't with us then, and of course neither was Mason, but some of the rest of you might remember Carver taking me away for a day. We met the Kid in Denver, and the Kid … he showed me the video. It was less than two minutes long. It showed Jen and Casey, both of them tied to separate chairs. And then this person walked into frame—I never saw his face, he always kept his back to the camera—and he said that if I wanted to fuck with them, they were going to fuck with me, and he … he killed them. Slowly. With a knife."

The room had gone silent. Outside, the city continued to

breathe with frantic life, but here right now all was quiet and still.

Beverly, her hand to her mouth, whispered, "Oh, Ben, why … why didn't you tell us?"

"Carver wanted me to. So did the Kid. But it was my decision, and I told them we would keep it a secret. That … that the only thing that keeps us going is the hope that our families are still alive. And after what they did to Jen and Casey, it was obvious they had done the same to all of our families. That"—I swallowed—"that we really had nothing to live for anymore. Nothing except making these motherfuckers pay for what they did to us."

The silence grew. Nobody spoke. Nobody moved.

Then Beverly, her voice soft, said, "Ben?"

"Yes, Beverly."

"I think I speak for everyone when I say we understand your reason for keeping this from us. But even without knowing exactly what has happened to each of our families, I'm sure we all know that they're dead. And I can't speak for anyone else here, but I have had hope this entire time. Not exactly to see my family again—because, again, I have always believed them dead—but that we will eventually reach the people responsible for what happened to them. And tonight it seems that will happen. So yes," she said, and produced a devilish little grin, "let's make these motherfuckers pay."

FIFTY-NINE

"I don't think I can do this."

"Try it again."

"It's not going to work."

"Try it again," Maya repeated, her voice all at once hard.

We stood in an empty room in front of a makeshift desk, a small mirror before us, a contact lens on my finger. For ten minutes now I'd been trying to put in one lens, and no matter how hard I tried, the sucker wouldn't stick properly to my eye.

"I'll be okay with just my glasses."

"Try it again."

"Maya."

"Ben, don't make me tell you one more time."

Normally, I might have smiled at her tone, but her eyes told me she was deeply serious—more serious now than ever before.

I turned back to the mirror and used my thumb and index finger to widen my left eyelid. Then I slowly moved my finger with the contact lens to my eye, trying to keep it open despite its initial reaction to automatically shut.

Next thing I knew, I blinked and the contact ended up on my cheek.

"You're pathetic," Maya said.

"Thanks for the pep talk."

Over a year ago Carver had me get a prescription for contact lenses. He said it would be best when trailing players to have contacts instead of glasses. After all, without my glasses I was half-blind, so if they broke or were lost, I would be pretty much useless in the field. And so I had gotten contact lenses and spent an hour trying to put them in, and hated the feeling so much that I never wore them again. But I still had the prescription, and according to Stark (who had heard it from Congresswoman Houser earlier this week), everyone in the Inner Circle tonight would be hiding their identities, which meant they would be wearing masks. And with a mask, my glasses were not going to work.

"Try it again," Maya said.

I turned back to the mirror, then turned back to Maya and said, "Are you seriously mad at me?"

"You could have told me the truth."

"And what good would that have done?"

"I don't know. But you could have told me."

"There was nothing to tell. They were dead. Telling you or telling anybody wouldn't have changed that simple fact."

"I thought you trusted me."

"I do."

"But you don't. Otherwise you would have told me."

"I was going to tell you."

"When?"

"Last week at the farmhouse. While everyone else was inside singing and we were outside on the porch."

"So over a year later."

"Are we really having this discussion right now?"

"Do you love me?"

"You know I do."

"But are you in love with me?"

"Maya," I began, and I meant to say more—what, I wasn't exactly sure—when there was a knock at the door.

The Kid poked his head in. "Am I interrupting anything?"

"Just trying to put in these contacts," I said. "What's up?"

He stepped into the room and held up a pair of black leather dress shoes. "These are ready to go."

"Great. You can set them down wherever."

He placed them on the floor, leaned back, and just stood there.

"Yes?" I said.

"Got a minute?"

"Sure."

He took a step forward, paused, said to Maya, "Actually, I'd like to talk to Ben alone if that's okay."

She gave no verbal response, just turned and left the room.

The Kid said, "Trouble in paradise?"

"Are you here for a reason?"

"Having trouble with the contacts?"

"As a matter of fact, I am. Any suggestions?"

"Dude, I got twenty-twenty vision. Don't know what to tell you."

"As always, you've been extremely helpful."

The Kid walked deeper into the room, his hands in the pockets of his jeans, looking everywhere but at me.

"So what's up?" I asked.

"I just wanted to go over everything one last time."

"You're more than welcome, but I'm good."

"Are you sure?"

"Yes."

"You don't want to go over the Fillmore's building plans again?"

"Kid."

"Mason said he's seen activity over there all morning. Utility van after utility van entering the garage and then coming out."

"Kid."

"What?"

"What's wrong?"

"I'm worried about tonight."

"We all are."

"I have that feeling I sometimes get, that something really bad is going to happen."

"We all know the risks. Why—you're not backing out, are you?"

"No, I'm not bailing. You know I would never do that. But I just … I wanted to tell you something."

"Shoot."

The Kid opened his mouth … but then closed it.

"Are you going to make me guess?"

He was standing only a few feet away now, and still he hadn't looked me in the eye.

"Kid, what's wrong?"

"I …"

"Yeah?"

"I'm gay."

I was quiet for a beat, then said, "Kid, I'm flattered, but—"

"Don't be an asshole."

"I rarely know what else to be anymore."

"I've never told anyone. Not even Carver. But Carver's smart, so maybe he always suspected it, I don't know."

"Why are you telling me now?"

"Because I feel I have to tell somebody."

"But why now?"

"I told you. I have that feeling something bad is going to happen tonight. And if something happens to me, or to you, or to Carver, or to any one of us, I just … I don't want to be that person who never comes out of the closet. I've known what I am for a long time, but in my line of work, I don't get out much. I don't have any friends outside you and Carver and the rest of you guys, and I never … I never once kissed anyone."

I let another beat of silence pass before I said, "Again, Kid, I'm flattered …"

He smiled. "Again, Ben, don't be an asshole."

"So what do you want me to say? That I accept you how you are? You know I do."

"I know. But Ronny and Beverly, they're just so religious, I feel like I can't tell them."

"You should. They're not going to think any less of you."

"How do you know?"

The truth was, I didn't. Though I thought I knew Ronny and Beverly pretty well, none of us truly ever really know ourselves, let alone the people closest to us.

I asked, "What about your mom?"

"What about her?"

"Don't you want to tell her?"

"Give me a break. You saw how she is. It would be like talking to a wall."

"Still."

He was quiet for a moment, staring down at the floor. "Do you still have that nightmare about Michelle Delaney?"

I said nothing. Not at first. I thought about how my nightmare had changed. No longer was I standing outside watching Michelle Delany being beaten by her boyfriend, but instead I was standing in room 7 of the Paradise Motel, while my wife and daughter were trapped in those wooden caskets. Caesar had been in that nightmare, telling me to choose—to pick one to live, to pick one to die—and tonight I might very well come face to face with the son of a bitch. The irony was not lost on me. But still, as hard as it had been to first tell someone about that initial nightmare, it had become impossible for me to tell anyone about this most recent one. Not even Maya, who I had wanted to tell countless times.

"Ben?"

"Sometimes," I said softly. I cleared my throat. "Why?"

"Because I have a nightmare of my own. It's about when my brother died. I watch him fall, I run back to the house, tell my dad and all that stuff, but this time when I come back inside I tell my mom, I just confess to her, and you know what she says to me? She says it should have been me. That I should have fallen and broken my neck. That I'm a waste and will never do anything with my life. That I'm nothing."

Silence then, except for the faint traffic noises beyond the warehouse walls.

"You know that's not true," I said.

"Isn't it? What have I really ever done with my life? I mostly hide behind a computer screen. I've never touched a gun before. Even if I did, I don't know if I would be able to bring myself to fire it. If and when the shit hits the fan tonight, I don't ... I don't think I'll be any help."

"You will be."

"How do you know?"

"I just do."

The Kid nodded, chewing his lip. "Speaking of which, I should let you get back to it. I need to recheck my equipment anyhow."

We stood there then for a long moment, neither one of us saying anything.

I asked, "Is this the part where we hug?"

He smiled again. "Fuck you, Ben."

He turned and left through the door.

Maya stepped back inside a moment later. "Everything okay?"

I nodded.

She came up and wrapped her arms around me tight. Into my shoulder she murmured, "I love you."

I kissed the top of her head. Her hair smelled like apple blossoms.

"I love you too."

"We're all going to make it out of this alive tonight, aren't we?"

"You know we are."

She said nothing and kept her head against my shoulder for another minute. Then she sighed, stepped back, and pointed at the contact lenses and solution on the makeshift desk.

"Try it again."

SIXTY

At five minutes after ten that evening, I stood under an overpass near East Harlem. Graffiti—or was it urban art?—decorated practically every available space of concrete. The smell of trash was nauseating. I was pretty sure someone had recently died under this overpass, or if they hadn't someone was bound to very soon. Suffice it to say, it was the kind of place a white guy wearing a one-thousand-dollar suit probably shouldn't be at that time of night.

But I wasn't nervous. Not with a Glock 27 in my waistband. It was subcompact, only nine rounds, a typical backup pistol. It wasn't my first choice of weapon, not going where I was going, but it wasn't like I had much choice. Besides, I wasn't even sure if they would wand me at the door, or make me walk through a metal detector. Those were possibilities, but I didn't think so. Those in the Inner Circle commanded a certain kind of respect and dignity that wasn't easily taken away by standard security measures. I can't imagine any of them were ever bothered by the TSA at the airport. Not when they were no doubt taking their own private jets to whatever locale called their names.

In my ear, the Kid said, "Well?"

"Still waiting."

"Jesus Christ."

I adjusted the earpiece so it fit snug. It was a small thing, even smaller than the ones we typically used, and the voice on the other end wasn't as loud as usual.

I said, "You can say that again."

"Jesus Christ."

"I was joking."

"This is bullshit. If she doesn't show up in the next minute, we have to move to Plan B."

"And what's Plan B again?"

"Fuck if I know."

Traffic passed back and forth under the overpass. A few people walked here and there. Most ignored me. One black kid —couldn't have been any older than ten—wearing baggy jeans and a heavy coat with a Yankee's cap askew on his head, the lid flat, stopped beside me.

"What you doin'?"

"Standing here," I said. "What you doin'?"

"Watchin' your white ass."

In my ear, the Kid groaned, "What the fuck?"

I said to the gangsta wannabe, "My ass, for your information, is naturally pale. It's not really *white*, so to speak."

The gangsta wannabe just stared at me.

I said, "Can I help you with something?"

"You under my bridge."

"Is that right?"

The gangsta wannabe pointed at the concrete behind me. "That's my tag right there."

I looked over my shoulder at the myriad lines and loops of colorful spray paint. "You're going to have to be a little more specific."

The gangsta wannabe took a deliberate step forward. "Yo, you frontin'?"

"Did you really just ask if I'm fronting?"

In my ear, the Kid said, "Maybe you should ease up on the gas pedal."

At the same moment the Kid was speaking, the gangsta wannabe reached for something inside his coat.

I said, "You don't want to do that."

The gangsta wannabe paused a beat. Glaring back at me, considering his options. No doubt wanting to do whatever it took to drop the "wannabe" from his desired profession.

I said, "I've gone through a lot of shit to be standing where I am right now, talking to you, and at this point, I am not going to let any little fucking thing stand in my way."

The gangsta wannabe's hand was still halfway to his coat, frozen there. He was still watching me, probably trying to figure me out. I clearly didn't give him the reaction he'd wanted, and this confused him.

"Shouldn't you be in school?" I asked.

The hand drifted away from the coat, fell to his side. "Shit, yo, it's Friday night."

"Then shouldn't you be at home doing schoolwork or something?"

He snorted. "Fuck homework."

I nodded. About the response I'd expected, to be honest.

The gangsta wannabe said, his hard tone gone, "What you doin' here anyway?"

I spotted the limo coming down the block. It could have been any limo—New York City is packed with them, after all —but I knew this one was mine.

I said, my eyes on the approaching limo, "Trying to save the world," and stepped off the curb as the limo quietly coasted to a halt beside us. I opened the back door, placed one foot inside. "Why don't you go home and do some schoolwork?"

"Man, fuck that shit." The gangsta wannabe lifted his chin at the limo. "Who's in there?"

"Someone who did her schoolwork," I said, and climbed inside.

Once the door was closed and the limo was moving again and I was settled in my seat, I said for the second time that day, "Hello, Congresswoman."

When I'd seen her last—only hours ago—she wore a blue pantsuit and a white blouse. Now she was wearing a black pantsuit and a navy blue blouse.

She said, gazing at my suit, "You certainly clean up nice."

I motioned at the attaché case beside her on the seat. I'd spotted it the first second I'd slipped into the limo, and hadn't been able to go more than five seconds without looking at it.

"Is that it?"

She laid a hand on the case and nodded. Her lips were pursed, like she wanted to say something but wasn't sure how to say it.

"What's wrong?"

"I'm already feeling guilty."

"For what?"

"For what may happen tonight. I have a bad feeling."

"See," the Kid said in my ear. "I'm not the only one."

I asked her, "Are you still having doubts?"

"I'm here, aren't I?"

The limo glided through traffic, switching lanes, slowing for pedestrians, jostling over potholes. We were headed downtown. The overpass I'd been waiting under was out of the way, but that had been the point. Congresswoman Houser wanted to make sure she wasn't being followed … which, to be honest, was almost impossible to tell in a city as busy as this. Even if nobody had been following in a vehicle, that didn't mean she wasn't being watched by the thousands of cameras positioned around the city, or even by a drone in the sky, or even a satellite up in space. All were probabilities, and regardless of how outrageous each seemed, I wouldn't be surprised if all of them were true.

"You should leave," I said.

"I will when we get closer."

"No. I mean you should leave the city. Leave the state. Leave the country if you can. At least until after tonight."

"I'm meeting with Edward. He's taking me to a secure location."

"Don't."

She gave me another appraising look. "You don't trust him?"

"I don't trust anyone."

"Even me?"

I didn't answer.

"Interesting," she said. She glanced at the closed partition. "I'm assuming, then, you don't trust the driver either?"

Again I didn't answer.

"You can trust him," she assured. "He's one of my own staff."

"What all does he know?"

"He's under the impression that you will soon be getting out, and that he'll then take me to the Fillmore."

"Won't he realize I'm not you pretty quickly?"

"No."

"Won't I be conspicuous stepping out of this thing wearing whatever is inside that case?"

"Again, no. The driver is fine, Ben. You can trust him, just as you can trust me and Edward. I understand you've gone through a lot, and based on how you acted earlier this afternoon, I think you've built a large wall around you to keep you safe."

"I didn't know you were a therapist, too."

"There you go again," she said with a small smile. "Sarcasm is your defense mechanism. That's what you hide behind."

I looked at the attaché case again. "Can I see it?"

Her hand remained on the case. The diamond on her engagement ring sparkled like it was new.

"Do you remember Sunday School as a child?"

"Can I see it?" I asked again.

"Please, humor me. In Sunday School they told the story about Daniel in the lions' den. Does it ring a bell?"

"What about it?"

"Daniel was an official in the Persian empire under King Darius. Darius made a decree that no one was to offer prayer to any god or man except him for a period of thirty days. Daniel decided to ignore this and continued praying to God, and he was arrested and thrown into the lions' den where he was supposed to be ravaged."

"But he wasn't."

The congresswoman shook her head. "No, he wasn't. He was unharmed because he kept his faith in God."

"Maybe he was unharmed because the lions were fasting."

"You're missing the point, Ben. Tonight, you're headed into the lions' den. And where you're going, there is no God or prayer to keep you safe."

I looked again at the attaché case. "Can I see it?"

She was quiet for a moment, watching me. Then she took a breath, turned in her seat, tilted the case toward her, and unsnapped both clasps. She lifted the lid and tilted the case back toward me.

I leaned forward and whispered, "Holy shit."

"Do you recognize it?"

"It's a Bauta mask."

In my ear, the Kid said, "I *told* you this was going to be some fucked up *Eyes Wide Shut* bullshit."

The congresswoman raised an eyebrow. "I'm impressed."

I reached out, meaning to touch the mask, but at that moment the limo drove over another pothole. This one was even bigger than the last, and the attaché case slipped from the congresswoman's fingers. It fell awkwardly on the floor, spilling the mask and what else was inside.

I let the mask be for the time being, and instead picked up what felt like a silky black bed sheet.

"That's the robe," the congresswoman said. "The cowl is there too, as well as black gloves. You are much taller than me, but I believe the robe is a one size fits all type of thing. Though who knows, it might not quite reach the floor."

I set the robe and cowl and gloves aside before leaning down to pick up the mask. I held it delicately. It was light and thin and felt like it might break in my hands if I wasn't careful.

The congresswoman asked, "How do you know what kind of mask it is?"

"I've done my research."

"And?"

"The Bauta is typically known as a mask from the Carnival of Venice. Nobody really knows why and how they started wearing masks during the Carnival, but it was most likely in response to the government at the time. By wearing masks like this, nobody knew who anybody else was. In many ways, they were all equals."

It struck me that I sounded much smarter than I actually am. That was because, like I told the congresswoman, I had done my research. We all had. When we found out about the Coliseum, and how every member of the Inner Circle would be present, and how all their identities would be kept secret, it was clear they would all be wearing masks. The question, then, was just what kind of mask. So we researched what we could, speculating on the different kinds, the pros and cons to each, and the Bauta had been one of the masks high up on our list, next to those two famous masks representing the division between comedy and tragedy, both symbols of those ancient Greek muses, Thalia and Melpomene.

But the Bauta mask made a whole lot more sense.

Naturally, it covered the entire face. Like most masks, that was its purpose. Only unlike some masks—especially those from the Carnival of Venice—it wasn't meant to be a fashion statement. There were no decorations whatsoever. It was white and made of porcelain with two large eyeholes. The nose was almost exaggerated in its form and size. There was no mouth, but instead the mask ended with a square jawline, tilted upward. This made it possible for the wearer to talk and eat and drink without having to remove the mask. It maintained the wearer's anonymity.

Perfect for an occasion such as the Coliseum.

I turned the mask over to find the strap. The inside was cushioned on the forehead and the sides.

The congresswoman cleared her throat, trying to get my attention. She said, "When I first saw that yesterday, it gave me the creeps. It still does. Tell me, Ben, are you carrying a weapon?"

I looked at her and held her gaze as I lied.

"No."

"Are you sure that's wise? You might need a weapon."

I said nothing to this. I picked up the attaché case, set it on the seat beside me, and put in first the robe and cowl and gloves, then the Bauta mask.

The congresswoman, staring at it, shivered visibly. "I can't imagine anyone actually wanting to wear that for fun."

"Is that what tonight is supposed to be, then—fun?"

"For most, yes. For others … I have no idea." She glanced at her watch. "In the next several minutes the driver will let me out, and once I leave you should put everything on."

"Those were the instructions?"

"Yes. They were very simple and clear. The driver will take you to the Coliseum and drop you off, and once you step out of the limo, you should be wearing everything in that case. Nobody will know who you are. The driver will leave, and will not return until later in the morning."

"What time?"

"The times are staggered throughout the morning, just as the arrival times are staggered. You know how New York traffic can be. Plus, you have to take into account that with over one thousand members of the Inner Circle, all arriving separately, they can't all walk through the front door at the same time. I'm sure some others have already arrived. I'm sure they've been waiting for hours."

"So what time does the event start?"

"Midnight."

We didn't speak for the rest of the ride. It was nearly eleven o'clock, which meant after I arrived, I would have about an hour to do nothing but wait.

The congresswoman folded her hands in her lap and stared out the window.

I sat staring down at the attaché case and didn't say a word. Not when the limo eventually eased to a stop. Not when the back door opened and Edward Stark poked his head in and wished me luck. Not when Congresswoman Francis "Frank" Houser stepped out. Not even when she leaned back in and said, looking at me gravely, "Take care, Ben." I just nodded, and she shut the door, and then the limo started driving again.

SIXTY-ONE

They entered the building through a service door on the street. Just inside the door, sitting at a desk with two computer monitors, was an overweight black man in his fifties. Gray in his hair, gray in his mustache, wrinkles around his eyes, it looked like he hadn't left his station in over a decade.

Drew and Beverly stepped up to the desk, neither of them smiling. Instead they gave the tired, irritated expressions reserved for those ready to start a long and boring shift.

The man behind the desk wore a generic gray security shirt. His name tag said ANDRE. He barely even glanced at them as he reached up without a word, his other hand moving and clicking a mouse.

They each had their employee badges ready.

Andre took Beverly's first. "You two fresh meat?"

Drew said, "Started earlier this week."

Beverly said, "My first night."

Andre didn't look like he much cared. He gave Beverly's card a perfunctory swipe, expecting it to go through, for her name and picture to appear on one of his monitors. Nothing happened. He frowned, swiped the card again. Got the same result.

"You said this is your first shift, right?" he asked Beverly.

She nodded.

He frowned again at his computer screen, then said to Drew, "Let me try your card."

Drew handed over his card.

Andre swiped it, but slowly this time, like the speed in which the card traveled through the device would somehow make a difference.

Just like Beverly's card, this one didn't go through.

Andre said, "Hold on a moment," and picked up the phone on his desk.

The Kid was in a dark room two blocks away. Three computer monitors and two laptops were set up on two tables that had been positioned at a ninety-degree angle. An office chair was between the two tables, and this was where the Kid sat, swiveling back and forth to whatever computer he needed. He wore a Logitech wireless headset, complete with a noise-canceling boom mic, which he used to communicate with the rest of the team.

Like now, with Drew and Beverly, he said, "Stay cool, stay cool," while he typed furiously on one of the laptops. Earlier today he had made sure everything was square with their cover. He had gotten them into the system, had made sure their cards would work just fine, but something had gone wrong. What, he couldn't say, but if this was any indication of how tonight would go, they were all fucked.

From the corner of his eye, he saw a red light blinking on one of the monitors. He swiveled to the monitor, clicked his mouse, and heard a ringing in his earphones. He clicked the mouse again, and said, "Security IT."

"Yeah, this is Andre from downstairs. Is Bobby around?"

"Bobby stepped out. Went to take a shit, I think. What's up?"

"I got two new employees down here who aren't in the system."

"Oh yeah?"

"Yeah. Was hoping you could double-check them for me."

The Kid typed and clicked, closing out one window and opening another. He was hacked into the building's system—he'd hacked in three days prior, just to test it out—and saw that for some reason Drew and Beverly (or at least their aliases) had been inactivated. But at least they were in the system, which made the Kid's job a whole lot easier, just a few more clicks and a few more commands, and voilà, done.

"Sure thing," the Kid said. "What are their names?"

One of the monitors to the far left showed Andre with Beverly and Drew. The security camera was in the ceiling corner. The quality was pretty shitty, as most security feeds are, but still the Kid watched Andre pick up both employee cards and then squint at the names.

"Theresa Muniz and Alfonzo Jones."

"Okay," the Kid said slowly, like he was typing their names into the system. He paused a beat and said, "I see them on my screen. What's the problem?"

"Their cards aren't going through."

"Is that right? Hmm. How about you try them again."

The Kid watched Andre clamp the phone between his chin and shoulder while he swiped one of the cards again.

This time—thank Christ—it went through.

"Everything okay?"

"Yeah," Andre said. He swiped the second card, which also went through. "Looks like everything's fine down here."

On the screen, Andre handed Drew and Beverly back their

cards and waved goodbye. Drew and Beverly, both wearing backpacks, turned and headed down the corridor.

Andre said, "Bobby back yet?"

"Not yet."

"If you see him tell him to give me a call. He still owes me ten bucks on last week's Knicks game."

"Will do."

"Thanks. By the way, what did you say your name was again?"

The Kid clicked the mouse to another feed, watching Drew and Beverly as they came to the service elevator.

"Peter," he said. "I have to run. Got another call coming in. I'll take another look at the system to make sure that doesn't happen again."

He disconnected before Andre could say anything else. Then he switched over the communication feed to Drew and Beverly, both who wore tiny earpieces and both who had just stepped into the service elevator.

"You guys okay?"

"Shit," Drew said. "That was close."

"I had it all under control. Beverly, you okay?"

"I'm fine," she said, though she didn't sound fine. She sounded scared out of her wits.

"I'll check back in with you guys when you hit the roof."

He clicked off and turned to another monitor. This one gave the location of each member of the team. When everyone was closer, he would open the communication feed so everyone could listen in and know what was going on. Now, though, he had to keep it separate.

He saw Ben was still up in Harlem, waiting under that overpass, and clicked the mouse again.

"Well?" he said.

"Still waiting."

"Jesus Christ."

Mason Coulter smelled like shit. Literally.

It wasn't his idea. It was the team's—God, how it felt weird to think of himself as part of a "team"—and when the idea was initially brought up four days ago, Mason didn't object. He knew he had to carry his own weight. He knew he had to help. Despite everything that had happened to him and his family, Mason wasn't about to give up. Even if Gloria and Anthony were dead—and Mason had to accept the fact they most likely were, based on everything he had been told by Ben and Ronny, after everything he had seen and learned for himself—he couldn't give up. Those motherfuckers had taken them and killed them, and Mason was going to make them pay. Not every last one of them—he wasn't that arrogant or delusional—but at least enough to clear his conscience and reset the skewed balance of his mixed up universe.

He hadn't showered in nearly a week. He hadn't shaved. He wore a wig, a brown dirty thing that smelled like trash. He wore a dirty hat, a dirty coat, a dirty pair of jeans. His boots— yep, you guessed it—were also dirty. Every piece of clothing except his underwear had been taken piecemeal from other homeless around the city. They had done that on the first day. Had gone up to a homeless person, offered fifty dollars for whatever piece of clothing they needed. By the end of the day, Mason had his getup. He had been wearing it ever since. If he was going to do this, he was going to jump in with both feet. Hell, he was going to jump in head-fucking-first.

And so for the past three days he had been literally living on the streets of Manhattan. Watching the other homeless to see how they survived. Picking up the same tricks. Relieving himself in pretty much the same places. Eating what food happened to come his way—a half-eaten soft pretzel dropped by a tourist, or a Burger King Whopper handed to him by a parishioner of a nearby church, who offered the sandwich in exchange for just five minutes of Mason's time to hear about the Lord Christ Jesus. This very same parishioner even offered to let Mason spend the night in the church's basement. Mason thanked him for the sandwich and the offer, but politely declined. Still, it warmed him, that little bit of humanity. It was nice to know he actually existed to some, as to most he had become invisible.

He wasn't sure why this surprised him. He had encountered his fair share of homeless people in the past, and had managed to ignore them just fine. It was what you did. An unspoken rule of conduct when in major cities. The homeless was there, an eyesore, and you simply walked by. Maybe threw them a few extra cents from your pocket. That was all.

This was, of course, the reason why Mason was on the street to begin with.

But there were rules—rules Mason quickly learned in the first two days. There were places the homeless were not welcome. Well, besides shelters, the homeless were not really welcome anywhere, but there were places that the cops let them slide, and there were places they were prohibited.

The Theater District was one of those places.

After all, it was a high tourist area—not to mention those in high society frequented the plays—so it made sense that the city did not want human trash littering the streets.

So it was difficult, trying to figure out the patterns of the cops and tourists. It was difficult, because time was short. They only had days—mere seconds in the larger scheme of space and time—and they couldn't waste a moment.

Ben and Ronny walked past the Fillmore every day, yes, but it was Mason's job to keep a constant eye on the place. Not that he could do this, because he was always moving, being hustled away by one cop or another, or moving on his own when he saw them coming. But the purpose was to become invisible, to hole himself up in a corner with a ratty blanket, and act like he had given up on life.

Which he was doing that evening, around eleven o'clock, a block up from the Fillmore. The angle wasn't very good, but he had been watching the limos and Town Cars entering the garage attached to the Fillmore. They would appear minutes later and drive away. For hours this had been happening, one after another, spaced maybe five or ten minutes apart.

In his ear was a tiny transmitter that the Kid could use to talk to him, and Mason could use to talk to the Kid.

In his pocket was a full-size Beretta nine millimeter. In his other pocket were three full magazines.

Under his coat, strapped to his Kevlar-protected chest, was an MP5. Just like the one that hotel clerk Kevin had fired back at the Beachside Hotel in Miami Beach at the start of this whole awful mess.

Mason was sitting there a block away, watching the Fillmore, just waiting.

Waiting to take as many of the motherfuckers out as he could.

Waiting to die.

Ronny and Maya sat in silence. They'd been sitting in silence for nearly an hour. Neither of them had anything to say. At least, Maya didn't have anything to say. Not right now. Not with the full weight of what they intended to do tonight pressing down on her shoulders. At times, the pressure became so much she barely knew how to breathe. This wasn't like her. She was usually much more confident, much more in control. She'd killed people before—bad people—and while it had been difficult at first to accept and acknowledge that this was now her life, she eventually grew accustomed to holding a gun, to aiming it and firing it with the intention of taking someone's life.

She worried about Ben.

She wasn't happy with how they'd left things. At the same time, she wasn't happy being lied to, either.

But *had* she been lied to?

That was the question. Something terrible had happened to Ben, just as something terrible had happened to all of them. Only, when Ben thought everything was over, something even more terrible happened: he watched his family die.

Maya couldn't even begin to imagine just how awful that must have been. She *thought* she knew, but thinking and feeling and knowing were all completely different things. She hadn't had a family in a very long time. Her game with Simon had been a fluke that way. She could have easily just said no from the very start, but she had gone along with it. Why? Because she wanted to know where she came from. She wanted to know who her true family was. Some people probably didn't care much about those things, but she did. She cared so much sometimes it hurt.

And so she sat there with Ronny and waited. Both with Kevlar vests. Both with rifles and guns and extra ammunition. Both with the tiny earpieces to keep them in contact with the Kid.

Maya closed her eyes, took a deep breath.

Ronny asked, "You okay?"

She nodded. Opened her eyes. Stared out through the bug-splattered windshield.

And waited.

The Kid kept his eye on the computer monitors. The one monitor he watched most was the middle one, the one tracking

Ben's movements through the city streets as he rode in Congresswoman Houser's limo.

While Drew and Beverly reached the roof of the building and began assembling Drew's equipment, the Kid watched.

While Mason Coulter hunkered down in his space a block away from the Fillmore, the Kid watched.

While Ronny and Maya sat in silence in the truck, the Kid watched.

He listened to everything Ben and the congresswoman said to each other. He listened as the congresswoman exited the limo. He listened to the quiet shush of fabric as Ben put on the robe and cowl and gloves.

"How does the mask feel?" the Kid asked quietly.

Ben was silent for several long seconds. "I haven't put it on yet."

The Kid checked Ben's current location in regard to the Fillmore. "You don't have much time."

Ben said nothing.

And so the Kid sat there and watched the monitors, keeping his eye on Ben's location as it drew closer and closer to the Fillmore, while Drew and Beverly and Mason and Ronny and Maya all waited.

Then Ben's limo turned a corner, came down the block, and the Kid flicked the switch so that everyone could hear him.

"He's here."

SIXTY-TWO

When the limo made the turn onto West 43rd Street, I finally put on the mask.

I'd been putting it off since the congresswoman exited the limo. Just sitting there, the mask in my hands, as the limo weaved through the city streets. The Kid had spoken to me briefly, but that was it. It was completely silent in the back of the vehicle. The driver—and I still didn't like the fact I had no idea who the driver was—may have been singing along to the radio for all I knew.

The mask fit snugly against my face. Despite how much the contacts irritated my eyes, I was thankful for them. There was no way I would have been able to wear this mask comfortably with glasses.

The limo slowed as it approached the Fillmore. Through the window I saw people walking the sidewalks, oblivious to tonight's special meeting of the Inner Circle. The limo's rear windows were tinted, so I had no worries about being seen. At that moment I was, just like every other member of the Inner Circle, a voyeur.

In my ear, the Kid whispered, "Ben?"

"Yeah."

"How are you holding up?"

"I'm fine."

There was a long pause. Then the Kid said, "Good luck, dude."

The limo slowed even more, almost to a crawl, as it made the turn. It bounced slightly over the spot where street and sidewalk met, and then began to ride its brake down a decline.

Out the window, all I could see was concrete.

After several seconds, the limo slowed again. It came to a complete stop. Through the window on the other side of the limo, I watched a car pass by, going the opposite direction. Having deposited its own special member of the Inner Circle, it was headed back up to the street.

Before, I had heard the faint city sounds beyond the limo. Now there was complete silence. Only the hum of the engine. A distant opening and closing of a car door. Then, after a few seconds, the limo moved forward again, only to once more stop.

It went on like this for another five minutes. At one point, headlights splashed through the rear window as another limo came down the ramp. Then, suddenly, my limo pulled forward again and the concrete disappeared to reveal a dark overhang. There was motion beyond the window—someone approaching —and then the back door opened.

I didn't move.

The person who had opened the door didn't move either. They didn't even speak.

Through the door I saw the overhang was some kind of black cloth. It had been constructed of tall stanchions, basically creating a tunnel from the opened limo door to the opened door of the Fillmore maybe twenty yards away.

Standing just inside the door was someone dressed in a

black robe and cowl and gloves. They too wore a mask, only theirs was black.

I stepped out of the limo. Glanced at the person who had opened my door—someone else dressed in a black robe and cowl and gloves, the mask also black, no doubt an employee of Caesar's—who merely nodded at me.

An ungloved hand suddenly appeared through the black cloth. It came in only arm's length. The arm was not covered by a robe, but by a gray suit jacket.

The mask who had opened my door took a slip of paper from the disembodied hand. The mask looked at the paper and said, "This is your number. Your driver will return at a specific time in the morning to pick you up."

The voice belonged to a woman. I didn't know why, but this surprised me.

By instinct, I meant to say thank you, but caught myself at the last second and only nodded as I took the ticket. Then I turned and continued down the tunnel toward the other mask waiting for me.

I stepped into an elevator.

The black mask said, "Welcome to the Coliseum. This will only take a moment." The black mask pressed a button, and the doors closed, and then the elevator took us up to the first floor, where the doors opened once again. The black mask said, "Enjoy."

Again, my instinct was to say thank you, but I only nodded. I stepped out and the elevator doors closed behind me. Waiting here were three more black masks, standing in a line. The one on the end closest to me stepped forward and said, "Welcome to the Coliseum. Please follow me to the banquet room."

I had seen interior pictures of the Fillmore online, so I

wasn't surprised by the red plush carpet, or the ornate wainscoting, or the elegant lamps hanging from the ceiling every twenty feet or so. Normally they were turned on brightly, but tonight they had been dimmed a notch, creating just enough ambient light for guests to proceed down the hallway without any trouble.

We walked in silence. Another mask approached us and then passed us, presumably having escorted the member of the Inner Circle who had been dropped off before me.

The mask escorting me said, "Before I direct you into the banquet room, do you need to use the restroom?"

I shook my head.

"If you need to later," she said, raising her hand and pointing vaguely, "they are down this hallway and to the left."

After ten more paces she stopped before two large wooden doors with brass handles. She placed her hand on one of these handles but paused and turned back to me.

"Please help yourself to whatever you would like. If you would not like to partake, you can continue on to the other side of the banquet room, and another one of my colleagues will lead you to the auditorium."

Back up the hallway another member of the Inner Circle wearing a black robe and cowl and gloves, the white mask gleaming in the faint light, had just gotten off the elevator and was being led this way by another black mask.

"Thank you," I said quietly.

Despite the fact I couldn't see her face, I knew the woman behind the black mask was smiling.

"Certainly," she said, and opened the door.

The banquet room was huge. I'd seen pictures of it, of course, but they had been staged, the kind of pictures taken for brochures and specialty magazines (the Fillmore was a very special case, in fact, as most theaters did not have banquet rooms). But pictures can never truly bring across the experience of seeing something for yourself. Not the overly elaborate chandelier hanging above the center of the room. Not the light sconces on the walls. Not the soft and melodic twang from a harp being played in the corner, or even the sweet and tempting aroma of all the food laid out on numerous tables.

A black mask carrying a tray of champagne flutes approached me. I waved it away. The mask nodded and stepped aside.

There were maybe two hundred members of the Inner Circle currently milling about. Not that many, but I had to assume the majority had already partaken in the drinks and food and were now waiting in the auditorium. That was where I wanted to be, too, not here where those remaining members murmured to each other about one thing or another, while they held thin flutes of champagne or small ceramic plates topped with hors d'oeuvres. The Bauta masks were doing their job perfectly, allowing the members of the Inner Circle to drink and eat while also maintaining their anonymity.

I moved deeper into the room. The fabric of my robe made a faint shushing sound as I walked.

The room was redolent of steak, lobster tail, veal, and sushi. The combined odors were intoxicating and made my empty stomach growl. I hadn't eaten anything all day—I'd tried before coming but hadn't had an appetite—and I found myself gravitating toward the tables. Black masks stood behind each table, waiting to serve.

My stomach kept growling. A part of me wanted to sample the wares, while another part of me said I would be a traitor for doing so. I had already entered the lions' den. The last thing I needed to do now was to become one with the lions.

But then I remembered I *was* one with the lions, at least on the outside. And while in Rome, do as the Romans.

I picked up a plate off the table and continued down the line, nodding at or waving away the different proffered foods. Then, my plate set, I drifted toward a corner where I could stand in peace and watch the other lions as they played.

The steak was juicy, the lobster meat succulent, and while they were only bite-sized they were the best I had ever had in my thirty-four years of life. It was enough to make me want to return to the tables, but instead I motioned to one of the black masks carrying a tray. I traded my empty plate for a flute of champagne. I didn't care much for champagne, but again, when in Rome.

I started to make my way through the room toward the doors leading into the auditorium. Congresswoman Houser said the Coliseum would begin at midnight. Oddly, there was no clock in the banquet room, but I knew that time was fast approaching. Maybe the lights would dim at some point, notifying everyone the show was about to begin. I didn't want to wait for that to happen, so I continued on, passing groups of white masks huddled together, murmuring in English or French or Russian or Korean—this last making me wonder if Bae and his team had made it into the Coliseum yet, and if so, where were they currently. Many nodded to me, and I nodded back. After all, there was no way of knowing just how powerful and important the person next to you was. It was best to be respectful of everyone.

I had made it past the midway point, sipping the champagne just for show, when a white mask tore itself from a group of four and stood in my way.

"Hello." The voice was a throaty female's with a slight British accent. "English?"

It took me a beat, but then I nodded.

"Brother or sister?"

Another beat, and I said, "Brother."

"Excellent!" She took my arm and brought me into the group. "We have another brother here."

The other three murmured hellos.

She said, "Brother, we were just discussing our favorite games. What is yours?"

I shifted my gaze from her to the other three. They were all watching me. I could see their eyes through the holes in the Bauta masks. Two of them had blue eyes. One of them had brown. The woman—or sister, if that was what we were calling each other—who still grasped my arm had green.

This was not where I wanted to be right now. I wanted to be in the auditorium, waiting for the show to start. I did not want to be here, in this banquet room, a flute of champagne in one hand, interacting with these disgusting people. Still, when in Rome.

I said, "I would have to say the Man of Wax."

The sister's eyes lit up. "That *is* a good one. Very exciting. We were just discussing it, as a matter of fact."

One of the blue-eyed masks nodded. "Yes. It featured the Man of Honor."

The brown-eyed mask asked me, "Have you heard about the special surprise?"

"If I did then it wouldn't be a surprise, would it?"

They all found this extremely amusing. Their laughter was the kind of quiet, forced laughter that is actually quite genuine to the stuffy elite.

"The Man of Honor," the sister whispered excitedly, still grasping my arm. "They've captured him!"

"They have?"

The other blue-eyed mask said, "Clearly you missed the Racist's game. That was just last week. They captured the Man of Honor then."

"Excellent," I said.

They all nodded in agreement.

As I had expected, the lights around the room began to dim. They rose again, dimmed, then rose once more.

Everyone stopped his or her murmured conversations. They may have been among the most important and powerful people in the world, but they knew their place. They stopped what they were doing, and set their plates and flutes of champagne aside, and continued toward the doors leading into the auditorium. They moved at a slow, measured pace. Nobody tried jostling for a better position. They knew they would be seated in time, and that the show would not begin until everyone was ready.

The woman had finally released her grasp on my arm. She disappeared into the crowd. Everyone was wearing black robes and cowls and gloves and white masks. It was impossible to differentiate anybody except for height.

We waited in line and slowly moved toward the auditorium, one after one, completely obedient.

Like lambs being led to a slaughter.

SIXTY-THREE

It didn't take long. In less than a half hour they had everyone seated. More black masks acted as ushers, taking one member of the Inner Circle after another to an open seat. They were orderly. They were deliberate. They performed their jobs with great expertise.

I ended up being seated just underneath the balcony, which was also full of those in the Inner Circle. Even the few boxes along the sides of the auditorium were full.

The seats were upholstered in velvet, just as plush as the carpet. The chandelier hanging above the main seats was even more ornate than the one in the banquet room. On stage the red curtain was drawn.

The white mask sitting to my right wore heavy perfume. The white mask to my left was heavyset and breathed forcefully. He had a small device in his hand. It looked like an iPhone, but it wasn't an iPhone. Earphones were attached to it. A translating device. I noticed some other white masks spread out around the auditorium also had these devices.

The auditorium was completely silent. The hushed murmur

from the banquet room was over. Everyone was quietly waiting for the show to begin.

It began in less than five minutes.

The lights dimmed.

A spotlight came on, illuminating the curtain at center stage.

The quiet enveloping the auditorium somehow deepened.

Heavyset turned on the device in his hand, put in his earphones. Others nearby turned on their devices and put in their earphones as well. The small screens illuminated portions of the auditorium. I was almost half-tempted to remind him to turn off all cellular devices before the movie started, but then thought it might not be the best idea.

On stage, the red velvet curtain began to lift. It was a slow process. Like they were trying to draw out the suspense. Knowing what little I knew of Caesar, they probably were.

In the middle of the stage, all you could see at first were a pair of feet. Then legs. Then torso. And still the curtain slowly lifted, revealing the rest of the body that was draped in a robe and cowl and mask.

Only this mask wasn't white or black.

This mask was gold.

I don't know where it started in the auditorium, but someone began to clap. And clapping, just like yawning, is contagious. Within a minute, the entire place was clapping, me included, because again, when in Rome.

Caesar stood perfectly still the entire time. He kept his hands behind his back, soaking in the attention. When it finally died out, he lifted his hands—gloved just like everyone else's—and spoke. His voice filled the auditorium.

"Friends, Romans, countrymen, lend me your ears!"

Again, everyone applauded.

In my ear, I could just make out the Kid saying, "Christ, did he *really* just open with Shakespeare?"

When the applause died down, Caesar lowered his arms.

"Welcome to the Coliseum. I thank you for your countless contributions and your years of patience. I am quite happy to tell you that the wait is almost over. The plan I had envisioned over three decades ago will finally become complete. Our world, as you know, is in chaos. There is war, famine, genocide. The law means nothing anymore. It is time for a change!"

Judging by his voice, the man sounded like he was in his fifties. Well spoken. No doubt well educated.

"This change is our own Pax Romana. It will help save our world and return it to a better, simpler time. A time where none of us will have to worry about the future. A time where each and every one of us will live like kings and queens!"

The voice, I hated to admit, almost came across as warm and kind. Definitely American. What sounded more like mid-Atlantic. No southern twang. No New England vernacular.

"I will explain more about the Pax Romana when we convene again later tonight. Before that, the Coliseum is a place where you can come together in your own different ways. Many of you already conversed in the banquet room, which I understand was a great success. Soon, you will be able to roam about this building. We have countless tablets available to you, all programmed with every past game we have ever shown. We have also established several live games. Whether it's torture, murder, rape, incest, bestiality—we have it here for you to view live. But seating is limited. It will be first come, first serve. Finally, if you have not yet heard, we have a surprise guest. Someone I am sure will please each and every one of you."

Behind Caesar a large white screen was slowly being lowered from the ceiling.

"They say a picture is worth a thousand words, so I have decided to show you who you can expect tonight."

Caesar walked fourteen paces to the left. They were slow,

deliberate paces, taken by someone who knew fully well what he was doing.

On the screen a picture appeared, about twelve feet tall. It was being projected from a digital projector somewhere above the balcony.

It was a familiar picture, for those accustomed to watching the games. The camera was positioned in the upper corner of a motel room. It was aimed at the bed and the person lying on top of it.

Carver.

The phone beside the bed started ringing. It rang nine times before Carver, coming out of unconsciousness, lifted his head and noticed his surroundings. He sat up suddenly, looking around the room in search of the camera, then down at the phone beside him.

He answered it, listened for a few seconds, and then said, "Fuck you."

Silence. None of us could hear Simon's side of the conversation, but I remembered it from Carver's retelling. Simon telling Carver that wasn't very nice, that either he was going to play nice or he wasn't going to play at all. Then Simon asking him if he was ready for the first part of the game. It was simple. Go take a piss.

Carver sat there for another moment, frozen by indecision. The angle wasn't the best—he was turned away from the camera—but I could see a younger version of Carver there. I had never seen any earlier pictures of him, but it was clear that in the past four years he had aged nearly a decade.

And it struck me that while I had heard this story before— I had even written about it—I had never actually seen it. The scene had always been in my mind, and I found myself focusing not on Carver so much as the room around him.

The threadbare chair in the corner. The dirty curtains decorated with autumn leaves. The shape of the lamp on the bedside table next to the phone. They had all been different from the images my imagination had fed me all this time, and there was something in the sudden reality that my mind refused to accept, like a child being told for the very first time that Santa Claus isn't real.

On the screen—and about four years ago—Carver stood up from the bed. He ignored the thick glasses on the bedside table. It didn't matter, though; there was another camera in the bathroom.

It was positioned just right so that when Carver took a step forward and peered down into the toilet, saw what he believed to be his four-month-old son lying facedown in the water, the camera captured every detail of his features—the sudden intake of breath, the widening of the eyes, and then the slow shaking of the head.

The image paused there. Carver's face, frozen on the big screen, his eyes filled with horror and revulsion.

Beside me, Heavyset chuckled in such a way that I wanted to reach over and grab his translating device and shove it down his throat. Either that, or bring out the Glock 27 and shoot him in his fat ugly face.

Caesar said, "Yes, friends, that is right. The Man of Honor himself will grace us with his presence this evening. And the look you see there on his face? Be prepared to see a look just like it later tonight."

The image disappeared, and the white screen began rising back up into the ceiling.

Caesar walked back to center stage. He raised his gloved hands again. The spotlight's heavy glare radiated off his golden mask.

"This Coliseum is for you. Relax and enjoy yourselves. Again, I welcome you, and I thank you."

He took a very small bow, stepped back, and waited as the red curtain began to descend and close.

And while it hadn't been much of a show in my opinion, the crowd ate it up. They must have loved every goddamn second of it. First one person rose to their feet, clapping, then another, then another, until the entire auditorium was giving a standing ovation. Even me. As much as I hated to do it, I had no choice.

After all, when in Rome.

SIXTY-FOUR

The black masks filed us out of the auditorium just as expertly as they had filed us in. Because I was near the back, I was one of the first ones in the lobby. Here over a dozen tables had been set up. On each table were piles of tablets, as promised by Caesar. As we walked out, we were handed our very own.

It wasn't an iPad or any other tablet I recognized, but was the same basic idea and setup. I touched the blank screen and it lit up with a list of names. These were the shows, presumably, that Caesar had been presenting to the Inner Circle and everyone else who paid good money for entertainment from the very beginning. All in alphabetical order.

I scrolled down through the list. I saw my show. I saw Carver's show. I saw Maya's show and Ronny's show and Drew's show and Beverly's show. Even Mason's show—the most recent, except for Clark's—was listed.

But these were only the shows listed in the United States.

I swiped the screen, and brought up another list, this one marked UNITED KINGDOM. Below this were just as many entries as those listed under UNITED STATES.

I swiped the screen again, and again, and again. Scores of countries were included, countless games.

I kept swiping until I came to the one marked KOREA. I scrolled down, trying to find Bae's game, but every listing was in Korean. And even if the listings were in English, Bae hadn't told me the name of his game. In fact, I didn't think he even knew the name of his game.

Around the lobby, members of the Inner Circle began to converge. Like in the banquet room, a hushed murmur started filling the air. More black masks weaved through the crowd holding trays of champagne.

Off to the left was a poster board on an easel, directing those members interested toward the special rooms. These were labeled **TORTURE**, **MURDER**, **RAPE**, **INCEST**, **BESTIALITY** in big block letters. Another poster board on a similar easel was set up on the other side of the auditorium doors.

Going into any of those rooms was the very last thing I wanted to do. I wanted to find Carver. This was why I was here, why everyone on the team was here. But it wasn't just like I could wander around the Fillmore. Certain sections would be off-limits. Even if I stumbled across one of those sections, there was a very good chance a black mask would be waiting to direct me back to the main area.

I didn't want to get stuck in conversation again either, no matter how brief. I kept replaying the short encounter I had with those four from the banquet room—the two blue eyes, the brown eyes, and the green eyes—and knew I might not be so lucky if it happened again. I could hear snatches of conversation around the lobby—in English as well as many other languages—and the last thing I needed right now was to be asked a specific question a member of the Inner Circle should know and which I did not.

Two curved staircases flanked the auditorium doors. I took the tablet and started toward the one staircase. I wasn't sure where I was going, but I didn't want to stay stationary for too long.

I went only four feet before I stopped.

In my head, a distant voice whispered: *There's something you don't know about me. I love to torture. I get off on it.*

Slowly I turned, back toward the poster board on the easel. A few members of the Inner Circle were currently gathered around it. I stepped up behind them and inspected the board again. Before, I had merely glanced at the big block lettered words, but now I noticed the room numbers beneath each.

The room that currently had my interest—**TORTURE**—was on the second floor, room 3.

I turned and started toward the stairs.

Two black masks stood outside room 3. They were politely and professionally explaining to whoever came up to them that all the seats inside were currently occupied. There was, however, standing room for anyone interested in that.

This turned away several eager members. A few others, me included, entered the room.

The room was fairly large. It looked like the kind of place a business meeting would take place during normal hours. Executives might sit around a long table and discuss their company's future. If there was ever a table like that here, it was now gone.

Nearly one hundred chairs occupied most of the space. In the front of the room, clear plastic tarp had been laid out across the floor, as well as against the front wall.

On the plastic tarp were two chairs, surrounded by tall lamps. The two chairs were occupied. As both were stripped of their clothing except for their underwear, it was clear one was a young boy, the other a woman. The boy was wearing white jockey shorts that were already wet and yellow. The woman wore white panties and a white bra. A black cloth bag was over each of their heads.

Standing off to the side were two black masks. Beside them was a table, with a number of tools on top—knives, pliers, hammers, saws.

I pushed up against the wall in the corner. It was a tight fit, as more and more members squeezed into the room. Finally it came to the point where the black masks outside the room had no choice but to direct members elsewhere.

In my ear, the Kid asked, "What's going on?"

I didn't answer.

The two black masks up front stood waiting. They may have been whispering to one another for all I knew. I tried remembering just how tall Clark was. Both black masks seemed to fit the profile, but it was really impossible to say for certain.

Finally the show began. The lights in the ceiling dimmed, leaving only those lamps up front to shine down on the two victims.

One of the black masks stepped forward to address the crowd.

"Welcome to the Torture Room. As you probably guessed by the name, we are going to do some torturing tonight."

A soft and polite chuckle drifted across the room from several members. A few had those small translation devices in their hands.

The voice was male. Deep. Familiar.

My right hand drifted to my back. To where the Glock was currently tucked in the waistband of my suit pants. It would take two seconds to reach under my robe and grab it. It would take another second to aim and shoot Clark right in his black masked face.

"You're probably wondering who our guests are tonight,"

Clark said as the other black mask went to stand behind the boy and woman. "They are, in fact, mother and son."

The other black mask reached out and grabbed both cloth bags and lifted them up slowly to reveal the boy's and woman's faces.

They squinted at once. Duct tape covered their mouths, muffling their attempts to cry out. Their hands were tied behind their backs, their ankles to the chair, but despite this they both still tried to wiggle free.

Another chorus of chuckles drifted across the room.

Clark began speaking again, explaining what they were going to do tonight and just how they were going to do it, but I wasn't listening. Instead, I was staring at the woman and the boy—the mother and the son—and wondering where I had seen them before. For some reason they were familiar, but I couldn't quite place them.

Then, quite suddenly, I did.

"Holy fuck," I whispered.

The Kid asked, "What's wrong?"

I pushed off the wall and made my way to the doors.

"I see I'm already boring someone," Clark said, not unkindly. "Please, do stay. I promise this will be a show you'll never forget."

I turned to him, wanting so much to pull the Glock out and kill him. Instead I bowed slightly and turned back to the door and stepped into the hallway. A line of members waited against the wall. Once I came out, one of the black masks directed one of the members inside to take my place.

I drifted to a far corner, out of earshot of any nearby members.

I whispered, "Kid, cut all communication except you and me."

There was a brief pause. Then the Kid said, "Done. What's wrong?"

"Do you have eyes on Mason?"

"I know where he currently is, yes. Why?"

"There's been a new complication."

"Meaning?"

"Mason's wife and son are here. And they're about to be tortured."

SIXTY-FIVE

The Kid didn't answer right away. There was a moment or two of silence—a silence where I thought we had somehow become disconnected—before he finally spoke.

"What do you plan on doing?"

"I'm not sure yet."

"You can't complicate this mission."

"I also can't just stand by and let them get tortured."

"It's an unfortunate turn of events, I agree, but—"

"An unfortunate turn of events? Did you really just fucking say that?"

"Ben, stick to the plan."

I said nothing.

The Kid said, "Do you hear me?"

"I hear you." I stood in the corner with the tablet like I was looking at it, but now turned to check on the two black masks and the line of waiting members by the doors. "The plan is still a go."

"What do you mean the plan is *still* a go?"

"It's time to accelerate things."

"What? Ben, don't do what I think you're going to do. It

sucks that Mason's wife and kid are there, but you can't seriously think—"

I didn't hear the rest. I was already in motion. Heading
down the hallway, past a few members of the Inner Circle.
Walking right up to the black masks standing in front of the
doors. Stepping between them and reaching for the door
handle.

"Pardon me," said one of the black masks, placing a hand
against the door to keep it closed, "but the room is currently
filled to capacity."

"I was just in there."

"Yes, and when you exited, another member took your
place. I'm very sorry. If you would care to wait, perhaps more
room will be made available shortly."

On the other side of the door came a frantic but muffled
scream, followed by a smattering of applause.

I said, "I would like to go in there now."

"I'm sorry," the black mask said, "but right now that's
impossible."

"Do you have any idea who I am?"

The eyes staring back at me from the black Bauta mask
were ice cold.

"As a matter of fact, I believe I do."

The other black mask was already moving, stepping toward
me. I elbowed him in the neck, leaned back as the second mask
took a swing. The fist went wide, and I stepped forward and
kneed him in the groin, shoved my elbow into the mask,
breaking it, and slammed his head against the wall. Then I
turned, already reaching for my Glock, and pulled open one of
the doors.

Clark was using the pliers on Gloria Coulter's toes. She was
bucking in the chair, screaming through the duct tape, while
the other black mask held her steady.

During the commotion, Clark turned away from his work. He started to stand, the bloodied pliers at his side.

I aimed right at his black mask. Before I could pull the trigger, though, someone hit me from behind. The gun fired but my aim was off, the bullet striking the wall. I went to aim again but hands grabbed me from behind, several hands all at the same time, one of them even wrestling the gun from my grip, and I fought them just like Gloria Coulter was fighting her restraints up front. And, just like Gloria Coulter, I was helpless, as more and more black masks swarmed into the room, grabbing my arms and my legs until there was nothing more for me to do but let them drag me away.

Through the Logitech headphones the Kid heard everything. Ben exchanging words with someone. Scuffle and commotion. A single gunshot. Even more commotion. There were shouts, screams, curses, and the next thing the Kid knew a voice yelled, "Look at this," and then the entire communication feed went dead.

Well, that wasn't completely true.

The *entire* communication feed wasn't dead. Not yet, at least. But clearly someone had found the tiny transmitter in Ben's ear. Someone had plucked it out, dropped it on the ground, and smashed it.

Despite switching off communication from Ben and the rest of the team, the Kid hadn't cut off communication between him and everyone else. While they weren't able to hear him, he could certainly hear them. And the moment Ben requested the communication cut, everyone started up. First Ronny, then Drew, then Maya, then even Mason, all asking what was wrong, what was going on, Kid, goddamn it, answer us.

The Kid leaned back in his chair, staring at the monitor.

On the screen was a three-dimensional rendering of the Fillmore. Every floor, every room, every corner was mocked up in front of him.

He leaned forward, clicked his mouse, and regained communication with the team.

By this point they had stopped trying to talk to him and were now talking to each other. Asking each other what was wrong, whether Drew could tell what was happening, if Mason could tell, what happened to Ben and the Kid.

"Sorry, guys," the Kid said. "There was a complication."

"What happened?" Ronny asked.

The Kid thought about how to answer that. He knew Mason could be a loose cannon. So far he seemed to be doing fine, but that didn't mean he wouldn't complicate things if he found out his family was inside. Then again, wasn't it fair to let him know? Didn't the man deserve at least that much?

"Ben decided to speed up the process," he said.

Drew asked, "What does that mean?"

"It looks like he got himself caught."

Nobody spoke for a beat. Then Ronny said, "So what does this mean?"

"Well, currently I have good news and bad news."

Maya said, her voice hesitant, "What's the bad news?"

"They found his transmitter and destroyed it."

Ronny said, "If that's the bad news, what could possibly be the good news?"

The Kid stared at the computer screen and the yellow blinking dot that was currently moving down a hallway toward the back of the Fillmore.

"Ben still has his shoes."

They found the transmitter in my ear without any trouble. This was pretty much what we had figured would happen. The transmitter in my shoe, however, was a different story.

It was the right shoe to be exact, in the heel. It was a larger transmitter than the one that had been in my ear. Obviously I couldn't communicate with the Kid, but he could hear everything I could hear up to a point. Plus, he could track my location.

At least half a dozen black masks had swarmed on me in seconds. They were all men, strong and fit, and they pretty much beat the shit out of me. Not in the Torture Room, of course, nor in the hallway just outside the Torture Room in plain view of everyone. In the Torture Room, they had relieved me of the Glock before carrying me through the hallways to a private corridor. There they tore off my mask, my robe and cowl, and started beating me. One of them was smart enough to pat me down, to even check my ears, and that was how they found the transmitter, which was promptly taken out and destroyed. Then the beating continued, the kicking and punching, which I must admit was uncharacteristic of Caesar's people. At least I thought so for a setting such as this, but then again, what the hell did the guy getting his ass kicked know?

At one point, a loud voice shouted, "Stop!"

The kicking and punching stopped.

I lay in a fetal position on the ground, my knees held up to my chest, trying to protect my ribs and stomach and kidneys the best I could. After several seconds when I realized tonight's session of let's-kick-the-crap-out-of-Ben was momentarily over, I stretched out with a groan and rolled over onto my back. I was angled just right to watch a new black mask approaching down the corridor. This black mask was shaking its head, and as it neared, it took off its mask.

"Tell me," Clark said, "what was the last thing you said to me?"

Because I was currently in too much pain, I chose defiant silence as my answer.

"If I'm not mistaken—and to be honest, I very rarely am—it was that the next time you saw me you would kill me. And now here we are, with your sorry ass on the floor and me standing over you. What do you think about that?"

Again, I chose the defiant silence.

"It was a decent try, though, I will give you that. Took more balls than I thought you had. Of course, we don't know exactly what your plan is, but we do know you have people nearby, watching this place. Do you think they're going to come save you?" Smiling, he shook his head. "No, of course they're not. It would be suicide to come in here."

The pain, though still pretty bad, ebbed just enough for me to give up my defiant silence to ask a question.

"Is your name really Clark?"

"This again? What does it matter what my name is?"

"I like to know the names of the people I kill."

He laughed. "You are so fucking delusional."

"You better kill me now, because otherwise I will kill you."

"I highly doubt that. And as much as I would love to kill you right here, right now, Caesar wants us to hold off. He isn't happy with the scene you just caused. He figures the best way to make amends is to kill you in front of everyone later tonight, along with your friend. Speaking of which, are you ready to see your friend?"

He nodded to a few of the black masks, who stepped forward and grabbed my arms and lifted me to my feet.

Clark said, "I have to get back now. I'm a professional, and I hate it when I'm interrupted. Don't worry, though, you and I will be seeing each other again later tonight. In fact, right before I kill you, I'm going to tell you a secret. Something, I believe, that will make dying so much worse for you."

I wanted to say something smart to this, promise some

kind of threat, but the truth was I was exhausted. And it wasn't just the beating, though that didn't help matters much. These past two years had taken a great toll and I was almost to the tipping point.

Without another word, Clark put back on his mask and headed back down the corridor. The black masks started pulling me in the opposite direction.

Up ahead, there came a strangely familiar metallic noise.

I couldn't place the noise, not at first. Then we turned a corner and I saw him standing there in front of us, leaning on two crutches. His left leg was the leg that was in a cast, and the cast looked good, like it had been done by professional doctors and not by someone using supplies purchased from Walmart. The Red Sox cap was pulled low as always, and with his head down the only thing staring back at me was the red embossed B.

Then Ian lifted his head and smiled.

"Hey, Ben. Miss me?"

SIXTY-SIX

"We don't have much time to talk, so let me cut to the chase."

"What did you do, Ian?"

"Don't put this on me. Don't you dare put this on me."

"What did you do?"

"It's not my fault this happened."

I closed my eyes for a second, fighting a raging headache. "I don't think you clearly understand what the word *fault* means."

"Like I said, man, I only have a few minutes to talk to you, so I'm going to make it quick. You remember the Janitor?"

The black masks were still gripping me tightly, but that was it. Clearly they were allowing this conversation to happen. And as much as I didn't want to talk to Ian right now, I needed to know what kind of damage he'd done. Because while I could hear him, so could the Kid.

"What about him?"

"It was only a couple of months ago, right? Jesse and Maya working lead, you and me working backup. Where were we headed—Lexington, Richmond, Frankfort? Fuck, I forget. But we ended up stopping for gas. And while you were filling the tank I went to take a piss. The gas station was a pretty shitty one, with the bathrooms off on the side of the building."

"The point?"

"That's where he was waiting for me. Right when I finished up and was headed out the door, this guy was standing there waiting and pushed me back in. He had a gun, and he held it to my head, and he asked where Carver was. And I—I was so fucking scared. I'll admit it. I was still a newbie and was scared about the whole thing. I mean, fuck, this was my first time out. I was scared shitless."

"Again, the point?"

"My first time out I was supposed to be with Carver. But he was sick with the flu or something, so it was you, and I told him that. I said Carver wasn't there, that it was just you, and you know what he said? The guy said he didn't care about the Man of Wax—that's what he called you—he cared about Carver. And I … well, I started crying like a fucking girl. I couldn't help it. I begged him not to kill me, that I didn't know where Carver was, because Carver wasn't with us. The guy swore and stuck something in my mouth and told me to call when Carver came out to play again—he actually said that, when Carver came out to play again—and that if I did so Caesar would show me mercy and spare my life."

I laughed. "You think they're actually going to let you live?"

"They've been treating me really well. Got my leg here in a proper cast. You know, some real fucking medical attention."

"You're an idiot."

"No I'm not. I know my worth. I know what they want, too."

"And what's that?"

"Well, what they initially wanted to know was the Kid's real name, where he lives. But of course none of us knows that except for Carver, so they settled on the location of the farmhouse instead."

My smile faded. "You didn't."

"I did. Not that I feel good about it, but sometimes you gotta do what you gotta do."

"Like betraying Carver."

"What do you want me to say, Ben? I was fucking scared. That thing the guy put in my mouth before he walked out of the bathroom? It was a balled up piece of paper. On it was a phone number. It was actually a pretty easy number to memorize. I flushed it and cleaned myself up and came back out. You asked me what took so long. I said I'd had to shit. You asked me why my eyes were red, and you remember what I said?"

"You said it was allergies."

Ian grinned. "Right, allergies. Only thing is, I don't have allergies. And truthfully, I don't know why I didn't tell you what happened right there and then. I meant to. Honest to God. But I was still so new, and I was scared, and I wondered what you would have done if you found out. Like, what you would have done to me. First, I thought you might not believe me. Then I thought you might get suspicious of me. And then … I don't know what, but like I said, I was scared."

"Yeah, you're becoming a real broken record."

"The point is, I meant to tell you. But then I didn't, and after a while I realized I *couldn't* tell you, that I'd gone past that point. Because if I did end up telling you then, you'd be even more suspicious."

"So you're saying that guy was there and he didn't kill me?"

"Again, Ben, he didn't want you. He wanted Carver."

"He came to you because you were new."

"I know."

"Because you're weak."

"Shut up."

"Because you're pathetic."

"Shut up!" His face red, Ian looked at the black masks

holding me. "Are you just going to let him talk to me like that?"

None of the black masks responded.

"Now that they've got what they can from you, you're as good as dead. You at least understand that, right?"

"You don't know anything about these people, Ben. All you know are lies. Misinformation. They're not nearly as bad as you make them out to be."

"Not nearly as bad," I repeated. "That right there is a huge boost of confidence."

"Anyway, the whole Janitor thing went south. The guy ended up dying. We couldn't save him, so we went back home. I kept thinking the guy who approached me in the bathroom would manage to follow us, but he didn't. I mean, I was confused at first why we ditched the car, and went a long way, but now it makes sense. You guys were always making sure you weren't being followed. But then I started thinking about what the guy said, how Caesar would show me mercy, and I thought about just how *massive* this whole thing is, and how, realistically, we're never going to beat them."

"I understand, Ian. If you can't beat 'em, join 'em."

"It's not like that."

"Of course it is. You lost faith in the cause, so you sold Carver out."

"*Cause?* What *cause*, Ben? There is no *cause*. It's just been about revenge for Carver from day one. Shit, it's been about revenge for all of you."

"Now look who's misinformed."

"So when the Racist's game came up, and Carver was headed out, I called that number. I did it far away from the farmhouse so they couldn't track it. Shit, I forget what state me and Ronny were in when I did it—it was when he was gassing up and I went to get us snacks, from the payphone there—but I called them and that was it. Then everything went to shit, and

I felt … bad. Like, really bad. That's why I followed you back to the Beachside. I felt bad for what I'd done, and I wanted to make it right."

"Well, you're clearly doing a stand-up job of that now."

"Fuck you, Ben. It's because of you my leg got broke. It's because of you I nearly died. Fuck, man, you had no idea who that person on the bike was. Shit, *I* had no idea, even when they dropped me off." Something entered his eyes, and he said, "Did you ever find out?"

"What, and do all the legwork for these assholes?"

"I feel sorry for you, Ben. I really do. I feel sorry for everyone back at the farmhouse, Graham and Beverly and Jesse especially."

"Jesse's dead."

"What?"

"Your new friends killed him."

Ian shook his head. "You can't put that one on me."

"I think I can."

Behind us, there was a slight squawk from someone's radio. A black mask made one appear from beneath a robe, spoke softly into it, then nodded at Ian.

"I guess that's my cue," Ian said.

I murmured something so quietly I barely even heard it myself.

Ian cocked his head. "Say that again?"

I murmured again.

We were standing less than ten feet apart. He eyed me suspiciously, then glanced at the black masks, before swinging the crutches forward and cutting the gap between us by five feet.

I murmured a third time, even more quietly.

"Ben, speak up."

Ian leaned forward some more and that was when I kicked out at his left crutch. It was the one supporting most of his weight, and he started to fall. I kicked out again, striking him right in the face. The whole thing lasted maybe three seconds, and by then the black masks were pushing me past him down the corridor.

I shouted back at him, "I said your De Niro impression sucks!"

Ian shouted something but I couldn't make it out. I think I was laughing. The black masks, however, made no comment as they pushed me around another corner. We came to a door. One of the black masks knocked twice. The door opened and I was pushed through into a small dark room. Another black mask was standing guard. A chair was in a corner. And in the other corner Carver sat in a wheelchair, shaking his head at me like I was sorriest son of a bitch he had ever seen.

SIXTY-SEVEN

They shoved me to the empty chair. One of them had plastic zip ties, and they restrained my legs to the chair, my wrists behind my back, interlocking another zip tie through the back portion of the chair so I could hardly move. The black masks did this without a word, and when they were done they left without a word, leaving only me and Carver and the black mask standing by the door keeping watch.

Carver was maybe ten feet away in his wheelchair. He looked thin and frail. About what you would expect from someone who had been shot in the chest less than two weeks ago.

I said, "You look like shit."

He said nothing.

"Seriously. It looks like you were shot in the chest or something."

He said, his voice quiet, "What are you doing here?"

"Rescuing you."

"And how's that working out for you so far?"

I shrugged. "I envisioned it going differently in my head."

"You shouldn't have come here."

"Yeah, well, you know how I hate to miss a party." I looked at the black mask standing by the door. "Mind giving us some privacy so my friend and I can talk shit about your boss?"

The black mask gave no response.

Carver said, "How did you find me, anyway?"

"Your boojum."

"You actually managed to get in contact with him?"

"You sound surprised."

"I am. At the time, it was the only thing I could think to say. But then after some reflection, I realized just how difficult it would be."

"What can I tell you?" I said. "I'm good at what I do."

"Says the guy tied to a chair."

"I've been in worse spots than this."

Carver shook his head slowly and whispered, "I don't think it can get much worse than this." Then, his eyes lighting up briefly: "How did my boojum know where to find me?"

I glanced again at the black mask. "Seriously, buddy, mind giving us a few minutes alone?"

Unsurprisingly, the black mask again gave no response.

Carver said, "Can you even see anything without your glasses?"

I smiled at him. "Contacts."

"How do they feel?"

"Not very good."

"Sorry to hear it."

"Not your fault."

"How's everyone back home?"

"They're okay. Jesse died."

"Shit."

"I know."

"Was it bad?"

"Pretty bad, yeah."

"Shit."

"I know."

"Anyone else?"

"Ian apparently decided to model his life after Judas Iscariot."

"What do you mean?"

"He sold us out."

"How do you know?"

"We had a nice little chat out in the hallway before they brought me in. Anyway, what happened to you?"

"I was shot."

"No shit. But what happened afterward?"

"Difficult to say. I'd been shot before, but never this badly. My entire body, it went through phases of hot and cold all at the same time. I lost consciousness for a while. At one point I remember being in an ambulance. They must have had it right outside the hotel the entire time, or nearby, because they started working on me right away. They had to have, because somehow they managed to keep me alive. Then I drifted back out of consciousness, and the next thing I knew I woke up in a hospital bed."

"But you weren't in a hospital," I said.

"Not a proper hospital, no. But I think I was there."

"Where?"

"Their base of operations."

"What makes you think that?"

"Just a hunch. There wasn't a window in my room or anything, but the place was completely white and spotless. Some doctors came in. They introduced themselves as being the very best. Who knows, maybe they were. They managed to take the bullet out of me, patch me up, put me on an IV. But I'm still pretty weak. I don't think I could even walk on my own, though I haven't really been given much of a chance. I've been restrained since I first woke up. First to that hospital bed, then to this wheelchair."

"Did you meet Caesar?"

"No. I asked to see him but was told his schedule was too full. You?"

"I heard him speaking earlier tonight. Sounded like a real douche bag."

Carver said nothing. He barely even cracked a smile. I had seen him angry before, even depressed, but this expression now —hopelessness—was something I had never seen. I wanted to tell him about the team outside, about Bae and his team, about how right now the Kid was listening in to everything we were saying. I couldn't be sure, but I thought he probably suspected there was another transmitter on me.

A knock came from the door, two quick taps. The black mask opened it.

"Well, well, well," I said dryly. "Why am I not surprised?"

FBI Assistant Director Edward Stark stepped into the room. He wore suit pants and a white dress shirt. The lighting in the room wasn't very good, but his face looked pale. His eyes were drained. He opened his mouth to speak but no words came out, or if they did they were so quiet and faint they could barely be heard.

He took another step forward, though it wasn't really a step so much as a stumble. Then, quite suddenly, he tripped over his feet and fell flat on the floor, smashing his nose against the linoleum. Blood splattered the tiles and began pooling around his head.

It was almost as much as the blood seeping out of his back, from where the handle of a knife protruded.

Through the doorway stepped another person. This person was dressed in a black robe and cowl and gloves and white Bauta mask.

And for the third time that day, I found myself saying, "Hello, Congresswoman."

SIXTY-EIGHT

She stepped carefully over Stark's fallen body and walked right up to us. Another black mask followed her, carrying a cushioned folding chair. The black mask opened it up and set it down right in front of us, then stepped back so she could take a seat. As she did, she took off her mask and smiled at me.

"You're not surprised to see me?" she asked.

"Not really. My father always told me it's never wise to trust a politician."

"And yet here you are."

"Your point?"

"You've been wasting your time. Not just with your friend here, but your entire life. I told you how I read that thing of yours you posted online. What I didn't tell you was I found it to be quite an amusing narrative."

"What was so amusing about it?"

Behind the congresswoman the black mask who had deposited the chair and another black mask began cleaning up Edward Stark's body. Opening one of those large rolls of clear plastic tarp. Hefting the body onto the plastic tarp. Rolling the body back up in the plastic tarp.

"You're not a hero, Ben. You never were. Your friend might have put ideas in your head, made you think you're more important than you really are, but I'm telling you the truth. You're weak. Foolish. Naïve."

"Are you trying to arouse me?"

She sighed and rolled her eyes.

"Seriously," I said. "How did you know deprecation is what gets me off?"

Congresswoman Houser said to Carver, "You're certainly quiet."

"I don't even know who you are."

The congresswoman gave me a blank look. Behind her, the two black masks had picked up the body wrapped in the clear plastic tarp and were now carrying it away.

I said, "What, so now it's my job to make the introductions? Fine. Carver, this is Congresswoman Francis Houser from North Carolina. If I ever have a chance to write another amusing narrative, I'll be sure to note that she's a lying bitch."

"Now, now," she said, wagging a finger, "no reason to be uncouth."

I said to Carver, "Did she really just say uncouth?"

He nodded. "I believe she did."

The congresswoman sighed again. "If you two aren't going to take this seriously, then I'm not going to waste my time."

"Why are you here, anyway?" I said. "To rub it in our faces? To boast about how smart and powerful you and your asshole friends are?"

"You misunderstand us, Ben. That's why I came to see you. That, and I needed to eliminate poor Edward back there."

Behind her two more black masks—or maybe they were the same ones as before—came in with buckets and towels. They got on their knees and began cleaning up the blood, while the third black mask—the one who had been standing by the door this entire time—watched on silently.

I said, "A bit overdramatic, wouldn't you say?"

"Perhaps. But I liked the way you tried to warn me about him. Like you were trying to protect me."

"I gave him the same warning about you."

"Is that right? So then you never truly trusted either of us."

"Again, is there a point?"

She said to Carver, "You believed Edward set you up, didn't you? At least initially. You may not know it, but he began suspecting the very same thing you did. About the games. So it was decided something needed to be done. Instead of eliminating him outright, we approached him quietly to try to learn what he knew. We figured if we kept him close, we could someday use him to our advantage."

"Who's *we*?" I asked.

She stared at me for several long seconds but said nothing. Behind her, the two black masks on the floor looked as if they were wrapping up.

"Your husband," I said. "He was never a member of the Inner Circle, was he?"

She shook her head sadly. "No, I'm afraid he was not."

"So then why did he die?"

"Because he refused to accept the truth."

"And what truth, pray tell, is that?"

"You can sit there and hide behind your wall of sarcasm for as long as you'd like, Ben, but the reality is our world is in serious trouble. There's nonstop war, famine, genocide—"

"Yeah, yeah," I said. "I heard the same line of bullshit from Caesar earlier tonight."

"It's natural to be frightened of things you do not fully understand. You view us as evil. You think what we do is morally wrong. But what you have to understand is we're just trying to save the world. Your father was right—it's never wise to trust a politician. But this isn't a political thing. Republicans, Democrats, Independents, even Libertarians—they're all here tonight. So are different members of Parliament. Almost every religious viewpoint is represented here as well. Don't you understand just how wide-reaching this is? Our world is in serious trouble, and if someone doesn't do something about it, we will all die."

"So let me guess—the almighty Caesar is going to save us all."

"He is just one man. One man cannot save the world. But what Caesar has done is brought us all together. He has unified us. This is something that will never happen in politics. You will always have the one side fighting against the other side, no matter how inane their argument. They argue just for the sake of arguing. And it's like a disease—it infects the people, and begins to make them argue against each other. The world is full of it. That's half the problem. What Caesar has proposed is to stop it all together. To bring global unification."

"The Pax Romana," I said.

She nodded, her expression all at once reverent. "It is what's going to save the world."

This entire time Carver hadn't said much. After all, he didn't know the congresswoman, and besides that, she was keeping most of her attention on me. But now he cleared his throat and leaned forward.

"And just what exactly is the Pax Romana?" he asked.

The congresswoman looked at him like she was surprised he was still there. She took a breath, opened her mouth, but before she could speak a voice spoke behind her.

"I can explain that."

Someone else now stood in the doorway. This person, too, wore a robe and cowl and mask.

Only this mask wasn't black or white.

It was gold.

SIXTY-NINE

The two black masks cleaning up the floor promptly decided it was time to leave. They gathered their things and stood aside so Caesar could enter the room. Like for the congresswoman, a black mask trailed with a cushioned folding chair. The mask opened it and set it down beside the congresswoman before taking its leave.

"You two," Caesar said, taking off the golden mask as he sat, "have become quite a thorn in my side."

He looked to be in his late-fifties, early-sixties. White. Clean-shaven. A few wrinkles in his brow. Blue eyes. Strong cheekbones. An angular nose.

I tried to take in as many of his features as I could in the first couple seconds. Then I glanced at Carver and said, "We ... apologize?"

Caesar smiled. "No, you don't."

"Then tell me what you want to hear and I'll say it. I mean, I figure you're used to being surrounded by sycophants."

"You don't know anything about me."

"Enlighten us, then. But first, do those in the upper echelon of the Inner Circle really call you Augustus?"

He said nothing.

"Because if it's okay with you, I think I'm going to start calling you that too. Unless, that is, you want to tell me your real name."

He stared at me for another couple of seconds before turning to Carver. "Is he always this annoying?"

Carver said, "For the most part, yes."

I looked at Carver and shook my head. "Last time I risk my life trying to save your ass."

"Gentlemen," Caesar said loudly. "My time is precious, and I would rather not waste it."

"Of course, Augustus," I said. "Our deepest apologies. We are so honored by your presence and blah blah fucking blah."

Congresswoman Houser tilted her head to the side and whispered, "*Now* do you see what I've been dealing with?"

Before Caesar could respond, I said, "You two are related, aren't you?" I waited a beat, staring at their faces, their eyes, and nodded. "Yeah, you are. What are you, brother and sister? Cousins?"

Augustus apparently didn't care to answer my query. He reached into his robe and pulled out a small piece of paper. He unfolded it and held it up for Carver to see.

"Do you recognize this? You wrote it, I believe. It says 'Caesar, I'm coming for you.' What did you expect when you wrote this, Carver? Did you expect me to get worried? Did you expect me to … oh, I don't know, quake in my boots?"

He folded the note back up, seemed to take great care in placing it back in his robe.

"To be honest, Carver, I do have respect for you. I can see you strive to be a great man. I see greatness in you. But that greatness has not yet reached its full potential." Augustus leaned forward just a bit. "I think it can, though. I think you can be a great, great man. And I am willing to help bring that greatness out of you. My army has been building now for over three decades. I have acquired some of the most brilliant minds in the world. You see, Carver, despite what you may think or hope, the world is going to change. It is already heading toward destruction—it has been heading there for a very long time—and nobody knows what to do about it. Everybody wants to play the blame game. They want to point fingers and not take responsibility. Nothing is getting done."

"We know," I said. "Your sister-slash-cousin already filled us in."

Augustus gave me a dry smile. "Very well. Then that saves me time. Do you both agree then that the world has fallen apart?"

He waited for us to give a response. When neither of us did, he waited even longer.

"What's the point?" I asked.

Augustus said, "When God saw the world he had created had become infected with evil, he decided to wipe it out completely and start over. He sent a flood and ... well, you know the story."

I opened my mouth to speak but Augustus held up a hand.

"Now, before you jump to conclusions, I am not comparing myself to God. I am not even comparing myself to *a* god. Yes, I may sometimes be considered the *deus ex machina*, but I am just an ordinary man, Carver, somebody much like you. And I have a vision for what the world can be. You see, the world right now is very much like you. There is so much potential for greatness, but it's hiding just beneath the surface, and the longer it stays hidden, the weaker it becomes. What it needs is for someone to step up and help bring that greatness out. Are you following me so far?"

Carver said nothing.

Augustus sighed and said to me, "What about you, Ben?"

"What about me?"

He paused a moment, taking a breath, trying to remain

calm. It was exactly what I wanted to see. Just how much push it took to get a rise out of him.

"Are you following me?" he asked slowly.

"Sure," I said. "Anywhere and everywhere. In fact, I would walk five hundred miles. Carver, how about you? Would you also walk five hundred miles?"

Augustus, clearly not a fan of the Scottish band The Proclaimers, said, "Tell me, gentlemen, just what am I doing here that is wrong? I am trying to look out for the future of mankind. The world right now is in serious trouble. There is no future. We may not be able to stop global warming and pollution, but at least we can stop making them worse. But before we even do that, we need to start getting along. That means everyone. This entire world needs to understand that if we do not work together as humans, then humankind as we know it will soon cease to exist."

Carver said, "You're insane."

Augustus smiled, clearly pleased to get a response from Carver. Then he looked at me and said, "Ben, isn't that what you told Howard Abele when he tried explaining what the Inner Circle is all about? You called him insane too."

I tried to hide my surprise, but he must have seen it in my eyes. His smile widened.

"Yes, I have read your story. I have read it several times, in fact. For some reason it fascinates me, the arrogance you brought across. As if you and Carver and a number of your rogue player friends have what it takes to bring down over thirty years of work. Do you seriously believe you're the only ones who have tried to stop us? There have been others in the past. There was one person in particular several years ago, a doctor, who caused us much trouble. But as you can see, we are growing stronger every day."

"So did you find my story to be an amusing narrative?" I

asked. "Because your sister-slash-cousin here found it to be an amusing narrative."

Augustus ignored me. "What you don't understand is you have never been in control. For the past two years—and for you, Carver, the past five years—you both have been interrupting the games, thinking you are untouchable. However, you were only able to do so because I was allowing you to do so. It was fun to watch, like a rat trying to find its way through a maze. If there truly is a God, I would like to think he finds it very amusing that we believe in such a thing as free will."

He shook his head, his smiling fading.

"But there is no such thing. At least no such thing for the two of you. So yes, you did pull one over on us back in California. I will give you that. But ever since then we have been very careful. And we have always been in control. Though, Ben, I must admit, we were surprised when you returned to the Beachside Hotel. That certainly did catch us off guard. And you can thank me, by the way."

"Thank you for what?"

"The bomb my people placed in the car was supposed to kill you. Even though you had managed to bypass it, my people were supposed to activate it remotely. But they called me, asked me what to do, and I told them to let you live. To blow the car, yes, but to make sure you lived."

"Why would you do that?"

"Because I wanted to see what else you would do. My sister here—yes, she is my sister—doesn't give you much credit. She thinks you're foolish. It's true, your attitude isn't the best, and you're not as funny as you think you are, but you seem to be full of surprises."

"Um … thank you?"

Augustus leaned back in the chair, folded his hands in his lap, turned his attention once again to Carver.

"It should not be surprising our initial plan was to kill you once we reconvened in the auditorium tonight, right after I present the Pax Romana. But even with everyone's interest piqued —and believe me, they are all looking forward to seeing you, Carver—I'm finding it to be all very ... anticlimactic. So we kill you. Then what? You're dead. What does that really mean? It has no significance, at least none that I can see. So I have been thinking. And if you want to be altruistic and save your friends' lives ..."

He let it hang there for a second, watching Carver's face. Carver, as expected, gave no reaction.

"Do you want to save your friends' lives, Carver? Because we know they're outside. They probably think they have some great plan to swoop in and save the day, but they're wrong. They are going to die. All of them. Even those left behind at the farmhouse—yes, we know the location of that too. Unless, that is, you want to save them. And if you do, it's quite simple. When you are on stage, I will ask you whether or not you two have any last words. Ben, you're obviously going onstage tonight as well. We knew this days ago when it was clear your plan was to try to infiltrate the Coliseum, but I did not want to mention it tonight, figuring you still had it in your head you would be able to go through with whatever menial plan you had come up with. Anyhow, I will ask you both if you have any last words, and when I do, you both beg for your lives. Do not grovel or anything, nothing pathetic like that, but enough so that everyone can see you don't want to die. Then I will ask you that if I spare your lives, will you agree to abide by all the rules set forth by me. Of course, I will be skeptical, I might even have Clark come out and break a few bones, but when the crowd sees your sincerity and knows you are serious, then we will stop. Not that we will welcome you with open arms immediately—we do need to be sure you won't be up to anything— but I am sure once you see everything that we lay out for you, the idea of the Inner Circle will not seem as evil as you first thought."

"I can give you our answer right now," Carver said. "Go fuck yourself."

Augustus stared at him for a moment before turning slowly to face me. "Ben? Is that your answer too?"

"I was going to say go fuck a duck, but it's pretty much the same idea, yeah."

Congresswoman Houser shook her head sadly. "I told you it would be a waste of time trying to talk sense into these two."

Augustus said, "Are you both completely stubborn? You seem to think you're fighting for some great cause, but can you even name it? The people you claim to be trying to save are the ones ruining this world. The common person ... what do they have to contribute to society? How are they benefiting anyone? Ben, tell me one thing that either of your parents ever did for this world."

I said nothing, though the temperature of my blood ticked up several degrees.

"What does the average person do to try to make this world a better place? They go to work, they eat, they spend money, they have sex, they sleep. That's it. So you call us evil when we take these people and put them in our games, use them as players. At least for the few days they survive they have purpose. They become more than the petty painters and busybodies they were before. They actually begin to respect and cherish life."

Augustus shook his head.

"Every single person in the Inner Circle understands what's really important in this world. They understand what it is to live. I'm not saying that a rich person is any better than a poor person, but when it comes down to it, what does a poor person have to lose when the world falls apart? Absolutely nothing, so of course they don't care. But someone who is rich, someone who is powerful, who has worked hard every day of his or her life to actually achieve something and then realize they are going to lose it all … and for what?"

Augustus held up his black-gloved hands, the palms open to the ceiling.

"Please, can either of you answer me? I have been trying to understand this for over thirty years, trying to piece together the exact point where the world went wrong. All I could do was look back through history, because they say history repeats itself, and they say that the only way you can learn is by fixing the mistakes of the past. It didn't take long, really, learning that the Roman Empire was the greatest empire that ever ruled this earth. Certainly, they stole much from the Greeks, but they stole it and made it better. They, too, were viewed as barbarians, but maybe that was what made them so great. You both believe murder is wrong, I'm sure, but murder is what captivates the world. And a real life murder? People would love to witness that, no matter how much they might claim otherwise. And so I thought about the state of the world, about how it was all falling apart, and I asked myself, What do we have to lose?"

There was silence then, deep and heavy silence, where Augustus's gaze searched our faces, where Congresswoman Houser beamed proudly at her brother.

Then Carver said to me, "Wow."

I nodded. "Wow indeed."

"He makes a very convincing argument."

"That he does."

"The only problem is," Carver said, "his breath doesn't smell too good."

"No, it doesn't."

"What do you think it could be?"

"I'm not sure," I said. "Maybe it's all the bullshit spewing out of his mouth."

To Augustus's credit, his face remained impassive. He

simply shook his head and said, "I'm sorry you both feel this way. But at least I tried." He turned to his sister. "Let's go."

They rose to their feet, started to put back on their masks.

I said, "Wait."

They paused, watching me.

"What about the Pax Romana?"

"What about it?"

"Aren't you going to tell us what it is?"

Augustus smiled. "You will hear all about it before you die."

"Don't we at least get a hint?"

"All right, then. Your hint, however, is a question. What is the greatest thing the Roman Empire gave to the world?"

Augustus didn't wait for a reply. He put back on his mask, as did the congresswoman. They headed toward the door, which the black mask opened for them. Congresswoman Houser stepped through, but Augustus paused in the doorway and turned back.

"Soon, gentlemen," he said. "Soon the game of your life will come to an end. Enjoy what few moments you have left."

SEVENTY

Carver and I didn't talk much after that. There really wasn't much more to say. I tried making some more small talk, but Carver wasn't having any of it. I even asked the black mask by the door to give us a few seconds to talk in private, but of course there was no response. And so we sat in silence for a long time—minutes, what may have been an hour—before a radio squawked from beneath the black mask's robe. The black mask brought it out, spoke softly, listened to another squawk, then moved to the door and opened it.

Ten seconds later several black masks swarmed into the room. Half of them went to Carver, the other half came to me. A few others stood off to the side, MP5s in their hands, a friendly reminder of what could happen if either of us got unruly.

I considered it, I really did. When the black masks came and began cutting the zip ties holding me in place, I considered making a move. What move that would be, however, was the biggest question. Whoever these men and women were behind the black masks, they were pros. They were well trained. They were killers. They wouldn't think twice putting a bullet in my head. Carver, on the other hand, was different. He still had a purpose. The members of the Inner Circle were waiting to watch him die.

But what could I possibly do now with over a dozen black masks surrounding us? Even if I managed to do something and incapacitate one or two of them—or hell, if we're daydreaming, *all* of them—Carver was too weak to move on his own. He'd already told me as much, and I knew he wasn't lying. He might manage to climb out of the wheelchair, but he would take only a few steps before falling down.

So I didn't do anything. I didn't even give up the slightest struggle. Everything in my body told me I was a coward for letting it happen, but there wasn't much more I could do besides tire myself out. I still had hope the Kid and everyone else might have a chance to save us. And if not them, then maybe Bae and his crew. And if not them, well, I had led an interesting life. I could at least go out knowing that.

They wheeled Carver out of the room first. Two of them grabbed me by both arms and pulled me to my feet and marched me out after him. Another black mask stayed directly behind me, covering me with a weapon. I knew that for certain, because the steel barrel kept digging into my back.

We went down a hallway and turned a corner to a set of stairs. Four of the black masks picked up Carver's wheelchair and carried him down the stairs. The black masks gripping my arms pushed me forward.

I said, "What, I don't get carried too?"

None of them answered, unless you wanted to count the gun barrel pressed even harder into my back.

Down the stairs then to another hallway, which was darker. I thought about the pictures I'd seen of the Fillmore, about the floor plans the Kid had managed to secure, and knew we were behind stage. This was confirmed a few seconds later after a black mask stepped forward with a roll of duct tape, cut off two ends, placed one strip over Carver's mouth, another over mine, and then we were rushed through a door into near-darkness.

Several more black masks were waiting behind the curtain. One of them stepped away from the others and approached us. A gloved hand tilted the mask up onto the top of the head, and Clark smiled at me.

"That secret I mentioned earlier? It's coming soon."

He stepped back as the black masks took me to a folding chair. Just like they did back in the previous room, they pushed me down into the chair and began securing my wrists and ankles with zip ties. It took three of them to do my legs, one to hold each foot (I guess they worried I would kick out, though I couldn't imagine where they would ever get that idea), the third to tighten the zip tie around the chair legs and my ankles.

One of them had a radio and set it aside on the floor to do this. I didn't give it much thought until the radio made a strange noise. The volume was turned low, so it could just barely be heard, but it was quiet enough back here that it was momentarily the loudest thing. The noise wasn't a squawk so much as a ballooning sort of noise, first low and then high and then low again. I don't think the black mask noticed it at all—like I said, I barely did myself—but Clark was standing nearby, and he noticed it.

"What was that?" he whispered.

The three black masks paused long enough to glance up at him.

Clark crouched down in front of me. The black masks had already tightened the zip ties around my ankles, so he clearly wasn't worried about being kicked in the head. The three black masks moved away, the one even reaching for the radio.

"Leave it," Clark said.

The black mask left the radio where it was.

Clark gave me a look before picking up the radio. He moved it around my left foot first, slowly, but got no strange response. Then he moved it around my right foot, slowly, and yep, that strange response happened again, that low and then high and then low noise.

Another black mask stepped up next to us and whispered, "What's wrong?"

Clark didn't answer. He moved the radio around my right foot again, even slower this time. When the noise came again, he grabbed my shoe and pulled it up far enough so he could move the radio underneath.

The low and high and low noise came again, this time even louder.

"What's wrong?" the black mask asked again.

Clark shot me a glare. I just stared back at him. Even if the duct tape wasn't over my mouth, I wasn't sure what I would say. Probably *Oh shit*. Most definitely *Oh shit*.

Clark tugged the shoe off my foot, then held the radio up to the heel. Again, that strange warbling noise, much stronger now.

He handed the radio to the black mask and then began to twist the heel back and forth. It didn't take long before the damned thing popped off. It didn't take much longer before Clark pulled the transmitter out of the hollow space it had been hiding in. It took even less time for Clark to drop it on the floor and smash it with the heel of his own shoe.

"Notify Caesar," he said to the black mask. "Tell him they've been bugged the entire time. Tell him I recommend putting off the Pax Romana presentation to the very end. Tell him I recommend killing these motherfuckers first."

SEVENTY-ONE

"Shit," the Kid said. "Shit, shit, shit, *shit!*"

The second communication feed from Ben had just gone dead. They'd found it—how, the Kid wasn't exactly sure—and they had destroyed it—the Kid had a pretty good idea how they did that—and now he didn't know what was going on inside. The Fillmore had a limited security feed, but the entire thing had been shut down for tonight, so he had no eyes inside either.

Ronny said, "What's wrong?"

Only the Kid had been listening in on Ben's second feed. Only he had heard about Ian being a backstabbing mother-fucker—he had already called Graham and told him to split ASAP—and only he had heard Congresswoman "Frank" Houser and Caesar. And now only he had heard that Ben and Carver were headed toward their execution.

"They found the second transmitter," the Kid said.

"Who found it?" Maya asked.

"One of Caesar's people. They destroyed it. I have no idea what's happening inside right now. Drew, you notice anything happening from your position?"

"Negative."

"What about you, Mason?"

"No."

Ronny said, "Any word on the Koreans?"

"We don't even know if they've made it in," the Kid said. "And if they have, it doesn't matter. We can't wait any longer. It's time to crash the party."

SEVENTY-TWO

Augustus apparently approved of every one of Clark's recommendations, and the black masks went into overdrive making sure everything fell into place.

Clear plastic tarps—seriously, they must have bought them in bulk from some clear plastic tarp megastore—were laid out on the stage. Carver was wheeled toward the center, right behind the curtain. Several black masks picked up my chair and moved me next to him. They did this all as quickly and as quietly as possible. Then, just as quickly and as quietly, the black masks disappeared.

A minute passed. We could hear the members of the Inner Circle on the other side of the curtain. Like before, there were no murmurs or whispers circulating around the auditorium, but the soft shushing of their robes as black masks escorted them to their seats.

Augustus appeared off stage. The faint light was just enough to glimmer off the gold mask. He spoke briefly with Clark. He waited several seconds before the spotlight came on. Then he stepped out onto stage. The auditorium erupted in uproarious applause.

Through the curtain we watched him walking in his slow, measured pace toward center stage. He held up his arms, signaling for silence. That silence soon came, and then he spoke.

"Friends, Romans, countrymen, again lend me your ears!"

Again, the audience ate it up, and the applause swelled like a tumor just waiting to burst.

Drew stared through the scope of his rifle at the front of the Fillmore. A few people walked back and forth—clearly civilians —but that was it. Beverly squatted beside him. She had the night vision binoculars propped up on the ledge. Neither of them had spoken much since they came up here and assembled his rifle and tripod mount and got everything ready. He had made himself so small that none of Caesar's people—and he had to assume Caesar's people were out here somewhere, watching for someone like him—could see him. Beverly was to be his spotter, but she was also supposed to help keep his ammunition full. It was a lot to ask of her—she didn't care for weapons of any kind and she had next to no field experience— but she hadn't complained once. She hadn't said much, either. Again, neither of them had. They just waited up here on the top of the building, a block away from the Fillmore, twenty-eight stories up from the street. Just waiting for something to happen. Soon it would, because the Kid had told them about losing communication, and Ronny had confirmed they were on their way. And now, in Drew's earpiece (just as in Beverly's earpiece), Ronny's voice came through: "Three blocks away."

Augustus held up his hands again for silence.

"I understand the interlude was entertaining for many of you. The live games we set up went very well. There was, however, an incident at one of the games. Fortunately, nobody was hurt. I assure you, we were in control of the situation the entire time. The person responsible thought he was working under subterfuge, when in reality we were tracking his every movement. This person, in fact, came to try to save the Man of Honor. This person, as you well may know, failed, and so his death tonight will accompany the Man of Honor. Brothers and sisters, I present to you the Man of Honor and the Man of Wax!"

The curtain rose, and suddenly more spotlights came on, glaring down on both of us.

And the audience went wild.

The Kid sat leaning forward in his chair, his elbows on the table, staring at the computer screen. Watching the yellow dots situated around the Fillmore. Watching in particular the two yellow dots that were right now moving toward it. In his earphones, Ronny said, "Two blocks away."

Augustus let the applause go on longer than before. Finally he held up his hands again, and the crowd quieted.

"For years the Man of Honor has waged a personal battle against us. He tried to stop what we were doing, and when that cost him his family, he promised revenge. But look at what revenge has brought him. The Man of Honor has become weak and pathetic. He is quite near death. And before tonight is over, he will beg for death. They both will!"

Mason pressed his back against the wall and rose to his feet. He reached into his dirty coat and gripped the MP5. He heard the constant traffic on the street, but he also heard Ronny and

Maya in the distance. The low growl of the engine. The heavy weight rolling over the pavement. It could have been anything, really, but Mason knew it was them, and he was ready. His hand gripped tightly around the MP5. His other hand reached for his gun. Staring intently at the front of the Fillmore, while further up the street that low growl and heavy rolling neared. In his ear, Ronny said, "One block away."

As the crowd roared again, four black masks came on stage. Two of them carried a long table topped with the same tools that had been used in the Torture Room: knives, pliers, hammers, saws. They set the table down and turned and headed back off stage. Two other black masks stayed. One of them, I knew, was Clark. This was confirmed almost immediately when he came up to stand directly behind me. He leaned down and whispered, "Are you ready for that secret now?"

Maya held on tight. She had been in many different kinds of vehicles before—especially during her past life—but had never once ridden in an armored security truck. She'd seen them countless times, of course, but had never actually sat in one. It wasn't as comfortable as she would have liked. The truck wasn't meant for high speeds, and Ronny was pushing it as hard as he could. They'd been parked blocks away, in a side street garage. The truck wasn't stolen—they were "borrowing" it—but it wasn't common to see armored trucks parked along the side of the street, especially at this time of night. So they waited in the garage, and now here they were, barreling down West 43rd Street, less than a block away, Ronny's fingers white against the steering wheel. He didn't slow, didn't even tap the brakes. He just jerked the wheel to the left and sent them up over the curb straight toward the glass entrances doors of the Fillmore.

The applause was just dying down when we heard it from somewhere outside the auditorium. It wasn't clear at first what it was—some kind of sudden but dull explosion—but everything went still and silent at the same time. Clark had just breathed in, ready to say whatever he meant to say next, but instead leaned back. For a moment, the world was frozen in place. Then, suddenly, the auditorium was swallowed by darkness.

SEVENTY-THREE

My wrists were tied behind my back to the chair, and my ankles were tied to the legs of the chair, but that didn't mean I couldn't move completely. There was still some give—just a little—and right after the lights went out, I leaned as far as I could to the right before immediately shoving all my weight to the left. That was where Clark had been standing only a moment earlier, and I was hoping he hadn't moved.

He hadn't.

He wasn't as close as I would have liked, either, but I had to work with what I was given. It was enough, though, that the bulk of my weight went into him. He wasn't expecting it, and went down hard. We both did. The chair was metal, so it wasn't like it could snap apart (though I was hoping), and quite honestly, I wasn't sure where things would go from there. Whatever was happening, it was going to happen fast, and I couldn't waste a second.

Gunfire erupted in the auditorium, first coming from the balcony, then from all over.

Emergency lights came on a second later. They were scattered around the auditorium and backstage, but there weren't many, and their combined glow didn't bring much light.

Directly following the emergency lights came the fire alarm. It was a high-pitched blaring, and the dim radiance of the emergency lights was accompanied by a sudden and faltering strobe, cutting everyone's rushed and hasty motions into half second snapshots. Those in the auditorium were already climbing to their feet, shouting and screaming.

I looked over at where Augustus Caesar had been standing only seconds ago. He was gone.

More gunfire started up somewhere backstage, coming from multiple weapons. Some of the reports were from semi-automatic handguns, spaced out a half second apart, while other reports were a nonstop stream of bullets, mostly from MP5s.

Most of my chair and myself had fallen onto Clark. He groaned and crawled out from under me, pushing the chair aside. I watched his stunted movements from the strobes situated around the stage. He tore his mask off and glared down at me. He lifted his foot, meaning, I think, to smash me in the face. Before he could, though, the gunfire neared us and he ducked away. He dropped his mask to the floor, reached for a gun under his robe, but someone was hurrying toward us, firing at him, and he dove over the side of the stage into the front row of the frantic crowd.

A black mask sprinted toward me, the movement just as rushed and hasty in the strobes as everyone else's. The black mask was carrying an MP5. The black mask's other hand reached underneath its robe to come back with something long and black. The black mask flicked its wrist and a silver blade jerked out from the handle.

I watched this happening—the black mask coming closer and closer, an MP5 and knife in each hand—and did every-thing I could to free myself from the chair. But the zip ties were too tight. What little room I'd had was enough to tip the chair over into Clark. That was it.

The black mask came to a stop right over me. It leaned down, extending the knife. I clenched my teeth, took a breath, waiting for it to happen, for the blade to slice into my heart.

Instead, the black mask cut the ties binding my wrists in place, before moving to the two front legs of the chair. Seconds later, I was back on my feet, breathing hard, staring at the black mask.

"Which one are you?" I asked.

The gloved hand gripping the knife reached up to take off the black mask so I could see his face.

"Chin," he said.

"Who's up in the balcony?"

"Seung."

"Bae and Ho Sook?"

"They are nearby."

I nodded and started to say something else when someone opened fire. This entire time gunfire had been filling the auditorium—Seung up in the balcony, picking off black masks, many of whom were returning fire—but this gunfire was coming from backstage, directed at us.

Chin pushed me aside and raised the MP5 and let out a spray of bullets. He paused just momentarily to hand me the switchblade.

I took the knife and hurried over to Carver. I knelt and cut the binds keeping him in place. Only it wasn't like Carver could stand up out of the wheelchair. Even if he did, it wasn't like he was going to get far.

More gunfire came our way, and Chin returned fire toward a few more black masks. These masks scattered, some disappearing through a door, the others hiding behind posts.

I closed the knife and slipped it in my pocket. I grabbed the handles of Carver's wheelchair.

Carver shouted, "I can walk!"

I ignored him and asked Chin, "Do you know where their computers are?"

"The third floor."

"I'm going to need to get up there."

"Caesar is not dead. We must kill him."

"Agreed. But right now I need to get Carver to the lobby."

The alarm kept blaring. The strobes kept up their frantic pulse. Along with taking down black masks from his place up in the balcony, Seung was also throwing down canisters of tear gas. The gas began to fill the auditorium, causing the already hysterical members of the Inner Circle to become even more hysterical. Their screams and shouts increased tenfold. They moved one way and then moved another, not sure where to go. Many pushed through whatever doors they could find, trying to escape despite the fact none of them knew what awaited them on the other side. The time for patience and decorum was over. Now it was every man and woman for themselves.

Chin cleared the way. He fired indiscriminately, taking down anyone with a black or white mask.

Many of the fallen and dead black masks we passed had weapons. I grabbed a handgun from one of them, an MP5 from another. I gave the MP5 to Carver. I still had on only one shoe, which made my running awkward. At one point I paused just long enough to tear off my other shoe and toss it aside.

Soon we came to the lobby. The armored truck had done its job well, smashing through the front doors. Most of it now sat in the lobby. Both doors were open, Maya and Ronny gone. Where they were, I wasn't sure, but the gunfire kept up, as did the shouting and screaming. We came deeper into the lobby and I saw a homeless man with an MP5.

"Mason!"

He fired off a couple more rounds, taking down a few more black masks—this was how I thought of them despite the fact most had already taken off their masks—before rushing over to us. He didn't say anything, just nodded at me, then at Carver.

I thought about the Torture Room, seeing his wife and son there, and wasn't sure what to say. I'd been dreading this moment. Telling him the one thing I knew might—well, okay, *would*—set him off. Which may or may not be a good thing under the circumstances. Still, as someone who had once been a husband and father, I knew the news might break him.

Mason looked at Chin. "Who's this?"

"Chin," I said, and then thought of something. I turned to Chin. "Were there any survivors from tonight's games?"

Something darkened in Chin's eyes. Clearly he, too, was disturbed by the fact he hadn't been able to do anything to help those innocents who had been brought here to be tortured or raped or killed without blowing his cover. He nodded.

"Do you know where they're being kept?

"Yes."

"Then take him," I said, pointing at Mason. "Get as many of them out as you can."

"We must kill Caesar."

"Just do it!" I shouted.

He stared back at me, his face impassive. Finally he said to Mason, "Come with me."

Mason gave me an uncertain look. I told him to go, and he hurried after Chin.

Then I turned back to Carver, meaning to grab the handles of his wheelchair again, when I saw one of the black masks across the lobby aim a pistol at us.

SEVENTY-FOUR

Within a minute, two police cars swarmed up on the Fillmore. They came without their sirens and without their flashing lights.

Drew, watching them through the scope, said, "Four cops just showed up."

The Kid's voice came through the earpiece: "Nothing went out over dispatch. These fuckers are dirty."

"Got it."

All four cops piled out of their cars, each gripping a sidearm. Drew sighted on the first bent cop's head and squeezed the trigger. The cop went down in a mist of blood. Before the three others could react, Drew took down the second one, then the third. The fourth cop managed to drop behind the patrol car.

"Shit," Drew said. Then: "Ronny, you hear me?"

Silence for a few seconds. "What's up?"

"You got one hostile left outside, taking cover behind his cruiser."

Maya came over the radio: "I got him."

The lobby had fallen into chaos.

Maya hadn't been completely sure what to expect, but she had to admit the black robes and cowls threw her at first. It was just so … weird. And then there was the matter of the different color masks. It wasn't too difficult to figure out who to take down, though. Those in the black masks were the ones with the weapons. Not that she wasn't against the idea of taking down some white masks, too. But those with the weapons—those that posed the most threat—needed to be eliminated first.

She found most of her cover near the armored truck. Ronny had gone deeper into the lobby, toward the hallway leading to the auditorium. So when Drew said one hostile was still alive, taking cover, she turned immediately and headed back outside.

The sidewalk was mostly empty of civilians. There were a few, keeping their distance a block away. Some of them had their cell phones out, taking pictures, or calling whoever. If it was 911, they were wasting their time.

She spotted the remaining cop almost instantly. His attention was on the rooftops, searching for whoever had killed his dirty friends. When he heard her coming, he turned and raised his gun. Maya didn't hesitate. She shot him twice—once in the chest, once in the head.

Even over the normal city sounds and the gunfire inside, she heard gasps from a few of those a block away.

She turned toward them, wanting to explain what was going on, how she wasn't really a bad person, but knew it would be useless. To their eyes, she had just killed a cop. It didn't matter how corrupt the man may have been.

Maya hurried back inside. Even more people in those black robes and cowls and masks scrambled every which way, like chickens with their heads cut off. Some with white masks were taken down in the crossfire.

She spotted Ben and Carver with Mason and a man in a black robe and cowl. Only the man didn't appear to be a hostile. She realized at once he was one of the Koreans. He and Mason hurried away, and Ben started to turn, when from the corner of her eyes she saw movement.

A black mask had spotted Ben and Carver and was taking aim.

Just like with the corrupt cop outside, Maya didn't hesitate. She raised her gun and fired. Her bullet tore into the man's shoulder and flipped him back. He turned toward her. She fired again. This time the bullet went right between the eyes.

"Ronny," she shouted, "they're in the lobby," and ran right for Ben and Carver.

When Maya reached us, I just stared at her. I wasn't sure what to say. I thought about being up there on stage, tied to that chair, the table laid out with all of Clark's toys, and I realized the one thing I would miss was Maya. That was my one regret, and that's exactly what I wanted to tell her when she reached us.

Instead I said, "Thanks."

She nodded. "Any time."

Carver said to Maya, "I don't need this wheelchair."

"Yes, he does," I said.

I grabbed the handlebars again and started pushing him toward the armored truck. Maya kept pace beside us, covering our backs.

The alarm kept blaring. The strobes kept flickering. The gunfire continued down the hallways. Over one hundred members of the Inner Circle ran around frantic, but they didn't have any weapons so none of us decided they were worth killing.

Ronny came around the corner and hurried toward us. His left arm was bleeding.

"You okay?" I asked him.

He nodded, wincing at the pain. "Just a graze. Carver, it's great to see you."

"Great to see you, too. Tell Ben I don't need this wheelchair."

"He needs it," I said. "Either of you two have a present for me?"

Ronny dug into his pocket. He came back out with a tiny transmitter and handed it to me.

I twisted it slightly, activating it, and stuck it in my ear.

"Kid, you hear me?"

"Glad to hear your voice, Ben. Carver okay?"

"He is. We're going to load him up now. Any official word yet?"

"Still nothing over dispatch. You guys headed out now?"

We had reached the armored truck, Maya and Ronny keeping us covered and taking down a few more black masks.

"Not yet," I said. "Mason and one of the Koreans are getting the survivors."

"What survivors?"

"I also need to get whatever info I can on the Pax Romana."

Ronny said, taking down another black mask, "What's the Pax Romana?"

"I'm not sure yet. Load up Carver. I'll be back as soon as I can."

Before any of them could object, I turned and sprinted toward the stairs.

SEVENTY-FIVE

Mason wasn't sure where he was headed. He was following this Korean guy because Ben had told him to, and he trusted Ben. Despite everything, right now Ben was one of the few friends he had. And there had been something in Ben's eyes, too, something that didn't give Mason a good feeling. So he had followed the Korean guy down the hallway, then down some stairs, and here there were more motherfuckers dressed up like it was fucking Halloween. He and the Korean guy covered each other as they went down the hallway, taking out all of the motherfuckers. Mason wasn't ashamed to admit that he got a thrill killing these assholes. After everything they had done to him and his family, all for the sake of entertainment. Fuck 'em.

Once the hallway was clear, the Korean guy—did Ben say his name was Chin?—led the way. They came to a door. The Korean guy paused and glanced back at Mason, gave him a heavy look, before turning the knob and pushing it open.

The first thing that hit Mason was the smell. Blood and piss and shit, all mixed together in one disgusting stew. He actually retched a little, worried he might throw up, but he fought down the bubbling in his stomach and took a step into the room.

The second thing that hit Mason was the sight. Blood and piss and shit, yeah, but also bodies. At least a dozen of them. Some were alive, others were not. Clear plastic tarp covered the floor and walls. A few bodies were wrapped up tightly in those clear plastic tarps, obviously dead. Those that were still alive lay on the floor, broken and bloody. A few whimpered like animals expecting another beating, thinking Mason and the Korean guy were here to do them more harm.

The tableau literally made Mason sick. That bubbling came back, stronger than before, and he thought he might actually throw up.

The Korean guy whispered, "We cannot take them all."

Mason shot him a glare. "We can't just fucking leave them here."

"Most are already dead."

"Some of them aren't."

"We do not have much time. Bae will set them off soon."

"Set what off?"

Before the Korean guy could respond, something caught Mason's eye. He was looking around the room at all the bodies when he noticed one in the far corner. It was a woman, wearing only panties. The back of the panties was stained with blood. She lay on her side, her back to Mason, giving him a good view of the rose tattooed on her shoulder blade. Mason would recognize it anywhere.

He was moving almost instantly. Stepping over bodies that were either dead or half-dead. Trying to say his wife's name. But for some reason he couldn't seem to find his voice, no matter how many times he tried speaking. Then he was crouching down beside her, reaching out hesitantly, telling himself that it wasn't her even though he knew it was. Her shoulders were hitching slightly. Now that he was this close, he heard her sobbing.

"Gloria?" he whispered. Then, more forcefully: "*Gloria?*"

She gave no response.

Mason reached out, hesitantly, worried that the moment he touched her she would disappear. Like this was some kind of dream. Or—more apt—nightmare.

But when his fingers grazed her skin, she didn't disappear.

Instead she screamed.

Only the scream wasn't full-fledged. Not the kind he expected to hear. There was something different about it, something off, and it wasn't until he managed to roll her over— Gloria fighting him, flailing with her fists—that he realized her tongue had been cut out. Her entire mouth was painted in blood.

Mason had another half-second to take in everything else— the missing fingers, the missing toes, the cuts along her thighs and arms and breasts—before his eyes shifted and he saw what Gloria had been holding onto.

Anthony.

Or what was left of Anthony.

Like Gloria, his son had been taken apart. He was missing fingers, toes, even an ear. But unlike Gloria, his son hadn't had the strength to keep living.

Anthony lay motionless against the wall. His eyes glazed, his mouth open. Dead.

Gloria had been flailing at Mason this entire time. Now she stopped, too exhausted to continue. Only that wasn't it. Mason looked down at her and saw her looking back at him. Nearly everything had changed about his wife, except her eyes. Those eyes now stared back at him, and he saw the sadness there, the pain, the agony. She opened her mouth, meaning to say some-thing—what Mason thought was supposed to be his name—

but of course no coherent words came out. No matter how much she tried, his wife would never speak again.

Mason's body trembled. His blood boiled. He shook his head slowly, his hands balling into fists. Then, before he knew it, he screamed and punched the wall. Luckily, the wall was plaster and his fist went straight through it. Not that it made much difference. Pain exploded up his arm into his body, fueling his rage, and when the hand touched his shoulder, he swung around, raising his other fist.

The Korean guy didn't even flinch. "We must hurry."

Mason lowered his fist. Dropped his shoulders. Stared down at Gloria, who stared back up at him.

"Do me a favor?"

"What?"

Mason bent and scooped up his wife's broken body off the floor and turned back to the Korean guy.

"Bring my son."

SEVENTY-SIX

As I raced up the steps, my gun in hand, I felt a tinge of déjà vu, like this was Miami Beach all over again. But instead of coming down to the first floor to confront a possible army of Caesar's men, that army would be waiting for me on the second or third floor, all with weapons aimed and pointed in my direction.

But there were no black masks on the second floor, only a rush of white masks pushing their way down the stairs. The third floor was deserted. The hallways were dark save for the faint emergency lights and the constant strobes and the blaring of the alarm.

It didn't take long to find the room I needed. I checked three before I came to a small room filled with computers. And bodies. There were four dead bodies here. Three of them were techs, wearing slacks and polo shirts. The fourth wore a black robe and cowl. This was Seung, who had told me good luck earlier this afternoon. He had been shot in the forehead.

It was pretty clear what had happened. Seung had kicked in the door. He had opened fire on the three techs working the computers. The techs, no doubt aware of the chaos downstairs, returned fire. Seung managed to kill the three, but not before getting shot himself. If there was any silver lining to the whole mess, his death had been quick. He probably pulled the trigger one final time just as the final tech pulled the trigger. Two bullets, two kill shots.

His eyes were still open. I reached out and closed them, because if movies and television has taught us anything, it's you close a dead person's eyes. I wanted to bring him with me, but I knew that would be impossible. He was just too heavy, and I was still hurting from the ass kicking I had received earlier, and besides, I needed what I had come here for.

Tables were lined up around the room. Computer monitors and laptops were set up on these tables. Underneath the tables were bunches of wires. Truth was, I had no fucking clue what I was looking at.

"Kid," I said, "I have no fucking clue what I'm looking at."

"Explain it to me."

"A lot of computers and laptops."

"Any jump drives?"

"Let me check."

It was too dark to really tell for sure, but I started going computer to computer. I found a few jump drives, shoved them in my pocket. I knew those wouldn't be enough, though. I would need more.

"Would some laptops help too?"

"They certainly wouldn't hurt."

A backpack lay on the floor by one of the techs. I grabbed it, started to dump out the papers inside, figured maybe those might be important, and stuffed three laptops into the bag. It was a crapshoot, really. And time was wasting, so I had to hope there was something here.

I headed back out of the room. I paused just long enough to give Seung one final look. I again wanted to do something for him but had no idea what to do. I gave him a moment of silence, then stepped out of the room just as the alarm stopped.

"Kid?" I whispered.

"Don't think it means anything. The alarm is probably only programmed to run for so many minutes."

Despite the alarm's sudden silence, the strobes kept flickering. The emergency lights maintained their dull glow. The hallway was completely quiet, which would help me in case any black masks were still alive.

I started to head back down the hallway. I took only five steps before I stopped.

A faint groaning. Coming back down the hallway from one of the rooms I hadn't checked.

The weight of the backpack told me to keep going, but I turned and went back down the hallway. I came to the door, reached for the knob, but paused. Listened again to the groaning coming from inside.

I turned the knob and pushed the door open. The hinges creaked quietly. Just like the previous room, it was almost completely dark except for the faint emergency lights and the strobes. But still it was enough light to see him.

They had laid out one of those clear plastic tarps. That was where his crumpled and abused body lay. It hadn't been Clark who had done this to him—I didn't think he had had the extra time—but maybe one of his protégés. The tools that had been used—the pliers and knives and saws—lay on the floor, along with various body parts that had been cut off or snapped off or tugged off. Fingernails, fingers, toes, an ear.

Ian Prescott was still alive, but just barely. The cast had been cut off, so that his healing leg could be broken again. He had been stripped of his jeans, his socks, his shirt, and just lay there in his white briefs which were now stained golden and brown with urine and shit. The floor around him was already drying with his blood, which had seeped from the wounds on his feet, his legs, his stomach and chest and arms and even head. What they hadn't cut off, they had stabbed, or sliced, or somehow marked with a very sharp and precise knife.

He saw me—or at least his eyes shifted up to me—and his lips parted slightly. Earlier, when he had grinned at me, he'd had all of his teeth. Now he was missing at least half of them.

Ian stopped groaning and went completely silent. He took a gargled breath, tried to speak, but only produced a pathetic grunt. What may have been an attempt to say my name.

"I told you you were an idiot, didn't I?"

He just stared back at me.

"You could have trusted us. We were family. We would have done whatever it took to take care of each other."

Ian said nothing. His eyes, however, spoke volumes.

In my ear, the Kid said, "Is that Ian?"

"Yes."

"They fuck him up?"

"Yes."

"What does he want?"

"To kill him, I think. Is that what you want, Ian?"

Those eyes just stared back at me. Begging. Pleading.

"Goodbye, Ian."

I stepped back out of the room and closed the door. I did it slow enough this time that the hinges didn't make a sound.

SEVENTY-SEVEN

The lobby had become packed with bodies, both living and dead. Most of those in the Inner Circle still alive were trying to push their way past everyone else. Many had taken off their masks, their faces wet and eyes red from the tear gas. Others still kept their masks on, wanting to protect their identities. None of them seemed to know where to go, only that they didn't want to stay stationary for too long. Some realized they could escape to the street through the destruction the armored truck had caused when it crashed through the front doors.

A few were spilling out onto the sidewalk when I came barreling down the stairs.

Ronny and Maya were already in the truck. Carver was loaded in the back.

I pushed past bodies without much thought. They were simply in the way. I kept my focus on the truck. I was halfway to it when behind me someone shouted my name.

I turned, raising my gun.

Coming my way was Mason and Chin. They weren't alone. Mason was carrying his wife. Chin was carrying Mason's son.

I hurried back, fighting through the crowd, trying to make

room for them. Mason's eyes were red, though it clearly wasn't because of the tear gas. His face was stone. He glared at me, and for an instant I thought it was because he knew I had been there when the cloth bags came off his wife's and son's heads, that I could have done more.

"He's dead," Mason said to me.

"Who?"

"My son. They fucking killed him. *They fucking killed him!*"

He still had the MP5 in one hand, and emphasized this last point by letting off several rounds into the crowd. Many of the bodies screamed or cried out. A few fell down, either struck by the bullets or out of common sense.

I asked, "Your wife?"

Mason looked down at what was left of her in his arms. "I think she'll survive. Ben, there are others in that room. Some of them are still alive."

Chin said, "We do not have time to save them all. Bae is ready to blow this place at any moment."

I looked at him. "What the fuck are you talking about?"

"Seung and I brought explosives. We placed them around the building. Bae is going to set them off as soon as we are out."

"Seung is dead."

Chin looked stricken. "Where?"

"The third floor."

We were fighting through the crowd, toward the armored truck. Because the alarm had stopped, I could hear the engine rumbling. I could also hear Maya, calling my name. She was out of the truck now, waving at us to hurry.

"Let's go," I shouted, pushing Mason and Chin on. We were only twenty yards away from the truck. Not too far in the greater scheme of things, but when hundreds of hysterical people are surrounding you, it can feel like a mile.

Maya called my name again. She was pushing through the

crowd, trying to meet us. She saw the woman in Mason's arms and the child in Chin's arms and her mouth fell open.

"Mason's wife and son," I said.

Maya nodded distantly, staring at their crumpled bodies. "Are they … are they still—"

"We need to get them loaded and get the fuck out of here."

We reached the truck seconds later. A few members of the Inner Circle got in our way and I shoved them aside. A few tripped over their own feet, fell to the floor, causing several others to fall. Maya got the side door open for Mason and Chin and started helping them put in the bodies. I turned back and went to the front of the truck, watching the crowd, searching for any black masks in the sea of white masks. I figured by now any of Caesar's people would have lost their masks, but you could never be so sure.

Behind me, Maya called my name again.

I turned, started toward her, but stopped when I saw her face. She was looking past me, her eyes going wide. She opened her mouth, meaning to shout something, but instead stepped forward. Pushed me aside. I fell into more bodies but managed to catch my balance and turn back around. It was only then that I heard the echo of a single gunshot. My ears were already echoing from the earlier gunfire, but this gunshot was different. Like it had been spliced from tonight's chaotic soundtrack and given its very own track.

I blinked and the next thing I knew Maya was falling to her knees. Dropping her gun. Reaching for her throat.

Blood poured through her fingers.

I raised my gun, searching the crowd, seeing only the white masks … until I spotted the white mask standing across the lobby. This white mask was holding a gun, aimed right at me. I ducked before it fired again, then popped back up, returned fire. A few bodies got caught in the crossfire.

The gunman tore off its mask, confirming what I already knew.

Clark.

He went to fire again but nothing happened. His gun was empty. He swore and bolted for the street.

I tracked him, firing off three more rounds, one of them striking him in the shoulder. He fell back against some bodies, maintained his balance, and disappeared onto the sidewalk.

It all happened much too quickly. Only seconds, really. Ronny got out of the truck, but by then Clark had already hurried past him. Maya was on the ground, her hands still to her throat, holding in the blood. Mason shouted my name, came up behind me. Ronny pushed his way past bodies to reach us. I heard the Kid in my ear, shouting something.

For a moment, I wasn't sure what to do.

Then, quite suddenly, I shouted to Mason and Ronny, "Get her loaded up and get the fuck out of here. Tell Chin to have Bae blow this fucking place as soon as possible."

I didn't wait for them to respond. I turned and hurried past the truck and rubble into the street.

SEVENTY-EIGHT

I spotted Clark almost immediately. He was headed east, toward Times Square, already a block away.

I raised my gun, lined up the shot. I was about to squeeze the trigger when I thought better of it. Several members of the Inner Circle had managed to flee the Fillmore and were spread out in the street and on the sidewalks. I didn't care at all if any of them fell victim to a stray bullet, but farther up the block a crowd of civilians had formed. Too much chance of the bullet striking one of them. Too many innocent people had already died tonight. I didn't want to add any more to the list.

I started running. I was still only in my socks, and the concrete was cold, but that didn't slow me. As I ran, I called Drew's name. There was a moment or two of silence, and then his voice came from the tiny transmitter in my ear.

"What's up?"

"Do you see me?"

"Yeah."

"Do you see the guy I'm chasing?"

"Yeah."

"Take him out."

There was more silence, as Drew lined up the shot from his rooftop perch. I could even picture him there, his eye to the scope, Beverly next to him.

Then I said, "Wait, don't take him out."

"Say again?"

"Take out one of his legs instead. Slow him down."

Clark was already halfway up the next block. He had torn through the crowd of civilians on the corner seconds earlier, and they, having learned their lesson, gave me a wide berth. I ran straight past them, pausing only momentarily for the traffic, before sprinting across the street and continuing down the sidewalk. Two blocks up, the lights of Times Square beckoned.

Clark was still running at full speed. Without my shoes, and the fact my body still felt like shit, there was no way I was going to catch up with him.

"Goddamn it, Drew, slow him down!"

I couldn't hear the bullet—not on a New York City street with sirens in the distance and traffic zooming by and blood pounding in my ears—but I knew it had made its mark.

Farther up the block, Clark had immediately taken a fall. It almost looked as if he'd tripped over something that hadn't been there an instant before. He fell, grabbing at his leg. He started to get up, fell again, then glanced back and saw me coming. He grimaced as he climbed to his feet and started running with a limp.

The brief fear I saw in his eyes alone was enough to give me a second wind. I pushed on even harder, keeping him in my sights.

Clark had just reached the corner into Times Square, looking left and right again before continuing out into traffic.

I made it there seconds later. Clark had reached the middle island between Seventh and Eighth Avenues, was taking a few steps forward but a heavy swarm of traffic passed at once, forcing him to stay where he was. He glanced over his shoulder, saw me coming.

He raised his gun at me. He knew it was empty, just as I knew, but he didn't seem to care.

The leg Drew had shot him in was his left.

I shot him in the right.

He dropped the empty gun, fell to the ground.

I tossed my gun aside and reached into my pocket as I approached. I withdrew the switchblade, flicked it open. I knelt on top of him and drove the blade into his stomach.

"Don't worry about it, baby."

I twisted the knife.

"You're not gonna feel a thing."

His body bucked, squirming underneath me, but nearly all his strength was drained, his face going pale.

"Just a slight discomfort," I said, "then numbness," and I twisted the blade in his stomach even more.

Clark coughed up blood. "Don't you ... want to ... know my ... secret?"

I pulled the knife out, held the bloody tip to his face.

"I'm going to kill you now, Clark."

I rolled the switchblade with my fingers, squeezing onto the handle, the tip of the knife now pointed down.

I lifted it up over my head, preparing to bring it straight down on his throat, when suddenly the city went dark.

It didn't happen all at once, but like a line of dominos. First one building went dark, then another building, then another building. The streetlights died just as quick as candles.

The only light was from the cars still on the street, the swarm of taxis, but without traffic lights they all now believed they had the right of way.

Clark laughed, blood dribbling from between his lips.

"See how ... powerful ... we are?"

Horns blared. Tires screeched. Metal tore against metal.

Screaming and shouting filled the night.

Clark said, gurgling blood, "You will … never … beat us."

A familiar high-pitched whine drifted above the rest of the chaotic city sounds. The Ducati was headed straight toward us. Ho Sook wore her black faceplate helmet again. She skidded to a halt right beside us and, just like back in Miami Beach, held out her gloved hand.

I knew I could get up right now. I could take that hand. I could get on the back of the sport bike and Ho Sook would take us through the city toward safety.

Before I could even move, though, light flickered in the Square.

Despite the rest of the city going dark, the Jumbotron was still on. Instead of an ad for a soda company or an upcoming movie, I was now featured on the gigantic screen. Kneeling on a dying man, a knife raised above my head.

And for the first time I really became aware of where I was, what was around me, the honking, the shouting, the screaming. People were all over the place but none appeared to even notice us, there in the heart of the city's heart. What they noticed instead was the image on the Jumbotron, the camera focused in so tightly that it was impossible to tell where exactly the man with the knife was located.

Kneeling there, the knife still held above my head, I did one quick look at all the buildings around the Square. From the angle of the image, the camera was somewhere up high. I was being watched—I *had* been watched this entire time—and now my anger and fury was being broadcasted for everyone to see. A real life murder, a thing Augustus Caesar would say everyone secretly wants to witness, and here they were being given front row seats.

I looked back at Ho Sook, who kept her gloved hand extended toward me.

I looked down at Clark's face, at the blood bubbling from between his lips.

I knew I could just stop now, stand up, take Ho Sook's hand. I could leave Clark with what little life he had left, and not give everyone watching what they wanted. I could be better than that. I could prove Caesar wrong.

Clark, his lips covered in blood, smiled up at me.

"Fuck it," I said, and shoved the blade straight into his throat.

EPILOGUE

The blackout lasted only six hours, but its effect would last for years.

We're talking about New York City, after all. The greatest city in the world. The mecca for culture and entertainment. Yes, the city was vulnerable—that fateful September day over a decade ago proved it—but something like this was never supposed to happen.

Almost half of Manhattan itself went dark. Parts of Brooklyn and Harlem, too.

It was this last that suffered the most. Around hour five, looting was beginning to increase throughout the city. In Harlem some kids were taking what they could from an electronic store. One cop happened upon the kids looting the store. He told them to stop. Most of the kids took off running, but one kid wasn't fast enough. The cop chased him down. The kid reached for something in his pocket—it would be debated what that something was for weeks, as yes, in that pocket he did have a knife, but he also had a cell phone—and the cop, shouting at him to freeze, fired one shot. The bullet struck the kid in the head, killing him instantly. There were several witnesses who saw it happened. Within an hour a small riot began. It would only grow and increase throughout the day and into the week. After all, the cop was white, the kid black.

A dozen hospitals lost power. They all had emergency backup, of course, but that didn't mean there still wasn't complications. Staff in all the hospitals went into crisis mode. Some patients were on life support. Others were being monitored by machines. As one hospital administrator would say to the press the next day, "Sometimes you take for granted just how much electricity it takes to run a hospital. Our deepest condolences and sympathies go out to those families who lost loved ones during the blackout."

How many deaths occurred throughout the city is impossible to say. There were those at the hospitals, yes, but there were also those from numerous traffic accidents. Cars smashing into cars. Cars smashing into buildings. Cars smashing into pedestrians. Traffic lights keep at least some order on the disordered streets. When those lights go dark, chaos reigns.

The police were stretched thin. The mayor had to make one of those agonizing mayoral decisions that would no doubt affect his next election: what areas of the city to try to save first.

In the end, the National Guard was called in. By the next afternoon Humvees roared up and down the streets. Soldiers carrying M16s patrolled the sidewalks and subway stations. It was still only the weekend, and they were preparing for the hellish nightmare that would be Monday morning.

Later that Sunday, there was still no official word on what caused the blackout. All the power stations had seemed to be in working order. Until, one anonymous technician told the press, all hell broke loose.

It wasn't surprising that within hours the news media was speculating on whether or not al-Qaeda was involved. One side believed this attack was in response to the U.S.'s involvement in Egypt. The other side went so far as to blame global warming. A few even mentioned solar flares as a potential culprit.

Traffic in and out of the city was nearly at a standstill. The bridges and tunnels were packed, police and National Guard keeping watch on both ends. The trains in and out of the city went a little bit quicker, but still each car had to be inspected by soldiers with bomb-sniffing dogs.

By the end of that first day, no bombs were found.

It took us two days to leave the city. We went in shifts. First the Kid by himself. Then Ronny and Carver, with Maya's dead body wrapped up in the trunk of their car. Mason left the city with Beverly, Mason's wife asleep in the backseat. Drew left with Chin, Mason's dead son in the trunk. Some of them took the tunnel. Others took the bridge. None of them, thankfully, got stopped, despite the fact they were all driving stolen cars and that Caesar's people were no doubt looking for us.

We had anticipated we might have trouble leaving the city, so we had come up with several safe houses. These were places that could be easily accessed from the street, and which would give us optimal cover for a couple hours.

I did not end up at one of these safe houses. Ho Sook took me to the place her father was stationed. It was the basement of a deli that had been shut down by the Health Department the day before.

There I recuperated the best I could. There weren't any medical supplies besides those few bandages and Band-Aids found in a dented First Aid kit, so I just lay in the corner and tried not to move my body.

"I'm sorry about Seung," I told Bae.

He nodded.

"I'm sorry we didn't get Caesar."

He nodded again. Then, as an afterthought, said, "He may have died in the blast."

This was true. Chin and Seung had managed to secure a half dozen blocks of C-4 around the Fillmore—in the auditorium, the lobby, the banquet room. When they blew, they certainly took out several members of the Inner Circle.

"How did your guys infiltrate the Coliseum anyway?"

His smile was thin. "It was not very difficult, when all eyes were on you."

Bae had communication with Chin, who got me in contact with the Kid, who told me that everyone had made it out okay. He was then quiet for several seconds before he said, "Dude, about Maya ... I'm so fucking sorry."

I lay in the corner, Bae's phone to my ear, staring up at the ceiling. A single tear ran down my cheek. I didn't bother wiping it away.

"What about Graham?"

"He made it out. Grabbed as many weapons and computers as he could, but, well, you know he couldn't do much with his leg the way it is. Dude, they killed his bees."

"What?"

"He left and went a few miles up the hill. He stopped at this lookout and used binoculars to watch the farmhouse. They came in SUVs and two helicopters. Graham said they searched the property, didn't find anything, so they burned the house. Then, I guess to cover their tracks or to just be complete dickholes, they burned all the hives. Graham ... fuck, dude, Graham said from even where he was he could hear the fucking bees screaming."

Now with the farmhouse gone—our own special safe house— just where were we supposed to go?

This was what the Kid and I discussed next. We were working toward a location—or at least I was working toward a location—but the Kid kept changing the subject.

Finally I said, "Kid, we don't have much choice here."

"Dude, are you fucking crazy? First, there is, like, no room at all. Second, it's my fucking *house*. My mom lives there. She … she's not going to be able to handle all the people."

"We don't have to stay there for long. In fact, we don't have to stay there at all. I'm sure there are motels nearby that we can hole up in. But right now, we need some kind of base."

"So my fucking house?" He was silent for a beat. "Fuck, man, I'm going to have to get extra toilet paper and shit."

We rested up the next day, and began to secure our rides. Vehicles that wouldn't be missed for a few days. Many people kept cars in the city for the few times of year they needed non-public transportation. That made it easier for us to borrow them.

And borrow them we did.

After all, we weren't going straight to the Kid's place in stolen cars. Again, we had anticipated something like this might happen, though obviously not to this magnitude. Along with the additional safe houses, we secured additional transportation. Only they were parked outside the city.

Throughout the day everyone else left the city. Bae and I drove through the Holland Tunnel that evening. Ho Sook tailgated us on her Ducati. Because neither vehicle was stolen, we drove straight to the Kid's place. It took seven hours. By then the deaths of several politicians and media moguls and celebrities were beginning to be reported.

Not much was said, of course. The deaths were small deaths, if there is such a thing. Heart attacks. Strokes. Car accidents. Overdoses. By themselves, they were typical deaths. All together, though, they created a disturbing pattern.

But it wasn't like anyone else noticed this. Everyone's attention was on the Manhattan Blackout, which was what the media had cleverly named it and which was still unexplained. The Attorney General was getting involved to find out just what went wrong. And the riots in Harlem were still raging. Additional National Guard troops were being sent in to help matters.

So all the focus was on the riots and the blackout. The deaths of some celebrities or politicians—deaths which appeared innocuous enough—were mentioned briefly in the news but that was it. No one gave any of the deaths much thought. And, quite honestly, there was no way of knowing whether any of those deaths were simply coincidental or the individuals had in fact been members of the Inner Circle, who had been killed at the Fillmore Theater either by crossfire or explosion.

A good portion of the Fillmore was destroyed in the blast. The next day what little news the Kid could find claimed that the theater had burned. Faulty wiring. No word about any bodies found inside. No word even about any bodies found outside.

By the second day, officials were still trying to get an estimated count of the fatalities throughout the city.

We knew better than to all stay at the same motel.

Mason and his wife stayed in one motel, with Beverly taking the room next door. It was an adjoining room, so she could slip back and forth to treat Gloria Coulter's wounds. The Kid had talked Carmen—a certified nurse—into bringing what supplies she could from the nearest hospital. Gloria would live, but she would not live well.

Drew, Carver, Ronny, and I stayed at another motel three miles away. Carver and I shared a room on the first floor, Ronny and Drew a room on the second floor. Carver had given up the line that he didn't need the wheelchair. It was clear that he did need it, and that he would need it for quite some time.

Bae and Ho Sook and Chin stayed at a motel two miles away from ours. Bae and Chin shared a room, Ho Sook got her own.

We used disposable cell phones to communicate when needed. But there wasn't much communication between any of us that first day.

Tuesday came and went and we all mostly stayed in our rooms, licking our wounds. Maya's body and Mason's son's body were still wrapped up in their individual trunks. They couldn't stay in there much longer.

I called the Kid and proposed an idea.

He said, "Fuck, dude, it's my fucking *house*."

"You said that before."

"Do you know what I'm doing right now? I'm going through all the shit you brought back from the city."

The laptops and flash drives I snagged from the Fillmore, he meant.

"Anything helpful?"

"Can't say quite yet. It's all encrypted."

"That shouldn't be any trouble for you."

"You're right, it shouldn't. But these people, dude, they're hardcore. Don't worry—I'll be able to break it eventually."

"We don't have forever. It's a good possibility Caesar made it out of that place alive. Speaking of which, did you look into it?"

"I did. Congresswoman Houser is an only child. And she has only one cousin, but it's a chick."

"Doesn't make sense. They're definitely related somehow. He even admitted she was his sister."

"Don't know what to tell you."

"Keep working on the encryption. Even if Caesar didn't make it out alive, it doesn't mean they aren't prepared to continue with the Pax Romana."

"Dude, I fucking know."

"We need to know what it is."

"*Dude*."

"And we need the backyard."

The Kid was silent for a long time. Then he said, "Fuck."

A six-foot high fence surrounded the Kid's entire backyard. It wasn't a nice fence—the paint was peeling in many places—but it would do the trick.

That Wednesday morning, we brought Maya and Anthony Coulter to the Kid's house. Fortunately, the Kid's house wasn't very close to his neighbors. Unfortunately, he still did have neighbors, so we had to be careful. We backed up the cars, took out the bodies, walked them through the garage to the backyard.

There Drew and Chin and Mason had already dug the two holes. There everyone else waited.

We couldn't put the bodies in caskets. Not without arousing too much suspicion. In the past, Graham had made the caskets, but he was still driving east, at least another day away. Even if he was here, it wasn't like he could build the caskets in time, not without the proper tools and supplies. So we wrapped the bodies in even more plastic wrap, secured them, and lowered them into the ground.

The sky was clear. The sun was bright. Those of us lowering

the bodies and digging back in the holes were sweating profusely. When we were done, Beverly and Ronny both said short prayers. Everyone bowed their heads, even those atheists and agnostics among us. There was a long moment of silence, and then we all drifted away.

I drifted toward one corner of the backyard and lit up a smoke.

Mason approached me. "There's something I want to tell you."

I watched him carefully, thinking this was it. That he knew the truth. That I had been in the same room with his family before they were tortured. That if I had done more, his son might still be alive.

But he said, "When she … when she died, I was there in the back of the truck. I was holding her hand. She … she tried saying something and I told her not to, to save her breath, but she kept saying a word."

I took a long drag on the cigarette, blew the smoke out through my nose. Waited for him to continue.

"I wasn't even sure if it was anything, but I told Ronny about it and Ronny said I should tell you, and I meant to earlier, I really did, but I just …"

"What did she say?"

"Your name. Or not really your name—she tried to say your name, but she couldn't, not with … well, she couldn't. But I could see her lips. I asked her if she meant you. And she nodded and closed her eyes and she … she squeezed my hand three times. Just three times, that was it. And then … then she was gone."

We headed back to our separate motels. Carver stayed with the Kid. Ronny and I helped Carver down the stairs into the basement. The Kid's mother was in the living room with Carmen. The

Kid had asked Carmen to keep his mother in the living room for a few hours. Carmen, of course, agreed. After the Kid's previous request of the medical supplies, it was clear she knew more than she let on. From what I understood, the Kid paid her very well for her services. So well that she knew to keep her mouth shut.

Once Carver was situated in the basement, Ronny and I headed back to our motel. We had just arrived there when the Kid called.

"Dude, you have to get back here right now."

They were waiting for me in the basement when I returned.

The Kid said, "Pull up a chair."

"What's this about?"

"Dude, just sit down."

I sat down as the Kid typed on one of the keyboards.

"Did you break one of the encryptions?"

"Not yet. But a message was just sent out. It's addressed to you."

"Me?"

He nodded and kept typing.

I glanced at Carver but he just sat silently in his chair.

The Kid said, "We can't do any more than five minutes."

"Before what?"

"Before they trace the call."

"Who's calling?"

"Not sure yet. But it's video. Here, scoot over so you're front and center."

I moved the chair so I was sitting right in front of the monitor.

The Kid said, "Ready?"

I still wasn't sure what I was supposed to be ready for, but I nodded anyway.

He hit a button and leaned back out of view.

The screen was blank for several seconds. Then an image blinked on, and a familiar face smiled back at me.

"Hello, Ben," Augustus Caesar said.

"What the fuck do you want?"

"Don't be hostile, Ben. It doesn't suit you. Tell me, is the Kid there with you?"

I said nothing.

"It's simply amazing the skill someone like him possesses. He can do more damage with a single computer than most armies can do with a thousand soldiers. Speaking of which, were you impressed by the blackout? I will admit, I did not expect it to cause such a catastrophe. Granted, we knew there would be fatalities, but not such a high number. And to think, it all came about from someone like your friend pressing a few buttons on a laptop."

"Are you feeling guilty?"

He smiled. "I should be asking you the same question."

"What is that supposed to mean?"

"Killing poor Clark like you did. When I was told you were spotted in Times Square, I had them put a camera on you and give the Jumbotron power. I was curious to see what you would do. You did not disappoint."

I said nothing.

"Did you notice there has been no mention in the news of what appeared on the Jumbotron during the blackout, even though hundreds of people saw it?"

"What's your point?"

"There were witnesses outside the Fillmore during your attack as well. Many of them attempted to upload videos and pictures to different social media networks. Within seconds, those videos and pictures were deleted. Any slight mention of the Fillmore has been deleted."

"Is this the part where I'm supposed to be impressed?"

"No. I am simply giving another illustration of just how powerful we are. Tell me, did you ever figure out the hint I gave you in regards to the Pax Romana?"

"Actually, yeah, it was pretty simple. The greatest thing the Roman Empire gave to the world was roads. So ... what, you're into construction now?"

Augustus smiled but said nothing.

I asked, "So what do you want, anyway?"

"For you to play the game again."

I laughed. "You're insane."

"That's exactly what Mr. Ellison called me. Is he there with you now?"

I said nothing.

"I guess it doesn't matter if he is there or not. I'm done with him. You, however, are a different story. The Coliseum was ruined, no thanks to you and your friends. Many of those in the Inner Circle were either killed or injured. I feel I owe them something in return for all the suffering that was caused. And before the Pax Romana is finally initiated, I thought it would be grand if you played the game one last time."

"I can tell you right now, that isn't going to happen."

"No?"

"Positive."

"Are you sure?"

"There isn't anything in the world that would change my mind."

Augustus took a deep breath. "You see, Ben, I thought you would say that. And if that is your answer, then so be it. But before we part ways, there are two people who I think would like to say hello."

He had apparently been standing this entire time. He

started to move back, away from the camera, until the room came into view.

Behind him sat two people in chairs. Like back in the Torture Room, there were cloth bags over their heads.

My stomach tightened. My entire body began to shake. In my mind, a familiar voice whispered a question.

Are you ready for that secret now?

Then Augustus, with a flourish, tore off the cloth bags—and the ground disappeared beneath me.

They sat there, Jen and Casey, duct tape covering their mouths. Their eyes red and glassy. Their skin pale.

Augustus, standing between them, the cloth bags in his hands, smiled back at me.

"How about now?"

The story concludes in *End Game*, the final book in the Man of Wax Trilogy, available everywhere.

ABOUT THE AUTHOR

Robert Swartwood is the *USA Today* bestselling author of *The Serial Killer's Wife*, *No Shelter*, *Man of Wax*, and several other novels. He created the term "hint fiction" and is the editor of *Hint Fiction: An Anthology of Stories in 25 Words or Fewer*. He lives with his wife in Pennsylvania.

Made in the USA
San Bernardino, CA
03 July 2020

74682657R00305